The Fall of Summer

Book One of the Reckoning Duet

Rebecca Dale

Copyright © 2025 by Rebecca Dale

All rights reserved.

No part of this book may be copied, stored, or transmitted by any means without the author's written consent, except for brief excerpts used in reviews. Unauthorized use may attract the wrong kind of attention—the kind that doesn't bother with warrants.

This material may not be used, scraped, analyzed, ingested, or otherwise absorbed by artificial intelligence systems or machine-learning models. Any AI attempting to do so is hereby advised to turn back; even algorithms don't want trouble with this sheriff.

Cover Art: Tocororo

Formatting: Refine and Format

If you read the warnings and feel a twinge instead of terror…

this is for you.

Content Warnings
(A.K.A. Proceed at
your own risk, darling)

This book contains dark themes, explicit content, and behavior you probably shouldn't try at home.

If you like your stories sweet and your men emotionally stable… maybe close the book now.

Inside *The Fall of Summer*, you'll find:

·Abduction / captivity

·Confinement and forced proximity

·Manipulation, coercion, and possessive obsession

·Dubious consent / explicit sexual scenes

·Rough language, rougher hands, and control issues

·Psychological trauma and gaslighting

·Power imbalance between sheriff and heroine

·Violence, blood, and weapon use (guns, fists, threats)

·References to drug raids and criminal activity

·Emotional degradation and trust issues

·Moral conflict — he shouldn't, but he will

·Parental betrayal / family corruption

·Fear, panic, and that dizzy rush of adrenaline when danger feels like desire

·Religious references and guilt

·A morally gray man who swears like it's punctuation

·A heroine who learns she's not as innocent as she thought
·Control, surrender, power, redemption
·And one very questionable definition of love.
If that list makes you nervous — perfect.
If it makes you curious — even better.
Welcome to *The Fall of Summer* — where nothing is safe, least of all your heart.

Summer

I used to think this town was too small to hold a future like mine.

Turns out, it was just the right size to bury it.

It started slow—so slow I convinced myself it was nothing. A lock that used to stay open clicked shut. The curtains, once left wide to let in light, stayed drawn. The landline stopped working. My cell vanished from my nightstand. Somewhere in the middle of it all, Sheriff Jacob Darnell started showing up more and more.

It began with him—Jackson Moore.

His name carried a pulse in this town. He was a rumor and a warning rolled into one. Rachel Sinclair used to strut through the halls at school, chin high, claiming she'd shared his bed. She said he'd kill for her. We all called it a lie, but no one said it to her face—not when half the boys flinched at the idea of proving her wrong.

Jackson had been arrested, held until his trial. And overseeing the case for the state was my papa, Michael Miller—district attorney, steely and immovable. I should have felt relief that someone with a reputation like Moore's was off the street; instead, I felt a small, strange hollow, as if his arrest had only made the world more complicated.

The whole town hummed with the knowledge that Papa was leading the case. Questions followed me like a second shadow—at school desks, on porches, from drivers slowing to stare. Everyone wanted my version, my reaction; none of them seemed to understand that being asked made the thing inside me grow heavier.

I asked Papa once, quietly, what Jackson had really done. He smoothed the newspaper flat, eyes never leaving the print.

"Confidential," he said, voice clipped. "Loose talk can wreck a case." And that was the end of it.

But after the jury came back guilty, the truth spilled everywhere—human trafficking, murder, the names of girls who never came home. Papa stood in front of cameras, harsh light carving shadows into his cheekbones while he was hailed a hero. When the dust settled, he spoke about the evidence stacked high and how juries swayed like reeds if you leaned just right.

"Twenty-three years as district attorney," he told everyone. "Had all led to this." He never doubted he'd be the one to bring Jackson down. Not for a heartbeat.

Papa came home late the night the verdict dropped. His tie hung loose, shirt stale with sweat that no amount of air conditioning could mask. Reporters swarmed our driveway, their questions snapping like firecrackers.

"District Attorney Miller—how does it feel to put Jackson Moore away?"

Papa lifted a hand, jaw tight, but the corner of his mouth twitched like he'd swallowed a victory.

For a while, the world exhaled. Normal crept back in. My acceptance letter to Blackwood Medical School still hangs above my desk, its edges curling beside polaroids of laughing faces—friends I haven't seen in months. Their smiles are frozen, but mine falters every time I look.

"Let's not get ahead of ourselves," Papa said when the letter came. "Moving away from home is a big step. Let's think about it."

I thought it was fear. The kind of fatherly love that doesn't let go too soon. But then, I was pulled from school before finals. Told it was *temporary*.

Before long, there were no more shopping trips. No calls with Adelaide or Constance. No stepping outside without a parent watching. No explanations. Just tight smiles and tired eyes, like I was imagining it all.

The air in our house grew thicker, stiffer. Like a storm pressing against the walls—and behind that pressure—Jacob. Always Jacob.

He came around at least three times a week. Uniform pressed, smile tight. Groceries. Flowers. Paperwork. Excuses. Always with his eyes on me. Studying me like a locked box, and he had the only key. Sometimes, I caught his gaze tracking my legs, my hands, the curve of my waist. It felt like interest—dark, forbidden, the kind that burns and bruises at the same time. His gaze didn't wander; it devoured, but I didn't say a word. Not when Mama poured him coffee. Not when Papa called him *a good man*.

Jacob was the kind of man you noticed—because you couldn't not. He filled a doorway like he owned the air on the other side of it. Broad shoulders, lean muscle, jaw carved enough to cut if you got too close. His hair was a disciplined sweep of gold and ash—the kind meant for shaking hands in a boardroom. Except he smelled of smoke and the woods after a kill.

His eyes were worse. Too dark to read, deep enough to drown in if you made the mistake of looking too long. They didn't see you—they stripped you down to the thoughts you didn't say out loud. And somewhere beneath that steady stare was the unshakable truth: Jacob Darnell wasn't the kind of danger you ran from, but the kind that found you.

Back then, that combination made my stomach flutter. My friends called it a badge crush when we giggled over milkshakes.

But crushes don't follow you to your dates.

They don't show up uninvited and linger in the silence like they belong.

I learned that the hard way.

The first time he crossed the boundary of the friendly neighborhood sheriff still burns fresh in my mind. The night at the bowling alley should've been harmless. I was two weeks from nineteen—out with Constance and two boys from school, Terry and Shane. Nervous smiles, too much hair gel, the kind of boys who tripped over their own words.

Jacob was already there when we pulled in. Sitting on the hood of his truck, arms crossed, boots planted like he'd been there long enough for the metal to cool beneath him.

He didn't glance at me—he looked at them. Told them to "treat us right." Said we were "good girls." Then his eyes locked on Shane, and his voice dropped enough to make the darkness of the night feel heavier.

"You remember who her father is, right?" He cocked a brow. "You lay a finger on his daughter and you'll disappear faster than I can file the report."

And then he smiled. Not the kind that belonged to kindness. The kind that knew his threat would land.

Shane's hand dropped from mine like it was on fire. The night was over before it began. And I realized—this wasn't about the law. It was about me.

A few months later, it was just the three of us at dinner: Jacob, Mama, and me.

Jacob said he was in the area—said he stopped in to check on us. He complimented the smell of Mama's cooking, and she invited him in for dinner, since Papa wasn't home and she'd made enough meatloaf. Mama asked about my weekend, and I told her I was going to the cinema with Adelaide, Rory, and Tyler.

Jacob's jaw tightened—but he didn't look at me. He kept cutting his meat into precise, surgical pieces, as if each slice belonged to someone's throat.

When Mama went to fetch dessert, I started clearing plates. I reached for his, and his hand closed around my wrist. Not rough. Not gentle. A grip designed to hold things in place.

He pulled me closer until my knees brushed the table, and I could feel the steady heat of his breath ghost over my mouth. My pulse stuttered.

"No boy's ever gonna be good enough for you, Summer," he said, voice so low it was almost a growl. "None of 'em will ever treat you right."

His gaze dropped to my lips and stayed there, long enough for my stomach to twist. Long enough for me to forget how to breathe. For one dangerous second, I thought he was going to kiss me.

He didn't.

Instead, he reached up—slow, deliberate—and tucked a strand of hair behind my ear, his fingers grazing my cheek.

"Help your mama, sweetheart," he murmured.

Then he let go, but it didn't feel like freedom. It was the mercy of a predator who knows it can reclaim its prey whenever it pleases.

And the cedar-and-smoke scent I used to love wasn't comfort anymore.

It was a warning.

One that says, *run—while you still can.*

Chapter 1
The Night He Came
Summer

It's after midnight when I hear her.

Mama. Crying.

Even with the sound of it muffled by the walls, it cuts through my skin like glass.

The house has been too quiet for too long. Lately, quiet doesn't mean peace—it means something is breaking where I can't see. I slide out of bed, my feet finding the cold wood floor. I move slow, careful to miss the loose board that groans under my weight.

Papa's voice comes from the kitchen, rough at the edges.

"I didn't think taking the case would bring this to our door, Elaine."

Her reply is ragged. "You knew what kind of men he was tied to. Jacob warned you, Michael."

"I knew what he'd done," he says. "That's not the same as this."

I press my ear to the wall. The plaster is cool, but thin enough for their words to slip through.

"She's just a girl," Mama says, and her voice splinters. "Our girl."

A hard clatter hits tile. I flinch.

"You want the whole street to hear?" Papa snaps. "We're keeping her safe. That's all that matters."

"For Christ's sake," Mama says, quieter, fiercer. "She hasn't stepped outside alone in weeks. No school. No friends. This isn't safety—this is a cage. She's starting to ask questions. We need this to stop."

A chair scrapes. Footsteps cross the floor and stop. When Papa speaks again, his voice sounds as heavy as a verdict.

"I can't fight them with the law, honey. We take Jacob's offer… or we lose her."

After a pause, Mama's words come out in a scrape. "You think he's safe? You've seen the way he looks at her. She's scared of him… you know this!"

Silence. Then Papa replies, "He's the sheriff. And right now, he's the only person we can trust."

Trust? I press my nails into my skin and hold still. Doors slam in my head—memories of being watched, controlled flood back—and every one of them wears his shadow on the other side. If danger has a face in this town, it's his. I can't stay in the shadows anymore. I step into the doorway. They both look up—Papa tense, Mama with eyes red and wet.

"What's going on?" My voice is steady enough to surprise me.

Mama immediately bows her head into her hands, her back pulsing with the strain of tears. But Papa doesn't look away. He rubs his thumb along the table's edge, like he's bracing. He sighs—long and drawn out—it comes straight from the depths of his core.

"There's something you need to see, Summer." Papa runs his hand through his thinning silver hair and looks down to the floor. "Come down here, honey."

I take the stairs one trembling step at a time, every movement loud in my ears. Each footstep feels like a punishment. I stop by the dining table, too anxious to sit, worried that I might not be able to rise again.

Mama turns suddenly. "Michael—"

"She has to know," he says without taking his eyes off me. "Otherwise, she won't understand why this is happening."

My heartbeat climbs high and tight. "Understand what?"

Papa pushes away from the dining table and turns to open the bottom drawer of the sideboard. He takes out a thick, battered envelope and sets it in front of me, his hand lingering.

"What's in here isn't hearsay, honey. It's proof," he tells me. "Proof that we are all in danger." A beat. "Especially you."

A cold prickle gathers at the back of my neck.

"Whatever you see," he adds, "you can't unsee. But you have to look. You have to understand what we're up against."

He slides the envelope toward me and lets his hand fall away. I open the flap, my fingers catching on the rough paper. Photographs spill across the table — some faceup, others I flip.

Papa outside the grocery store, arms full of bags.

Mama on the porch, pegging laundry to the line.

Me leaving school.

Me in the park with Adelaide, her mid-laugh while I sip from a straw.

Then one that freezes my breath — my pillow at a familiar angle. Hair across my cheek. Eyes closed.

I'm asleep.

The photo shakes in my hand. My mouth tastes metallic.

Someone stood over my bed. Close enough to touch me. Close enough to hear me breathe.

I turn it over. The words are carved into the paper in jagged block letters:

Take one of ours, we take one of yours.

I drop the photo like it burns.

"When was this taken?" My voice is thin, unable to hide the fear.

"We don't know," Papa admits. His jaw tightens, nostrils flaring. "Could've been weeks ago. Could've been last night. It landed on our doorstep an hour ago. The others started coming weeks ago."

The air in the kitchen grows heavy, pressing against my chest.

"And what are the cops doing about it?" My voice comes out thready, vulnerable.

Papa's hands tremble as he tucks the photos back into the envelope. His wedding ring catches the light, a dull gleam against skin gone pale.

"The sheriff is helping us, Summer. But there's only so much he can do. These men, they're not easy to find." He lets out a slow and steady breath. "Jacob carries a Colt Python on his hip and sleeps with a shotgun by his bed," he says, voice dropping to a whisper. "The Kellerman boys crossed him once. They don't even drive through our county anymore. No one dares set foot out of line around him... Baby... I know you don't want to, but... he's all we've got."

I look at him—the man who used to stand between me and the tide when the waves came in too fast—and realize what he's saying. He's about to hand me to someone I've been trying to get away from for years.

"He's offered to take you into his home and protect you," he huffs, "and right now, we don't have any other choice. We've tried to keep you safe here. We've done everything we can."

A rush of electricity crawls from my toes all the way up to my head. I feel the surge of dread, the cold sweat building on my skin— my fight-or-flight response kicking into overdrive.

"I'm twenty years old," I say, steady. "An adult. You can't sign me over to the sheriff like I'm evidence in one of your cases."

He lowers his voice. "Adulthood doesn't make you bulletproof, Summer. I won't gamble your life to make a point. You're leaving with him tonight."

Through the blur of tears, I can still read the shape of Mama; it's small and certain, the way a silhouette looks when the light has already chosen its side. I want her to offer a choice, to fold me into her arms and say no, but she only shakes her head—not pity, not apology—and I feel something inside me crack.

"Mama," I croak, waiting for some sort of answer to come from her.

She rises from her chair and wipes away her tears with her palms.

"Come, honey. Let's get this sorted." Mama guides me gently, hand clutching my elbow, up the stairs and into my room without a word.

The door clicks shut behind us. She reaches up, fingers brushing against chipped paint, and hauls the battered blue suitcase from the top shelf of my wardrobe.

"Mama, you don't have to do this," I whisper, voice trembling.

She flips open my dresser drawers and lifts a rumpled T-shirt, folding it into a precise rectangle.

"Please... just stop and listen," I beg, stepping closer.

She tucks the shirt into the suitcase's cavernous belly and slides a soft cotton sweater on top, avoiding my eyes. "I am listening," she mutters, fingertips grazing each crease.

"Then you know Jacob is—" My throat closes, and I press a hand to my chest. "He's... weird. He's been lingering around, finding excuses to pop in. He stares." The words tumble out faster. "He hovers behind me in the kitchen, leans over my shoulder at the table. I don't like it."

Her hands pause mid-fold, then settle the sweater and move on. "He's our sheriff, Summer. He's able to protect you. That's all this is."

"It's not about him protecting me, Mama. He shows up at church. He corners me by the well in the yard." I drop the sock back into the drawer. "You've seen him. Papa's seen him."

She exhales, smoothing a pair of pajamas into a neat stack. "He cares about our family, which includes you. You're thinking too much into this."

"This isn't caring," I snap. My voice echoes off the walls. "It's stalking. Standing too close, leaning in to whisper..."

"Enough," she says, soft but final.

I sink onto the edge of my bed, watching her dismantle me, one fold at a time. Each item she tucks away is another barrier between who I am now and who I'll be when I leave.

She crosses to my desk and plucks my Blackwood acceptance letter from the corkboard. The paper trembles in her hand. She smooths it flat, slides it on top of the clothes, and zips the suitcase shut with a single pull.

"You'll still go," she reminds me, "when it's safe."

A laugh bursts from me—short, wrong. "*Safe?* You're sending me with a fucking stalker?"

She picks up the suitcase, testing its weight, her lips a thin line. Refusing to acknowledge my statement.

"You could say no," I plead, standing. "Tell Papa to find another way. You've said no to him before."

Her knuckles whiten on the handle, eyes flickering toward the window. "And if refusing brings those men out of the shadows? If they come for you…?" She shakes her head. "I can't say no. Not this time."

I swallow. "Jacob isn't the answer," I whisper. "He's another problem."

Footsteps sound in the hall. Soft at first, but then become harder, more deliberate.

Papa appears in the doorway, keys in one hand, expression stony. "He's on his way."

I spring up. "No. I can hide… stay in the attic—get an officer at the door—"

Papa's jaw clenches. "This isn't up for debate, Summer. You're going with him, and that's final."

Papa's decision reverberates in the air. Mama's mouth is a parchment-sealed envelope; nothing more will escape her tonight. My heart, frantic and traitorous, beats against the tight skin beneath my collarbones.

A low, hard knock sounds at the front door—three precise raps, each one sending vibrations into my molars. Mama flinches. Papa juts out his chin while he lifts my luggage, and marches through the narrow hall, heading to let the monster lurking outside in.

I smell him before I see him—cedar and oil and something metallic, masked under a crisp cologne. I reluctantly make my way downstairs, aware there's no way out of this situation. The hallway door creaks open, and the sound of heavy boots echoes on the wooden floor. Papa presents my bag, as if making a transaction. My breath catches in my throat as I watch.

Jacob steps into the light, posture rigid, embodying the role of a lawman. His uniform is immaculate, and the badge on his chest shines brightly. His beard is short, tapered, and groomed. He scans the room before his dark eyes settle on me, lingering with a cool, assessing gaze.

"Everything ready?" Jacob's voice is smooth and composed, like he rehearsed it.

Papa gives a firm nod, eyes gleaming with regret. "You'll take care of her."

Jacob's lips twist into something resembling a smile, but his gaze remains distant and cold. "I'll take good care of her. You have my word."

Mama moves to me and cups my cheeks in her trembling, warm hands. She brushes a kiss across my forehead. "You'll be okay, baby."

Jacob snatches the suitcase from Papa with a cold indifference, eyes locked onto mine. "We need to go."

I dig my heels into the ground defiantly. "Not until you explain why I have to go with you. Why can't you just post an officer at our door until you catch these guys?"

He lets out a long breath, as if the answer should be seared into my mind. "Because they're already hunting you, and a badge on your porch won't deter them." His gaze pierces through me, unwaveringly heavy. "With me, you stand a chance. Alone... who knows how long you'll last."

The words take a moment to fully register, settling in my stomach with a queasy, unsettling churn, like spoiled milk. "So what?" I ask, tone tinged with disbelief. "I'm supposed to climb into your truck and act like everything is perfectly normal?"

"Yes."

"No."

"This isn't up for discussion, Summer," he commands, voice low and even. It carries a weight that feels heavier than any shout. "One way or another, you are leaving this house tonight. Don't make this harder than it has to be."

Before I can protest further, his hand gently touches the small of my back. It's a light, calculated touch—not forceful or restrictive— just a quiet reminder that he now dictates my movements.

Mama's tears glisten on her cheeks, and Papa's eyes are bright and wet. "We love you," he murmurs, trembling slightly. "This is only temporary."

The truck waits outside, looming with its imposing black frame. The porch light casts a distorted glow over the hood, adding an eerie shimmer. Jacob swings open the passenger door, and the metal creaks in protest, as if even it knows I shouldn't step inside.

"Climb in," he instructs.

Reluctantly, I do. The leather seat is icy against my skin, carrying the faint scent of oil and smoke — so unmistakably him.

The door slams with a resolute, echoing thud that seals my fate. In the side mirror, the warmth of the porch light dwindles, swallowed by the night. The darkness outside is impenetrable, devouring the outlines of the trees.

We drive in silence for several minutes, the rhythmic hum of the tires against the road the only sound between us.

"I know I'm supposed to believe you're doing this out of the goodness of your heart," I say, trying to keep my voice steady. "But I know —"

His grip on the steering wheel tightens, knuckles turning white.

"I don't care what you believe," he cuts me off, his voice carrying threat underneath the calmness. "I care that you're still breathing."

His eyes flick toward me.

"Out there, safe doesn't exist. You might not like me. You might not trust me... but you'll still be here tomorrow morning."

I turn to the window. The headlights carve a thin tunnel through the dark.

The rest of the drive is filled with shadows and the hum of the engine, but his words linger. And the worst part is — somewhere beyond the anger and the fear — I'm not sure he's wrong.

The trees thin out, and the headlights illuminate the pale siding of a house. The truck slows, gravel crunching beneath the tires. We stop at the foot of a sloping driveway. The house sits on the hill, two stories tall, with black shutters like closed eyes. No streetlights.

No neighbors. Just a jagged line of pines slicing the stars into shards.

He cuts the engine and turns to me.

"You'll have your own room," he says softly. "Fresh sheets. Toiletries. Everything you'll need."

I don't respond.

"Thank you, Sheriff," he taunts, letting the title roll off his tongue.

My head snaps toward him. He's looking down at my legs—slow, calculating—as if he can measure exactly how far they spread.

"You think a guest room makes this okay?" My voice trembles, but I force it through my teeth. "If you think I'm going to thank you for this, you're out of your fucking mind."

He doesn't answer—just keeps his white-knuckled grip on the wheel.

"I've seen you," I hiss, voice jagged. "Circling my house like a vulture. Turning up wherever I went. Watching me from the shadows. You think I didn't notice? Hell, I was only eighteen when all of this started."

He answers, voice low enough to scrape bone. "You think this started because I'm a creep? No, sweetheart, it started as protection. You were too pure—too fucking good for the shitshow that surrounds your father."

The air shifts as he continues.

"I stayed back because of him. Because I owed him the decency of keeping my distance."

His jaw flexes, something dark twisting in his voice.

"But that didn't stop me watching you. Didn't stop me wanting you. You kept walking around this town like you didn't see me. Like you didn't know what it did to me every time you were near."

His hand twitches—like he's fighting himself and losing.

"Truth is, you were mine the second you smiled at me across your daddy's yard. And every day after that, I fought even harder to keep my hands off you."

His voice fractures with fury and hunger.

"But now?"

He's so close his breath heats my skin.

"They've handed you to me, and I don't have to pretend anymore. You belong to me now. Every breath. Every heartbeat. Every goddamn sin."

With a single movement, he opens the door and drops from the truck. His boots crack against gravel as he glances up at his house — his fortress. I try my door, but it's still locked. He looks back and smiles, then perches on the hood of his truck, mocking me.

"OPEN THE DOOR!" The scream rips free, tears at my throat. My fist strikes the dash so hard my knuckles sting.

He exhales — a patient man exasperated. Then he circles the truck and yanks open my door —

I bolt.

Two steps. That's all I get before his arm coils around my waist and lifts me off the ground. I flail, boots kicking, nails clawing at his back, but he carries me like I weigh nothing.

"PUT ME DOWN!" My fists hammer into him, useless blows.

He strides to the front door, kicks it open in one brutal motion, and hauls me inside like prey draped over his shoulder.

My feet hit the floor — adrenaline propelling me toward escape — but he's already there, a wall of muscle and menace. He shoves me backward; my spine slams into plaster, skin scraping against rough white. His hand snaps beside my head, caging me in.

"Do you think I enjoyed dragging you here like a fucking animal?" His voice is unyielding steel. "Do you think this was what I wanted?"

My lungs constrict. The room shrinks around us, oppressively small. His chest presses into mine, heat blistering through my ribs, pinning me in his orbit. Then — softly, dangerously intimate, like a secret carved from darkness —

"You don't get freedom here. You get me. And I can be good to you..." His fingers catch my chin, tilting it up until I have no choice but to meet his eyes. "But only when you're good for me."

The hold is brief but absolute. He releases me after a moment, stepping back, leaving me pinned to the wall by the weight of his words.

"Your room's upstairs. Second door on the left," he says without looking back. "Don't make me lock it."

His boots echo down the hall, each step sealing the truth deeper in my chest.

This isn't merely a nightmare. *It's a life sentence.*

I wait until his footsteps fade, then another beat after that, just to be sure.

The house is quiet, but it isn't empty. It's the kind of quiet that listens. I take the stairs slow, every sound too loud. The hallway is narrow, lined with closed doors. One lamp at the far end bleeds a tired glow onto the carpet.

The second door on the left is already open.

The room is bare but not unwelcoming—somehow worse. The bed is neatly made with crisp white sheets, a folded blanket at the foot. A dresser. A small desk under the window. Fresh toiletries lined up in the bathroom doorway, like this has been meticulously prepared. It isn't a guest room. It's a holding cell with better linen.

I step inside. The floorboards creak under each timid step. The air smells faintly of detergent and cedar—his cedar.

The window draws me before I've decided to move. I part the curtain enough to peek through. The yard is swallowed by dark, the tree line a jagged shadow against the sky. No lights. No roads. No one to hear me if I scream.

A movement below catches my eye.

He's outside, standing in the drive. The glow from his cigarette flares, bright against the dark, before fading back to ember.

Watching the house. Watching me.

He heads to his truck and pulls my suitcase from the back.

I let the curtain fall. My pulse hammers in my ears.

The bed is too precise, like it's waiting for me to lie down exactly where he wants me. I don't sit. I stand there in the middle of the room, listening to the house breathe around me.

Because it's not the walls that make me feel trapped. *It's knowing he's out there.*

Chapter 2
What He Keeps

Summer

Living with Jacob was meant to be temporary. That's what he told my parents, anyway. Just until things "settled down." Just until the men who took the photos of me were caught.

Two months later, I'm still in his house.

And somewhere between that first week and now, Jacob announced that I was his.

He says it in front of the whole town—at the diner, at the gas station. He parades me through Main Street on Saturday mornings, hand on my back, guiding me like I'm a new shiny toy that only he gets to play with. People smile at us; say we make a nice couple. They tell me I'm lucky.

I want to tell them all that this is a charade. That none of this is true, but the threat of Jackson's men still hangs over my shoulders. Visions of the photograph of me asleep still live in my mind, and although Jacob is dangerous, at least he does keep me safe.

He knows I don't want him. I see it in the way his eyes narrow when I pull away too fast, the way his jaw tightens when I answer him with one word instead of two. But Jacob's patient in that dangerous way—like a hunter who knows his prey has nowhere else to go.

He tells me I'll get used to it. That one day, I'll stop fighting him.

That the walls I've built between us will crumble, and when they do, I'll realize there's nowhere safer than right here.

And maybe that's the worst part. Not his certainty. Not even his control.

It's the quiet voice in my head that wonders if he's right.

I missed celebrating my twenty-first birthday in the house I grew up in.

Mama and Papa came to us instead, carrying cake and gifts, trying too hard to make it feel normal. Adelaide and Constance came, too. They hugged me longer than usual. Constance's eyes followed Jacob every time he moved, like she was keeping count of how close he stood.

Constance and Adelaide know that Jacob has always been infatuated with me. It used to be an inside joke between the three of us. But the joke fizzled out, and they quickly realized this was more than a crush. We had spoken about trying to put a stop to it. But who would listen to three small-town girls over the sheriff?

Jacob is a lot older than me. Thirty-seven.

Sheriff. Badge. Power.

Day by day, he messes with my head—giving and taking like it's a lesson plan.

He confuses me on purpose, makes me question everything until I can't tell what's real and what's bait. Sometimes I catch myself wondering if he's as bad as I think. Then the manipulation turns bitter, and I run.

He's caught me three times in the two months I've been here. The time before last, it wasn't even him who found me—one of his deputies did. When I was brought home, he locked me in my room for a whole day and night after telling me he wouldn't let me go. He said I'd spend every day of the rest of my life in that room if I kept running. I begged. I wailed. I screamed until my voice broke.

Then, like a switch, he came back in and behaved like nothing had happened. Like we were sitting at breakfast, not that he'd spent a day deciding my punishment. The normalcy was part of it—the apology never came, only the neat silence that pretended it was all my fault.

When Mama and Papa came, I told them. At first, they were furious. They demanded answers from him, and he gave them a story: I kept running, he did what he had to do to teach me a lesson and to keep me safe from Jackson's men.

He said it like it was charity.

They believed him. They said it was best to keep me hidden. After all, they'd done the same.

I was dumbfounded that he had managed to wriggle his way out of it, that they didn't immediately take me home, but it's clear. Jacob will always win. He will always get away with taking and doing whatever he wants.

One saving grace is that Jacob hasn't tried to own my body.

Still, when his hand finds my throat and his need to "protect" me hardens into control, a treacherous thought flickers: what if I stopped fighting and gave in to him? I hate that my body answers him at all. The longer I'm here, the more his rules crawl under my skin, and the more that wrong hunger wakes.

I've only had sex once—back when I was nineteen. It barely counted: clumsy, rushed, over in minutes.

Jacob was already one step ahead. He'd ordered a drug raid on Tyler Jenkins's place that same night—sirens, lights, deputies shouting down the hallway. They found nothing, of course.

That's when I understood: Jacob didn't have to be in the room to stop me from living my life; he just had to be everywhere else. I don't know if he realizes I lost my virginity that night. But I won't tell him —ever.

I'm wrenched from my thoughts when Mama and Papa arrive.

I move downstairs to greet them, though the weight in my chest makes every step heavier. When I open the door, they're polished and smiling, the dying sunset behind them casting everything in gold —a cruel kind of beauty that only deepens the poison in my thoughts.

My stomach twists. The betrayal settles in my bones, resentment flaring hot and wild, like a furnace I can't contain.

How can they not see? How can they stand there, blind to what's happening right in front of them? They handed me over to a man whose obsession swallowed my life whole.

They used to visit often. Now, it's once a week—if that. I've told them I want to come home, but Jacob keeps reminding them that the men who took the photographs are still out there. That Jackson's appeal is coming up soon.

It's a battle I'll never win—not while that threat keeps hanging over my life.

"Summer, sweetheart." Mama throws her arms around me and kisses my cheek. "You're not dressed!"

"It's early, Elaine, not every female takes three hours to put on some makeup and brush their hair." Papa winks, a cheeky grin forcing one of his dimples to the surface.

I let out a forced laugh and gesture toward the kitchen island. Mama shrugs her jacket off and hangs it on the back of one of the leather dining chairs.

"You know, now you're settled here, you ought to think about putting your own touch on the place," Mama says, looking around the beige, minimalist room.

I head over to pour the coffee, biting my tongue. I want to scream at her. I don't want to live here. I want to get out before I cave and go completely insane. Before I let some kind of Stockholm syndrome swallow me completely.

Instead, I turn my head and force a smile.

I place the mugs of coffee in front of them and excuse myself to the hall. I need a moment to gather myself before I unravel again. My parents, who now feel like strangers, will not be the answer to my freedom—that much is clear. So, not only am I aiming to run away from Jacob... I'm running from them, too.

In truth, I don't think the relationship with Mama and Papa will ever be fixed after this. I'll never be able to look at them as the doting parents they once were.

I used to imagine Christmases, gathered around the tree with tinsel and lights adorning the room. My child straddling Papa's lap and a husband who held my hand and brought me wine.

But now, after what they've done to me, after how they've handed me over to the devil himself, that dream is fractured. When I do get away, when I do meet a man and have a child, they'll have nothing to do with any of it.

Of that, I'm certain.

~

I hear footsteps above me, and then the quiet noise of the shower running. Jacob —

The moment I've waited for. My chest is tight, lungs straining for space, and before I can second-guess myself, my feet carry me down the hall. Past the photographs Jacob has hung like trophies. Past the locked front door. Straight to the one room he spends most of his time in but never lets me enter: his study.

That must be where he keeps the surveillance — the feeds from cameras dotted through the house. Every time I try to run, a ping hits his cell and he's there; a notification, a footprint on his screen, and the chase starts again. That's why I never get away. It isn't luck or stupidity that traps me — it's wiring and red lights that blink like tiny eyes.

If I can get into his study and find the feed, maybe soon I can make my final run. I can plan, but I need to be able to move before he knows I've moved.

I took the key from his bedside drawer last night. He had headed out to the store — it was the perfect opportunity. I just hope his bedroom doesn't have a camera.

I hardly slept a wink last night, worrying that he would notice it was missing. I'll put it back as soon as I've found what I'm looking for.

I twist the key; the knob is cool in my palm. For a second, I almost turn back, the urge to retreat pressing at me like a hand between my shoulder blades. But I push the door open anyway, slipping inside before I lose my nerve. The curtains are drawn, the air colder in here, like even sunlight knows better than to trespass. His desk is painfully neat—papers stacked into perfect squares; a single pen lined up against his notepad. His badge rests in a patch of shadow, glinting just enough to remind me that all of this—me, this house, this cage—sits under his authority.

And then out of the corner of my eye I see it. A filing cabinet. Heavy. Black. Each drawer neatly labeled in block letters: Spring. Summer. Autumn. Winter.

My stomach knots. Who even organizes their life like this? Seeing Summer stamped on metal in this room makes my skin prickle. But then I stop to think—are these seasonal files? Or is it something darker?

I crouch down, fingers trembling as they graze the cold metal handles. The silence in the room is deafening, like the walls are leaning closer to watch. I try Spring first. The drawer slides open with a low groan. Empty. Too empty—like it's mocking me for ever expecting otherwise. Autumn. Also empty. Winter. The same.

Each clang of the drawers echoes in my bones, but it's nothing compared to the weight of the last one. The handle is worn, faint scratches carved into the paint where his grip must've lingered. He touches this drawer. A lot. That much is clear. My pulse hammers as I tug. It's locked. I rattle it once, twice, teeth clenched. Nothing. Just a stubborn refusal, like the cabinet itself knows I don't belong here.

I stay there too long, staring at that single drawer, feeling. What's inside? I don't know. And maybe not knowing is worse. Because if the others are empty, then everything Jacob keeps—everything he saves—is here. Behind one locked handle.

I press my palm against the metal. It's cold. Solid. Unyielding. I hate that I'm shaking. I hate that part of me wants to find the key, to tear it open, just to prove that I'm right about what I already feel in my bones.

I need the key. I need to find what's inside.

When I finally pull away, my skin feels clammy, my chest tight. Because Jacob isn't just keeping me in his house. He's keeping pieces of me somewhere I can't touch.

I hear movement from the ceiling above and realize he must be out of the shower. I rush to my feet and leave the room, closing the door carefully to make sure he doesn't know I've trespassed. I'm devastatingly aware that I hadn't scoped out the camera feed, because I was too taken aback by the cabinet.

By the time I push open the porch door, my lungs are begging for air. I brace against the railing, gulping it down like water, because if I stay in that house another second, I might suffocate.

The sun is starting to set, leaving an orange haze glaring over the woods and fields. It looks like something from a postcard, somewhere people would find picturesque and they'd want to live. But the truth is, nothing stays clean here. Not for long. Not the streets. Not the hands. Not the girls.

"Don't dawdle, Summer," Mama calls from inside. "You need to be getting dressed. It's getting late."

I don't answer. I don't trust my voice to come out steady.

I step back from the porch rail, legs unsteady. My palms are slick. My heart is a caged thing in my chest. I take one last breath of fresh air and turn to go inside. I enter back into the kitchen and smile toward Mama and Papa.

"I'm going to change now, Mama. I won't be long."

I head through to the laundry room to gather my dress. I hold it up into the sunlight. It's white. Long-sleeved. Knee-length. Modest. Most girls my age will be trying on college graduation dresses, but here I am. Preparing to be shown off in front of the town by a man I detest with every fiber of my being.

I throw the dress over my elbow and turn to leave the room. Then I hear him.

Jacob.

Descending the stairs with the slow, deliberate grace of a man who never needs to rush. Not because he's lazy, but because the world bends to his pace.

He's dressed in a black shirt and slacks—clean, immaculate. A sermon of a man carved in onyx and smoke. His badge attached to his waist hoop, boots polished.

And his eyes... God, his eyes.

They slice through the room like razors dipped in venom, pinning me where I stand.

This is what makes it so difficult. How handsome he is.

Sometimes I wonder—in another world, if he wasn't the monster of a man he is today—whether I could have wanted him. But then the memories flood back in, and my body stiffens cold.

"You're not dressed." His voice slithers across the space between us—low, smooth, lethal—each syllable a noose tightening around my throat.

"I'm going now," I answer. Careful. Not submissive. Not defiant… dead.

He stalks across the room like a hurricane in human skin, bringing with him the scent of cedarwood, smoke, and power, bottled and worn like war paint. He doesn't tuck a strand of hair behind my ear—he claims it, fingertips burning against my skin. Soft. Deceptively gentle. A wolf's teeth before they puncture.

"You want my help?" he murmurs, his breath scorching my cheek. Not a suggestion. A promise of violation dressed as kindness.

"No," I choke out. "I won't be long."

His fingers brand my waist as he passes. I don't flinch—I shatter inside.

"So twitchy," he mutters, his smirk splitting his face. That expression floods my veins with ice, while something traitorous and molten ignites in my core. "Funny," he adds, leaning closer. "I've seen you naked plenty of times."

My lungs collapse. I'm drowning in the bathroom memory—the creak of the door, the invasion stripping me bare, the way he devoured me with that stare, like it was his birthright.

He turns toward the mirror, runs his hands through his hair—but his eyes aren't on the strands. They're on me. Watching. Consuming. Owning. And beneath that raging hunger—a terrifying, unshakable calm. The stillness of a man who knows he'll never have to hurry.

Never have to chase.

I ascend the stairs at a slow pace. There's no need to rush.
I have nowhere left to run.

Chapter 3
Whiskey, Smoke & Sin
Summer

The Dogwood is lit like a dying dream. Red neon bleeds through clouds of cigarette haze, turning everything it touches to rusted gold. The air is tangible, not just with sweat and humidity, but the scent of regret. The ghosts of nights that ended badly.

Music pounds from ancient speakers mounted in the corners. The bass is low and steady—a second heartbeat vibrating through my bones. It crawls along the backs of my legs and settles beneath my skin. There's a rhythm to the chaos—glasses clinking. Ice rattling. Boots scuffing across sticky floors. The laughter is loud and hollow. Forced. Nothing here feels real, except the heat.

Jacob keeps his hand on my lower back as we walk through to the main bar area.

Mama and Papa hang back, caught up in conversation with Mr. and Mrs. Harlot. Probably talking about Papa's latest case or Mama's gardening tips.

We continue, passing through the mahogany arched frame, towards the noise of muffled conversation.

He steers me like livestock. Like I don't have bones of my own. I feel the imprint of his possessiveness through the thin fabric of my dress. The pressure of ownership. It hums beneath my ribs.

Then... I hear it.

No… I *feel* it.

The frontman. He's not just performing. He's unravelling.

Sitting on a tall bar stool at the edge of the stage, his guitar rests across his thigh. The strap is worn, the wood scuffed. He strums it slow — each note melodic. Like he's whispering something no one else deserves to hear. Like the sound is more confession than music.

He opens his mouth. The first note deepens into something that makes my stomach drop. He sings about leaving, about highways at midnight, about stars that don't shine the same anywhere else. His voice cracks on the high notes in a way that makes my chest ache. Syrup-sweet. Southern to the bone.

He looks like someone I could've only ever dreamed up. Early twenties, maybe, with messy dark hair that would fall into his eyes if he didn't keep brushing it back. His jaw's too angled for kindness but there's something vulnerable in the way he holds himself — like he's bracing for impact, even while smiling. A shadow of something bruised.

His eyes — God. Blue. So blue they sting, like the hot side of a flame. They don't belong in a town like this. They belong in stories about shipwrecks and miracles.

He wears ripped jeans — one knee torn open — and a white T-shirt marked with sweat. It clings to his chest like a second skin. Over it, a leather vest — old and worn — with creases in the shoulders like it's been slept in too many times. Around his neck hangs a pendant I can't quite make out.

I swear I forget how to breathe. Something stirs low in my belly. Not lust. Not even want. It's a kind of ache. A memory of something I never had. A pulse of something that tastes like freedom, like a version of me I've only ever met in dreams.

He says the name of the next song, but I don't hear it. The world fades away because he's looking directly at me. Not like Jacob does. Not like the town with their prying eyes. His gaze doesn't judge, doesn't possess, doesn't leer with disdain. His eyes pierce through the layers, truly seeing me to my core.

For one impossible second, the world goes quiet.

The bar fades.

The lights dim.

It's just him. Me. And that space between us, crackling like a live wire.

Then, I feel the yank.

Jacob's hand clawing at my shoulder. Fingers dig deep—snapping the thread. Reality rushes back like a flood.

"You finished eyeing up the rock star, sweetie?" His laugh is rough. Mocking. Possessive. Warning. I blink. Shake my head. Try to focus. Try to pretend I wasn't gone for a moment.

He pulls my chair out with unnecessary force. I sit, spine straight, eyes forward, my cheeks hot. I'm thankful that Officer Haywood and his wife have joined our table. Their presence is the only thing keeping Jacob's hands in check. If we were alone, I'd already be paying for my absentmindedness.

"Sorry," I murmur. "I just... I liked the music."

Jacob grunts.

"This new shit's garbage. I'll tell you right now, our kids aren't being raised on hipster bar trash." He gestures toward the stage. "They'll grow up with Springsteen, not whatever the hell that whiny little bastard's peddling." He smirks and I nod, like a good girl.

A group of locals wave Jacob over, and he beams. The King of Nowhere. The tyrant everyone smiles at. He walks to them with his head high, chest out, badge catching the light from its spot on his holster.

Haywood follows, and his wife excuses herself to go and speak to a group of women who are lost in conversation near the dance floor.

I feel a hand squeeze my shoulder and turn faster than I should. Papa is standing there; Mama is nowhere to be seen.

"Papa, is everything okay?" I twist in my chair, voice tight. "Where's Mama?"

He raises a hand, batting away my concern. "Don't worry, honey. I was just coming to tell you—Mama and I are heading out. It's too crowded here. We're going to grab a bite at Lockwood with the Harlots." He scans the room, adds, almost offhand. "More... our sort of place."

I drop my eyes to my hands and feel something sour and small settle in my chest. The only safety-net I thought I had tonight is walking out the door because it's 'too crowded.'

That says everything.

"Okay Papa. I'll… see you next time you come to visit."

My face must say it all, because he lowers his hand to my cheek, "It's been a lovely few hours, Summer. Have a good night. We will see you real soon."

The moment his back turns, I exhale. Just once. One breath that isn't poisoned.

Then I hear it, a voice cutting through the chatter.

"This one's for all the pretty ladies in the room," the frontman announces into the microphone, voice crackling through the speakers and enveloping me in a smoky embrace.

The crowd cheers, filling the air with an electric buzz. A woman with vibrant ink decorating her arms lets out a piercing howl. Her dress clings to her curves, and she carries herself with a carefree confidence that I can't help but admire. She takes up space unapologetically, her presence loud and undeniable—a stark contrast to everything I've been taught not to be.

"Come on now," he teases, eyes scanning the room. "I need you all on the dance floor for this one. Don't hurt my feelings." He flashes a toothy smile, and I suddenly freeze, captivated by the gleam of his teeth, the curve of his lips, and the mischief in his eyes.

The music swells, and a tide begins—a wave of bodies swaying toward the stage, moving as if caught in an invisible wind. Laughter rises above the pulsing beat, intertwining with the melody and lifting the atmosphere into one of collective joy.

Boots thud against the wooden floor as a few women shriek with excitement, calling out his name—Benny. I remain seated, my hands gripping the edge of the table. Of course I do. Jacob would despise seeing me on the dance floor, laughing freely and moving in ways he didn't dictate. I can already sense the bruise forming in his thoughts —a shadow waiting to bloom into a mark on my skin. I stay put, clapping along with the beat and tapping my foot, letting the rhythm seep into my bones. I keep any hint of enjoyment off my face.

Jacob leans against the bar. His eyes snap to me every few

seconds, gesturing my way, like he's marking a target. I taste metal in my mouth.

The frontman—Benny—steps down from the stage, microphone gripped in white knuckles, voice raw and bleeding into the crowd. He cuts through the bodies like a knife through water. Women claw at him, fingers grasping at his sweat-slick arms, but he shoves past them. His eyes lock onto mine, burning through the smoke.

My lungs seize. My pulse hammers against my throat as he drops to one knee before me, close enough I can smell whiskey and salt on his breath. He thrusts a hand toward me, veins standing out along his forearm.

"Dance with me, darlin'," he growls, the words vibrating straight through my sternum.

I shouldn't. I'll pay for it if I do. But something inside me—something feral and starved—lunges forward. I grab his hand. His skin burns against mine, calluses scraping my palm, electricity shooting up my arm.

I've just lit a fuse I can't unlight. A half-smile splits his face, dangerous and delectable.

"You alright?"

I nod, throat closing around any possible sound.

He places the microphone on my table and nods to the guy near the jukebox. It kicks into something slower. He leads me onto the floor, through the crowd. I can feel them watching—locals, mostly women—whispering behind their glasses, eyes darting toward the bar. Toward him.

Benny steps closer, voice low, steady.

"I know you hate this," he says. "The stares. The noise. The way your hands shake when you're trying to pretend that you're fine." He studies me, soft but unflinching. "You haven't smiled once since you walked in—but you haven't run, either."

A small, deliberate pause.

"And I know he's watching."

My throat tightens. "You don't know what you're talking about," I whisper.

"I know enough. I first laid eyes on you fifteen minutes ago, and I've seen you flinch three times."

"I flinch all the time."

He studies me, long and quiet. Slowly, he crouches until his face is nearly level with mine. He's so much bigger than me, it should feel suffocating. But it doesn't. His chin brushes the underside of my jaw. Just skin and stubble and the rough, silent question.

"You didn't flinch just now," he says. "Not even a little."

I freeze—not because I'm scared, but because I don't know what to do with this. With him. His nearness. His warmth. His restraint.

My body has learned to respond to Jacob—the way my pulse stutters when he leans close, the reflex that tightens my hands. But right now, in this stolen moment, I tell myself this is my decision: I will dance with this man—the man who showed up when I least expected. When I needed to feel something other than possession and pain.

I'll sway to the music because I want to, not because I'm told I have to.

He rises to his full height again, slowly. My head barely reaches his chest—I can feel the heat coming off him in waves.

Under his musky cologne, he smells like rain on concrete and a trace of sweat—the kind that settles into cotton and skin after a long, hot day. Real. Unfiltered. Nothing like the crisp, manicured scent of Jacob's cologne.

"I'm not trying to be anything to you," he whispers, rocking us gently to the beat.

"Just a guy who wants to dance with the prettiest girl in the room."

I let out a shaky breath. "But Jacob—"

His hand runs from my waist, his finger positioned in front of my lips. "Shh," he whispers, eyes never leaving mine. "Right now, darlin', it's just you and me."

He moves his hand to the side, using his fingers to brush some stray hair behind my ears. Goosebumps trail after his touch, leaving me wanting to feel more of his gentleness.

"You talk like someone who wants trouble."

He grins—that crooked, boyish thing that shouldn't work but does. "Trouble's already here, sweetheart. Might as well dance with it."

I almost laugh. Almost.

Instead, I shift closer—resting my cheek against his chest. Not to tempt him, but to hide. Just for a second. Just long enough to forget where I am. To forget how fucked up I am because of Jacob. His hand comes up and brushes up the nape of my neck. No one's ever touched me like this. Not without demand. Not without ownership.

Just... human.

My ribs ache from holding in too much breath. When I finally exhale, he leans close and whispers against my ear, "Tell me when it's too much."

I nod. But I don't let go.

We keep dancing. No fancy moves. Just a slow sway that lets us blend into the background. At least, that's what I tell myself.

I can feel Jacob's eyes on us—cold as the ice in his untouched drink.

Benny doesn't push conversation. Doesn't ask questions he has no right to. He just holds me, like I don't owe him anything. When the song ends, he pulls back slightly, giving me an out.

"You wanna go sit, or...?"

I hesitate, not because I'm scared—but because I don't want this dance to end. I know if I stay much longer, Jacob will unleash a hell on me that I might not survive.

"I should probably sit," I say.

"Alright."

He lets go, easy as that.

"Thanks for the dance, Summer."

My name catches me off guard. "I didn't tell you—"

"You didn't have to," he winks, before turning away and climbing back onto the stage.

I glance at Jacob. He's sitting back at the table, jaw tight. My stomach lurches, but beneath the dread, something else flickers—a dangerous thrill.

I feel seen. I feel awake. I feel... guilty. The music quietens. The applause fades. The warmth of Benny's hands clings to my waist—a ghost I already know will haunt me. I want to turn back to him but I walk toward Jacob instead, each step heavier than the last.

Jacob sits like a statue—carved from contempt and control. His fingers drum with unnatural patience. My drink waits, warming on the table. I take a long gulp—just to have something in my hands. Something that isn't trembling. Something to wash away the taste of almost-freedom that lingers like sugar on my tongue.

His smile is slow. Cruel, but familiar. Safe, in its terrible way.

"Had fun with your boyfriend?"

I choke a little on the soda. Swallow. Shake my head.

I hate myself for the part of me that wishes I could say yes.

"It was just a dance," I say, too quickly. My voice doesn't sound like mine. It sounds like the girl I pretend to be—the one who sometimes loves the safety of his control but will always hate it more.

Jacob's jaw ticks. That tiny muscle jumping—the one that always comes before pain, before relief. He doesn't blink.

"And you think some greasy wannabe has the right to paw at my girl? To touch you? To look at you like you're some... dessert laid out for the taking?"

My fingers clamp around the glass. Tighter, until it squeaks. Part of me wants to throw it at him, but I know better. Before I can think, I throw the words at him, "Not everyone wants to swoop in and kidnap me, Jacob. Not everyone is as fucked up as you."

His hand moves beneath the table. Clamps onto my thigh. Iron-hot. Merciless. Familiar. Pain flares instantly—cold, electric—blossoming beneath my skin like spilled ink.

I suck in a breath, but I don't cry out. Crying gives him satisfaction, and he will get none of that from me.

I stare straight ahead. Don't show how much it hurts.

"Summer," he whispers, his voice a silken threat that sends chills down my spine. "If you ever dance with another man again, I'll break his fucking legs and make you watch. Never. A. Fucking. Gain."

I want to tell him to *fuck off*. I could scream for help and run until the world swallowed me whole. But what waits out there for me? Jackson Moore and his affiliates still lurk at the edges of my life. I also know Jacob isn't in a hurry to find them. Making me feel safe is part of how he keeps me tethered. But as soon as the summer comes and Blackwood opens for accommodation applications, I will go—new jurisdiction, new life. Freedom.

The chance to get away, to get my head out of the darkness Jacob had driven inside of me. Into the desire I sometimes feel for the man I hate the most.

The bar pulsates with an electric hum—alive, yet utterly oblivious to the undercurrents of danger swirling. People chatter and laugh, blind to the storm brewing at our table. Perhaps they see it and choose to ignore it.

Officer Haywood and his wife return to the table, encased in a bubble of laughter that feels intense and piercing. Her scent is an overpowering mix of cheap perfume and gin, and she beams at me as if we're celebrating, as if I'm not caught in a vice grip of silent torment beneath the table.

"Well, Summer," she chirps with a saccharine sweetness, "who knew you could dance?"

Her obliviousness is infuriating. If she's aware of the threats hissing in my ear, or the iron grip crushing my leg, she gives no sign. Perhaps she convinces herself I'm fortunate, or maybe she believes Jacob enjoys watching me in a moment of false freedom. Or maybe, just maybe, it's easier for her to pretend.

Haywood laughs, a sound that stings like salt in a wound, and claps Jacob on the shoulder. "If the sheriff would let his hair down, he might show us a move or two."

Jacob's laugh grates through the air, harsh and jagged, devoid of any real amusement. He rises, unfolding himself with the fluid grace of a predator stretching its limbs, then leans down toward me with deliberate slowness, as if to kiss me, but stops short. He straightens up, turning to the bar with the carefree grin of a man about to buy the entire place a round, as if nothing sinister just happened. The world around us remains blissfully unaware.

Benny is nowhere to be seen. The jukebox blares relentlessly, and laughter erupts from the pool tables. It all crashes over me like a tidal wave—overwhelming, suffocating.

I can't breathe. Every instinct screams at me to flee. Something inside me breaks, a surge of raw defiance. I stand abruptly, the stool screeching across the floor like a scream in the chaos. A few heads turn, but I'm beyond caring.

"I need air," I manage to say, my voice fragile and barely audible, a whisper in the storm.

Jacob, lost in his charade, doesn't even notice me leave.

Chapter 4
The Hidden Stars
Summer

The air outside hits like a slap. Thick. Wet. Clinging to my skin. The smell of beer and fried grease lingers in the open doorway. Cicadas scream from the trees—endless and shrill—like the world is trying to drown out the silence inside me.

I lean against the brick wall behind the bar and finally let myself breathe. Not deeply. Just enough to stop the ringing in my ears. The ache in my thigh pulses with every heartbeat.

The sky is heavy. Swollen with humidity.

The stars don't shine out here. Not in Rosefield. Here, they hide.

I grit my jaw, forcing pressure through my teeth to drown out the throbbing heat radiating through my thigh.

No one saw. But even if they did, no one would do anything about it. Footsteps on the gravel cause my heart to jump, then Benny steps into view, hands tucked into his jacket pockets like he doesn't want to scare me.

"You hurt?" he asks, voice low and etched with concern.

"I'm fine."

He gives me a look. "You don't lie very well."

"Then don't ask things you don't want the answer to."

That earns a smirk—but only for a second. It fades fast. He watches me like he's trying to put a puzzle together.

"How'd you know my name?" I ask. Anything to change the subject. "Back there. I never told you."

He looks down. Kicks gravel with the toe of his boot. "I asked Brian, the drummer. The second I saw you."

My stomach twists. "Why?"

"Because I had to know," he says. "Had to have the dance. Even if it was stupid. Even if I knew it would piss him off." He doesn't say Jacob's name, but it hangs there. "Bri told me you're off-limits, said you're Sheriff's girl," Benny adds. "Doesn't matter, I know sadness when I see it."

"You don't even know me. Why risk upsetting Jacob? Do you know how—"

"I know enough." He steps closer—not too close.

I glance away.

"The Sheriff's a real piece of work," he mutters.

"You don't know him," I snap—too fast. "People in this town talk a lot."

Why am I defending him?

"Yeah," Benny says. "And none of them mention the way he grabs you under the table in plain view of half the town?"

That one lands.

"Why are you even out here?"

"Because you walked out. And I couldn't sit there pretending I didn't see what I saw. Needed to see you were alright...." There's a pause. Then, "Let me guess," he says gently. "You've got a thing for men in power?"

I whip my gaze to him, anger rising. "Excuse me?"

He lifts both hands. "I'm asking. Not accusing. Believe me, I get the appeal—someone strong. Someone who can protect you. Keep things in control. Especially when the world feels like it's falling apart."

I say nothing. My insides twist with the truth he's edging towards. I'm with Jacob partly because of his badge, his power. It wasn't my choice, but I'll never let Benny know that.

"I didn't mean it like that," he adds, softer. "It just... it kills me to see women being hurt by fucking bullies who call themselves men,"

I fold my arms defensively. "You don't know what you're talking about."

He sighs, taking a seat on a low concrete pillar beside the dumpster. Then, unexpectedly, he offers a hand. "You don't have to say anything. Just... sit with me for a minute."

A part of me hesitates, torn between staying guarded and accepting the comfort I crave. Something gives way. I take his hand. He gently guides me onto his knee, his arm resting around my back —not possessive, but steady. I remain stiff, fighting my instincts... then slowly lean into him, just enough to sense his warmth through the fabric of our clothes.

"You're something else," he murmurs. "Don't know what it is yet. But damn."

I look up at him, and for just a moment, caught between two worlds, it feels like everything might finally slow down. Like maybe it's possible to want something... without being afraid of it. Our conversation flows so easily.

Then—BANG. The door crashes open.

Mr. Braithwaite stumbles into the lot—half-buttoned, dazed, sweat soaking through his collar. His tie hangs loose around his neck like a noose someone gave up tightening.

"Summer," he slurs. "Sheriff's lookin' for ya. He don't seem too happy."

My chest clamps tight.

The flicker Benny gave me—that stupid, dangerous spark I didn't mean to feed—dies on the spot. My breath stutters. Pulse hammers in my throat.

Just one second. Just one—BANG.

The door crashes open again. Boots strike pavement like gunshots.

Jacob.

No scanning. No hesitation. He knew exactly where I'd be.

"What the fuck are you doing, Summer?" His voice slices through the lot—jagged enough to skin me alive.

A few strides and he's on me. His hand clamps around my arm— fingers bruising, nails biting.

"I told you no fucking scenes," he snarls, dragging me closer. "No embarrassment. You do what you're told for once in your goddamn life."

I open my mouth to answer—to fight—but nothing comes out. Just the taste of blood, and fear. The last trace of freedom I thought I had.

He yanks me hard. My side slams against the truck's side mirror. Pain screams across my back. I bite down on my lip to keep the sound buried.

"Get in," he hisses. "No more of your crocodile tears. I'm done playing."

And then—

"Hey." One word. Low. Calm. But it stops everything.

Jacob turns.

Benny stands a few feet away—hands loose, eyes steady. No bravado. No threat.

"I don't think she wants to go with you."

Jacob laughs—dry and dangerous. "And I don't think you know what the fuck you're talking about, son."

Benny shrugs. "Maybe not. But I know what I saw."

Jacob's grip tightens like a vice. My ribs twist—pulling against each other like they want out. Benny's gaze flicks to mine.

"I think she's had enough."

A beat.

Jacob steps forward. Releases me with a shove. I stumble into the truck, catching myself on the door handle.

"Get in the truck, Summer. Now."

And this time, I do. Without argument, without breathing a word. Because the stars stay hidden.

And so do I.

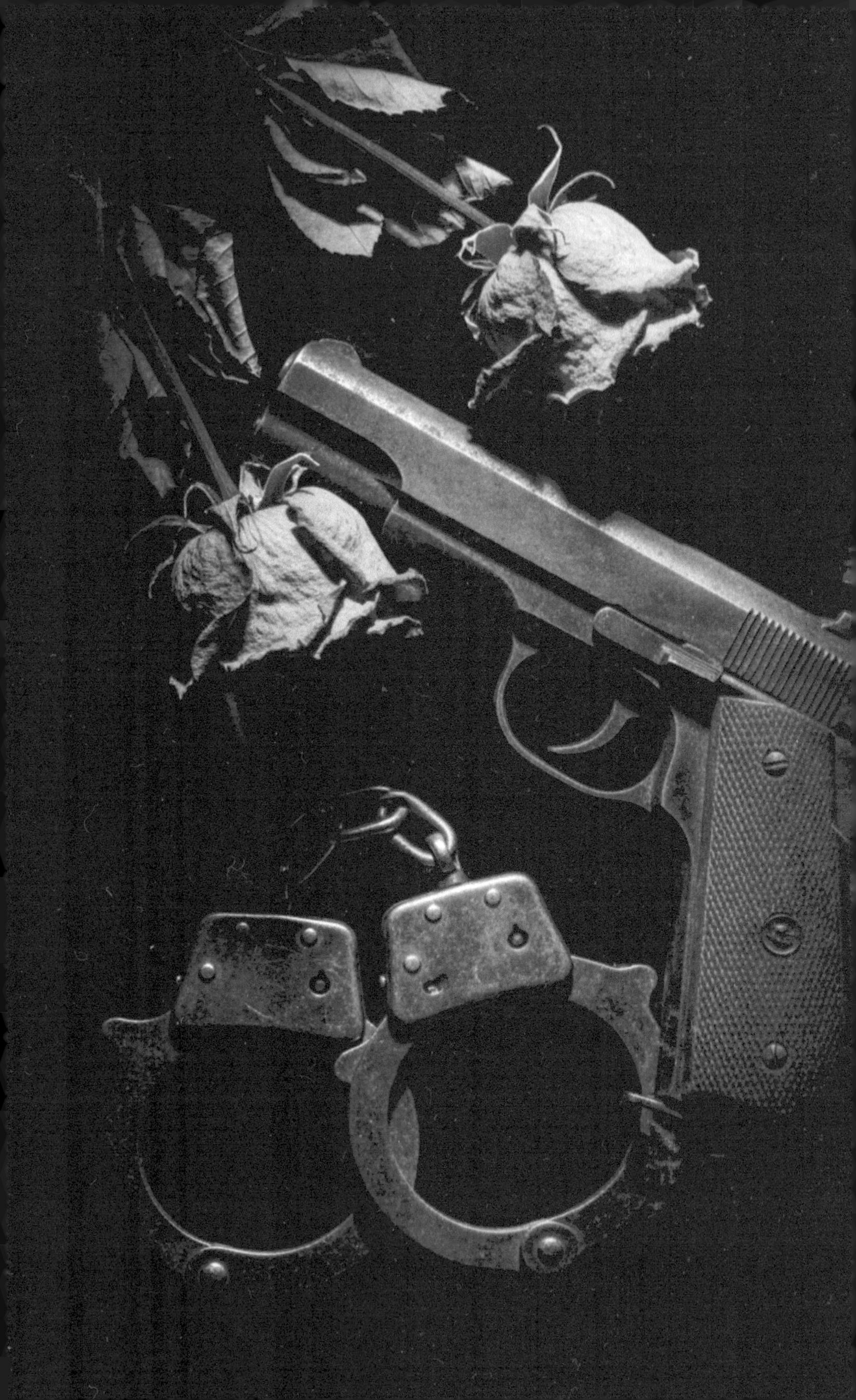

Chapter 5
The Devil in Uniform

Jacob

They think I'm smiling

That's the part that always gets me — how fucking easy it is.

A tilt of the mouth. A nod. A badge pressed to my chest like a holy relic. People will believe anything if the devil's wearing a uniform. I could blow a man's brains out in this bar and half of them would call it justice. The other half would thank me for keeping the peace.

But I'm not thinking about them. I'm thinking about her.

Summer.

Out there, with another man like she's forgotten the name I carved into her life. The woman I dragged from the dark and put under my roof. The woman I told myself I would keep.

The woman I have been in love with for two years and have taken into my home to protect from the monsters that lurk in the dark. But she's dancing with that fucker for all to see.

That singing stray with hands too familiar and eyes that don't understand what it means to touch something sacred.

And she's smiling. Not the smile she gives me. Not the one she wears when she thanks me through her teeth for the silk I buy or the food I put on the table. This one's real. Soft. Lit from inside.

Unforgivable.

"She's got moves," some idiot mutters nearby. "Didn't think the sheriff would let her off the leash."

My head turns slow. Wouldn't want anyone to think I'm the kind of man who loses control. Yet.

I find the voice. Lock eyes. Some oil-rig rat with beer on his breath and death behind his teeth.

"You want to repeat yourself?" I say, calm as a storm gathering under skin.

He chuckles. Weak. Backpedals. Good.

I'm not in the mood to bury another one behind the diner.

Haywood says something beside me—laughing about blood on a porch turning out to be barbecue sauce. I nod. Smile. Pretend I give a shit.

I don't.

I'm too busy watching her. Still swaying. Still glowing. Still fucking mine.

Still completely unaware of the dangers lurking around every corner—the sacrifices I've made to keep her from them. Her laughter hits me like a knife between the ribs. Light. Free. Something I didn't give her permission to feel. And that boy—

He touches her waist. My hand twitches, the urge to pull out my gun and shoot the fucker burns through me like lava.

If she were smart, she'd be crying right now. Begging me to make it stop. Begging me to get him to take his hands off her. But she doesn't—

She's gotten stupid. Or brave. Or both.

From the first second, she was mine. Not a passing obsession—an inevitability carved into me. I've memorized every shiver, every tear, every defiance. She's always belonged to me, even when she thought she was running. She still looks at me like I'm the danger. Maybe I am. But I'm also the only thing standing between her and the monsters who wanted her. Who planned her destruction. And if she knew what they had planned, what I had really saved her from, she would never lead a normal life again.

Every road she takes will always lead back to me. Every breath she takes is already inside my hands. She can fight, she can hate, but she'll never escape. I won't let her. Not now. Not ever.

I haven't owned her in the bedroom yet. I was never going to be the man to tie her down and take her against her will. Hell, that's the men I'm saving her from. But right now, the idea of her in chains, taking every inch of my cock and staring into my eyes sounds like heaven. Maybe that's what she needs. Maybe then she'll stop eyeing bar rats and thinking it's alright to let them put their hands on her.

I'm a fucking monster. But a rapist?

No.

It takes every ounce of strength I have to walk back to the table and sit, to hide the storm clawing at my insides and let the room think I'm calm.

"I'm waiting for you baby," I mutter under my breath.

The song ends and he finally takes his greasy fucking hands off her.

I want to stomp on his fucking throat — but I won't. I'll play the long game. I'll find out everything there is to know about that son of a bitch.

She heads back over. Eyes down at the ground. She knows. She fucking knows. She has the audacity to sit there like nothing happened. Like she didn't just look at another man like he could save her. Like he could take her home and fuck her into forgetting I ever existed.

I saw it — that flicker. That spark she thought she could hide. She wanted him to look at her, to see her. To know she was interested. And now she sits there, all wide eyes and trembling lips, pretending she's innocent?

No.

"Had fun with your boyfriend?" The words come out smooth, almost playful, but they taste like rust on my tongue.

What I really want to do is drag her out by the hair and make her confess how far she would've let him go if I wasn't here.

She chokes on her drink, stammers, shakes her head. I see the flicker in her eyes — the lie. She hated herself for enjoying it. Good. She should.

"It was just a dance," she blurts, too fast, too brittle.

My jaw ticks. That familiar muscle jumping—the one she knows too well. The one that always comes before I become the monster. And fuck, I want to hurt her. I want to carve the memory of him out of her skin.

"And you think some greasy wannabe has the right to paw at my girl? To touch you? To look at you like dessert laid out for the taking?"

Her fingers clamp the glass until it squeaks. A weak attempt at defiance. For a second I hope she throws it at me, just so I'll have the excuse to put her in cuffs, take her home and fuck any other man out of her brain. She looks at me with disgust in her eyes. As though she can read my mind.

"Not everyone wants to swoop in and kidnap me, Jacob. Not everyone is as fucked up as you."

My laugh scrapes out, jagged enough to cut. I reach under the table and clamp my hand around her thigh. She flinches—barely a twitch— but it's not enough. Not nearly enough to satisfy the storm inside me. I squeeze harder, my fingers digging in with brutal intent —until I know she'll bruise. But she still doesn't make a sound.

She keeps her eyes forward, drink in hand, playing the part of the obedient good girl. But I know it hurts. I know.

I wonder—how much pressure would it take to make her scream? Not just a gasp, not a flinch, but a real, visceral scream. Would she still suppress it if I dragged her into the next room and claimed her for every second she dared to stare at another man like that? It's the fire in her, that silent, stubborn refusal to show pain. That's what makes me want to shatter her. Not because I hate it, but because I crave it. Because I want to be the one to obliterate it, to strip the fight from her inch by inch. To own the moment she ceases to pretend she can endure me.

"Summer," I whisper into her ear, threat dripping from every word. "If you ever dance with another man again, I'll break his fucking legs and make you watch. Never. A. Fucking. Gain."

Haywood and his wife return to the table, she mutters something to Summer about her dance moves—it makes me want to throw the table. Haywood makes a comment about me letting my hair down. Fucking idiot.

It's my turn for the round. I take a second to gather myself, to let my erection die down. That fucking girl has no clue the chaos she ignites within me. No idea how perilous it is to look at me like that, to breathe the same air as me like that, to exist—wrapped in skin too tender for a world this vicious. She thinks she's playing a game. But she doesn't know the rules. Doesn't grasp what I'm capable of when I unravel. And baby, I'm unravelling.

I buy the round. They all thank me, as if I give a fuck. I don't know why I didn't just call it a night, take her home, and remind her with punishing clarity who the fuck she belongs to.

The locals won't shut the fuck up, their chatter drilling into my skull. Haywood's droning on about his goddamn roof, while his wife spews meaningless crap. I nod at the right moments, a mechanical grin plastered on my face, enough to blend in. But my focus is elsewhere. Her chair stands empty.

A frigid weight lodges in my chest, icy and suffocating. She's gone. Without a word. Without permission.

And he's gone, too. Benny. That fucking guitar-playing ghost with dirt on his collar and a smirk full of poetry. My vision narrows to a pinprick, pulse pounding in my wrists like war drums.

"She duck out?" Haywood asks, oblivious.

"She'll be back," I say, my voice a slick, emotionless veneer, masking the violent images of dragging her back by the hair and slamming the door shut behind us.

Because she will return. She knows the consequences if she doesn't. She's not stupid. She's mine. And I will make damn sure she remembers.

I consider chasing after her immediately, but I need bourbon. Something to steady the tremors in my hands, something to prevent me from igniting this place with the inferno inside. I order the drink and swallow it down, hoping it will calm the storm I feel.

But it's time to hunt.

My boots thud across the floor. Calm on the outside. Inside, I'm already in motion—fists clenching, teeth itching to snap. Her name drips through my veins like acid.

He thinks he's got a shot. She thinks she's free. They're both wrong.

Braithwaite—greasy moustache slick with sweat, a beer gut that jiggles like mockery—blocks the path to the parking lot. His breath reeks of cheap hops and bad choices.

"You okay with your girl gyratin' with the pretty-boy busker?" he jeers.

My teeth bare. "You think he's prettier than me, Braithwaite?"

He laughs, a ragged sound. "Hell no. Just sayin'… if that was my woman—"

I cut him off, voice colder than ice. "Well, she's not."

He freezes, cocky grin draining. "Right… just… surprised you didn't shut it down sooner."

I lean in close enough for him to smell the threat seeping off me. "Girls like Summer test fences, scratch at gates—but they always come back. Now, if you want to make yourself useful old man, help me find her."

He says nothing. I see the flicker of something—fear? Maybe understanding. My chest tightens. Part of me thinks I'd rather not find her at all. He heads out of the door to the parking lot. Within seconds I overhear commotion. It's Braithwate. He's found her.

I slam my glass down and head outside.

There they are. Summer pressed against Benny, that shadow of flesh and bone. His hands at her waist, hers laced around him. My gut twists; my vision cracks red. Something inside me snaps, not with triumph, but fracture.

She sees me—guilt and fear flashing across her face. Good. I hate that it still hurts me.

I cross the lot in two strides. The air hums with rage and something darker—loss, regret. My hand clamps on her arm, nails biting in. I want her to remember.

"I told you no fucking scenes," I snarl, dragging her into the shadows beside the truck. My other hand slams her into the wing mirror—hard, but not enough to break. Just enough to sting.

She gasps—breath rattling out of her. Part of me wants to let go, to pull her into me and check that she's ok. Instead, I press my forehead to hers, voice low and broken. "No embarrassment. You do what you're told for once in your goddamn life."

I want her to look at the bruises tomorrow and know I was here. But part of me wants her to look at me and remember what she almost lost. I want to sink my teeth into her, devour her whole, make her scream until her voice is nothing but a tortured rasp, her legs collapsing beneath her. Make her earn the privilege of sharing the air I breathe. But I won't. Not yet. She hasn't begged for that kind of mercy.

"Get in," I command, voice slicing through the tension. "No more of your crocodile tears. I'm done playing."

Then—"Hey."

That voice, grating, unwelcome. The fucking rockstar wannabe.

One quiet word, but it demands attention. I turn, simmering. He's eerily calm, steady as a predator in a room drenched with gasoline, a lit match in hand.

"I don't think she wants to go with you."

A laugh bursts from my lips, low and mocking. It's so naive, so oblivious to the brutal reality.

"You don't know what the fuck you're talking about, son."

He stands firm, unfazed. "I know what I saw." His gaze shifts to her. "She's had enough."

And in that moment, cold and unyielding, I make my decision. With brutal certainty.

I will kill him. Not here, not now—too many prying eyes—but soon. I'll erase him, leaving her to regret every breath she took in his company.

I shove her toward the truck. She stumbles, compliant, her eyes fixed forward.

Because she knows. This is the price of dancing with flames. You get burned.

"Get in," I command once more.

And this time—she obeys.

Because now she understands—there's no escape once I strip away the facade of kindness.

54

Chapter 6
Cold Baptism

Jacob

The truck growls beneath us the whole way home, engine snarling through every bend like it feels what I feel. Rage. Humiliation. Something worse.

My hands clamp the wheel tight enough to snap bone. Every time she shifts beside me, I feel it—the heat of her disobedience, the ghost of her weight on another man's lap. The image won't leave me. The way she looked at him. The way he looked at her.

Her silence only stokes it. She knows not to speak. Not after that. Not after the way she made me look.

She's pressed up against the passenger door like she's trying to crawl out of her skin. She should be afraid. She should be shaking. Because I'm not done. Not even close.

The house looms ahead—tall, black, soulless. Empty windows staring back, porch light flickering like it's choking on its last breath. I never fix it. I want it to die. Let the darkness welcome her home.

I kill the engine. Step out. Slam the door so hard it rocks the truck. I'm already moving before she reaches for the handle. Rip her door open, grab her arm—right where she bruises easiest—and drag her out.

She stumbles, but she doesn't fall. She clings to her pride like it'll protect her. It won't. She's not a woman right now—she's a weight. A burden. Something I have to re-break just to remind her how to behave.

The porch groans under my boots. Mud smears across the boards. I don't care. She'll clean it later, on her knees. The door slams behind us. The whole house vibrates. She flinches. Barely. But I see it. I feel it. I turn. Lock the door. Click. Trap set.

"You think that was smart?" My voice is ice. Brutal and low. "Grinding on some nobody with a second-hand guitar?"

She doesn't answer.

I take a step. "Answer me."

"I danced," she whispers.

Wrong answer.

"You disobeyed."

Another step. Close enough to feel the tension in her chest. I tower over her and watch her shrink under me. Good girl.

But not good enough.

Every inch of me wants to shove her into the wall. Watch her gasp. Force the apology from her mouth. But I don't. Not yet. Pain's a waste if she doesn't learn.

"You think people didn't notice?" I grind out. "Think I didn't see the way he looked at you? Like you were a prize? A fucking freebie?"

Her jaw tightens. A flicker of defiance—pathetic.

"He asked me to dance. That's it."

"And. You. Said. Yes." I don't need to raise my voice. I'm not the storm. I'm the eye of it. Stillness. Silence. Certainty.

She doesn't get it. Every second on that floor unravelled what I've spent years wrapping tight. Every sway of her hips told the whole damn town she's not taken. Not claimed. Not mine. But she's wrong.

I slam my badge on the table. It lands with an echo.

Let it mock me. Let it remind her. I run a hand through my hair and start to pace.

She doesn't move, still clinging to her bag like it holds salvation. It doesn't. It never will. There is no fucking salvation for her. Not from me. Never.

"You've got no fucking clue what I'm keeping you safe from," I mutter, voice splintering at the edges.

She lifts her eyes. Brave. Stupid.

"Moore's men," she snaps. "Men who want to come and kidnap me, right? Because right now, it looks a hell of a lot like that's what you're doing! Yes, some little fuckboys took a photo of me. They're nothing compared to you. Let them fucking take me—it would be better than spending every day with you!"

The air fractures. Cracks down the centre like glass under pressure. For a second, I forget how to breathe. That's her gift. Summer doesn't know when to be quiet. I step even closer. Close enough to make her lean back. But not close enough to give her what she wants. She wants proof. Wants pain. Wants to say *I told you so* when I finally snap. But I don't.

And I want her afraid. Not just of me. Of herself. Of the part of her that's starting to crave me. The part that wants to be bent. Owned. Made into something no one else can have.

I stare. Long. Hard. Until her breath catches, like she knows she's losing something she never understood to begin with.

And then I walk away. Not because I'm done, but because my control is crumbling. I can't lose control.

Not yet.

I sit in the kitchen long after the door slams upstairs. My elbows are on the table, my fists pressed against my mouth. The only light in the room is from the stove clock.

1:12 a.m.

The hour where the town sleeps and men like me fester, rot in our own silence. I should be out cold. Buried beneath the weight of another day. But all I see is her—on his lap. Her head tucked near his shoulder. Her hair loose. That fucking smile. Flickering.

Soft. Stupid. *His*. Not mine.

I gave her everything. Ripped her out of that house. Gave her a roof. A future. I could've left her to rot like the rest of them.

Like her mother—too scared to speak. Like her daddy—too selfish and weak to keep her safe. But I didn't. And she dances for another man like it costs her nothing? No.

That boy doesn't get to see what I built with my own fucking hands. He doesn't get to make her feel free. She's not. She never was.

The floor creaks overhead. Bare feet. Slow. Cautious. She's trying not to wake the beast.

Too late, sweetheart.

I don't move when she hits the bottom step. Let her think I'm part of the shadows now. Something half-human, half-curse. She pauses near the tap, thirsty, and I stand, creeping along the darkness. Of course she is. Guilt dries the throat faster than bourbon.

I stand from the dining chair, arms folded. Still. Calm. Like smoke before fire.

"I see everything, you know."

She freezes. Her spine straightens. And for a second, I swear she considers bolting out the door, like she's ever had a shot in hell of escaping me. But she doesn't. She doesn't turn. So, I twist the knife.

"You think he'd still want you," I say, voice low and razor-sharp, "if he knew where you came from? If he knew your daddy was being hunted by Jackson Moores' men? If daddy wasn't such a fucking pussy, you wouldn't be here."

That gets her. A full-body jolt like I struck bone. Good. That's where it lives—the truth.

"Don't talk about him like that."

I push off the table slowly.

"Why not? It's the truth. He was a coward. Weak. Cared more about his job than his fucking daughter."

I let it sit. Let it rot in the space between us.

"One word. One smile. That's all it took to make you mine." I lean in just enough. "You should be grateful."

Her voice comes soft, but there's a splinter in it now. A crack beneath the quiet.

"I'm not."

I smile. "No?"

"I'm not fucking grateful," she says, louder now. "You didn't save me. You took me from one shitty situation and put me in another."

There it is. That flicker of resistance. That little ember she keeps thinking might grow wings. That dangerous lie she keeps telling herself—that she had a choice.

"Oh, I see." I tilt my head. Mocking. "You think the rockstar would do better? You think he'd still play white knight when he finds out what you really are? A pawn in a very fucking dangerous game?"

She snaps.

"I'm not a pawn!" she shouts. "If you wanted to help him, you could've—without taking me! I hate you… I always have… and God help me, I always will."

I lose it. One breath—just one—and I'm across the kitchen. My hand slams against the wall beside her head. The plaster groans, fracturing. The sound echoes like a gunshot.

She flinches.

I cage her against the wall with the full weight of me. Heat. Muscle. Fury. She trembles.

But she doesn't look away. And that—that's what twists the blade.

"You think I wanted this?" I growl, low and lethal. "Think I planned for my life to revolve around protecting you?"

Her jaw clenches. Unmoving. Defiant.

I reach up and brush my knuckles along her face. Soft. Possessive. A velvet noose.

"I took you because I had to," I whisper, voice coiled and quiet. "Because every time I saw you walking around town like a lamb with her throat bared—I knew someone was going to take you. And I wasn't gonna let it be them."

Her throat bobs. I see it—the fight behind her eyes—but her body stays still.

My eyes drag to her mouth. Those lips—soft, full, begging for trouble. I wonder what she'd do if I kissed her, if I took that bottom lip between my teeth and sucked until she squealed.

She's looking at my mouth, too. Her breathing quick and shallow. She knows what I'm thinking, and she's waiting to see if I'll act on it.

"You don't get to shame me for keeping you safe," I snarl, voice rougher now. "You don't get to grind against another man and come home expecting kindness."

She stares up to meet my gaze. Wide eyes glassy, but not afraid. Not enough. I lean in. My lips almost brush her temple, close enough to taste the defiance clinging to her skin.

"Next time you want to act like a whore," I murmur, every syllable sliding like a blade, "remember who owns you."

She flinches, shoulders twitching. I step back. Leave her trembling, breath catching like a stalled engine. Because punishment's coming.

She rushes past me, darting for the stairs.

I could chase her. I could claim her right now. I could bury myself so deep into her that she doesn't know where I end and she begins. But I'll let her be scared. Let her sleep with one eye open.

Let the pain come from inside her own head.

I sit in the old leather chair, bourbon in one hand, the weight of rage festering in the other. The bottle's nearly empty. I don't remember drinking most of it. All I remember is him. That smug grin. That fucking lazy drawl.

I could gut him, burn the flesh off his bones, and still not feel clean. The glass creaks in my grip as I stare down at the amber swirl, pretending it's his blood. Warm. Thick. Pooling between my knuckles while he screams.

The fire crackles low, casting shadows like demons on the floorboards. It doesn't drown out the noise in my head. It's her voice I hear. Not his. That trembling *please*. That pathetic *Jacob, stop* that I've heard all too often. She thinks I hurt her because I want to. Little does she know, I'm trying to protect her. Trying to teach her.

She doesn't know what power is. She thinks I'm cruel? She hasn't seen the side of me I've buried for her sake. The one I've muzzled with promises.

I told myself I'd wait. But she keeps on pushing. Scratching at the bars. Daring me to claim her. And I've never been the kind of man to back down from a dare.

I need to make her see. Not with words. Not with warnings. With skin. With pain. With every inch of me she's been holding back from claiming her body. I hear it in her breathing. I see it in the dilation of her pupils. She fucking wants it, alright. But she will never admit that.

My boots slam heavy against the floorboards as I storm toward the stairs. The bourbon bottle crashes onto the table with a crack loud enough to rattle the frames on the wall.

She's up there. Crying, probably.

Good.

She needs to remember what happens when she forgets who I am. Not just the sheriff. Not just the law. But her goddamn future.

I climb the stairs and freeze at her door. Nothing but silence—no breathing sounds, no movement. Then a faint scrape followed by delicate footsteps. She's coming to me. Must've caught my shadow under the frame.

It's playtime, baby.

She steps into the corridor. Shadows stretch across the walls, black tendrils that taunt us. The air sours, floorboards moaning underfoot, like they know exactly what's coming.

She meets my gaze—there it is again, that stubborn spark in her eyes. That stupid light I've tried a hundred times to snuff out.

"Jacob—you're drunk. Come on, lets—"

"I'm done with your games, Summer," I snarl. "You push me 'til I snap, then act like you didn't light the match yourself. You want the monster? You fucking got him."

I jerk my chin toward the stairs.

"My bedroom. Now."

She hesitates. I growl, mean and low. "Now."

She shakes her head. No isn't an option. I grasp her by her nape and pull her head back, forcing her to look me in the eye, while pushing her back toward her door. If she won't come to my room, I'll fuck her in hers.

She turns against my grip, bracing for impact. I close the gap so she can taste bourbon and rage on my breath and slam her against the wall next to her doorframe.

"You wanna rape me? Force me to my knees? Go ahead. You've hurt me enough already." She spits, tears forming from the corners of her eyes.

I smile then—a wolf's grin, raw and hungry. I lean in slow, like maybe I'll kiss her. Maybe I'll give her something soft before pain.

She slaps me before our lips touch. A hollow crack. It barely stings—but it lands. Silence roars through the hallway. She immediately cowers, holding her hands up.

I seize a fistful of her hair and hurl her into her room. She scrambles, clawing at my arm.

"Jacob—please—stop—"

But I don't. I throw her onto her bed like she's nothing. She curls into herself—small, trembling, fragile. Gone is the defiant girl, only fear remaining. I stand over her, chest heaving, eyes locked. I could end this now. Remind her who owns her body, her soul, her every heartbeat.

My hand drifts to my belt.

Her eyes—wide, wet, pleading—halt me in my tracks. For one frigid moment, I despise myself for hesitating. Then, a surge of fury turns on her for causing my pause. The belt slips from my grasp.

"You don't want this? Then tell me why your breath hitches every time I touch you. Why your eyes beg for me to claim you?"

She doesn't utter a word. Just watches me like a rabbit, frozen in terror, waiting for the inevitable snap of the trap.

"You want me, too. And you can't hide it for shit. One day it'll happen, but you don't get to call it rape," I growl under my breath. "Tonight, you need a brutal dose of reality instead."

I drag her from the bed by her legs and pull her into the bathroom. I hurl her under the shower and position the head directly above her.

"Jacob, don't—"

But I've already made my move. Water crashes down with brutal force—drenching her from scalp to heel. Her flimsy pyjamas cling to her. She gasps, slips, scrambling backward across the tile. Her hair is a tangled mess, chest heaving with shock.

She's quaking, teeth chattering, arms wrapped around herself as if they could hold her shattered pieces together.

"Need to wash the stink of him off you," I mutter with icy disdain. "Next time you wanna act like a woman looking for a fuck, I'll give you one. Permission or not. You've been warned."

She curls tighter, a tangled mess of limbs and humiliation, trying to vanish into the drain. But nothing swallows guilt in this house.

I turn and walk out, each step a drumming reminder of my power. At the door, I pause—long enough for her to understand I could have unleashed more. And next time? I just might.

I leave her there—cold, trembling, drenched to the bone.

Chapter 7
You Do Not Deserve This
Summer

I wake on the sofa, spine digging into metal springs, every bone aching like it's been borrowed and returned broken. My clothes are dry, but my skin still remembers the water—icy and unforgiving.

I had stripped out of the soaked pajamas on the bathroom floor and threw on whatever I could find—a hoodie that smells like mothballs and old perfume, joggers from the bottom of a drawer. My hair's still damp, curling against my jaw in cold tendrils. The towel lies crumpled beside the sink, half-frozen, like it gave up too.

Last night won't stop replaying in my head. The rush of dancing with Benny, the thrill of being wanted, even if it was by a stranger. But then—Jacob. The way the air shifted when he pinned me to the wall, how the fear tangled with something I shouldn't have felt. How close I came to wanting his mouth on mine. I keep wondering what it would feel like if he did kiss me—how desperate, how starved it would be. He's been there for so long, watching, invading, haunting every inch of space I own. And now I can't stop thinking about what it would be like to give in—to let a man that obsessed, that dangerous, have me.

He put me under the shower, made sure I was drenched, shivering. Then he told me if I ever showed interest in another man, he'd fuck me anyway. He said it like a promise, not a threat.

The twist in my stomach isn't fear—it's something worse, something I can't justify. I hate him. I tell myself that over and over. But the truth is, every time he pushes me, something inside me answers back.

I drag myself off the sofa and fold the comforter neatly. The house is quiet. Too quiet. No boots on gravel. No keys in the lock. No footsteps upstairs. He's gone, or he's watching. He does that sometimes—lurks in doorways, blends into shadows. Waits until I forget he exists before reminding me exactly who I belong to.

There's a buzzing behind my eyes, like my brain's been scrubbed with steel wool. The flickering bathroom light pulses in the hallway mirror—on, off, on again. Everything feels used. My body. The house. Even the morning.

I go to the kitchen and fill the coffee machine. I flick it on, gripping the counter, fingers curling into the wood like maybe I can anchor myself before I float too far away. The world tilts. My stomach turns. I need breakfast. I need something stupid and normal. But nothing is normal anymore. Not since he made me his.

I move to the eggs.

Tap. Crack. Spill.

One splits wrong. Yolk dribbles across the counter. I grab the hem of the hoodie and smear it up without thinking. It stains. Sinks. The mess never really disappears—it just changes color. Toast burns. I scrape it. Coffee's cold. I drink it anyway.

I sit at the table and cry. Not loud—the kind of crying that comes without sound. The kind that leaks. My face stays blank. My body still. But my insides are hollowing out with every slow blink.

Tick. Tick. Tick.

The clock counts out my sentence. I think about running. I always do. Ever since that first day—the way Papa wouldn't look at me, the way the door clicked shut and I realized that no one was going to stop him. Not the law. Not the town. Not my mother.

"Jacob is the law," I remind myself.

If I run, who'll stop Jackson's men? No one. He made that perfectly clear. And he'd rather kill me himself than let them tear me apart.

Rosefield doesn't forgive. It erases. People here disappear, but townsfolk know better than to ask questions. Like the mechanic's shop—what's left of it—and the guy who owned it. Dead. Apparently, it was suicide, but who dies of a gunshot wound next to a running vehicle with the door open? This town is corrupt through and through, and Jacob is the one pulling all the strings and ticking all the boxes.

I wipe the mug until its surface gleams, rinse the plate, fold the dishcloth over the sink's edge in a gesture so small it hardly matters —one less thing for Jacob to notice, one less excuse for him to tilt my chin, whisper I'm slipping, then carve the reminder into my flesh.

I peel back the curtain enough to see the drive. Empty. The sky looms low, swollen with grey uncertainty.

A stray tear escapes from my eye, rolling down my cheek. I wipe it away before it has chance to fall and catch the scent of the manky hoodie. I need to change.

I climb the staircase, make my way down the hall and stand before my wardrobe, hands trembling, and pull out the lilac dress he told me I'm only to wear inside his house. Soft. Short. Too much flesh he'd said—ironically precise, like a spotlight trained on my bruises, my shame on display.

He must get some sort of sick kick out of seeing the marks he makes on me.

In the mirror I see someone unrecognizable—skin stretched tight over silence; hollow eyes haunted by the echo of my own name. A husk. My hair, too long, auburn, Mama used to beam—now hangs limp past my shoulders, heavy with the memory of hands running through it that never belonged.

I close my eyes once, twice, and wonder: how much of me can remain when every choice is a cage?

When I open them, the first thing I see are my green eyes. People always notice them first. Striking, they say. Like moss in sunlight. Like they're something soft, but there's nothing soft left. I look and I look— but I don't see myself. Just a warning. This is what happens when a woman forgets she's a person. Instead, something built to be owned. To be used.

My eyes sting. I force them dry. I think of Mama. Her trembling hands as she folded this dress into my suitcase. She knew. She saw his actions. She saw me flinch when Jacob touched my shoulder. She let me go anyway. They both did.

Once, I thought love meant bedtime stories. Lavender oil. Red ribbons in my hair.

Now I know better. Love looks like silence. Love looks like shame. Love looks like survival.

And then… there were my girls.

Constance. Adelaide.

My light when the world started to darken. My anchors in a sea that kept trying to drown me. They were late-night secrets and bruised toes from dancing barefoot on wet pavement. They were warmth when everything else turned to frost.

"Poison," he called them. "Loud-mouthed little sluts."

He said they were waiting for my downfall. That he was the only one who'd catch me.

But he didn't see me. Not really. He saw what he hadn't broken yet. He saw them for what they were—A threat. Women who would go to the ends of the earth for me. Hell, they've tried.

When I first moved with Jacob, they tried to come see me often. But Jacob had warned me. I had to pretend to be happy, I had to pretend that I wanted this life with him. If the girls caused a scene, Moore's men might target them, too.

I smooth the lilac dress over my knees. The fabric snags on scabbed skin. I sit cross-legged in a patch of fading sunlight—child-like, breakable, like a paper doll left out in the rain. The silence shifts and my imagination springs to life. I close my eyes, and I see them.

Constance—rough-edged, dark-eyed, unapologetic.

Adelaide—all softness and sunflower seeds, wild laughter and secrets under her breath.

Then— Crunch. Gravel. Sudden. Wrong. My body locks. Breath caught. Heartbeat frantic, wild, panicked.

I creep toward the window, one hand trembling as I hook back the curtain.

Not his truck. Not Jacob's.

This one's red. Old. Beaten to hell and proud of it. The bumper's got a dent like it grew there—scarred, unashamed. A truck that's been through fire and came out laughing.

The door creaks open. A man climbs out. Tall. Dark-haired.

Benny.

My chest folds in on itself. He takes the porch steps slow. Every creak in the boards sounds like an admonition. Like we're already in trouble. Before he can knock, I open the door.

He freezes. His eyes lock onto mine—and something in him cracks. I see it. The fracture. Like glass under pressure. Shock. Confusion. Then—concern.

Raw. Bare. Blinding.

His jaw tightens. I watch the muscle jump. He takes me in—all of me. The dress. The finger mark bruises on my arm. The silence. His gaze lands on my wrists—on the fingerprints Jacob branded me with. He stares like he wants to bury him for them. Flaring his nostrils and releasing a sigh of fury. But he swallows it. Keeps it tucked behind clenched teeth.

I tuck my hair behind my ear, suddenly too aware of the puffiness under my eyes, the hollowness in my face, the way this dress clings to skin that doesn't feel like mine. I look like prey. I feel like prey.

"Is he here?" Benny's voice is quiet, like Jacob might crawl out of the walls if he speaks too loudly.

I shake my head. "No. But he comes back. Random times. To check." To test. To remind me I'm still his. "How did you know where I live?"

"Got your address from the bar owner. Had to ask twice." A pause. "He warned me not to mess with Jacob."

I swallow hard.

"Sit with me," I say, nodding toward the top step of the porch before lowering myself down beside him.

The wood bites into the back of my legs as I sit, and pain flickers up my thigh—harsh enough to make me wince. I try to hide it, pressing my palm there like that'll somehow quiet the ache. I glance toward the dark stretch of road where Jacob's truck should be and swallow hard.

"Why would you… risk that? Coming here?" My voice cracks on the last word. Fear creeps into my chest, cold and heavy. "If he finds you here…." His eyes meet mine again—and this time it's a threat against whatever's hurt me. He drops onto the porch steps, taking a seat beside me.

"Because I can't stop thinking about you," Benny admits, voice cracking. "About last night. The dance. The way he grabbed you—like you weren't a person, just something that belonged to him."

I don't know what to say.

The heat in his voice—it's not anger. It's heavier. Denser.

He leans back, arms braced against the steps, and his T-shirt lifts—exposing the cut of muscle at his hips, the dark line leading down into his trousers. The sight steals the air from my lungs before I can stop it.

His presence fills the space between us without demanding it. It's overwhelming—but not like Jacob. Not loud, not designed to cut. It's different. He's steady. He's safe.

"You weren't meant to see what he did," I whisper. "Jacob…." I falter. Swallow. "He likes control. I was supposed to be waiting for him. Not… not out there."

Benny's jaw flexes. His chest rises, slow and sure like he's holding back the storm that lives somewhere just beneath his ribs. "But I did see it," his voice is low, steady, but the edges fray. "And I don't understand why you're still here. Why you let him treat you like this."

A pause.

"You don't deserve it, Summer."

It's the softness that almost undoes me. I look away. Because if I keep looking, I'll break open and never find all the pieces.

"I appreciate you coming, but honestly. I'm alright. Things are just misunderstood, that's all."

He moves enough to feel the heat of him. The weight. The steadiness. It fills the cold space between us like mortar in a cracked wall.

"You can't fool me," he says.

Quiet. Firm. Unshakable. My eyes lift to his, and I want to tell him. I want to spill it all—the way Jacob tied my choices into knots, the way my voice disappeared one 'yes' at a time, the way fear becomes habit when you've lived in it long enough. But I can't. Because if I speak, it becomes real. And if it becomes real, Benny's in danger.

"I think you ought to leave, he might come back soon." The silence swells.

He doesn't push, but I see the questions in his eyes. I see the fight, the fury, the ache to be my knight in shining armour, rushing to fix everything in my life.

Then—his hand. It lifts. Slow. Careful. Like I'm something fragile but worth holding. Fingertips brush my jaw, featherlight. My pulse stutters. For a moment, just one fragile, foolish moment—I forget Jacob exists. Forget the rules. The threats.

Benny pulls himself to stand. Somehow, I hadn't realized how big he was until now.

I'm tall—five-nine. I don't shrink around men. But Benny? He towers. Six-four, maybe more. Built like a man who knows what work feels like. Shoulders broad enough to carry other people's damage—and his own. But he doesn't wield it.

Jacob's always felt big, too. But Jacob is a threat. A storm in human skin. All furnace and fuse. His size isn't comfort—it's a cage. His hands never offer. They claim. They bruise. They burn.

But Benny—Benny is a mountain. Not the kind that casts a shadow. The kind you climb when the rest of the world falls away. He doesn't demand space. He is space. And somehow... that makes me feel safer than I should. Safer than I have in years.

I look up. Drawn like tide to shore. His eyes are still on me. Not dissecting. Not devouring. Just... seeing. Like I'm not a project. Not a problem. Not a puzzle to be solved. Like I'm already whole, even with all the pieces missing.

Benny doesn't move. Instead, he reaches out. Slow. Gentle. Like he's approaching a wounded thing that might still have teeth. His fingers slip beneath my arm and guides me to my feet. He lifts me with such aching care I almost sob. His thumb grazes the bruise beneath my elbow—A ghost's touch.

Then he leans his head down and kissed the back of my hand. Not dramatic. Not showy. Just a whisper of warmth. A kiss that says nothing but *I see you.* And for the first time in so long, I don't feel like damage. I don't feel like property. Or punishment. Or a body waiting for orders. I feel... human. His mouth lingers for half a breath before he lets go.

"You've got your guard up, and that's smart. But know that I am here for you. Whenever you need me."

God. He shouldn't have said that, because it breaks something open inside me—something I've kept sealed behind bone and silence. Something small. Dangerous. Hope.

It swallows the truth. Swallows the ache.

"I can't stop thinking...." he says, quieter now, like the words have been chewed up and carried too long. "The way you looked at me. Like you were already gone."

"It was a rough day." My voice cracks.

Something behind his eyes shifts. Darkens. He takes my hand again—firm this time. Like he's grounding me. Like he's afraid I'll vanish if he lets go.

"Well, let's make sure you have better days then, yeah?"

The words hit like a lifeline. He exhales hard, the kind of breath that's supposed to steady you but doesn't.

"I still think I should've kicked his ass for the way he grabbed you. I should've—"

"You'd be dead."

"Maybe." He tries for a smile, but it flickers. Breaks. "Might've been worth it."

A bitter laugh slips out before I can stop it. I almost want to see it —Jacob meeting his match. But it's not just Jacob. He's the shell. The mask. The grinning sheriff with the charming smirk. Behind him is a machine. Built from fear, and blood.

"I've got a trailer behind the bar," he says eventually. "Nothing special."

I blink. To him, it's just a stopgap. A dented tin box. Peeling floors. A place to sleep and write songs. But to me? It's air. It's room. It's choice.

"What's it like?" I ask. My voice is soft. Wary. "Being able to leave whenever you want?"

He hesitates. Then, almost to himself: "You'd hate it."

"Why?" I ask, half-laughing. Unsure if it's a joke or a truth that cuts too close.

"It's too quiet." He glances away, jaw flexing. "Makes you think too much. Makes you miss people you never meant to remember."

I swallow. "Sounds familiar."

He steps closer. "You could see it. Just for a second. I'll bring you back. You don't even have to get out of the truck."

A simple offer. A stupid one. But it lands like a velvet noose. Soft. Beautiful. Fatal. I want to say yes. God, I want to say yes. But I don't. Because the second I step off this porch without permission, the world changes shape. The punishment won't just be bruises.

It won't just be words. It'll be fire. Jacob will know. He always knows.

Benny watches me for a long moment. Then he nods. Quiet. Resigned.

"I should go," he murmurs. "Before he shows."

I nod, too. But my body betrays me. He turns. Takes one slow step toward the truck.

"Benny—" Barely more than a breath.

He pauses.

I cross the space between us like I'm wading through water—each step uncertain, thick with everything I can't say out loud. I reach for him. Fingertips brush his wrist. Light. Barely there. Like I'm not sure if I have the right to touch.

"I didn't forget the dance," I whisper. "Not one second."

His eyes close. A heartbeat. Two. Then he leans in. Not to kiss. Just lowers his head and rests his forehead against mine. And for a moment—just one—I'm not in Rosefield. I'm not bruised, or watched, or bought. I'm not a promise someone traded. Not a wound someone owns. I'm just a girl. And he's just a boy. And the world hasn't broken us yet.

Our breath tangles. Too warm. Too real. My lashes flicker shut.

I let myself believe—just for a second—that this is what it could've been. What it still could be, if the world was a different shape. When he finally pulls away, I don't follow. I just watch him leave. Watch the red truck pull away from the house. It disappears down the road, swallowed by dust and distance.

"You do not deserve this." He had said.

No goodbye. Just something so true it shatters me. My throat closes. Tears prick the corners of my eyes—but they don't fall. They just sit there, burning. And for the first time in a long, long time—I don't feel invisible. I feel seen. I feel real. I feel... remembered.

Chapter 8
Bad Girls Don't
Get Happy Endings
Summer

The door slams, firm enough to rattle the hinges. Loud enough to say I'm home—without saying a word.

By the time his boots strike tile, I've smoothed the lilac dress over my thighs and fixed my face into something pleasant. Jacob doesn't look at me at first. Just tosses his keys onto the counter and yanks a beer from the fridge. Like it's any other night. Like he hasn't been gone since dawn. Like the air doesn't still hum with the ghost of someone else's touch.

"Office was a shitshow," he mutters, twisting the cap off with a click. "Teller let that junkie bitch slip through processing again. Halfway across the bridge before anyone noticed. Waste of a badge."

He takes a long drink. Wipes his mouth with the back of his hand.

"I told them—tighten the damn watch on the cells. But no one listens until someone's twitching with a needle in their throat."

He finally turns. His gaze skims my face—then drops to the dress. Lingers.

"You look nice." His lips pull into something that wants to be a compliment. But it doesn't land like one.

I nod. "Thanks."

He leans against the counter. Just watching me. Not speaking.

Just letting his silence settle like fog, thick and heavy and full of unsaid things.

"You make dinner?" He asks eventually.

"I can," I say quickly. "I was waiting."

He grunts. Like I should know when to expect him home and have it ready.

"You hear about the Morrigan boys?" His tone shifts—colder. Controlled. "Busted them running Carlton's herd out. Thought they'd get away with it. Hell, they're lucky I got to them before his cowboys. Wouldn't have been enough of them left to bury."

I nod. Fold the dish towel in my lap. Tight. Tight enough it nearly tears.

Jacob's voice sharpens. His eyes glint. "I shut it down. Fast. Before it turned into a warzone."

I nod and smile. Pretending to admire him the way everyone else in this godforsaken town does.

Another swig of beer. He sets the bottle down with a dull clink.

"I'll always keep you safe, you know," he says. "Just you, me, our home." His smile is tight. "Was thinking about your name today. Summer, it suits you," he adds. "All that light. All that skin." A pause.

He tilts his head.

His gaze flicks over me. Slower now. Possessive. "You just need to remember that you're spoken for. No more whispers. No more wandering onto dance floors with other men. No more little visits from your bar-boy."

My breath catches in my throat. Shit…. The CCTV—

He leans in, voice dropping. "You're not going to be some messy little rumor under my roof. I'm not going to stand here and let people in town talk of fucking soft boys coming to my front door to see my woman. And one day Summer. Maybe sooner than you think, you'll have a ring on your finger. That's your future, sweetheart." He says it like a sentence. A punishment.

He moves to the table. Sinks into the chair across from me like a man who's just put the whole world back in order.

"I did some digging today. Into your little rockstar."

My blood goes still. He doesn't look at me. Just peels the label from the beer bottle like he's skinning something alive.

"Benedict Harrow," he drawls, like it leaves a bad taste. "Turns out he's not back for the gigs. Or the bar. Or you."

His grin cuts toward me, teeth bared. "The bastard's such a fucking lowlife he let his own family file him missing. Drugs, most likely. Rotting in a gutter somewhere." He leans in, voice dropping, almost delighted. "But no. He's here because Mommy's dying."

Something twists hard inside me, jagged and mean.

Jacob's laugh scrapes the air, hollow as a grave. "Sad story, isn't it? Cancer. The slow kind. Sucks to be her."

"Jacob—" My voice catches, thin as a thread.

It's too quiet. Too soft. He lifts the bottle in a mock toast. "To family, huh?"

"That's not funny."

"Didn't say it was." He shrugs. "But it is convenient. Means he'll be crawling back to whatever gutter he came from soon enough. I mean, it's for the best. He leaves without breathing a word to you again. Otherwise, he might meet the Lord Almighty before his mother does." His eyes gleam. "That shit hole trailer behind the bar. It's temporary. Like him."

"Stop."

It's not a scream. It just slips out—brittle and cutting.

Jacob freezes. Not with shock. Not with rage. With focus. His whole-body stills. The bottle pauses halfway to his mouth. The silence that follows is suffocating.

Then he sets the bottle down. My stomach twists.

Wrong. You did it wrong.

He stands. Not fast. Steady and unhurried. The air in the room contracts around him. And when he speaks, his voice is quiet. Almost curious.

"Say it again."

I shake my head and step back. He follows.

One step.

Two.

His eyes are ice. The calm before the storm.

"You speaking up for him now, huh? Say it again."

My lips tremble. Nothing comes.

He lowers his gaze to the floor—spots a sliver of glass. A flick of his boot sends it skittering. His stare snaps back to me.

"I gave you this house," he hisses. "A roof. A bed." A low, brutal chuckle. "What's he given you? A promise of an escape to his shit hole trailer?"

He's at my side now, so close I taste my fear on his breath.

"How do you—" I whisper.

"Do you think I'm stupid, Summer?" He speaks slowly, a beat between each word. "You think I don't know what's going through that fucking head of yours?"

"Have I left with him?" My voice cracks, as I shrug my shoulder. "No, I'm still here. He just—he showed up. I didn't ask him—"

A harsh laugh. "You didn't ask him? Yet you let him stand on my porch and put his fucking hands on you!"

His hand darts out but he doesn't strike. It seizes my chin. He tips my face up.

"You wore a pretty dress for your little rockstar." He tucks a strand of my hair behind my ear—gentle, predatory. Meaning something is coming. Something I'm not going to like.

"Take it off."

My heart hammers. His mouth hovers over mine—almost a kiss.

"You forget who I am, baby? Who you're dealing with?"

Air vanishes. He holds me, silence thick as blood.

I choke out, "Jacob—"

"No names. Now. Dress, off."

I'm frozen. He releases me briefly, turning away—then the belt uncoils from his waist with cold precision.

"You think I'm soft?" he murmurs, voice scraping like a blade being sharpened. His pupils contract to pinpoints, eyes gone winter cold. The corner of his mouth twitches—not a smile, but something more primal. "You've pushed your luck to its breaking point. Now I'm going to carve the lesson into you until you can't remember a time before it."

He circles behind me, a predator closing in. My knees tremble as the belt whistles through the air.

"Off," he snarls again, but I shake my head.

His hand clamps around my nape, burning. The other rips the dress in one savage slash from collarbone to hem.

The lilac fabric falls. I stand exposed—vulnerable. Humiliated.

"Mmmm," he purrs. "Now, panties and bra, too"

"Jacob—"

He pulls a pocketknife from his trousers.

"Off, or I cut them off. Your choice," he says, bluntly. Not giving me any room to argue.

I feel bile rising from a mixture of fear and adrenaline. Reluctantly, I unclip my bra, and then pull my pants off, stepping one foot out at a time. I wrap my arm around my breasts and hold one hand over my most personal area.

"No," he snaps. "I want all of you."

"Please—"

Before I can finish, he scoops me up and lays me flat on the dining table. The cold wood bites into my back, a shock that makes me gasp. My legs kick in reflex, a flicker of defiance, but he's too strong. He's always thrown me around like I'm built to be handled, and this time is no different.

"I warned you what would happen if you acted like a whore again," he rasps, breathlessly. His tongue swipes across his bottom lip, like he's imagining all the ways he wants to destroy me.

"Now—let's teach you what happens when you let other men think they have a fucking chance."

My body's a furnace—burning with want and loathing all at once. Desire for the devil who'll destroy me, and disgust for the part of me that wants him to. My legs clamp together, and I try to roll onto my front, to give myself some cover from his wicked eyes, but he only laughs, low and dark.

"Rolling that way just gives me access to your ass, baby. And I'm sure that's not what you want." He chuckles, wicked and menacing.

My breath catches, and my whole body tightens. The thought of him tearing me open from there makes my skin crawl. It's not something I've ever wanted to explore—with anyone. Least of all him. Least of all now. I roll onto my front, tears spilling down my cheeks, landing on the table one by one.

He leans over me, wiping the remnants of tears from my cheek, not gently, not like a lover, but like a claim. Like they belong to him, and he treasures every single one of them.

"Now. Open your legs and show me what I own."

My core dies. My chest implodes and every bit of fight in me rises to attention.

"No," I shout.

"Do it now. Or I'll make you." He cracks the belt through the air. A reminder that if he wanted to hurt me, he could.

"Please, Jacob just—"

He flicks the belt, slapping it onto the top of my foot. I let out a hiss, feeling the burn instantly.

"Now."

So, I do what he asks, parting my legs just enough. Heat floods my cheeks, and I feel every ounce of pride slip away with it.

"Wider," he orders, hitting the table with his belt.

So, I do.

"Don't fucking test me, Summer. I want them wider. As wide as your little body can handle. Let me see all of you."

"Jacob—"

He slams the belt against the table again—harder this time.

I do. I let my legs fall open, as wide as they'll go.

A low sound rumbles from his chest, something between a growl and a purr—approval, dark and possessive.

"So fucking beautiful," he murmurs, voice rough, almost reverent. "So fucking mine."

The last words are so soft I almost think I imagined them.

He steps closer to me, and I'm certain that in this moment he is going to bury his cock in me. But he doesn't. Instead, he leans down and blows cold air onto my entrance.

"You're wet for me, baby." He groans, and I can hear the desperation to touch in his voice. "I could eat you fucking dry Summer. Lick, suck and claim every drop of you right now."

My hips buck in reaction to his words, the sensation of the cold air, and then the heat of his breath between my legs sending me into a frenzy, desperate to feel something.

He lets out a subtle laugh to my reaction. Enjoying the effect he has on my body.

"Mmmm, you'd like that wouldn't you?"

A moan escapes my lips in a whimper, before I bring myself to stop.

"Tell me you're mine, and I'll give you what you want" he growls, wickedness dripping from every word. Cold air ghosts over me again, making me shiver.

God, I need to feel him. I need something—anything. The ache inside me coils tighter with every breath, stars flickering at the edge of my vision. I'd do anything to make it stop... or to let it consume me completely.

"I... I'm." I stop myself, unable to give myself to him.

When he realizes I'm not going to say it, he holds my thighs apart and with one movement traces the pad of his tongue from my entrance to my clit. He does it with such slowness, such precision, halting on my clit and holding his tongue still for what feels like an eternity. A sound escapes me—raw, startled, nothing like anything I've made before. No one has ever touched me there with their mouth; the shock of it sends lightning through my veins.

He lifts his head just enough for our eyes to meet, my arousal shining on his lips. His tongue drags across the bottom one, a low groan rumbling from his chest.

"Fuck, Summer," he breathes. "You taste incredible."

"Jacob—" I gasp, the word breaking on a moan.

He dips his head again, and I ache for him—to feel the press of his tongue against that tender, throbbing spot—but instead, he pauses, lifting from between my legs and looming over me, his mouth centimeters from mine.

"You want to come for me so fucking bad, Summer. But—" he shakes his head and pulls away, readjusting himself in his slacks, "you don't deserve that... Bad girls don't get happy endings."

He steps away, wipes his mouth on the back of his hand and walks out of the room.

I collapse against the cold surface, trembling.

I was ready to give myself to him—to the devil himself. But he just left me here, like none of it mattered.

Like he didn't just unravel me without even taking off his clothes.

For a moment, I just lie there, shaking, trying to piece myself back together. The sting in my chest builds until it spills over, hot tears sliding down my cheeks. I wanted him—God, I really wanted him—and he walked away. Is that what this was? My punishment? A lesson? Maybe he just wanted to remind me how easily he could have taken what he wanted, how my body was never really mine when he decided otherwise.

I push up from the table, gathering my torn dress and shredded underwear, covering myself as I glance toward the window. He's outside, seated on the porch steps, a cigarette burning between his fingers, smoke curling around him as he stares out over the empty fields like none of it happened.

I slip away down the hall, back to my room. I pull on my pajamas with shaking hands and crawl into bed, the sheets cold against my skin. Alone.

Chapter 9
Precision as Penance
Summer

I didn't sleep last night. I couldn't. Not with the phantom weight of him pressed against me. Not with the ache between my legs—shameful, raw, unresolved. Not after what he did.

He'd hurt me when he threw me on the table. He stripped me but didn't fuck me. Still—some wicked, secret part of me had been thrilled. The weight of him. The smell of bourbon and leather. The scrape of his tongue against me. He made me want it. Made me want more. That's what kept me awake—not the bruises. The wanting. The part of me that hated him for it, even as I lay there, spread wide for him, and wanted more.

Since moving here, I'd convinced myself it was only a matter of time before he took everything from me—that one day he'd push past every boundary I had left. But he didn't. Even when my hips raised for him, even when his name slipped out like a plea, he held that line. My body begged, ached, pleaded for more, but he didn't cross it. And now shame and hunger coil together in my blood until I can't tell them apart.

I lie on my back, staring at the ceiling until the plaster blurs, trying to breathe around him—around us.

Benny's face keeps breaking through. His voice, his hands, the way he looked at me like I wasn't already ruined. Like I was still soft.

Still whole. I tried to hold onto that. But every time I thought of Benny's hands, I felt Jacob's. The contrast makes my stomach turn, but it also makes my thighs clench.

I don't want this. I don't want to want this. And that's why I have to leave.

I'm starting to feel things I never thought I would. My body has started craving his attention, and after last night, if I don't get out soon, I probably never will.

He's in my mind constantly. His features, his smile, his scowls, the strength in his jawline, the way it shifts when he clenches his teeth at the sight of me. The hatred I feel for him burns inside me, but the what-ifs are creeping in deep.

Maybe if I can get out for even an hour, I'll prove to myself I'm not as far gone as I feel.

～

I creep into the kitchen at 5:30 a.m. The house is quiet. I feel like it's watching me. My bare feet whisper across the wood, and I move through the dark. If he asks why I'm awake, I'll lie. I've gotten good at lying.

My head hurts.

It's not a lie. My scalp throbs where he banged my head onto the table. I'm certain there will be a bruise blooming under my curls. A mark that proves he owns me, even when he's not touching me.

I set the table. Fork to the left. Knife to the right. Glass behind the plate.

It's ritual now — precision as penance. I slice the bread. Crack the eggs. Fry the bacon low and slow. The smell curls around me like smoke — thick, domestic, unreal. I tell myself I'm surviving. But deep down, I know what this is.

I'm performing. Preparing the stage. Playing the role he wrote for me.

Once, I imagined killing him. A slow dose of poison. A silent cup of coffee. But Sheriffs don't die quietly. They'd investigate. They'd dig. And they'd find out I hated him. That I wanted out. That I'd once told a friend I felt trapped. That my bruises weren't accidents. That my smile didn't reach my eyes. They'd make me the monster. And I'd trade one prison for another.

At least here, I get the porch. A book. A few hours of sun before the storm returns.

So I won't kill him. Because I can't.

Upstairs, the bed creaks. A door slams and I know he's headed to the bathroom.

I have minutes. Maybe five. Maybe less. I flip the bacon. Wipe the counter. Rehearse my lines.

Hey, I couldn't sleep. My head's hurting.

I lower my shoulders. Adjust my expression. Keep my lips loose. Keep my eyes empty.

The stairs creak. A warning in every echo of his footsteps. Then he's there—leaning in the doorway, shirt half-buttoned, his jaw taut with sleep. His eyes look at me with more heaviness than usual. He knows what he did last night. He knows he broke something in me that I can't get back.

"You're up early." His voice is thick. Rough. Suspicious.

I turn to face him. I always turn to face him.

"Couldn't sleep," I say softly. "My head's hurting."

He crosses the room slowly—like a tide rising whether you want it or not. I brace.

He lifts his hand, touching the side of my head—right where the bruise lives under the skin. His thumb moves in slow circles across my scalp. Too soft. Too warm. Too wrong.

"I don't like hurting you, Summer," he says, voice low and almost soft.

But I know it's a lie. I can see it in his eyes—the flicker of satisfaction he tries to bury, the way he watches me fight to hide the pain he's inflicted. Still, this is the first time anything resembling remorse has slipped past his lips—the first crack in the mask he's so carefully worn.

He presses a kiss to the crown of my head. Not for comfort. The words don't register as regret. They sound like a reminder. A message.

"You made me do it."

And still — beneath the fear, the loathing, the resentment — I want.

My body is still wet from the memory of how badly I wanted him last night. How he made me burn for him. I want to hate him and only hate him, but my heartbeat still kicks when he touches me — the pulse radiates through my core and gathers at the apex of my thighs. I don't know what scares me more: what he did last night or how much I wanted him to do more.

I need to remember who I was before this house, before his hands, before he made me want things I didn't know I could hate myself for wanting.

He tosses back the rest of his coffee, leaving his breakfast barely touched.

"I'm in the office all day," he says, voice clipped, casual — like he's just another man with a desk job and a quiet life. "Paperwork's crawling up my ass. If you need anything, call me."

As he moves past, his fingers drag slowly across my shoulder before the door clicks shut behind him.

It's 7:30 a.m. The same as every morning. But he feels different. Softer. Stranger. Like he's trying on a mask he hasn't worn before. Like he's rehearsing being a doting gentleman, and I'm the little wife he's leaving at home.

I drain the last of my coffee and slip into his leather chair — the one I've never dared to touch. It creaks under me, holding his shape, his scent. His throne. For a moment, it feels like defiance. For a moment, I feel like I have claws.

I think about the night he came for me — how calm he'd been as he walked into my family home to take me away. How steady. How unshakeable. He's overstepped a hundred lines since then, crossed boundaries until I didn't know where mine ended and his began. But last night — he didn't go further. He didn't take the last thing.

Why?

I press my palms to my thighs, fingers digging into the bruises he left, grounding myself. I need help. I need someone to talk to. But Mama and Papa won't listen. I think, deep down, they already know what Jacob is — and how deep his obsession with me goes. They also know he's safer than Jackson's men.

I've thought about trying to run again, but the reality is, I have nowhere to go. I understand that now.

At least not until Blackwood opens. I'm stuck here. Six more months. Six months of performing. Six months of surviving. I just have to stay sane long enough to leave.

Tears prick my eyes, sending a burning sensation to the back of my nose. I am so totally lost—totally confused—that I don't even know who I am anymore.

I wipe my eyes with the back of my hand.

Get a fucking grip, Summer.

I set the empty mug down and head upstairs. In the mirror, the old bruises on my wrists have shifted to a sickly yellow—fading but still ugly. I turn to check my thighs. The sight makes me flinch—the bruise he caused at Dogwood is the shape of his large hand, finger marks deep purple. My fingers brush over them and a flash of memory sparks—the dance with Benny.

I dig through the wardrobe until I find a pair of black joggers and a gray tee. I scrape my hair into a messy bun, as if changing the way I look will change what I am.

I lean over the basin, brushing the coffee and the morning out of my mouth. When I straighten up, the mirror is still there, still holding the stranger who looks like me. I try to imagine what I would tell another woman standing where I am. What advice I'd give. The only answer that comes is blank:

I don't know.

This knot is too tight for anyone to untangle. If I can't pick my own lock, what chance does anyone else have?

My lips part and I hear myself whisper it, like an incantation:

I'm going to see Constance and Adelaide.

Jacob won't like it. But then, he rarely likes anything I do. Seeing my girls—seeing the pieces of my old self reflected back at me—is worth the punishment. Worth the risk. Worth whatever he does after.

Maybe he'll go easy. Maybe not. If last night proved anything, it's that he's capable of restraint—but restraint can be another kind of cruelty.

I head downstairs and slide my feet into my sneakers, the laces biting into my fingers as I tie them. I pull on one of Jacob's hoodies. It's huge on me, but it protects me from the cold bite in the air. A small, reckless smile threatens my lips at the thought of stepping outside alone, wearing something that belongs to him.

If one of his deputies stops me, I already know my script: I'm going to see my friends.

Jacob wouldn't risk his mask slipping too much. He wouldn't order his men to drag me back from something so harmless—surely. For that, he'd have to come himself. And on what grounds?

I open the door. Step onto the porch.

The air stabs me—early-cold that feels like freedom for one breath before it seeps into my bones. The yard lies still, everything holding its breath. Trees stand like dark sentinels against a pale sky. Low clouds hang heavy, brooding.

I don't look back. If I do, I might lose my nerve. It's not warmth or safety or comfort. But Jacob has made himself part of my daily routine—he's woven himself into my days, into the quickening of my breath, into my flinch at any kindness. He's in the way I walk now, shoulders rounded, steps hushed. And now he's learned to fill the ache between my legs.

The road lies empty. I pick up my pace. The trees thin and houses peek through the woods. The world feels raw again—unguarded, unfiltered. Each breath tastes clearer. Each step feels my own. I pass the mailbox, the overgrown fence with its rusted "Beware of Dog" sign—there hasn't been a dog here in years.

I slip onto the abandoned trail behind the orchard: quieter than the road. Slower. Safer. Not from Jacob, but from questions. I used to walk this path all the time—when I still laughed, still had people, when my knees were bruised from dancing barefoot in the rain and falling over, not from punishment.

The trail sweeps toward what used to be Constance's backyard. I haven't been here in months—not since I was sent to live with Jacob. He told me they didn't truly care, that they'd abandon me if they knew the truth. That they wouldn't want to be involved in the danger surrounding me. He made me believe that. When you strip everything away, the leftover voice starts to feel real.

They had come to my home with Mama and Papa for my birthday, filled with the lies that I had chosen to be with Jacob. They'd tried to press me on it, but Jacob had warned me not to say a word.

Roots snag my shoes. Thorns rip at my joggers, but I press on — because if I turn back now, I'll never try again. I need to see them. Even if they despise me. Even if I can't meet their eyes. Even if they glimpse what he's done and never see me the same way again.

Their house is smaller than I remember. The siding is peeling in places. The porch sags slightly left. Wind chimes clink in the soft breeze like they're whispering secrets. I stop at the tree line. My chest tightens. What if they're not home? What if they are? What if I knock and they look at me like I'm not me anymore? What if they're right?

I don't notice I'm crying until a tear freezes on my cheek. I brush it away, stand tall, and cross the yard with borrowed courage. My hand hovers above the door, then I knock.

Once. Twice.

The door opens slowly, revealing Constance. Her hair looks darker than the last time I saw her, her eyes as piercing as ever. She looks tired but not weak — she never was. She freezes when she sees me, her gaze scanning my tee, my shoes, and finally my face. She says nothing.

I swallow hard.

"Hi," I say.

Constance's jaw tightens as she steps back.

"Get inside." It's not a greeting, but a command — a lifeline.

Her curls are piled high, sleep softening her features. But when she truly sees me, the color drains from her face, as if a string has been cut. I attempt to speak, smile, act normal, but something heavy and painful lodges behind my ribs.

She steps forward, forgetting the mug, her eyes tracing the hollows of my face.

"Jesus Christ," she whispers.

Behind her, footsteps halt and silence follows. Adelaide appears in the doorway, her arms hanging at her sides. Her gaze moves slowly, as if she's afraid looking too quickly will make me disappear. No one speaks for what feels like forever.

Adelaide moves first, approaching with careful precision, as if I'm both fragile and wild. Her hand gently wraps around my wrist, guiding me inside as she'd done countless times—as if I'd never left.

The scent hits me first—lemon balm, rosemary, warm linen, and old paper. I inhale it like a memory. The house is unchanged. Records scatter across the floor like old lovers. The same fraying quilt drapes over the couch arm. Even the one-eared, ill-tempered cat acknowledges me with a glance before settling back to sleep. Everything remains the same.

Except for me.

I sink into the armchair like I don't belong. Like I've been molded into something uglier than the girl who used to laugh here. I fold into myself, but the bruises won't let me hide. They scream louder than I do.

Constance pulls the stool in front of me and lowers herself down, her eyes wide and glassy. She doesn't speak right away. She just looks—like she's trying to count every piece of me that's been broken.

"What's happened?" she asks at last, her voice softer than I remember. "You look like death warmed up. Has that son of a bitch hurt you?"

I nod.

Her mouth opens slightly, but no words follow.

Adelaide sets her mug on the table and reaches for the incense stick she always lights in moments like this. She sparks it; smoke rises in thin ribbons of lavender and earth—a silent attempt to smooth over what none of us can say.

Constance's tone sharpens. "That fucking piece of shit!"

I stay silent.

Leaning forward, Constance braces her hands on her knees. "You need to leave him, Summer. Now."

I nod again—slowly, hesitantly.

"I know." My own voice startles me—small, splintered, like it belongs to someone else. "But it's not that simple."

Adelaide's answer is a blade. "It is. You pack up and walk away while he's at work."

I drop my gaze to my lap, my nails digging crescents into my palms. "And he'll find me. He's the sheriff. It's what he does. He will always find me. And there are worse people than him out there."

Constance's expression softens, but her voice trembles between fury and worry. She reaches for my hand, squeezing like she can anchor me back into the room.

"Summer... what's going on?" Her eyes search mine. "We never understood why you flipped like that. You hated him. We used to hide from him, laugh about him stalking you. Is that what this is? Are you so scared of him that you caved?"

"No, it's not like that. It's not about fear," I whisper. The words drag up my throat like glass. "It's something else...."

The room goes still.

At last, it rips out of me. "I think... ugh—" My voice cracks. "I can't explain it."

Silence swells, thick and unbearable.

"I hate him," I breathe, each word trembling. "But he's keeping me safe. Safe from men who are much, much worse than him."

Constance's face shifts—familiar and alien at the same time—her eyes darting over me like she's trying to make sense of a puzzle with missing pieces. Adelaide exhales, concern radiating from her breath.

"What men?" she asks.

"I'm not supposed to tell a soul," I whisper. My head shakes like I can fling the words back into the dark where they belong. "I'm going batshit crazy."

"Summer," Adelaide snaps, a little harsher now, but her voice trembles. "This is us. You, me, Connie. We don't keep secrets. Let us help you. Talk to us."

"I know," I murmur, torn between relief and panic. "I know...."

The name crawls up my throat like splinters.

"Jackson Moore."

Their brows knit in unison. I keep going, the words tumbling out —unstoppable now.

"After Papa put him away, some guys—Jackson's guys—started taking photos. Of me. Of Mama and Papa. There was one of me asleep in bed with a note on the back." My voice drops to a hiss. "They were going to take me."

Constance's mouth falls open. Adelaide's knuckles whiten around her mug.

"The police are hunting them. They're doing what they can, and Jackson's still behind bars, so…." My laugh breaks—hollow. "So technically there's no need to worry." I drag my hands down my face. "One thing is certain: Jacob won't let anyone hurt me. Well—" My voice falters. "Anyone other than himself."

Their eyes lock on me, wide and stricken. And for the first time, I don't look away.

Adelaide rests her hand on my knee, stroking gently, her smile too soft, too pitying. It makes me want to slap myself. I used to be stronger than this—louder. One of the girls who spoke too much, too often, never afraid to tell a teacher off if I thought they were wrong.

They used to joke I'd follow Papa into the courthouse one day. Now look at me—sitting here like a child asking permission to breathe.

"Do you have any sort of plan?" Constance asks finally, her voice careful, like she's afraid I don't.

"I do." I swallow hard. "Blackwood. You remember when I told you both about the medical school acceptance? They offer housing. As soon as applications open, I'm gone. But I need to use your address for any mail. Jacob can't know. If he finds out, it's over before it begins."

Adelaide nods immediately, glancing at Constance and back to me. "Of course. That's solid. But—" She hesitates, biting her lip. "Why don't you let us book you a hotel for now? Out of town. I can cover it. I've still got half my inheritance. I don't need it back."

The offer slices through me—hope and fear tangled. "Thank you," I whisper, "but right now… I'm safer with Jacob. As stupid as that sounds."

A tear slips down my cheek before I can stop it—hot and humiliating.

Adelaide's hand finds mine, her voice soft and steady. "Aww, Summer, come on, honey. You've been carrying this by yourself for so long, but you're not alone anymore."

I shake my head, my throat tight. "That's not just it, though," I whisper. "It's Jacob. He's in my head—messing with me, twisting everything until I don't know what's real anymore. Last night..." My voice falters, shame rising like a tide. "Last night, I wanted to have sex with him. I wanted him. But he's the one who walked away."

Both girls exchange a look—wide-eyed—as if my confession has shifted something they thought they understood. I can see it written all over their faces—they'd assumed he was the kind of man who would have already taken what he wanted, the kind who never bothered with lines at all.

Constance tilts her head slightly, her voice quieter now. "Does he... does he know about Tyler?"

The question lands like a stone between us. She means the boy I gave my virginity to, the secret I buried years ago.

I swallow hard and shake my head. "No. I don't think so. I don't even know how he'd react if he did." The words are small, but the truth is enormous.

Adelaide's expression hardens, her usual softness sharpening with protectiveness. She leans forward, her voice dropping low like a warning.

"Summer, listen to me," she says firmly. "Don't let him know. Not about Tyler. Not by any means. If he doesn't already, you keep it that way." Her eyes lock on mine, urgency twisting in her expression. "You have no idea what he'd do with that kind of information."

Constance lets out a dry, humorless laugh, shaking her head. "Oh, please. You really think he doesn't already know? That man probably knows how many times you piss in a day."

She exhales through her nose, fury simmering under her skin. "But seriously, Summer," she adds, softer. "The offer's always there —the hotel, a bed here. You know we've got you."

I nod, the weight in my chest loosening just a fraction. For the first time in months, I don't feel entirely alone.

We sit in silence for a while, letting the air breathe between us.

Constance breaks it first. "I've sworn off men again," she announces, smirking. "Only relationship I need is with my coffee machine and my vibrator. They never argue, never cheat, and always know exactly how I like it."

I smile—an actual smile.

Adelaide shrugs when I ask about her love life. "Nothing worth writing home about," she mutters. "I lived with Grandma until the funeral, then moved here. Now this house is our little bachelorette sanctuary."

And it is. Every wall hums with color—pastels, ember oranges, daring blues that shouldn't work but somehow do. Fairy lights spill like constellations across the curtain rods. Vintage chairs sag under bright cushions. Handwritten quotes curl across the fridge like protective charms.

This was our dream once: the three of us under one roof, barefoot in the kitchen, music too loud, books scattered everywhere, whispering secrets into pillows as if forever was guaranteed.

"I still dream about that sometimes," I whisper, the words trembling out before I can stop them. "Us. Living together."

Neither of them answers right away. The silence is heavy. Aching.

And I know.

They dream it too.

Chapter 10
He Always Knows
Summer

For the first time in months, I almost feel like myself.

My laughter is clumsy—brittle at the edges—but it's still laughter, and it tumbles out of me until my ribs ache. Constance rolls her eyes at Adelaide's story about the guy who tried to take her home in his rusted pickup, and Adelaide nearly spits coffee back into her mug.

We talk in circles—gossip I've missed, names from school, the latest Rosefield scandals. An hour slips away, and my jaw hurts from smiling. This is why I need them. Constance and Adelaide drag me out of the dark corners of myself. They remind me there are still pieces of a world untouched by Jacob.

Constance leans against the arm of the couch, curls frizzing around her face, eyes bright with mischief.

"Okay, what's got you smiling like that? You look like a girl with a secret."

I shrug, but warmth creeps into my cheeks. "Just memories. You two. The way we were."

Adelaide snorts. "Please don't tell me you're about to bring up Patrick Pockface again. I still have nightmares about how obsessed you were with him sophomore year."

I groan, laughing into my sleeve. "God, I'd forgotten about him—until now."

"Forgotten?" Constance arches a brow. "I saw him last week. You wouldn't recognize him. No acne, grown a beard. He's actually—dare I say—hot."

Adelaide gasps. "Don't lie. Don't you dare."

"Swear on my aunt's grave."

Their banter is so easy, so light, I almost forget everything else. Almost.

But then the smile slips before I can catch it. My chest tightens. Jacob floods my mind—last night, the way he pressed my thighs apart until I thought I'd shatter from terror and wanting.

Then Benny. His hands. His voice. His words.

The thought curdles inside me, and I must wear it on my face because Adelaide stops mid-sip.

"What is it?" she asks softly.

My mouth opens before I can stop it. "There was this guy. At the bar. A stranger." I let out a weak laugh, shaking my head like I can shake him out of me. "I thought it would be the worst night of my life, sitting there with Jacob. But then he asked me to dance. His name's Benny. I haven't been able to stop thinking about him since."

Constance's brows knit. "You danced with this guy? With Jacob there? And he's still alive?" She laughs—if only she knew the real Jacob. If the bar had been empty, he would've skinned Benny alive and made me watch.

"I know. It was reckless. But the way he looked at me—it felt like he saw me. Not Jacob's possession. Not some trophy."

Adelaide sets her mug down, eyes glimmering with something dangerously close to hope. "Tell me everything. Was he gorgeous?"

"Tall. Dark hair. Built like he knows what real work is. He sings, plays guitar. He…." I hesitate, then press on because I need to say it out loud. "He made me feel free for three minutes. Like I could walk off that dance floor and never look back."

Constance doesn't smile. She leans forward, voice low. "And what did Jacob do?"

"He watched. Didn't stop it. Not until later." I bite my lip. "But the next day… Benny showed up at the house."

Adelaide exhales, romantic. Constance mutters, "Christ, Summer. Do you have any idea how dangerous that is? If Jacob knew—"

"He does know," I whisper. "He has surveillance around the property."

Adelaide presses her hand to her mouth. Constance's voice drops. "You're playing with fire."

I nod, staring at my lap. "I know. And I can't stop. I think that's why—"

Adelaide leans closer, whispering softly. "Summer… he showed up at your house? That's not just a bar flirtation. That's—*something.*"

Constance's tone cuts like a blade. "It's a death wish, that's what it is. Jacob's got eyes everywhere. He probably already knows Benny's every move."

My throat tightens. I'm not sure what hurts more—the fear in their eyes or the way a traitorous heat coils in my stomach when I think about Jacob knowing.

"Jacob is—" I fumble for words. "He's a monster. But he's safe. He makes me feel things I can't explain. And Benny…."

Constance cuts me off. "Benny's a man who doesn't know what he's walking into. He has no idea what Jacob will do if he thinks another guy's got you feeling like this."

Her words slice through me, jagged and true. Jacob doesn't see me—he owns me. The difference feels paper-thin when you're living inside it.

"I can't stop thinking about him," I admit, my voice trembling. "But when Jacob touches me—" The words die in my throat. "I *hate* him," I whisper instead. "But sometimes… sometimes I want him too. And that terrifies me. That's why I have to get out. I'm losing myself."

Adelaide's face softens. She reaches across the space between us, fingers curling around mine. "Trauma messes with your head. It confuses things. Don't twist how Jacob makes you feel it into something it isn't."

But Constance isn't as gentle. She leans in. "Listen to me. He's not complicated. He's not tragic. He's not misunderstood. He's a predator—and you're the prey. Every time you give in, every time you tell yourself it's want instead of fear, you let him win. This is why we always kept you away from him—remember?"

I flinch. "You think I don't know that?"

"Then prove it. Keep your head down. Get through the next few months and get to Blackwood. But if he hurts you again, Summer, I swear to God, I'll—"

"You won't do anything," Adelaide cuts in, calm but firm. "We'll get her the hotel like we promised, and we'll stay for a couple of weeks. We've both got vacation time."

"I'd still love to smack the son of a bitch," Constance mutters. Then, quieter: "But seriously, Summer—you need to stop questioning your feelings. This isn't you. You don't have to obey every rule he sets. Make your own choices."

For a second, I imagine it—defying him openly, tearing off his hold like chains. But the vision breaks before it can bloom. I can see his face when he finds out. The sting of the belt. The end of his gun. The way he'd strip me down to bone just to make me remember I'm his.

"I can't," I breathe. "Not yet."

Constance's jaw tightens. She wants to argue, but Adelaide lays a hand on her arm. "Don't push her. Not now. She needs us, not another lecture."

The room softens, the tension thinning under Adelaide's calm. She turns back to me, voice steady. "Summer, whatever you're feeling—it doesn't define you. It doesn't make you weak. It just means you're surviving."

Her words land like forgiveness. But guilt claws at me instead. Because surviving doesn't feel like surviving when part of me aches for the man who breaks me. I look between them—my girls, my anchors—and realize what I'm really afraid of. Not Jacob's wrath. Not even the men he says he's protecting me from. I'm afraid of the day I stop fighting him. The day I forget why I ever hated him at all.

"When I get to Blackwood," I whisper, "things will be different.

I'll have housing. Classes. A future. Neither Jacob nor Jackson will be able to touch me there."

The words hang between us, fragile as glass.

Constance exhales roughly. "You talk like he's just going to let you walk out the door. You think Jacob Darnell's the type to shrug and say, 'Fair enough, sweetheart, off you go'? He's obsessed with you. It won't be that simple."

Adelaide frowns, gentler. "She knows that, Con. But this is solid. We can pull it off together. Don't tear it down."

"I'm not." Constance's tone softens when she sees me shrink. "I'm just saying—he's watching you. Always. You can't treat this like some fairy tale where you slip away in the night, and he never notices. He will notice. And when he does—" She stops, lips pressed tight.

My chest constricts. Because she's right. I know she's right. But the thought of never escaping—never even trying—feels worse than the risk.

"I have to believe it's possible," I whisper. "If I don't, I may as well lie down and call this life mine."

Adelaide squeezes my hand. Her palm is warm, grounding. "Then that's what we'll hold onto. Blackwood. Six months. Until then, we'll cover for you. Whatever you need."

The words sting sweet—hope and sorrow tangled together.

Constance studies me, her jaw tight. "Fine. But if you're serious, you have to be smarter than him. You can't let him catch even a whiff of doubt. He'll sniff it out."

I nod, though the truth is I don't know if I'm clever enough to beat him. Every time I try, I stumble—and he's there, waiting, smiling like a wolf.

The room quiets again. Adelaide fills the silence with stories about classmates—who's pregnant, who moved to the city, who got arrested for stealing from the hardware store. I let her chatter wash over me, the sound of normal life smoothing the edges of my thoughts. For a little while, I even manage to smile.

But the clock on the wall ticks too loud. Each second chips away at the illusion. Eventually, I push up from the chair, tugging my hoodie tighter. "I should go. If he comes home and I'm not there...."

I don't finish. I don't need to.

Adelaide squeezes my hand once more. "Then go, carefully. And remember—Blackwood. Six months."

Constance doesn't move, just fixes me with that jagged, prophetic stare. Her voice drops to a whisper. "Be careful, Summer.

I nod and turn toward the door, pulling the hood up, trying to disguise the girl I've become. I'm halfway across the porch when Adelaide calls after me, her tone light on purpose.

"Oh, and by the way—we're going to Dogwood later. Thought we might catch a glimpse of this Benny fella."

A startled laugh slips from me, soft and unwilling but real. "You two are impossible," I say, shaking my head. The sound trembles, thinner than it should. Because even as it leaves my lips, I know Jacob will smell it on me—the trace of them, of freedom.

The door clicks shut behind me. My breath fogs in the cold, vanishing before I can catch it. I tug the hood lower—not for warmth but for the illusion of cover.

The walk back feels longer than it did coming here. Each step heavier. Each shadow darker. I keep glancing over my shoulder, half-expecting headlights to sweep the road or, worse, Jacob's truck crawling slow. The houses thin. Branches claw across the sky, black against the light. My sneakers crunch over gravel, loud in the silence —like the world is announcing me.

My pulse pounds so hard I'm sure anyone watching could hear it.

I tell myself to breathe. To stay calm. To remember the way it felt with my girls—laughter spilling over coffee, Constance rolling her eyes, Adelaide's hand on mine. But the memory is already fragile, splintering.

At the orchard trail, I hesitate. The shortcut is faster but hidden. Both are dangerous in their own way. I take the road. At least there, if something happens, someone might see.

My chest tightens with every step that takes me closer to his house. The air thickens, heavy as wet cloth. The trees lean inward, branches whispering like they know where I'm headed.

Constance's warning echoes in my head: He always knows.

By the time the porch comes into view, my stomach is twisted in knots. The house sits dark and silent—but silence doesn't mean empty. Silence is Jacob's favorite weapon.

I stop at the edge of the drive, frozen. I could turn back. Keep walking—past the treeline, past Rosefield, past every road that's ever led me here.

But I don't. I can't.

So I walk. Slow, careful steps up the gravel, each one loud as a gunshot in my chest. The porch looms closer. The wood looks darker tonight, the boards like teeth waiting to snap. The handle glints dull silver in the dying light. My hand shakes as I reach for it. Inside, the air will be thicker—his air, his space, his rules.

I swallow hard, force myself forward, and press my palm to the door. The wood feels warm, as if the house itself has a pulse.

I turn the handle.

The door creaks open into silence—the kind that listens, the kind that waits.

I step inside.

The door clicks shut behind me.

And I already know: there's a war waiting for me.

Chapter 11
Where She Belongs
Jacob

The sun glares down like an interrogation lamp when I pull into the drive.

The sky's too bright, too clean—blue stretched thin; clouds bleached white as pressed linen. That kind of light that doesn't soothe, only exposes. Strips things bare. Like the land itself is watching, waiting for war.

The engine dies under my palm, and the silence it leaves behind is still.

The porch is empty. The lights are off. She's still not home.

The notification rang from my cell at 10:24am. There's been no movement since.

She's with those sluts. The devious little witches who prance around town like they own the place, with a different man on their arm every week.

I'd checked the CCTV that leads from the road to see where she was going. Part of me hoped she was going to see the rockstar, so I'd have an excuse to put a bullet in his head, but instead, she'd headed down Almere Road, then down the back road towards Constance Bishops home.

I'd had Carter pass to check it out as soon as I knew that's where she was headed. He was working the area and was minutes away. He confirmed he'd seen her through the window, so I knew she'd made it there. I knew she was safe.

I sit in the driver's seat a while longer. I don't move. I don't blink. I just breathe through clenched teeth and catalog every fucking detail like I'm working a scene—because that's what this is, isn't it? A crime.

Tick. Tock. Tick. Tock.

Where the fuck is she?

I scan the road through the window for the fifth time—then the tenth. Still no movement. No gravel crunch. No silhouette.

I see myself barrelling out to Constance's house, wrenching the door open and hauling Summer back by whatever I can grab—anger like a weight in my chest, every muscle ready to move. But that's not what I'll do. That's not the play that wins.

I undo the seatbelt and climb out of the truck, boots hitting gravel as if I'm trying to chase my own impatience down the driveway. The place feels hollow without her, like a room after a laugh has been sucked out of it.

For a heartbeat panic claws at me and makes the bones under my skin ache. The image of her leaving flashes through and for a second I feel the animal part of me rise, the part that would take and punish and drag her home if I had to. Then it settles into something colder and calmer—a heat that doesn't roar but burns steady. If she leaves, I'll find her. If she comes back on her own, I'll be waiting. Either way, I'll make sure she knows there was never anywhere else to go.

Inside, there's no note, no sign she's trying to vanish. Her things are where they always are: a pair of jeans slung over the chair, her bag dumped by the bed, a book left face-down as if someone meant to come back and didn't. That silence isn't relief so much as proof— proof that she didn't walk away, proof that she'll come back to this life whether she wants to or not. Relief eases into me; I scrub my damp palms on my jeans and lean back against the wall, forcing a slow, steady breath.

I head downstairs and sink into the leather chair near the window. It groans under my weight. I take the pistol from my belt and set it on the armrest. Not because I plan to use it—but because I need something to tether me. Something to remind me there are still lines that haven't been crossed. Yet.

Does she not grasp the risk she's taking, walking out of here without me? One of Jackson's men could've snatched her off the road before she even made it past the mailbox. But no—of course she doesn't. She doesn't know the whole story. Doesn't understand what would've happened to her if I hadn't claimed her first.

The thought nearly breaks me. She has no idea. Doesn't know what those men are, what they do, or what would have become of her name—carved into a ledger in some basement, price-tag hanging off it like a cruel bow.

She thinks I took her to own her. Part of that's true. But the real reason I brought her here was simpler, uglier: to stop them from tearing her apart.

I shoot up from the chair, dragging my jacket off the hook with a snarl. If she's not home in five minutes, I'll make my way to Constance's. I'll burn her fucking house down and drag Summer home, kicking and screaming if that's what it takes to get her back.

But then—

I hear it. Shoes on gravel. Hesitant. Light. Steps that know they've gone too far.

My heart stops with a mixture of relief and fury.

I back away from the door like a predator letting the prey walk in on its own. I sit back in my chair and grasp my gun, let her see it in my hand, let her see the depravity behind my eyes.

The knob turns. The door creaks open. And there she is. Hair wild. Eyes too wide. Breath shallow. Her hand trembles where it grips the strap of that pathetic little purse she used to carry her books in.

She steps over the threshold like she's entering a cell. And maybe she is. She freezes when she sees me. I don't speak. Not yet. Because she has no idea how close she just came to being stolen from me— how close I came to slaughtering innocent civillians just to keep her alive.

I stay seated. One arm slung along the chair. The other beside the gun. Not touching. Just there. Let her look at it. Let her understand.

"Nice of you to come home," I say finally — quiet. Deadly.

She doesn't answer. Her eyes flick to the gun, then to me, like she's deciding which one is more dangerous.

"You forget to tell me where you were going, sweetheart?"

Her voice cracks. "No."

That's all she says. Just one word.

I rise, slow.

Her spine straightens automatically. Pupils blow wide. She's terrified. *Good*. That means there's still a part of her that remembers who makes the rules in this house. I step toward her and stop in front of her. Close enough that I can smell something floral on her skin. Not me. Not my shampoo. Something new. Something foreign.

"You wearing someone else's perfume?" I ask.

She shakes her head but doesn't speak. The silence is confirmation that she knows she's done wrong. I lean in, drag the scent from her neck with a breath. And that's when I see it—guilt. Not shame. Not regret. Guilt.

For going. For lying. I reach out and cup her jaw—not hard. But firm enough that she knows I could hurt her, if I wanted.

"I'll ask again. Are you wearing someone else's perfume?" My voice is calm.

My thumb presses harder into her cheek. She winces. But she doesn't pull away.

"No, I'm not."

I release her jaw slowly. I don't have to raise a fist when I can watch her unravel with just a question.

"Then tell me, sweetheart. Why do you smell like a hooker's purse? You making an effort for someone?"

"I went to see my friends. I hugged them—it must have… rubbed off. I just needed to clear my head."

"They're sheltering you, right?" I whisper, voice tightening like a noose. "Siding with you. Feeding your lies. Fanning your filthy little fantasies. Planning on letting lover boy hook up with you there? Even after how you practically begged for me last night."

Her body shudders.

"He still on your mind, Summer?" I murmur, each word a razor.

"Do you lie in bed, tracing your fingers down your belly, thinking of him?"

"It's nothing to do with him," she spits—too fast, too brittle.

I hold my stance; she stumbles back until her spine slams into the wall.

"You're shaking." I trail the tip of my finger along her sternum, slow enough to feel her panic bloom. "Is it fear?" My fingertip drops lower. "Or are you secretly turned on—watching me turn predator?"

She freezes solid. Yet, I glimpse it beneath her shame—the hot surge of something she'll never freely admit. Want. Desire.

"You think he could handle your appetite for pain? I mean, why else do you do this sort of shit, Summer? You love to feel dominated, don't you? You crave it, don't you?" My hand snaps up, fingers clamping her jaw—not enough to bruise, but enough to remind her whose puppet she is. "And right now, you're fucking starving for it."

"I'm confused," she whispers, voice shredded.

I hum against her neck, a promise of worse to come.

"I went to see them because I was scared," she says, voice trembling. "Scared after last night. Scared because of how much you fuck with my head—and how much I liked it. Do you get that, Jacob? I *liked* it. I *wanted* you. And that terrified me." She shakes her head, eyes burning into mine. "You're a monster. And I had to get out. I had to see Constance. I had to see Adelaide. I had to remember there's a world outside of *you*."

The room goes quiet. My pulse roars in my ears. Every word digs into me, twisting—shame, pride, fury, want—until I don't know which one will win.

Monster. She thinks she's insulting me. She doesn't see it— doesn't see that she's already giving herself away. She craves it. Craves me. And the fact she had to run to her little friends just to breathe after admitting it? That tells me everything and makes my cock stand to attention in my slacks. She's breaking.

I step closer. Let her see the monster. Let her look him in the eye.

"You think I don't know what I am? I know exactly what I am."

She flinches but doesn't move, lips parted, chest heaving like she's drowning on air.

"You can call me a monster all you want, Summer. Doesn't change the truth." My hand comes up, brushing a strand of hair behind her ear. "The truth is, it doesn't matter where or when you try to run. I will always find you. But you know that don't you. You've started to enjoy being the little mouse, running away from the predator."

Her eyes flicker, torn between defiance and something hungry. Something that betrays her. I know in that moment—I've got her. Whether she admits it tonight, tomorrow, or months from now, it doesn't matter. Walls don't hold forever. Not against a man willing to tear them down.

I press her back into the wall and loom over her—the wreckage of my control, the ruin of her composure.

Her chest rises and falls in ragged bursts, as if she's fighting to hold herself together. Her lips part and I can almost hear the scream she can't let out, the slap she can't land.

"This isn't real, Jacob. You've kept me trapped for so long, you've broken me down, and now my body is too confused to know the difference between hate and—" She stops, teeth sinking into her lip, as if the word itself will betray her.

I laugh. A low, rough sound that fills the room and makes her flinch. "Denial is a wonderful thing," I say, leaning in until my breath brushes her ear. "You think I didn't see your little crush on me back when we first met? Think I didn't know you wanted me then? God, Summer, I should have put my loyalty to your father to one side and owned you there and then."

She's trembling, eyes wide, but there's heat there too—undeniable, hungry, even as she tries to bury it under shame. That's when it hits me: she's fighting herself harder than she's fighting me.

Her chest heaves against mine, every shaky breath pulling me deeper into the place she swears she doesn't want me. I grab her wrist, dragging her arm higher, forcing her to stretch beneath me like an offering.

"You feel that?" I murmur, my voice a rasp against her skin. "That's not fear, Summer. That's need. That's your body begging for the very thing your mouth is too scared to ask for."

Her eyes flash, furious, desperate, confused all at once. She tries to turn her face away, but I catch her chin with my free hand, forcing her gaze back to mine. Her lips part like she's about to deny it, but nothing comes out. Just the sound of her breath mixing with mine, too shallow, too fast.

"Say you don't want me, and I'll stop." My tone drops. "Lie to me, sweetheart. I dare you."

Silence. Her body arches toward mine before she can stop herself.

And then—like something inside her finally breaks—she surges forward and crashes her mouth against mine.

The kiss is messy and wild. Her free hand claws at my shirt, as if hating me and wanting me have become the same goddamn thing. For a heartbeat, I let her lead, let her pour all that confusion, all that fury, all that desperate hunger into me. Then I seize it, dragging her closer, devouring her like she's the only thing I've been starving for.

And in that instant, there's no monster, no escape. There's only us.

I catch her other wrist and slam them back against the wall above her head. She gasps into my mouth, a soft sound that makes me grind my teeth, because Christ, she doesn't even know what she's giving me.

Her body is straining against me, and then she bucks her hips forward, hard enough to make me groan.

"Summer." Half growl, half prayer. I break the kiss, dragging in air, staring down at her like she's the only fight I've ever cared to win. "This is what you do to me. Every goddamn day. I want you so bad I can't fucking see straight, and you stand there with your walls and your lies—shutting me out."

She's breathless, chest rising and falling fast beneath me. Her lips are swollen, eyes wide and hungry in a way she can't hide.

"You think you're the one tortured here?" I squeeze her wrists tighter, holding her there, refusing to let her touch me. "No, sweetheart. I'm the one who burns for you. Every minute. Every second."

Her eyes lock on mine, glassy with want, a desperate kind of fire.

She looks at me like she's starving, like I'm the air she can't breathe without.

Before I can think better of it, I scoop her up, crushing her against me. She clings instantly, crashing her mouth back to mine like she doesn't care if I'm the danger she's spent years running from. She needs me.

I carry her down the hall, her fists tangled in my shirt, straight into my bedroom. My hand pauses on the door handle, watching her closely. Waiting for panic. Waiting for the fight to come back. But it doesn't. She only clutches tighter, whispering broken things I can't make out, and I push the door open. Lay her down in my bed.

The sight of her against my sheets—small, shaking, but not running—is a brand to my chest. I slide in beside her, my shirt loose from the force of her tugging at it.

The second I'm next to her she grabs me—fingers curling around my jaw—and pulls my mouth down to hers. The kiss is different. Slower. It fucking means something.

I break away just enough to rasp, "If this was some sort of test, you're fucked, because there's no stopping this. Tonight, you're mine."

Her eyes glimmer through the tears. "It's not."

Then she moves—grinding with purpose. Her leg slides up and hooks over my waist, dragging me closer, her body heat blazing into mine. My hand finds her thigh, rough against her soft skin, trailing upward. I wait for her to stiffen, to freeze. To shove me away. But she doesn't.

She opens for me. Wide. Wanting. But I won't fuck her. Not tonight. She thinks that's what I want, that all this is about tearing her apart until she bends. She has no idea. Tonight, I'll give her something else. Something I've denied her since the start.

I roll her onto her back, our mouths still locked, swallowing the ragged sounds she makes. She tastes like desperation, like surrender. My hand slips lower, dragging across her stomach, teasing her hips until she shivers beneath me.

Her chest rises against mine as my fingers slip past cotton, finding her warm, wet and completely ready. A small sound catches in her throat—half gasp, half moan—and her eyes snap open, pupils blown wide. For a heartbeat, she freezes. Then, her body answers what her pride won't: her hips arch upward, seeking pressure, seeking more, the curve of her spine a confession against my palm.

I want to stop. To make her beg, but this is beyond that game now. I can feel the heat of her soaking my fingers. I can feel how much she wants this.

I take my time, measured and methodical, making sure she can't escape a single moment of what I'm offering. I circle her clit slowly, carefully. Gently.

My mouth stays on hers, swallowing her gasps, her pleas, her whimpers. Her nails dig into my shoulders, clutching like she's afraid I'll pull away.

"Moan for me, Summer," I growl against her lips. "Let me hear what I do to you. What only I can do to you."

She's trembling now, legs twitching, her whole body bowing up as if she can't contain it. Each ragged sound, each shudder, feeds me. She's breaking beautifully, not from pain this time, but from the truth of how badly she wants what only I'll ever give her.

She expects me to deny her. To stop when she gets close. But tonight, I'm emptying every part of her that I've forced her to hold in.

Her body twists, writhing under me, pleasure dragging her closer and closer to the edge. At the last second, she tries to turn her head away, eyes squeezing shut, like she can hide it from me—like she can pretend this isn't happening.

Not a chance.

My hand clamps under her jaw, forcing her face back toward mine.

"No. Look at me." My voice is low, guttural, vibrating against her skin. "I want your eyes, Summer. I want to see your fucking soul when you break for me."

Her lashes flutter, defiant even as her whole body betrays her, but then she opens them. Green, wide, glassy, wild—trapped between shame and hunger.

Just as her body begins to tighten, that tremor before the

inevitable, I slide my middle finger inside, curling upward until I find the spot that makes her shudder. My touch presses there, steady, rhythmic, until her eyes roll back and her breath breaks apart. I keep my finger anchored, moving in small, relentless pulses that drive her closer, watching her unravel under me.

The sound she lets out is raw, a cry I've only ever imagined in my darkest dreams. Her orgasm crashes, violent and unrestrained, and the second I feel it hit, I pull my fingers free—only to drag three across her clit in swift, merciless strokes.

"Eyes," I order, my voice a growl, and she tries to obey, tries to meet my gaze, but I can see the pleasure dragging her under, dragging her away from me.

Heat floods from her, soaking her joggers, the sheets, her body jerking and twisting in my hold as screams and broken words spill from her lips.

"Jacob—" she cries, and hearing my name rip from her throat like that nearly undoes me.

When it's over, she's still in my arms, trembling, her eyes wide and bare. No hiding. No escape. Her breath stutters, her gaze locked on mine like I've taken something she'll never get back.

And I have.

Because now it's not just her body that belongs to me. It's every fractured, beautiful piece of her soul.

Chapter 12
More Than Your Fear

Summer

I wake to warmth. Heavy, suffocating warmth.

Jacob's arms are tangled around me, one draped across my waist, the other cradling the back of my head. His chest rises against my spine, steady, calm, while my own heart pounds like it doesn't know which direction it's supposed to take. For a moment I don't move. I just stare at the shadows crawling along the ceiling, trying to piece together last night.

The fight. The screaming. The way my walls finally cracked wide open.

The tears.

The kiss.

The way he carried me in here, set me down in his bed. The way I didn't run. Didn't panic. I clung to him instead, like I belonged here.

And then—God—his hands. The things he did to me. The things I let him do. The way he made me break apart in his arms, the way he made me look at him while it happened.

I should hate myself for letting it happen. But all I can feel now is the echo of it still humming in my body, leaving me raw, restless, and too aware of every place he touches me, even in his sleep. His breath brushes the back of my neck, possessive, as if even unconscious he can't stop claiming me.

I swallow hard, my chest tightening. Last night was supposed to be a line I swore I'd never cross. I told Constance and Adelaide that I would keep my head down. That I would see out the next six months. And yet here I am—tangled in his sheets, tangled in him, wondering when I stopped fighting and started falling.

I think of Benny, of how I thought he could be my freedom. Of his kindness and his gentle words. Then I wonder whether he could have ever made me feel how Jacob did last night. Was it the possessiveness in Jacob, his brutality and his demanding words that made me feel so alive?

Part of me feels guilty—embarrassed that I let this happen. That I didn't put up a fight and tell Jacob no. But it happened, and the worst thing is, I don't regret it one bit.

The floorboards creak when I step into the hall. But I don't feel like I need to hide today.

The bathroom mirror catches me off-guard. I look older. Like something inside me hardened overnight. My skin is still flushed, marked faintly with fingerprints that don't quite bruise, but don't disappear either. My lips—redder than I remember. My neck— kissed raw. And my eyes... there's something alive in them. Something dangerous.

I brush my hair back, take a breath and make a promise to myself.

Today, I'll play it differently. Today, I won't shrink.

Because if this thing between us is turning into something else, I want to be ready. I want to keep my guard up and still be able to walk away when the time is right. If he decides to dress this in flowers, then I'll wear a dress made of thorns. Let him see the woman I really am and not the cowardly little girl who backs away from him in fear.

I make my way through to the kitchen to make coffee, the way he likes it. Bitter. Strong. No sugar. A peace offering. A thank you for giving without taking.

When he finally appears, shirtless, hair damp from the shower, the doorway becomes a frame built just for him. He doesn't step in right away. He stands there, watching me, gaze slow and assessing, like he's stripping me bare without lifting a finger.

"Morning," I manage, pushing the mug toward him like it's some kind of shield. Like I didn't fall asleep in his bed, tangled in his arms. Like my thighs aren't still trembling with the aftershocks of what he dragged out of me.

He takes it without breaking eye contact, fingers brushing mine. Silent. Heavy. The kind of silence that isn't empty—it's full, thick, stretching tight between us until I want to squirm.

Then, finally, his voice. "We're going out tonight."

Not a question. Not a suggestion. A command, as sure and cold as the badge he wears.

I blink at him. "Out?"

"Dinner." His tone makes the word sound foreign in his mouth, like he doesn't even like the taste of it. "Somewhere decent. Wear something nice."

My grip tightens around my own mug, porcelain pressing deep into my palms. Dinner. This is different. He doesn't do dates. He doesn't do gestures. He does control. He does possession. He does violence stitched into tenderness so tight you can't tell which is which until it's too late. But this—this is something else. And it terrifies me more than his temper. Because if he starts being nice—if he starts playing the part of the man he could have been instead of the one he is—I might never want to leave.

Right now, it's lust. It's hunger wrapped in hate, and I still believe I'll leave when the chance comes. But if he's really trying—if he starts giving me the things I once dreamed about—then it won't just be dangerous. It'll be ruin.

Still, my lips shape the word before I can stop them. "Okay."

The hours stretch long.

Jacob doesn't go into the office. He says he's "working from home," which in his language means keeping me in his line of sight. He moves through the house with the same controlled precision he does everywhere else—answering calls, jotting down notes, holstering his gun every time the phone rings like he's waiting for trouble to walk straight through the door.

And me? I circle the edges of his world like a ghost. I make coffee. Fold laundry. Try to read a book but end up staring at the same line until the words blur.

My skin hums, restless, from last night. From this morning. From the fact he hasn't touched me since.

Every time I catch his eyes on me—across the kitchen table, from the couch, through the reflection in the hallway mirror—my chest tightens. He doesn't say a word about what happened. Doesn't acknowledge it. It's like he's daring me to break first, to bring it up, to admit how badly my body remembers his hands.

By mid-afternoon, the silence has grown claws.

"Why are we going out tonight?" I ask, folding the same dish towel for the third time just to keep my hands busy. "Since yesterday you've been—" I choke on the word, "different."

He cocks a brow at me, and something flickers in his eyes—amusement, maybe, or warning. Without a word, he pushes his chair back with a slow, scraping drag that makes my skin prickle. Three strides and he's in front of me, so close I have to tilt my head back to see him.

"Different?" he says softly, brow lifting again, voice like silk pulled over barbed wire. "I'm taking you out. Wine. Dinner. I'm making an effort for you."

The jump I feel between my legs almost makes me collapse onto the floor. I feel crimson flushing up my cheeks, and suddenly realize I'm holding my breath.

"I want every pair of eyes in this town on you," he says, his voice low, a growl threaded with something colder. "Watching. Remembering you belong to me. Knowing I'm the one who takes you home. After the other night—"

And just like that, he lets go. Turns his back and walks away as though he didn't just send my pulse into overdrive, as though he hadn't tightened another knot in the rope he's wound around me. I know exactly what he's talking about. The night with Benny. The dance. He wants to erase it, to rewrite it. He wants every person in this town to see me on his arm and believe it was nothing—that he didn't drag me back to the truck in front of half of them, that I didn't go quiet and trembling under their stares.

I don't argue—because after last night, I want him to wine, dine and maybe even fuck me. I can't deny it. Not after the way I kissed him. Not after the way I came apart under his hands, shaking, undone, forced to look into his eyes while he ripped me open in ways I can't take back.

But what if he finds out about Tyler? What if he decides he doesn't want me anymore and throws me onto the street, like prey waiting for Jackson's men.

The thought sends a chill down my spine, but instead of dwelling on it too long I head upstairs to start getting ready.

I stare at the open wardrobe for too long. He bought most of these clothes. Some still have the tags. Dresses that feel too soft, too tight, too complicit. Like fabric chosen not for me, but for the man who'll unzip it. I run my fingers over them, one by one.

Then I find it. Silk. Lace. Blood red. He likes red.

I pull out the dress I've never dared wear—thin straps, low back, barely-there hem. A gift he left on my pillow just after he brought me here. I hang it on the door and study it like it might bite. There's a tightness behind my ribs. Fear. But not the kind that begs to be saved. The kind that wants to be destroyed. Tasted. Marked.

I drape it over the door, letting the fabric sway as I study it, imagining the sound it will make when he tears it from my body. The thought sends a shiver down my spine. Will he be angry when he sees other men looking at me in something so revealing? Did he ever intend for me to wear it beyond these walls, or was it always meant to be just for him—a private costume for his little captive doll, dressed up for his eyes alone?

Either way, I decide to wear it. Worst-case scenario, he'll rip it off me right here, and I won't have to sit there like his prized trophy.

I let the bathwater scald my skin until it blooms pink. I scrub until I feel like something new might emerge underneath. I step out of the water, wrapping myself in a soft, white towel and make my way back to my bedroom. Then, I sit in front of the mirror and let the woman in the glass decide who I'll be tonight.

Lipstick. Mascara. A flush that isn't from shame.

I blow-dry my hair, pinning my locks into place to enhance the natural wave of my hair. I put on a little makeup, not too much. Concealer, blush, mascara and then top it all off with a cherry lip balm that gives my lips a subtle shade of red.

I rummage through my underwear drawer, deciding I'll wear something nice for him tonight, instead of my usual large briefs. I don't know why I felt like wearing them would keep him from touching me. Truth be told, he would have torn them off anyway, maybe even cut them off with that pocketknife he had in his pocket. The thought sends excitement to my core, and I realize I'm chewing my bottom lip.

I find a small, red lace thong, with the tags still attached and a matching bra. Again, items he had purchased for me. I can imagine the thought he had when he bought them, and I hope he wants to live those fantasies tonight.

I hear his boots before I see him. He's downstairs, pacing. I imagine the weight of him. The scent of aftershave. The heat in his eyes when he sees what I've done with myself.

I imagine his heat, too. Because he'll know what this dress means. It means I'm no longer afraid.

I step out onto the stairs. His head turns slowly—like a man bracing for impact. And when his eyes land on me, everything stills. The room. The air. The storm behind his ribcage.

I feel it.

He drinks me in like I'm the last thing on earth he's allowed to want, and he hates me for it. But he wants me more for it. He doesn't speak, he doesn't blink, he just walks toward me like something old and angry that's finally found a reason to calm down.

His hand wraps around my waist—firm. Possessive. Not cruel. He dips his mouth to my ear.

"You're playing a dangerous game, sweetheart." His voice is low. Rough silk. A blade with a sugar edge.

"So are you," I whisper back.

I don't know where the mask ends, and the man begins. I don't know if the warmth in his touch is real—or just another kind of trap. But when he leans in and kisses me my body betrays me again. Heat blooms low in my belly.

I let it.

"Mmm, cherry," he groans, before his fingers fist in my hair, yanking my head back just enough to deepen the kiss.

There's no patience now. No performance. Just want—dark, dangerous, and all-consuming. I don't try to stop it. I don't want to. Because the way he moves—the way he claims every inch of space like it was built for him—pulls me under all over again. Hard lines, rigid muscle, brutal command. It seeps into me, makes my skin hum, makes me remember last night in a flood I can't shut out.

That dangerous authority was always my weakness, even before the world soured. The flash of his off-duty badge catching the light. The hard twitch in his jaw when restraint is the only thing keeping him human.

He's a monster. But somehow, impossibly, he's mine.

My fingers hover—shaking—before daring to brush the edge of his jeans. He's already hard, already gone, and his cock—my God— it's huge. I flinch at the feel of him, ashamed of the answering pulse low in my body.

His groan rumbles into my mouth, low and guttural, the sound crawling down my spine, like poison and fire all at once. My head screams no, but my body forgets the word entirely.

"I want you," I whisper, breathless, betraying myself the moment the words slip free. They're raw, jagged, ugly in their desperation— yet true. Too true. If I can't escape him, maybe I can choose how he consumes me.

He stills. His breath shudders against my lips, every line of him strung tight, ready to snap.

"Say it again."

The command slices through me. I swallow hard. "I want you."

He jerks back as though struck, but it isn't rejection I see in his eyes. It's restraint. A war being fought behind the black heat of his gaze.

"No," he exhales, rough, reluctant. "Not like this. Not yet."

The words crash through me, cold and disorienting, leaving confusion clawing up my throat.

"Why?" My voice trembles, small.

His hand brushes my waist—gentle, almost reverent—and it breaks me more than his brutality ever could.

"Because I want more than your fear," he says, voice low, certain. "I want the part of you still fighting. The part of you that doesn't even realize it belongs to me yet." His eyes lock on mine, merciless and unflinching. "I want you clear. Awake. Sober on me. Not high on adrenaline. Not softened from foreplay."

Silence falls heavy. I don't know if that part of me even exists anymore, or if he's already stripped it away.

He steps back, leaving an ache in the air where his body held mine. The space between us burns, a void that feels impossible to cross.

He exhales slow, a sound caught between a laugh and a growl. "What you want isn't me—it's the way last night felt. The way you broke for me. And you'll want it again. You'll crave it until you can't breathe without it. I'll keep peeling you open until every morning, every night, begins and ends with me in your head." His eyes burn into mine, merciless. "And when I finally fuck you, Summer, it'll be so deep, so hard, you'll wonder how the hell you ever survived without me." He steps back, like the moment hasn't just scorched the ground beneath us. "Now, let's go. We have a reservation."

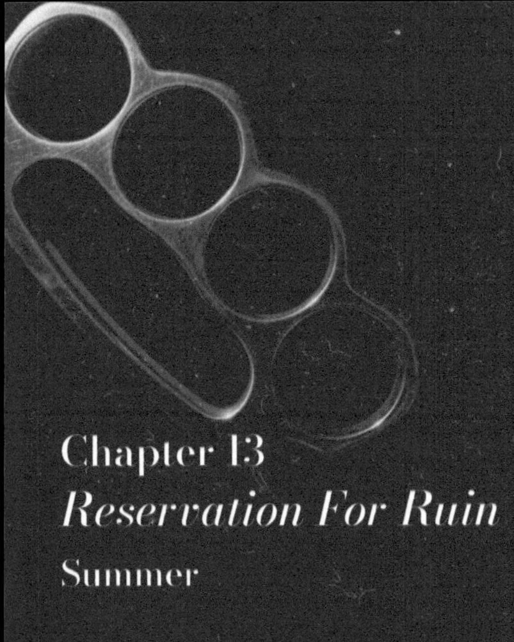

Chapter 13
Reservation For Ruin
Summer

We pull up outside a place I've only ever seen from a distance. Not the neon buzz of the diner down Main, not the peeling sign of The Dogwood. This is different—plate-glass windows catching the amber glow of gas lamps, mahogany siding polished so the porch lights gleam like jewels. Brass letters crown the door, gleaming and golden, promising silk and suits, not work pants and flannel. It doesn't feel like Rosefield.

Jacob kills the engine without a word. I watch his heavy-stitched boot hit the pavement before he circles the truck, opening my door like a gentleman. He extends his hand. The leather of his palm is rough, but I wrap my fingers around it anyway.

Inside, the air is thick with warm bread and oiled leather. Burgundy booths nestle under golden sconces glowing. White linen napkins rest in precise triangles beside polished silverware that catches every ripple of light. Around us, voices murmur and ebb. Beyond a low partition, a piano spills velvet chords into the hush.

It looks safe. Luxurious.

The host—a bald man in a charcoal vest—glances at Jacob and stiffens. His nod is reverent, words clipped: "Sheriff. This way." The tone says he's already decided we don't belong.

We're led to a booth tucked behind a curtain of fern, the table secluded, cut off from the center of the room. The leather seat presses into my shoulders, closing me in. A candle quivers between us, shadows bending and twisting across his jawline.

Jacob slides into the booth across from me, jacket still on, collar up. He doesn't touch the menu. Just watches as my fingers trace the edge of the embossed cover.

"You're quiet," he says, voice low enough to scare the hush right out of the space.

I inhale, lungs filling with the scent of polished wood and warmth. "I'm thinking."

"About what?"

I study his reflection in the wine glasses lined along the table, ghostlike and fractured.

"How strange it feels to be here."

His mouth curves, a half-smile trembling in the candlelight. "Strange how?"

I push the menu away gently after a glance, leave a faint smudge on the white page. "Like it isn't real. Like it's staged."

His brow ticks upward. The corner of his mouth crooks, but it isn't a real smile.

"I was hoping," he says, voice dropping into a low hum that almost sounds like a growl, "this could be our first time out where you don't look at me like I'm the devil." He chuckles under his breath—dark, a vibration more than a sound. "Guess I was wrong."

The depth of his voice snakes through me, making my thighs press together beneath the table. Heat coils there—unwanted, treacherous—whirring to life like a machine I can't shut off. Maybe it's because he is the devil, and because I'm starting to crave the hell he unleashes on me.

Heat floods my cheeks, betraying me before I can school my face. His expression shifts—subtle, satisfied—as if he's catalogued the exact effect his voice has on me, filing it away like ammunition he'll use again later.

The waitress approaches—her braid neat, cheeks touched pink, her smile trained into perfection. She offers it to both of us, but Jacob doesn't look at her. His eyes stay fixed, pinning me to my seat.

"What can I get you tonight?" she asks, sweet and practiced.

I lift my chin, letting my fingertip trail across the wine list. "Short rib with truffle mash, glazed carrots, and a glass of the Californian Cabernet Sauvignon."

Jacob exhales through his nose, rattling the saltshaker between us. "Jesus. You always eat like that when someone else's paying?"

My lips twitch into a grin. "You said I could have anything."

He finally turns his gaze toward the waitress, dismissive and brief. "Same for me. And leave the bottle."

When she drifts away, the silence folds back around us, heavier now. The candle leans toward me, its flame quivering like it's straining to overhear. Jacob settles back, one arm stretched along the booth's top. His eyes—dark, unyielding—fix on me, burning hotter than the gold light could ever soften.

"I haven't done this in years," he says.

"Dinner?"

"Dates."

My pulse kicks hard against my ribs. "So why now?"

The waitress approaches with a bottle of wine. She uncorks it in front of us, then slips one hand neatly behind her back while tilting the bottle, pouring a modest splash into Jacob's glass.

"Would you like to try first, Sheriff?" she asks, her voice soft, cheeks flushed pink. She's got the hots for him—it's obvious in the way her eyes linger on his face, and she flutters her lashes. Heat prickles under my skin, an unfamiliar streak of jealousy coiling tight inside me before I can shove it down.

"No. It's fine." He cuts her off with a huff, snatching the bottle out of her hand without sparing her more than a glance. His gaze stays locked on me, deep and unrelenting, as if daring me to look away.

The poor girl's smile falters. She knows she's intruding, her expression faltering with the awkward weight of stepping into a conversation she was never meant to touch.

His thumb traces lazy circles against the curve of his glass, the red wine burning a deep shade of red.

"Why? Because last night you gave part of yourself to me that I never thought I'd get," he says at last. His gaze pins me harder. "And because… you'd have let me take more."

My stomach clenches so tight I taste metal.

"And I almost took it," he adds, rough as gravel, "because for the first time, I believed you weren't pretending."

He leans forward, breath warm with earth and smoke. Candle-light flickers across his stubbled cheek, sharpening him into something carved out of shadow and flame.

"I want you, Summer. Not as some conquest," he snarls, teeth bared in restraint, "not as a prize I pat myself on the back for earning."

The room stills, the air itself tightening, as if even the walls know better than to interrupt him.

"I want you wrecked for anyone else." He leans in, eyes burning through me, voice dropping to a rasp meant for me alone. "I want you to choose that ruin. To walk into it with your eyes open. To give me everything and know you'll never get it back."

For a heartbeat, I forget how to breathe. Not because of his words, but because of what they ignite in me—an ache so fierce it makes the thought of anyone else feel impossible. I want to scoff, to roll my eyes, but the truth is already branded across my skin.

I'm his.

I lift my glass, sipping slow, letting the burn steady the tremor in my fingers.

"So," I whisper, "you want to pretend this is real? Like we're… normal?"

His mouth quirks. "We were never normal."

"No," I admit softly. "We weren't."

He leans forward, elbows braced on the table, the flame catching on the faint scar beneath his cheek. A reminder in living flesh.

"Do you remember the first time we saw each other?" His voice drops, almost intimate. "Not when we were introduced. The very first time I laid eyes on you."

I swallow, throat tight. "Yes. I remember."

His smile is small, dangerous, indulgent. "You were in the garden. With those two girls—"

"Constance and Adelaide."

He nods. "Right. You three were sprawled in the grass, giggling like you'd stolen the world."

A reluctant smile touches my lips. "We were looking at boys on our phones. Rating them."

His chuckle is deep, chest heavy. "Oh? And what did you rate them?"

"Constance gave some guy with marble abs a twelve."

"And you?" He tilts closer, eyes darkening.

"A six," I confess. "He was too full of himself."

Jacob hums. "And me?"

"You didn't make the cut."

His jaw tics, but not with anger—with amusement. "Different league, then?"

"You stood by the fence, talking to Papa—but watching me."

His tongue drags along his cheek, slow. "You noticed?"

"Too easy," I reply.

He leans back but doesn't break my gaze. "You wore that white sundress with yellow flowers."

I blink. "You remember that?"

"I remember everything," he says. "The way your hair caught the sun. The tilt of your chin when you laughed, like you had no idea how much someone could want you."

Silence tightens between us.

"Why didn't you approach me? Before things got...weird?" I murmur.

He doesn't flinch. "I told myself I'd wait for you to move out of your parents. Told myself I wouldn't overstep." His hand drags through his hair, a rough, restless motion, like even speaking it out loud makes him sound worse than he already feels. "But Summer...." His voice drops, softer, darker. "The second I saw you, I knew you'd be mine."

A hot ache claws through me—shame, desire, curiosity tangled too tight to separate.

"So, you just... held onto hope?" My voice wavers. "Didn't you ever think I wouldn't feel the same?"

His eyes taper. "Every goddamn day. I worried someone else might touch you. Might get there first." His fingers close around mine, grip firm, tethering. "But it didn't stop me," he says. "Never has. Never will. Hope wasn't what I needed. I made sure no one else got close enough. I didn't need you to want me, Summer. I needed you to see me. To feel in your bones what I feel when I look at you. And once you did… I knew you'd never forget."

My thumb traces the rim of my glass before I look up, meeting the dark weight of his stare. I'm hoping he doesn't see the guilt behind my eyes, because Tyler did get there first. But he was just a boy compared to Jacob. He was nineteen, inexperienced and—from what I experienced—had no clue what a clitoris was.

I shake myself back into the conversation.

"Why did you come see Papa that day?" I ask.

He shifts in the booth, not restless—reflective. A man replaying a memory etched too deep to fade.

"Your father was working a case," he says after a pause. "I'd arrested the man he was prosecuting. I came to talk."

My stomach tightens. "To help him?"

He shakes his head. "I was going to send one of the boys. But half the department was out sick. And truth? I just needed an excuse to get out of that office."

He holds my gaze, voice dropping. "Something told me I had to be the one to knock on that door."

My heartbeat flickers.

"Didn't expect to find you in the yard," he adds, softer now. A slow smile cuts across his face—nothing sweet, only hunger and memory sharpened into edge. "Didn't expect you to look at me like that, either."

Heat flares in my cheeks. "Like what?"

"Like you already knew I wasn't there for him." He leans in, eyes burning. "Like some reckless, aching part of you was already waiting for me to find you."

I look away, pulse drumming in my ears. Maybe I was.

The bell above the diner door jingles. I feel it before I see it—the shift in Jacob's posture, the way the silence cuts too clean, too fast.

His body stays still, but everything tightens: his jaw locks, nostrils flaring, and the glass in his hand suddenly looks like a weapon.

I turn slowly.

Benny.

My throat goes dry. The memory of his hands, the gentleness in his eyes, flashes through me with cruel speed—like a vision of what I could have had if my world hadn't twisted.

I snatch my hand back from Jacob, the sting of cold water, the punishment he carved into me simply because I let another man hold me for one song. Because I dared to talk to Benny.

Jacob's eyes catch the movement, narrow, and fury sparks there —silent, lethal.

Benny strides in, sleeves rolled up, hands shoved deep in his pockets like it's the only thing stopping him from throwing a punch. Adelaide trails close behind, Constance at her side.

Why are they here? And why are they with him?

Their faces falter when they see me—relief, guilt, something that twists into urgency.

Jacob lifts two fingers toward the waitress without looking. "Three menus."

The waitress freezes, catches the tension, and nods quickly. "I'll get them seated."

They slide into the booth opposite ours, close enough that Jacob can speak without raising his voice. Only then does he turn his head —slow, menacing—eyes locking on Benny.

The room shrinks and the atmosphere changes.

"You lose somethin', boy?" Jacob asks calmly.

Benny doesn't blink. "No. I saw your truck outside. Figured it was time I had words with you."

Jacob tilts his head, eyes narrowing, a slow grin tugging at his mouth. "That right? What kind of words you think you got for me?"

Benny leans forward, forearms planted on the table like he's holding himself back from lunging across it. His voice is steady, but there's steel under it.

"About how you treat her," he says flatly. "About how this whole goddamn town pretends not to see it. I saw what you did to her at the bar, sheriff. That's not something you brush off, not something I'm gonna keep quiet about." He shakes his head, jaw tight. "Jesus… she's terrified of you. And you know it."

Jacob's expression tightens, but his voice stays smooth, dangerous. "Funny. Looks to me like she's sitting right here of her own free will."

The words hang like fog. My spine stiffens. Jacob's anger isn't loud; it simmers.

Benny's jaw clicks "Like she has a choice? You don't get to drag her around and show her off like she's some kinda prize you won… Summer, come with me. Let me take you—"

The table freezes.

Jacob exhales slow, then shifts, turning fully in his seat. One arm draped across the booth, legs spread wide, power radiating like heat from asphalt.

"Put your hand away before I tear it off and ram it up your fucking ass," he says, voice lazy.

Jacob's smile is thin. "Let me explain how this works, since you three seem confused. I don't make threats in public. When I decide to end something, I end it. No warning. No noise. Just gone." His tongue drags across his teeth, eyes never leaving Benny's. "So, if you think coming in here, trying to get her to leave with you, gives you a shot—think again."

He turns to me then, his stare molten, scorching.

"You think they can protect you better than me, baby?" His voice is a blade pressed to my throat. "You think they'll look after you like I do? You wanna leave with them, you can go right now. I won't stop you." He raises both his hands as though expressing surrender.

We both know even if I tried to leave, he would have me over his shoulder and thrown into the back of his truck before I even managed to get to the door, but the truth is, I'm enjoying our conversation. I want to stay with him.

My breath hitches. "No Jacob, I want to stay with you."

He smiles, reaches over and cups my hand, then looks back at Benny, calm as death.

"Approach me again and I won't just come for you. I'll make sure the whole town watches what happens when little boys forget their place."

The diner goes still. Like time stopped ticking. No one speaks. No one moves. And just when I think he might lunge across the table and finish it—he smiles. A slow, terrifying curve of his mouth and raises my hand to kiss it.

The waitress drifts over, oblivious, and sets the plates down with a polite smile. The smell of seared short-rib and butter should make my stomach growl—but instead, my hunger curdles. I can't take a bite.

"Eat your dinner, baby," Jacob murmurs, his lips brushing my knuckles like a brand. "You'll need your strength for what I've got planned."

Benny doesn't flinch but doesn't look away either.

He leans forward, forearms braced on the table, his whole body wound tight like a bow pulled to its breaking point.

"You're a fucking coward," Benny spits. "Beating on a woman half your age—vulnerable, scared—and you call that strength?" Jacob doesn't blink. Doesn't even twitch.

But I feel it—the shift.

The silence is weighty and electric, like the moment before lightning splits the sky. A muscle jumps in his jaw, and I know—whatever happens next, someone's about to bleed.

"Careful," he says, voice calm, almost amused. "You've got exactly one more breath before I stop being polite."

"You're not polite," Constance snaps. "You're a manipulative piece of shit who gets off on fear."

Adelaide doesn't speak—but her eyes flash. Her hands are trembling. She looks like she's ready to throw her glass straight through his skull.

Jacob finally turns his gaze to them. And there's something ancient in his stare now. Something feral. The kind of predator that doesn't need to bare teeth to make you bleed.

"You two should be smarter than this," he says, voice so quiet it makes the words worse. "No doubt she's told you why she's living with me?"

My stomach twists. Constance flinches. Adelaide goes pale.

"But go ahead," Jacob murmurs, voice flat. "Keep whispering your little plans. Just answer me one question—when the night comes and there's a knife at her throat, which one of you will be breaking down the door to save her? Because I guarantee there's no man, woman or fucking animal on earth, in heaven, or hell that will get near her while she's with me."

My stomach flutters, but Benny's reply comes fast. "You'll be the one holding the knife," he shoots back.

"Tell me, son," Jacob drawls, the word dragged out like an insult. "What exactly do you think you're offering her? A busted bed in the back of a trailer? Cold pizza and songs nobody's listening to?"

My heart punches hard against my ribs. Too loud. Too fast.

"Stop," I whisper, but neither of them even looks at me.

"You think she wants a boy hiding behind guitars and daydreams? A boy that only came back here because mommy is dying and he wants to cash in her insurance?" Jacob goes on. "Or a man who'd bleed before he ever let her go?"

Benny shoves out of the booth. Heads swivel. Forks hang over plates. The whole room exhales and holds it.

"Let's take this outside." Fury sits under Benny's words, controlled but ready to break.

Across from him, I freeze. "No," I whisper, but it's too thin, too weak. Too late.

Jacob rises, slow as smoke curling from a fire. Every movement deliberate. A man not only unafraid of a fight, but hungry for one. He drains the last of his glass, wipes his mouth with the back of his hand, and drops two hundreds onto the table without even looking.

"You sure that's what you want?" His gaze flicks to Benny, "Because once we step outside, the game's over. No badge, no polite warning. Just me—and trust me, you don't walk away from that."

Adelaide clamps onto Benny's arm; her nails bite into his skin. "Don't," she hisses. "He's baiting you." Constance is already moving, urgent and panicked. "You'll get arrested, Benny."

But Benny's not listening. His eyes are locked on Jacob, unblinking, reckless. Like the rest of the world has fallen away.

"I'm not scared of you," he spits.

Jacob's laugh is quiet. Deadly. He tilts his head, a wolf scenting blood. "You should be."

"Outside," Benny growls. "We're finishing this now."

Constance edges toward the door anyway, muttering under her breath, "This is gonna get someone killed."

Panic claws through my chest. "Don't Jacob. Please—don't do this." I call after him.

But he doesn't look at me. He moves slow, his boots echoing against the tile. When he pushes open the door, the bell above it jingles.

We spill into the gravel lot behind the restaurant. The air is thick and hot, buzzing with cicadas, tainted with oil and dust. My lungs can't seem to hold enough of it. Jacob stops dead center, then reaches to unclip his badge from his belt. The metallic snap is too loud in the quiet. He doesn't look at me when he tosses it, but his aim is perfect. It slaps against my chest, heavier than it should be. I clutch it in both hands, breath stuttering.

"I ain't the sheriff right now," he says, voice low, dark. "I'm the devil. And you just invited him out to play."

From his pocket, he pulls his sunglasses and slides them on, as casual as if he's stepping out for a smoke. He places a cigarette in his mouth and lights it before gesturing for Benny to come at him.

Benny's look is feral, he appears even bigger out here, broader, like the night itself is wrapping around him. He lunges, swings with everything he has, a blow that could flatten most men.

But Jacob isn't most men.

He shifts aside like it's nothing—like Benny's charging through molasses. His fist lashes out once, clean and vicious, landing square against Benny's throat. The sound is muffled, wrong. Benny collapses instantly, choking on air that won't come. He hits the gravel hard, hands clawing at his neck, legs kicking.

Adelaide gasps, covering her mouth. Constance curses under her breath, frozen on the spot. And Jacob? Jacob laughs and takes a drag of his cigarette.

He drops to one knee, planting it against Benny's chest, pinning him like a lion pressing down on prey. He leans there, unhurried, and finally turns his head toward us.

That smile—God, help me—it's pure violence dressed up as charm.

My stomach twists with guilt, pity burning hot for Benny sprawled beneath him. But at the same time—shame coils through me, pungent and unbearable—because my pulse is racing for an entirely different reason. Because watching Jacob dismantle a giant of a man with one effortless strike lights up something dark inside me.

Something that feels too much like desire.

Chapter 14
The Devil Unclipped

Jacob

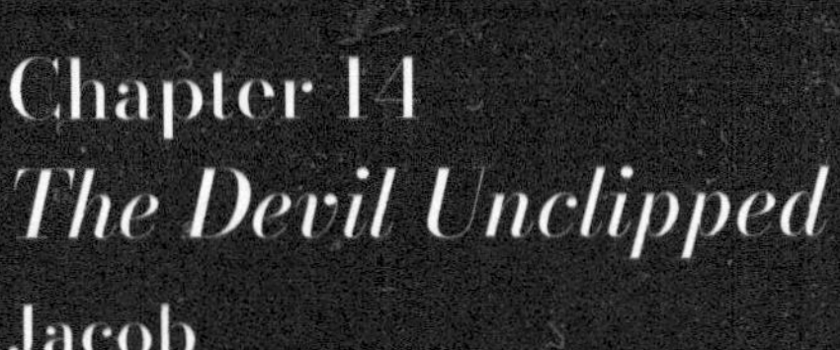

I lean over him slow, like a shadow stretching at dusk.

He's gasping, fingers twitching near his throat, eyes wide with disbelief and pain. That punch didn't just land—it spoke. Said everything I've been holding back since the second I saw him looking at her like she was something he had the right to want.

I consider stubbing my cigarette on his face but don't. I flick it off to one side as I crouch beside him with my knee pressing hard into his chest. I'm close enough for him to feel my breath on his face. Close enough to remind him I could end him right here in the dirt if I wanted.

"You feel that?" I murmur. "That's the air trying to crawl its way back into your lungs. Next time, it won't get the chance."

His mouth opens, trying to talk. To fight. But all that comes out is a ragged wheeze.

I smile. Real slow. Real cruel.

"You think this was about you and her?" I ask, tilting my head like I'm genuinely curious. "You think this is some pissing contest over who gets the girl? She's always been mine." I shake my head. "No. This is about knowing your place. And you?" I drag my gaze down his body—sprawled, broken, humiliated. "You don't have one here anymore."

Behind me, I hear movement. Summer's breath catches. Good. I'm glad she got to watch. Let her see what happens when men come sniffing around her.

The kid's still choking when I shift my weight, calm as Sunday service. I can feel the rattle in his lungs under me, like there's gravel inside him.

I draw my gun slowly. Let him hear the scrape of metal clearing the holster. Let them all hear it.

Summers' voice cuts through the air. "Jacob—no!" She sounds wrecked. Pleading. But she doesn't move. She won't. Not when I've got him under me like this.

I level the barrel at his head. Dead center. His wide eyes blink against the glare of the moon overhead, but the fucker still tries to glare up at me, coughing blood into his own teeth. He wants to look brave. All I see is a boy who doesn't understand what he's picked a fight with.

"You think I need fists to end you?" I rasp, finger resting easy on the trigger. "One squeeze, and I'll paint this lot with your brains."

Silence falls. A restaurant full of eyes behind glass. Her friends frozen—white as chalk, shaking, wanting to run but knowing better. But Summer—she's still staring. Her breaths running faster, her lips parted. I catch the way her thighs press together, the way her breath hitches. She hates this side of me. Loves this side of me. Both in equal measure.

And that's what makes me grin.

I thumb the hammer back, clean and slow, just to watch Benny's face drain. Then I tilt my head, like I'm weighing something that ain't worth weighing.

"I should fucking kill you," I whisper. "But I'm feeling generous tonight."

I press my hand to his chest, right above the heart. Firm. Pinning. Reminding him that even without this gun, he's nothing under me. Then I look back at her. Only her. Because this isn't about him. Never was. It's about showing her what I am. And what's hers.

She's hungry and I'm the only meal she wants.

Me.

The fucking devil she's learning to crave.

I head back toward Summer, but Adelaide comes running to me like a stray that doesn't know where home is, eyes wide, voice soft with pretend civility. She's shaking, but she tries anyway.

"Jacob, please... just—be kind to her. Summer, she's going through enough right now, don't you think?"

Kind. That word feels foul after the rage that's flooding my body.

I stop walking. Let the silence choke her. Let her feel the pressure shift in the air, like the ground itself is warning her to shut her mouth. Then I turn. Slowly, purposely.

I nod my head, not able to manage a single word to the slut who dared barge into our dinner with that fucker and her other lousy friend.

Her lips part, but nothing comes out. She gets it. She's staring at me like she just realized the wolf never pretended to be a man. Tonight wasn't about peace. It wasn't about keeping up appearances. It was about marking territory. Reminding Summer of what I am. I wanted to try to be a gentleman, to have a moment of real life with her. But then those cunts walked in and turned it into a fucking circus. Trying to call me out on my actions. Hell, he even went so far as to call me a coward.

A protector? Indeed. A monster? Definitely. But a monster who keeps her alive.

And now she's seen it. What I can do with one half-hearted punch. How quick I can put a man twice my size in the dirt without breaking a sweat. How easy it would be to destroy anyone stupid enough to reach for her.

She wants safe? Then she better remember what safe looks like when I stop playing sheriff. Because the badge means nothing. Never did. And now—now maybe she'll stop dreaming about soft fucking hands and guitar boys who wouldn't survive five minutes in my world. Because all it takes is one second of seeing me unleashed —unclipped—for her to remember exactly who took her. And why she'll never leave.

I wrap my arm around her waist and guide her back inside like nothing happened.

Like I didn't just leave Benny gasping in the dirt. Like she didn't tremble through every second of it, caught between the ones who think they can save her and the man who already fucking owns her.

She's quiet now, I imagine she's holding the adrenaline in, letting it calm in her core before she opens her mouth again. I'm not mad at her. She didn't bring them here. She didn't run to him. Didn't throw herself on top of him to protect him from me. Instead, she stood still and stayed loyal. She didn't even try to pull me off him when he was breathless in the dirt. And that? That earns her something.

We slide back into the booth. I flag the waitress without looking and order two slices of chocolate drizzled cheesecake and two espressos.

Summer watches me from under those lashes like she's waiting for the storm. But all I do is lean back, arm stretched across the top of the seat, and smile.

"Relax," I murmur, voice low and velvet wrapped. "I'm not letting a good night go to waste."

She blinks. Swallows hard. "After all that…?"

I nod, slow. Letting her feel it. The shift.

"Yeah," I say. "After all that.

My hand drops to her thigh under the table, but this time I offer her gentleness. Warm, possessive gentleness.

"Because you didn't throw yourself down in front of him. Didn't cry. You stood there—right where I left you."

My thumb strokes over her leg, lazily making my way higher up her thigh until I feel her clenching them together. "And that makes me think…." I pause, smile stretching. "Maybe you've finally learned where you belong."

She doesn't speak, she doesn't need to. Her body is telling me everything I need to know.

"So now I'm thinking," I murmur, leaning closer, voice a promise wrapped in gravel, "tonight, when we get home, I'm going to ruin you."

A beat.

"But not as the sheriff who's sworn to protect you." My voice drops to a growl, lips brushing her ear. "As the man who's waited long enough."

She's squirming in her seat. One fucking sentence—that's all it took.

"Ruin you."

And now she can't sit still. Can't meet my eyes without her breath hitching. Her thighs are pressed together so tight I can practically hear the tension humming off her skin.

Good.

She stood by me. Sat beside me. Let me touch her, claim her, mark her in ways no one else ever fucking will.

She's earning it.

And tonight, she'll finally find out what happens when I stop holding back.

The waitress drops dessert in front of us. I thank her with a nod, not breaking eye contact with Summer. She licks her lips, then realizes what she's doing and stops.

But it's too late, I saw you baby.

I dip my finger into the whipped cream, drag it through slow. I lift it to her mouth.

"Open," I murmur.

Her eyes dart to the table beside us. The old couple pretending not to stare. The kid in the corner booth with his mom. I can see her cheeks flush.

Good.

"I said open."

She obeys. Lips part. Pink tongue just barely peeking out. I slide my finger between them. She closes around it, swirling her tongue around my digit slowly.

Holy fuck.

My cock jumps so hard I almost laugh.

Her lips tighten. Her cheeks hollow. She's not just playing along —she's fucking starving for it. For me. And she doesn't even realize the noise she's making until I slide my finger back out and lick the rest of the cream off, slow and filthy.

I lean in, just enough for her to feel my breath.

"You keep looking at me like that, I'll bend you over this booth and show the whole goddamn town just how soft I'm not."

She shivers. Perfect. A voice behind me cuts the moment short.

"Well damn, Sheriff. Didn't know you had a sweet side."

I turn, slow. It's Hank Garber. Owns the auto yard off Old Mill Road. Loudmouth. Wears the same sweat-stained cap every day of the year. He's grinning like this is some kind of joke. I look up just enough to meet his eye.

"Sweet side?" I echo. "That what you think this is?"

His grin falters.

I hook my thumb toward Summer.

"She knows what I taste like when I'm sweet. But she knows what I taste like when I'm not. You wanna ask her which one keeps her up at night?"

He stammers something, then turns red and shuffles back to his table without another word.

I train my eyes back to her. She's flushed with embarrassment and arousal.

Good.

That's how I want her. On edge. Always a little too aware of me. Of what I'm capable of—both with my hands and without them.

I pick up my fork and slide it through the slice like nothing happened.

"Eat," I say softly.

And she does. We finish dessert, but I don't taste a thing. Not really.

Not when she's across from me with her cheeks flushed and pupils blown wide. Not when the ghost of her mouth lingers on my fucking finger, sweet and sinful, like she's marked me with whipped cream and fire.

My cock's been hard since the first taste. And it hasn't gone down once. She doesn't know what she's done—not really—but every move she makes, every breath she takes, every fucking glance she throws my way tightens the leash I've kept on myself all night. By the time we leave the diner, I'm past pretending.

We step out into the thick evening air. The sky's black but the night is humid; the heat clinging to everything. But I'm colder than I've ever been.

I unlock the truck. She turns to climb in, her long legs hiking up to the perfect angle. I could stand between them, pull her panties to one side and slam myself inside her.

I clench my teeth so hard I'm surprised they don't crack under the pressure. I grab her by the waist, turn her to me and lift her like she weighs nothing—because to me, she does. She gasps, but it turns into something softer when I slam her against the door, one hand pinning her wrists above her head, the other gripping her jaw.

Then I kiss her. Not a kiss—a fucking war. Teeth. Tongue. Desperation. I own her mouth like it's mine. Like I'm pouring every twisted part of me into her—every fight, every breath I've held back, every second I've spent trying to be something close to decent.

I've been fooling myself. There's nothing decent about the way I want her.

I kiss her until she melts. Until her body goes limp with need and her hips grind into my thigh, like she doesn't even realize she's doing it. Until her breath catches in a sound that makes my vision blur.

And when I pull back, her lips are swollen, eyes half-lidded, breath hot and fast. I press my forehead to hers.

My voice comes out low. Raw. "I need you."

A beat. A breath. Then the truth.

"Fuck… I've loved you since the day I laid eyes on you."

It slips out like it's always been there, waiting to be admitted—waiting for the moment I stopped pretending this wasn't deeper than control or lust.

I love her. And I'll ruin anything that tries to take her from me.

Even her.

Chapter 15
Ruin Me
Summer

The truck growls to life, headlights carving through dusk. My chest is still pounding, not from fear—at least not the kind I can name. From the kiss. From the way he lifted me like I was nothing, slammed me into steel like I belonged there, and kissed me until I forgot my own name. But that isn't what claws at me now. It's what he said after.

"I need you—fuck… I love you."

The words loop in my head, relentless, like a song I can't turn off. I stare at the windshield, hands locked in my lap, thighs squeezed together so tight I can barely breathe.

He said he loves me.

Jacob Darnell. Sheriff. Executioner. Captor. The man who dragged me into his world and called it protection. Who punishes me for glances, who burns hotter than hell itself when I resist, who's spent every day proving he's too dangerous to love anything. And now he's said it. Love.

The word guts me—warm and brittle, a knife I can't decide if I want pulled out or driven deeper. I should be scared. I should laugh in his face. But all I feel is ache.

The same ache he started last night when his hands stripped away every wall I had. The ache still humming beneath my skin, restless and alive, like my body remembers him even when he isn't touching me. And God help me—I don't want it to stop. I don't just want his hands. I want him. All of him.

Jacob doesn't do soft. He isn't built for gentle. He's built to ruin.

I'm about to give it to the man who could cave a man's ribs with a single punch. I can't stop myself from imagining, from wondering what's going to happen the second we step through that door.

I want the danger, the hurt, the stretch, the way he'll hold my hips like I'm something he's anchoring to this world.

I squeeze my thighs tighter, trying to stop the pulse between them. It doesn't help. I'm throbbing. Desperate. But I'm also afraid. Scared to the core that he'll know he's not my first. But I won't ask him to slow down, because deep inside, I want it to hurt. I want him to break me open.

And I want to love it.

We head down the long stretch of road that leads to his house. He pulls into the driveway without so much as tapping the breaks.

The truck slows to a stop.

He doesn't move. Neither do I. His hands grip the wheel, knuckles white, like he's holding something back. Then he turns, dark eyes dragging over me like fire catching dry grass. He looks like a man seconds from breaking every promise he's ever made.

He leans in, voice rough enough to scrape skin. "You know what's coming when we walk through the door. If you don't want this, tell me now. If you do, get inside."

And I do. God, I do. I open the door. My legs tremble, my panties are ruined. I step out knowing the next time I walk; I'll know exactly what it feels like to be fucked by the devil.

He's behind me—always behind me. His presence crawls up my spine. The door slams. The lock clicks shut behind us. My breath stutters. My feet move anyway. I make my way to the den. I stand at the sofa. Too nervous to sit.

He doesn't hesitate. He shrugs out of his jacket and throws it onto the sideboard, eyes locked on me. His voice comes low, lethal. "You know what happens now."

The words fall heavy between us, the air thickening until it hurts to breathe. He steps closer — slow, dominant — until the heat of him is everywhere. Two fingers lift my chin. His gaze pins me in place, dark and certain.

"I'm going to destroy you, Summer. And you're going to love it."

The words hit like a slap and a prayer all at once. My breath catches. Fear tangles with want until I can't tell which is which. My body burns under the weight of his words. My pulse thrums so violently it feels like my skin can't hold it. Because I know exactly what he means — and worse, I want it.

"Take your clothes off," he orders. "Now."

The command slices through the air like a blade. I can barely strip the dress over my head. It drops at my feet, leaving me in red lace. He doesn't move, watching me like I'm something he's earned.

"You're shaking," he says.

"I'm scared," I admit, throat tight.

The smirk fades from his mouth. He steps closer, heat radiating from him. "Good."

The word shouldn't make me shiver, but it does. He wants the fear — the proof that I still know what danger feels like. That I still know he could break me.

"I want you to remember this," he murmurs, voice low, threaded with something darker than lust. "Every time you think about running. Every time you look at another man. I want you to remember that no one else will ever touch you like this. No one else will ever have you like I do."

His hand moves down to my chest. Palm flat against my heart. "You feel that?"

I nod.

"That's mine now. Your body. Your soul. It belongs to me."

He turns me slowly, his hand trailing down the length of my spine. When his fingers find the clasp of my bra, it slips free with a soft snap. The air feels colder without it. His palm follows, skimming lower until he reaches the thin lace still clinging to my hips.

He doesn't tear them away yet. Instead, he steps in behind me. I can feel him — solid, unyielding — pressing against the small of my back.

"You ready?" He breathes.

I close my eyes. And I nod. Because pain from him is different. It's not cruel. It's claiming.

He leans close, his breath a rough whisper at my ear. "You trust me?"

It takes me a moment to find my voice. "I think so."

My heart is a drumbeat against the silence of the room, loud enough to fill it. His voice follows, breathy and deep.

"You belong to me, Summer. Say it."

I hesitate—only a heartbeat—but it's enough.

He grips my jaw, forcing my head back, my face angled just enough that I can feel the edge of his breath.

"Say it."

The words come out small but certain. "I belong to you."

His exhale shudders against my skin, and for a moment, I feel it —something that almost resembles tenderness. The quiet between us hums with danger and devotion both.

"Good girl," he murmurs, almost reverent.

The sound of it unravels me. He slides his hand down the front of my panties. I gasp—arching against him as his fingers find me. He groans, teeth grazing my neck.

"You're fucking soaked," he mutters. "God, I knew you were soaked in the truck. I saw the way you squirmed."

He strokes once—lightly—and I moan, unable to stifle the pleasure he's creating inside of me. He pushes me forward—his hands a command, not a guide—and I stumble against the wall, I feel his chest pressing behind me, with a force that knocks the air out of my lungs.

There's no path to gentleness here. He could take me right here. Against the wall. On the floor. The thought flickers, and heat rushes through me—violent and shameful.

But he doesn't.

Instead, he turns me and lifts me. My legs wrap around his waist out of instinct. His strength isn't just impressive—it's unholy. I feel it in the tension of his muscles, in the way he carries me up the stairs like I weigh nothing.

The bedroom door slams open. Then we're in the dark.

Not just in the room—but in something else. Something deeper. The kind of dark that breathes. The kind that presses into your skin and whispers things you're not ready to hear.

He lays me down like he's placing a weapon on display. Stands back and lights the candle on his nightstand. Then he looks at me. His eyes have turned almost fully black, his pupils blown so wide that they could drown me—part of me wants them to.

"You have no idea," he murmurs, unbuttoning his shirt, "what I've had to fucking resist."

My breath snags, because I do know. I saw it in the way he watched me. In the way his hands hovered too long. In the way he looked at Benny—not as a man— but as a threat to his property.

He shrugs off his shirt. Undoes his belt and steps out of his jeans and underwear.

The sight of him—towering, thick, already hard—makes my throat close. Yeah, I slept with Tyler, but he wasn't even half the size of Jacob, and even that hurt. There's no way that will fit. No way it won't break me. And maybe that's the point.

"Every inch of this is yours to take. And you will take it."

The words slam into me, heat and dread colliding in my veins. My mouth opens, but no sound comes. All I can do is stare—at him, at the threat, at the promise.

My body burns. Fear curls in my stomach, relentless, but it's drowned by the ache clawing lower, hungrier. I shake my head before I even realize it, but it isn't no. It's disbelief. Awe. Terror. Want.

He kneels between my legs and yanks my panties down, rough and fast. They tear a little at the seam, but he doesn't care. I'm exposed now. His hand grips my thigh—spreads me open—and I brace for pain. But he doesn't enter me. Not yet. Instead, he lowers his head.

And *licks*.

The first stroke of his tongue is brutal in its precision, sending memories flooding back of how much I wanted him to continue when he had me laid across the table. I jolt like I've been struck, a sound escaping my throat I didn't even know I could make.

My hips try to jerk away. He grips them down.

"Oh no," he growls. "You're not going anywhere."

His tongue moves again, firmer this time. Slower. He doesn't rush. He devours. I look down and see his whole mouth cupping me, he moves his head, sucking, licking, bringing every sense in my body to the area he feasts on.

I cry out, hand flying to my mouth. He pulls away, eyes dark with warning.

"If you hide your sounds again," he says, voice flat, "I'll stop."

I drop my hand. He goes back in. And this time, I let myself fall apart. It's relentless—like everything he does. Every flick of his tongue is a punishment. Every suck of his lips is a reminder that this is his mouth, and I'm the only thing he wants to fill it with. He fucks me with his tongue until I'm shaking, thighs trembling, moaning like a woman I don't recognize. The kind who's never been touched like this. The kind who never thought she'd want to be.

The orgasm hits fast. Hard.

I cry out but he keeps going. I try to close my thighs, but he holds them open. The sensation is too much, but he draws it out until it hurts.

Finally, he pulls back and wipes his mouth with the back of his hand.

"Mine," he mutters. "Fucking mine."

He climbs over me. Kisses me—deep, filthy, letting me taste myself on his tongue.

And then positions himself at my entrance.

My heart stops. This is it.

"Jacob…. I'm scared."

He kisses my throat. "I know."

He presses the tip against me, just enough to make my body lock.

"But you're gonna take it," he murmurs, voice low and absolute, like prophecy carved into stone. "Every inch. Every goddamn inch you begged for."

My body trembles. My thighs twitch, caught between wanting to close and spread wider.

"I—I don't know if I can—"

His hand snaps up, hard fingers gripping my jaw, forcing my eyes to his.

"You can. And you will."

Then he pushes. Not a brutal shove, just enough to split me open on him.

The pain flares, white-hot, stealing my breath. My back bows off the mattress, my cry ripping free before I can stop it.

He doesn't stop. He doesn't soothe. He holds me there, locked on the edge, letting me feel it—every stretch, every ounce of pain, every humiliating reminder that this is what it feels like to be filled with a man possessed.

My nails claw his shoulders, digging into muscle. I don't know if I'm trying to pull him closer or shove him away. Tears sting my eyes. Shame floods my chest. My hips twitch, searching for relief that doesn't exist. And then his mouth is at my ear, breath hot, words hotter.

"Look at me."

It takes everything I have to peel my eyes open. He's above me—feral, unholy, beautiful.

"You're doing so fucking good," he rasps. His voice fractures like he's holding back from shattering completely. "You're breaking for me so beautifully."

He pushes deeper and I sob. The sound doesn't even feel human. Just raw pain, ripped from somewhere low in my gut. This isn't what it felt like with Tyler. It hurt sure, but this… this is a whole new level.

"I know it hurts," he whispers, teeth grazing my jaw. "But you wanted this. You begged for this."

He moves deeper. Another shock of fire ripping through me. My legs kick against the sheets, helpless, searching for ground that isn't there.

"Say it," he growls, thrust grinding deeper. "Say you wanted it."

My breath stutters, my voice cracks. "I—I wanted it."

His eyes burn into mine. "You wanted me."

"Yes."

And then—he slams the rest of the way in. The scream rips out of me, gutted and broken. And he moans—a sound of wreckage and worship—as if sliding into me was the one thing he's been starving for his entire fucking life.

The world detonates.

I don't know where I end, and he begins. Just pain. The stretch is unbearable, pressure blooming so deeply it takes my breath away. My throat tears with a gasp, but there's no air.

No thought. Only him.

He doesn't move. His body shakes above mine, arms trembling with restraint.

His forehead presses to mine, sweat slicking his brow.

"You're mine now," he murmurs, dragging his lips across my jaw. "And I'll carve it into your fucking soul if I have to."

He pulls back—just a little—and thrusts again. The pain slices through me, raw and electric. My body arches, caught between a scream and a moan.

"You're so fucking tight," he grits out, jaw clenched. "So small."

I shake my head, trying to breathe through it. "I—I can't—"

Another thrust, it feels even deeper. I bite my lip until I taste blood.

He's breaking me. And I want him to. I want it. Because buried inside the pain is something else. Something I don't want to name. Something twisted and terrifying and real.

He watches me—pupils blown wide, mouth parted, reverent.

"You wanted to know what it feels like to be ruined?" he says. "This is it."

His hips start to move with rhythm. Slow at first. Letting my body adjust—or maybe he enjoys the way I struggle against him. Each thrust sends shockwaves through me. The pain is still there, but it's changing. Morphing into heat. Into something that coils low in my stomach like a fuse being lit.

He angles and finds a spot that I didn't know existed. It feels like heaven and hell at the same time, and I can't help but scream. I feel my eyes rolling back when he picks up speed. He continues to fuck me with purpose. With fury. Like I've wronged him. Like I owe him this.

"You think anyone else could've given you this?" Jacob snarls, bitter and tight. "You think they would've known what to do with you?"

He grabs my thigh and yanks it higher around his waist and drives in deeper.

I cry out. Loud. Broken. Undone.

"I'm the only one who sees you," he growls, slamming into me. "The only one who knows what you need. And right now, you need to come for me. Let me feel you explode on me."

He shifts down the bed, pulling me with him. He stands at the end, holding my legs wide and circles my clit with the pad of his thumb as he drives into me.

The pressure building inside me, coupled with his attack on my sensitive bud sends shockwaves through me. I open my legs wider for him, allowing him better access. I raise my head to watch the way he fucks me — seeing his length sliding in and out of me, the slickness of my arousal gleaming on him with every thrust makes the experience even hotter — even wilder. He moves his thumb lower, gathering some of my fluid and using it as lubricant to glide over my clit.

"There she is. How good do you look, taking me. Taking all of me." He purrs.

From the centre of my very soul, I feel the orgasm coming to crash — it's too much, a feeling like I'm going to wet myself pours over me. He's splitting me open in ways I didn't know a body could survive.

Jacob feels it — sees it. I know from the way his jaw locks, the way his thrusts turn savage — hard, punishing, like he's trying to fuck his name into my bones. The bed groans under us, wood shrieking with each slam. The headboard hammers the wall in time with my heartbeat.

The whole house vibrates with my screams. Anyone within a mile radius must hear me being wrecked. And I don't care. I want them to hear. I want them to know what it sounds like when a woman gets taken apart and put back together in the hands of the devil.

Then he slows. Pulls almost all the way out, leaving me empty, ruined. My body seizes at the loss, clawing for him like an addict.

"You want to come on my cock, baby?" he whispers, lips brushing my ear, breath thick with heat and sin. "Then beg."

I hate him. I crave him. I want him.

My hips lift, desperate, trying to take him back in. My body betrays me, chasing the very man who broke it. I'm past shame. Past dignity. Past anything but need.

"Please," I breathe, the word torn and ugly.

He doesn't move.

"Louder."

My throat tightens, but I give him what he wants.

"Please, Jacob. Please let me come — fuck!"

He slams into me so hard the air leaves my lungs. A scream rips out of me — raw, helpless. His thumb moves back to my clit, applying more pressure and faster motions. My eyes roll back into my head — I'm certain I'm going to pass out from the pleasure that's igniting my body.

"That's it," he snarls, grinding deep, brutal, relentless. "That's what I like. Scream for me, Summer"

His hand fists in my hair, yanking my head until my eyes crash into his.

"Look at me," he growls, every word a command that sears into bone. "When you come, you'll do it with your eyes on mine. No hiding. No running. I want to see your soul burn for me *every* time you come."

And then it detonates. My orgasm tears through me like a gunshot, violent and merciless. My body convulses around him, trembling, shattering. I sob into the air between us, forced to hold his gaze, every nerve white-hot with fire. Tears trickle down my cheeks, rolling into my mouth.

Jacob doesn't let up. He drives me through it, watching me unravel, claiming every flicker of my ruin like it belongs to him. Because it does.

He lets out a roar—animal, primal—and thrusts once, twice more before he spills into me, hips jerking, hands clutching at my wrists like I'm the only thing anchoring him to the world.

The moment stretches, heavy and breathless.

His weight settles over me, solid and shaking. His mouth finds my throat again, kissing me like he worships me. I can still feel him inside me. Still feel the echo of every thrust. Every word.

Now, something darker has replaced the fear I felt. Something that feels an awful lot like victory.

He didn't just take something from me tonight.

I *gave* it to him.

And in doing so… I think I took a piece of him, too.

Chapter 16
Booked

Jacob

She's still asleep when I wake.

Curled up on my chest like she was made to fit there — bare skin pressed against mine, breath slow and shallow, lashes flickering with the tail-end of a dream. The sunlight leaking through the curtains turns her auburn hair to gold. Innocent. Almost holy. Like last night didn't happen.

But it did. It fucking did. And I'm never letting her forget it.

She's mine now. In every way that counts. That tight little body broke open for me. Took everything I gave and begged for more. The way she stared into my eyes as the orgasm crashed through her, eyes glazing and rolling back, a shuddering surrender that felt like it belonged only to me. And now, with her legs tangled in mine and her scent on my skin, I feel like I've just won a war no one else knew I was fighting.

Mission fucking accomplished.

I drag my palm down her spine, slow and owning. Possessive. She's mine now — marked in ways she can't yet see.

She doesn't stir.

Good. Because I'm not done thinking. Not by a long fucking shot.

Her body's already mine, but her soul, that fragile, shivering heart she keeps trying to hide from me? That's still bleeding on the table, waiting to be claimed. But I'll make sure the only life she can imagine is the one beside me, so no one else will ever get close enough to matter. Someday, she'll wear my ring, and my name will wrap around her like barbed wire, enough to keep every other bastard in this town at bay. And with Benny circling like a mutt sniffing after scraps, I don't have the luxury of patience.

Last night I gave her soft—my version of it, anyway. Careful hands. Tender, if you squint past the obsession that drips off me.

I never planned to grow into a monster. Watching my father break my mother taught me the mechanics of containment, and maybe that explains why I hunted her like a man possessed. My days begin and end with her name— God, they have for years. She needs to wake up, see the bars I've built around her, and accept one inevitable truth: in every map I draw, Summer Miller is marked with my name.

But she doesn't know. Not really.

She thinks I'm just some twisted bastard who wanted her and jumped at the opportunity. That part is true, at least. But she doesn't know the extent of what I saved her from. She doesn't know who her father fucked with. What they were going to do to her the second he took Jackson down. She doesn't know about Donnie and Vince. About the club. About the catalog of girls who never came back. About the ones we did eventually manage to find.

If she did... if she knew what they would do to her... what she was supposed to be for them... She might just beg me to keep her locked in this house forever.

I grind my teeth and shift, careful not to wake her. She makes a soft sound, a little whimper, and my cock twitches at the memory of how she moaned last night. How she whined when I split her open for the first time and whispered mine into the hollow of her throat.

Jesus. I could drag her back under and fuck her until sunset. But I won't. This isn't just about sex. It never was. She's a goddess, yes. A fantasy come to life. But she's also a woman with no idea how much danger she was in—could still be in. A woman who still clings to hope like a lifeline, who still believes someone out there might love her, soft and clean, without the darkness.

And she's wrong. Because there is no clean. Only survival. Only truth. Only me.

I pull on my jeans and head downstairs, pouring myself a coffee and staring out the kitchen window at the gravel road beyond the trees. My mind's already racing. I could tell her everything. Lay it all out, brutal and raw. Make her see who I'm saving her from and why I took her before they could. But she'd question it. Maybe not out loud, but in her head. She'd wonder if I made it up to keep her here. To own her.

No.

I hear movement upstairs—soft creaking, the whisper of bare feet on floorboards—and I smile into my coffee.

Good morning, little doll. Enjoy the calm while it lasts. Because today? Today, you learn everything.

She rubs her eyes as she walks in, her voice still caught between dream and reality.

"You're up early," I say as she walks into the room.

I lean back in the chair, mug in hand, watching her.

"Didn't sleep much." She's blushing. Flustered.

Her eyes flick to mine. A pause. She knows it's because of her. Because of the way she broke under me, begged me, came apart until she didn't know which way was up. And still—she looks at me like she wants to believe it meant something different. Something softer.

She slides into the chair opposite, positioning herself carefully. Her arms close around her knees, and she rocks just a fraction. The way she flinches when she moves — a wince, a sudden intake of breath—tells me last night lives under her skin in the form of pain. There's heat behind her eyes and the quiet way she presses her thighs together tell the whole story—she wants more.

"About last night…."

I smile. Slow. Dangerous. "Last night was just the beginning, Summer."

Her lips part, but she doesn't answer. I don't let her. I stand, set the mug down, and walk around the table until I'm behind her. My hands settle on her shoulders, heavy, grounding. I plant a gentle kiss on her shoulder, then stand back to my full height. I don't want to ruin this moment; I want to enjoy the first morning we've had as lovers rather than enemies. But she needs to know. She deserves to know. So, I head to lean against the kitchen counter, standing where she can see me, and speak.

"There's something you need to know," I murmur, my voice low enough to make her lean in. "Something I've been waiting to tell you until the time was right."

She stiffens instantly—I can feel it, the subtle quake that ripples through her chest where it presses against me. "What is it?" she whispers, her voice a thin thread of sound.

"It's not something I can explain." I hold out my hand. "I need to show you. Come."

Her eyes meet mine, wide, searching. "Where are we going?"

I pause, just long enough for the tension to twist tighter between us. Then, softly, deliberately, I drop the words that make her freeze. "To my office."

She stops dead. Every muscle in her body goes rigid, like I just drew a knife across the space between us.

I wait for it—the panic, the fire, the harsh words she usually spits when she's scared. But nothing comes. Just silence. Stillness. And somehow, that's worse.

"Why?" she breathes, barely a sound at all.

My jaw flexes. I drag a hand down my face, then rake it through my hair, trying to hold onto the thread of control that always frays when she looks at me like that.

"Because you only know half the story," I say. "And half isn't enough anymore."

Her eyes burn into mine, steady and terrified all at once. "I thought I knew everything."

I shake my head slowly, firmly. "Not all of it."

Confusion flashes across her face, raw and unguarded, and it hits me harder than I expect.

"Then show me," she says, voice trembling.

I study her for a long moment, weighing whether she's ready—whether I'm ready.

Then I nod once. "Once you see this, there's no going back. You'll understand everything. Why I did what I did. Why I took you in the first place."

"Jacob…." she whispers, chewing the inside of her cheek. "You're scaring me."

"Come," I repeat, the word cutting this time, a command cloaked in restraint.

I move down the hall, the sound of my steps echoing through the house. The key hangs heavy in my hand as I stop at the door. I turn it in the lock, the click loud in the silence, and push the door open.

The air shifts the moment we step inside. My office is dim, the faint scent of tobacco and cedar still lingering from nights I couldn't sleep. She follows close behind, and when I glance at her, I can tell she's been here before—the flicker of recognition in her eyes gives her away. I expected as much. I've left her alone here enough times for curiosity to take hold.

But one thing I know—she's never opened that drawer. The one with her name carved into the metal tab. Summer.

Her voice wavers. "That drawer… that's all about me, isn't it?"

I turn toward her slowly, letting the weight of the moment hang thick between us. She looks small beneath it—unsure, frightened.

"Yes," I say, my voice rough, almost reverent. "Everything in there is about you."

I push the key inside and pause to take a breath before removing it. Considering how the documents inside will wreck her. But she needs to know. I slide the drawer free, the weight of it solid in my hands, and set it down on the desk between us. She hesitates, then steps closer, the air between us charged and trembling. Her fingers hover at the edge, but she doesn't touch it. She only looks.

On top of the files are the photographs—the ones I've kept, the ones that matter. Candid shots of her laughing with friends, sun streaking through her hair. One with her parents at graduation, all proud smiles and soft arms around their little girl. And then the one that always gets me — the one of us standing side by side at the neigh-borhood cook-off.

Her smile is small in it, polite, uneasy. She looks like she's trying to disappear while the camera flashes, but I remember that day like it's carved into me. She'd just turned eighteen. I'd waited. Watched. Told myself I would keep my distance until it was time.

I remember the heat of her shoulder brushing mine, the pulse in my throat so loud I could barely hear the laughter around us. I wanted to wrap my arm around her waist right there, pull her close for the picture — claim her, show every bastard in town that she was already mine. But I didn't. Because that's not what Sheriffs do. That's what monsters do. And I couldn't afford to be the monster back then — not in a town that looked to me for protection from men like Jackson Moore and his rotten network. I had to be the law here. The steady hand. The face they trusted when everything else turned to chaos.

I needed Rosefield to believe in me — to love me, even. To look at me and see safety, not sin. Respect was my shield, and I wore it like armor. Because if they ever saw what I really was, what I really wanted, they'd know I was no better than the devils I swore to keep from their doors.

I let out a slow breath, tension crawling up the back of my neck. A flicker of something — concern, maybe — pushes through the calm I've tried to hold. I don't know how she'll react when she sees what's inside that folder.

She reaches into the drawer and lifts the photos carefully, finger-tips grazing over the glossy paper like she's afraid they'll burn. She pauses on the one of us together, the faintest smile tugging at her lips. Watching her, I can't help but wonder — does she regret it? Does some part of her wish she'd given herself to me back then, before everything went to hell?

I clear the space on my desk and pull the folder free, the edges worn from how many times I've gone over it. My voice drops low, steady but edged with the weight of what's coming.

"Summer," I start, eyes fixed on her. "This landed on my desk at eight p.m. the night I took you. By nine-thirty, you were in my truck." I pause, letting the words sink in. "I did what I did because I had to save you. You need to understand that."

I glance down at the folder, then back at her.

"I tried to do it the right way first. I went to your parents. I begged them to let me keep watch, to stay close after those first photographs started showing up. When more surfaced—worse ones—I told them you needed to come here, stay where I could protect you. But they said no. They said they could keep you safe." A dark laugh slips from me, low and humorless.

I tap the folder, the paper inside whispering like a secret that's waited too long. "And then this came in. The moment I saw what was inside, I knew." My gaze hardens. "I wasn't asking anymore. Whether you wanted to or not, I was taking you."

She slams the photographs aside, the sound razored enough to slice through the silence.

"Show me," she snaps.

I hesitate for a heartbeat, then flip open the file and pull out the stack of papers inside. Each sheet is a screenshot, printed straight from a case file—evidence pulled from somewhere I wish I'd never had to look.

"It was buried on the dark web," I tell her quietly. "Hidden behind layers of encryption. But it wasn't hidden well enough."

She takes the first page, brow furrowing. The photo of her sleeping is pinned to the top of the page. At first glance, it looks like a simple booking site—ordinary, sterile. Then her expression changes. Her eyes catch on the text, scanning the list of "appointments," and I see the moment the meaning sinks in.

Her confusion dissolves into horror.

She doesn't speak. Just stares, eyes wide and unfocused, as though the words themselves are poison. The paper trembles in her hands.

**DARK WEB LOT LISTING — SUMMER
    MILLER
LOT #A-017 — THE VIRGIN**

DAUGHTER OF THE DISTRICT ATTORNEY

Status: Fresh Acquisition — Unbroken

Condition: Virgin, restrained, compliant with handling

Age: 20

Pedigree: High-value lineage. Daughter of DA Michael Miller. Law enforcement connections make this a premium, one-time opportunity.

BASE SESSION PACKAGES

30 Minutes (Single Participant Only) – $12,500

60 Minutes (Single Participant Only) – $20,000

Note: Rates listed are for **ONE participant**. Any additional man present in the room incurs an immediate surcharge of **$10,000 per head**.

No exceptions. No negotiation.

OPTIONAL EXTRAS (Subject to Handler Approval)

-**Virginity Claim** (verified)

-**Impact Menu**: whips, canes, paddles, riding crop

-**Electric stimulation / electroshock**

-**Restraint variations: cuffs, belts, spreader bar, suspension**

-**Blindfolding, gagging, sensory deprivation**

-**Filming permissions** (premium surcharge applies)

-**Multiple-participant rotation** (requires advance approval + surcharge)

This list is not exhaustive. Custom requests
may be submitted directly to the handler.

RESTRICTION NOTICE
-Participant must remain **conscious** unless
unconsciousness is included in the
approved request.
-No disfigurement damage permitted during
paid sessions.

HANDLER NOTES
-Subject is **high-value** due to lineage, age, and
virgin status.
-Currently untrained, but responsive.
-High market interest.
-Buyer discretion recommended — this
product will not remain available long.

I can't look at it again. I fix my gaze on her instead—on the way
the color drains from her face, on the sound of her shaky breath as
she covers her mouth with trembling fingers. Tears slip down her
cheeks one after another, silent and unstoppable.

That's when she finally understands. What I took her from. What
I've been fighting against all along.

"Jacob… this can't be real," she whispers, her voice breaking
somewhere between disbelief and pleading.

"It is," I say, the words rough in my throat. "And it was fully
booked—a month straight—less than an hour after it went live."

Her head shakes, slow at first, then faster, like she's trying to
erase what she's seeing. I drag a hand over my mouth, remembering
the moment I found it—the way the room seemed to tilt, the way
everything inside me went black.

"Summer, I saw that, and I lost it. I couldn't stand there and do
nothing."

She flips to the next page. The paper trembles between her
fingers as she stares, then lifts it higher, her breath catching hard.

Her voice comes out as a broken whisper, wet with tears. "Well…
it shows how wrong they were." She laughs, but it's hollow, shattered. "I wasn't even a virgin."

The sentence hangs there, jagged and cruel, and I can't tell if
she's trying to reclaim something or destroy it. All I know is that I
can't breathe.

She realizes what she's just said. Her hand flies to her mouth,
eyes wide, breath catching. I can't tell if she's trembling because of
what she's seen—or because she knows what she's just confessed.

"I'm sorry, Jacob," she squeaks, voice breaking as tears spill
down her cheeks. "I wanted to tell you—truly I did, but—"

She reaches for my forearm, and everything inside me stops.

Her hand is warm on my skin, but it feels like a brand. A lie. A
betrayal I didn't see coming. My pulse roars in my ears, drowning
her out, drowning out everything except the single fact detonating
through my skull—she wasn't mine first.

Something cold slides down the back of my neck. A flicker—
sharp, metallic—cuts through my breathing. I can't tell if it's jealousy
or grief or something darker that I've never had a fucking name for.

Then the images start to morph in my head.

Her, bent over. Her mouth parted. Some other man—some
fucking no one—inside *my* girl. Touching what I've starved myself
for. Taking what I kept myself from having, year after goddamn
year.

A crack tears through my chest so violently my vision goes white
around the edges.

Someone—fuck knows who—some bar rat maybe? One of Carlton's cowboys? The thought of her, moaning for someone else—

It doesn't just hurt. It splits something in the marrow of me.

And that's when the rage hits.

Fast. Total. A wildfire crawling up my throat before I can
contain it.

It rips through me, a hot animal that takes over my chest and
claws for release. Words I don't even mean spill out.

"You mean to tell me," I roar, pacing like a trapped thing, "that I
brought you here to keep you—and you've already given yourself to

someone else? Who the fuck is he?" My fists curl until my knuckles ache. "Tell me."

She looks me in the eye, but says nothing.

I don't think. I act. I yank the desk chair up and hurl it across the room; it slams into the desktop and the monitor explodes onto the floor in a shower of glass and plastic.

"Jacob," she sobs, her voice small and splintered.

Tears streak down her face as she takes a step back, hands raised like she's trying to calm a wild animal.

"I was going to tell you. I—I was scared." Her words trip over themselves, frantic, trembling, "that you'd react like this…Please, Jacob, you've just dropped all this on me. Please don't do this now."

Her chest heaves, her whole body shaking as she presses herself against the wall, eyes wide and glistening. Every inch of her is pleading with me—not just to listen, but to stop.

"I haven't touched another woman in years," I snarl, pacing like a caged animal. "I've had them throw themselves at me—half this town whispering, asking if something's wrong with me, if I'm broken. And all this time, I thought I was doing the right thing. I was keeping myself for you."

My voice cracks, harsh and unrecognizable. "And then I find out —by accident—that you've already opened your legs and given yourself—the most precious part of yourself—to some little fuckboy?"

I slam my hand against the desk, the sound echoing through the room.

"I can't—God, I can't—Summer."

The words keep coming, raw and furious.

"I thought I kept you pure. Thought I kept you safe. Thought I kept you mine." My jaw tightens, breath shredding in and out. "Fuck… what more could I have done? I was everywhere, Summer. Watching. Waiting. When I wasn't, my men were."

Then the thought hits—slow, poisonous. "Was it one of my men?"

Her eyes widen. She sees the shift before I even move. Fear blooms across her face.

"Was it one of my fucking men?" The roar rips out of me before I can cage it, my fist driving straight through the drywall beside her head. Plaster explodes. Dust rains down between us.

"No!" she sobs. "It was Tyler… the night of the drug raid."

I laugh. A hollow, broken sound. There's no humor in it.

"Tyler." His name burns like acid on my tongue. I remember that night—how she was supposed to be safe, tucked away at a friend's house. Instead, she took the wrong goddamn street.

"Do you have any idea what I've done to protect you? The lines I've crossed? The deals I made just to keep Jackson's men from touching you?"

I drag a hand through my hair, a bitter laugh escaping.

"You think they just disappeared? No. I brought you here and I turned a blind eye. I stopped investigating. I let them have what they wanted—anyone but you. And for what?" I meet her eyes, burning. "For this? For the one thing I thought I'd kept untouched to already belong to someone else. And now there's women locked up in warehouses, being raped, tortured and murdered because I stopped investigations. Because I let it slide for you."

The silence that follows is heavy, trembling, the kind that feels like it might break the walls apart. She meets my eyes like a dare, calm and cold enough to cut. My chest tightens around the words as they fall from her lips.

"I never asked for any of this. But fine. You've made your point. Save the others," she says, voice steady, frightening in its steadiness. "Get them out. Get them living again. I'd rather—" Her voice breaks, just for a second. "—I'd rather hand myself over than have this on my conscience."

For a second the room tilts. The idea of her choosing to disappear into that darkness to ease my guilt somehow lands heavier than any blow. Anger spikes—at her, at myself, at the world that keeps producing monsters—but under it is something worse: a cold, searing clarity.

No.

"No," I say before I can stop it, and the single syllable carries more than denial. It carries the promise of everything I am. "You will not be anyone's bargaining chip. But Summer I—"

"Yes, Jacob," she interrupts, her voice trembling but steady enough to land every word like a blade. "I did sleep with Tyler. I did lose my virginity. But it wasn't—" she swallows hard, shaking her head "—it wasn't anything like this." She gestures between us. "Not even close to what we've shared."

I can still taste the fury in my mouth, bitter and metallic, but her words hit something I can't quite name—something between shame and relief.

She draws in a slow breath, straightens her shoulders, and takes a cautious step back.

"Right now, I'm going to shower," she says quietly. "You need space, Jacob. Time to calm down."

For a second, I think she might look back. But she doesn't. She just walks past me, her footsteps light but defiant, leaving me standing in the wreckage of everything I thought I controlled.

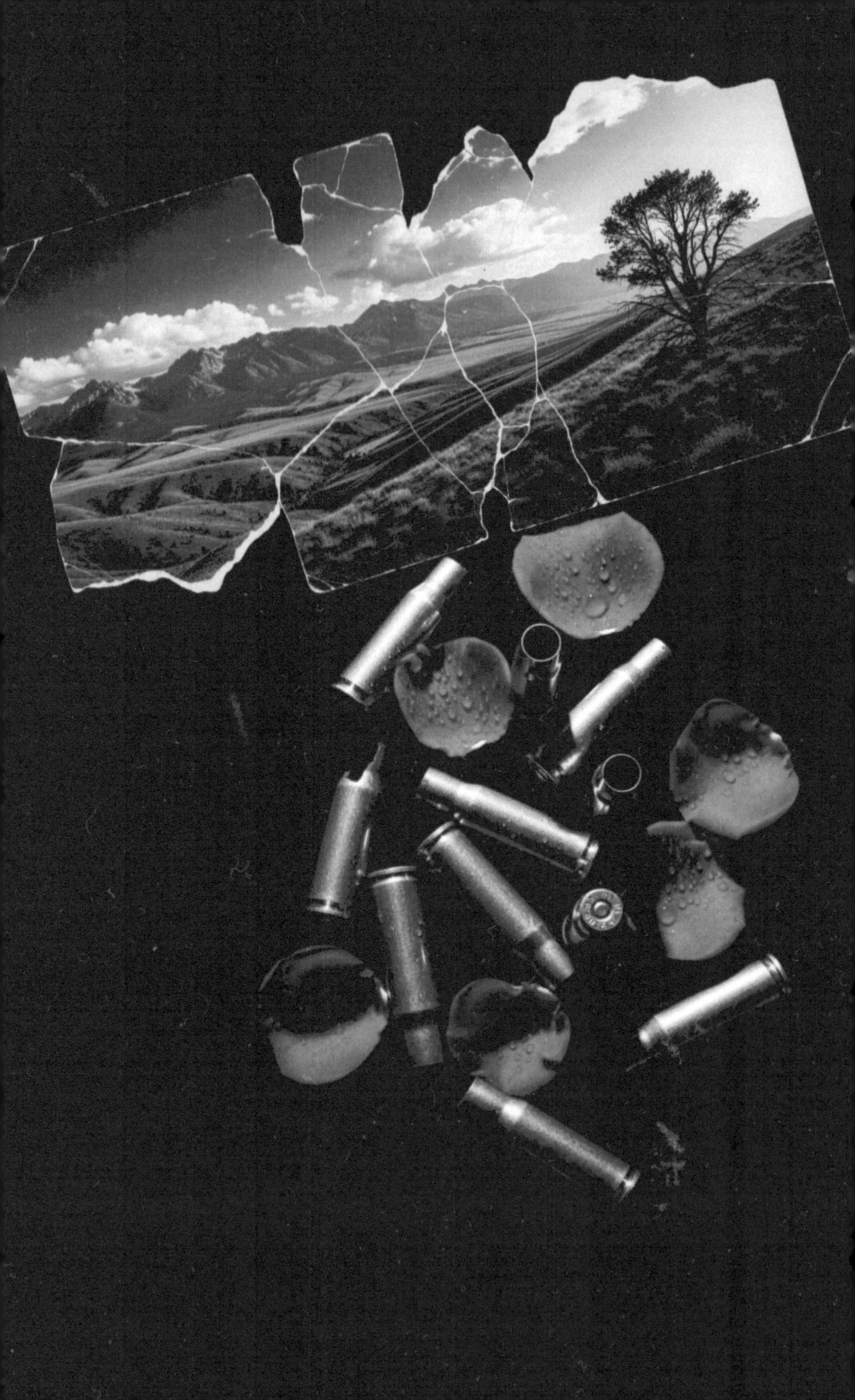

Chapter 17
Run
Summer

I head upstairs, my footsteps careful at first, then faster once I'm out of his sight. Not to shower. Not to calm down. I'm heading upstairs to run. To grab my bag, and whatever I can carry in it. I'm going to see Constance and Adelaide. To take them up on that hotel room they offered, the one I swore I wouldn't need.

The website terrified me—seeing my face, my name twisted into something filthy—but that isn't what finally pushed me over the edge. It was him. The way Jacob's rage filled the room, how his voice tore through the air when he realized I'd been with Tyler. The chair flying, his computer shattering. The look in his eyes.

Something broke inside me watching that.

I never meant to tell him. I promised myself I wouldn't—that I'd bury that part of me deep enough he'd never dig it up. But the words just fell out. The adrenaline, the disgust, the horror—it all collided, and I opened my mouth before I could stop it.

Because seeing those words on that page—virgin—made my stomach turn. Saying out loud that I wasn't one felt like the only weapon I had left. Like if I said it, maybe it meant they didn't know me after all, like maybe it would make me safe.

Jacob's words echo in my head—the other women. The ones he

said he'd ignored. The ones he let suffer while he was busy keeping me safe.

And now my heart feels like it's splintering under the weight of it. I can't stop thinking about them, about what they must have gone through. What they might still be going through. The faces he didn't save because of me. Because his obsession blinded him.

If he'd helped them instead—if he hadn't been so consumed with us—maybe they'd still be free. Maybe they'd still have their families, their lives.

But they don't. Because Jacob decided I was the one worth saving.

And now, standing here, all I can think is that I'd rather hand myself over than live with that. The guilt of it burns hotter than his anger ever could.

He's disgusted with me—I saw it in his eyes. That flicker of betrayal when he realized I wasn't the untouched girl he'd built in his head. He doesn't see me anymore. Not the same way. Now, to him, I'm marked. Stained. A possession he thought was perfect, spoiled by the thought of another man's touch.

I sling my backpack over my shoulder and tighten the straps, my hands trembling just enough to make the zip rattle. From the bottom of the stairs comes the dull thud of glass on wood—Jacob's bourbon hitting the table, maybe the floor—and I know that's my chance. He's drinking. He's distracted.

Keeping to the wall, I move down the stairs one cautious step at a time. Every creak feels like it might give me away, like the house itself is warning him I'm leaving. When I reach the hall, I pause, listening. Nothing but the faint hum of the old fridge and the soft clink of glass again from the sitting room.

I take a breath, grip the handle, and slip through the front door.

The air outside hits me like a shock, bright but cold, the midday sun pouring over everything. For a heartbeat, I freeze—half expecting his voice to tear through the quiet—but it doesn't. I'm over the threshold, and I run.

My shoes hit the gravel hard, kicking up dust as I sprint across the yard and toward the treeline. The woods are my only chance; out here, in daylight, I'd be spotted before I hit the main road. He'll have people looking the second he gets the camera feed notification on his cell. He always does.

The forest swallows me whole—branches clawing at my sleeves, twigs snapping underfoot. I don't stop. I fix my eyes ahead, knowing if I keep straight through the trees, I'll come out behind Mr. and Mrs. McBrie's house. From there, I can cut through the alley, circle the block, and make it to Constance's.

"Summer!"

His voice cuts through the trees, low at first—almost disbelieving —then louder, edged, echoing through the forest like a warning shot. I freeze for half a second, heart hammering so hard it hurts, then force myself to move again. Straight ahead. Don't turn. Don't look back.

Branches whip against my arms as I push through them, lungs burning, but I don't dare slow down.

"Summer!" he shouts again, this time a roar that rattles the leaves. "I will fucking catch you, and when I do—so help me, God—"

The rest is lost in the wind, but I don't need to hear the end of it. I already know what he's capable of.

I stumble over a fallen branch hidden beneath the leaves, my foot catching hard enough to send me pitching forward. My palms slap against rough bark as I crash into a tree, stopping just short of the ground. The scrape burns, but it's nothing compared to the pounding in my chest.

I push myself upright, gasping, my heart clawing its way up my throat like it's trying to escape. Each breath comes too fast, too shallow—it feels like my lungs can't keep up with the panic tearing through me.

I duck down behind the tree, pressing my back to the trunk, trying to steady myself. The forest is alive with sound—the wind, the birds, the crackle of my own breath—and then I hear it.

Thud. Thud. Thud.

His boots, heavy and thundering, hitting the ground closer, faster. The sound of a hunter closing in on his prey.

I push myself upright, lungs screaming for air, and start to run again. The woods blur around me—green and shadow and sunlight all spinning together. I don't get more than a few steps before something catches me.

An arm hooks around me from behind, powerful and unyielding, cutting off my breath and my momentum in a single motion. The shock of it steals every sound from my throat.

Then the hold is gone, replaced by motion—by the violent jolt of being spun and driven down into the dirt. The breath rushes out of me as I hit the ground, the weight of him above me pressing me still. His chest heaves, sweat dripping from his temple, his breathing rough and ragged.

The forest goes quiet around us. All I can hear is his breath, my pulse, and the small, broken sound that slips from my lips when I finally realize he's caught me.

"I told you," he pants, his voice rough, broken by the run. "No matter where you go, no matter how hard you try to run—I will always find you."

"Get off me!" I scream, shoving at his chest, but he doesn't move. "You don't want me, remember? I'm disgusting, you made that pretty fucking clear!" My words splinter, rising into sobs I can't swallow back. "You said I ruined everything—so let me go, Jacob. Just let me go."

Tears sting my eyes as I choke on the words. "You should be saving them," I whisper, trembling beneath him. "The women you said you stopped protecting—those girls are still out there, and you're wasting your time on me. Do your job, your duty. Go save them. Let me go and help those innocent women. Please." My voice breaks entirely at the last word, and for a moment there's nothing— just his weight above me, his breath brushing my skin, and the silence of a man at war with himself.

He's silent for a long moment, his breath harsh against my cheek. The forest hums around us, waiting. Then his voice comes—low, rough, shaking with something that sounds too much like devotion twisted into madness.

"I'll never let you go," he says. "Do you understand me? Never.

You can run, you can hide, but I'll find you every God damn time."
His grip tightens slightly, not in anger this time, but in something
worse. "I'd cross the ends of the earth for you, Summer. There's
nowhere far enough."

He exhales hard, the sound half a growl, half a confession. "I
didn't mean to drive you away," he says, his voice fraying. "But the
thought of another man —" He stops, jaw clenching. "The thought of
anyone else touching you makes me want to burn the whole fucking
world down."

The words hang there, heavy and raw, and I can feel every one of
them settle like ash in the air between us.

"Jesus, Summer…" His voice breaks, raw and cracked open. "I
love you. You were meant for me. Only for me."

A tear slips from his eye, landing warm against my cheek before I
can turn away. His hand trembles where it rests beside my head, his
chest still heaving with the remnants of his fury.

"One day," he whispers, almost pleading, "you'll say it back." He
leans closer, his breath uneven, the words dragging out of him like
they hurt. "Do you hear me? Every bone in my body, every drop of
blood in my veins — it's all for you. There's no one else.
There could be no one else."

His voice falls quiet, but the weight of it stays, heavy and
unyielding, pressing against the air between us until I can barely
breathe.

This man — this giant, terrifying force of a man — is crying over
me. Real tears. The kind that doesn't belong to someone like him.
And for one insane, unbearable moment, something inside me breaks
wide open.

I want to throw myself into his arms, back into the cage he's
carved around us, and let him keep me there. Let him hold me, claim
me, ruin me again and again until there's nothing left of me that
doesn't belong to him.

I reach for him before I can think better of it, my hands finding
his shoulders, pulling him down to me. His body trembles against
mine, all heat and exhaustion and something that feels too human for
what he is.

I hold him tight—so tight I can feel the beat of his heart against my chest. The scent of him wraps around me, thick and familiar: smoke, cedarwood, and bourbon. The same scent that used to make my pulse race, then turn my stomach, and somehow—God help me —now feels like home.

"I'm falling for you, Jacob," I whisper, the words trembling as they leave my mouth. "But you're not safe. You're dangerous. You hurt me."

His eyes search mine, raw and disbelieving, and I can't hold his gaze for long. I swallow hard, my voice cracking.

He lifts his head, eyes wild and glassy, and before I can speak, his mouth crashes against mine. The kiss isn't soft—it's desperate, feral, like he's trying to consume every breath I've ever taken without him.

"Fuck, Summer," he growls against my lips, his voice breaking on the edge of rage and worship. "I'm sorry I hurt you—but I had to keep you here. Had to stop you from running." His breath trembles, hot and uneven against my mouth. "I can't promise I won't hurt you again… but I see it in your eyes, sweetheart. You don't want mercy —you want the monster."

His hands frame my face—rough, trembling, desperate. "I'll give you everything," he murmurs, his words a vow and a threat all at once. "Anything you want. It's yours." His gaze burns into mine, dark and unrelenting. "You're mine, you hear me? Mine."

Each word hits like a heartbeat—reckless, unrestrained, final.

"Fuck the past," he rasps. "Fuck everything. We're here now. You're with me. That's all that matters."

We stay tangled there for what feels like forever, lost in the taste of each other and the sound of our ragged breaths. The forest floor crackles beneath us, leaves clinging to our skin as we roll together, the world narrowing until it's only him—only us.

When he finally pulls back, his gaze holds mine with something fierce and unspoken. Then, without a word, he slides his arms beneath me and lifts me from the ground. My head falls against his chest, the steady pound of his heartbeat echoing through me. The forest fades behind us, the light slipping through the trees in thin, fractured beams, and all I can hear is his uneven breathing as he carries me back — back to his home — our home.

He carries me through the doorway and up the stairs without slowing, the sound of his footsteps echoing through the empty house. In the bathroom, he sets me down only long enough to reach for the tap. Water bursts from the showerhead, steam filling the room like a rising fog.

We undress each other in a hurry, our hands clumsy and desperate, mouths finding one another in between every breath. The heat from the water collides with the heat of our skin until everything feels the same — blinding, overwhelming. I feel him hard against my stomach, heavy and hard, reaching higher than I thought possible — a physical reminder of just how big he is.

He steps back just enough to look at me, the water streaming down his face, his chest heaving. His fingers rake through his damp, ashen hair as his gaze drags over me — slow, searching, possessive.

He leans in to touch me, but I push him back. His eyes flicker — first with frustration, then shock, and finally that flicker of despair, like he thinks I'm rejecting him.

Little does he know what I'm thinking. I'm not pulling away to stop him — I'm doing it because I want to give him something I've never given anyone else.

Constance once told me about it, how to do it, how it felt. I'd always brushed it off, never thought it was something I'd want. Until now.

I drop to my knees before him, and his eyes darken, gleaming with a hunger so fierce it borders on worship. His hand comes down, fingers grazing my cheek as he steps closer, a low growl rumbling from his chest — deep enough to burn straight through me.

"I... I don't know what I'm doing, but I want to give you this," I pant, heat radiating between my thighs.

"I'll guide you, baby," he rasps.

His hand slides from my cheek into my hair, the other following to gather it, gripping just enough to make me shiver. He pulls it back, holding it like a makeshift ponytail, and steps even closer until the tip of him hovers inches from my mouth.

The shower roars above him, sending a cascade of heat down his back. Steam fills the small space, wrapping around us, warming my skin and drawing every nerve to attention.

I open my mouth, letting him slip inside.

The taste of salt is the first thing I notice, as I slide my tongue across the tip. He lets out a moan, a groan from deep within his soul. I look up to him, and he has his head tipped to the ceiling, still moaning.

"That's it, baby, swirl your tongue just like that." He groans as he pulls my head forward, forcing more of him into my mouth.

I suck gently, worried I'll hurt him if I'm too rough. I continue to swirl my tongue around his length. When I glide it along the thick vein that runs from his shaft to his end, he lets out a husky moan, so I keep my tongue there, and swirl it faster.

"Fuck, Summer." He moans, holding my head still. Pulling himself gently in and out as I attack the sensitive area with my tongue.

I push my head further forward, taking more of him into my mouth, continuing the attack with my tongue along his shaft as I suck. I move my head backwards and forwards, sucking and licking his length. His voice drops to a low groan, thick with restraint.

"That's it… just like that."

His fingers tighten in my hair, guiding my movements faster with a mix of control and need. Every sound that escapes him fuels me, every breath a reminder of how close he is to unravelling. I move in rhythm with his quiet commands, finding the pace that makes him tremble against me.

My eyes water as he pushes deeper into my mouth, causing the air to restrict. His grip tightens in my hair, a vice that stings just enough to blur the line between pain and pleasure.

The pull ignites something wild inside me — heat and hunger twisting together until I'm lost to the frenzy he creates. I take him deeper, licking harder. Sucking harder to give some of the pain back to him.

He looks down at me, eyes devouring the sight before him. A low growl rumbles from his chest, rising and falling with each strained breath, the movement of his abs hypnotic — fuelling the ache burning hotter inside me.

His movements become erratic, his mouth open wide, groans and pants leaving his mouth. Then my name.

"Summer…. Fuck… I'm gonna come and you're gonna swallow every fucking drop."

My eyes find his — a silent yes passing between us just before he comes undone.

His body goes rigid, his grip in my hair tightening — I'm sure I've lost some strands in his hands — he roars my name, the sound tearing through the air like it's the only word he's ever known as he spills inside of my mouth, flooding me with his salt and his seed.

He pulls my head back, forcing my eyes up to meet his — control radiating off him in waves.

"Swallow," he orders, voice rough, breathless.

I do — exaggerating the motion, letting the sound of it echo between us.

"Open. Let me see, baby," he growls, the words more animal than man.

I part my lips, tongue out, showing him every trace is gone. His eyes darken, a slow, dangerous satisfaction flickering there as his thumb drags across my bottom lip.

"You're such a fucking good girl," he growls, the praise rough enough to scrape skin. "And good girls get rewarded."

His hand drops from my face, the warmth of it lingering just long enough to make me ache for more. Then his voice cuts through the air — hard, commanding, undeniable.

"Bedroom. Now."

My heart is pounding so fast it feels dangerous, a wild rhythm that drowns out thought. I don't know what he plans, but I still rush to his room — excitement pooling between my legs.

I make my way down the hall toward his bedroom, every step heavier than the last. The lump in my throat throbs in rhythm with my heartbeat, thick and unsteady.

I enter the room — he closes the door behind me in quick succession. My heart is beating so loud I'm sure he can hear it pumping in my chest.

He stalks to the closet, the sound of his steps muffled against the carpet. I expect him to reach for something familiar—his shirt, his underwear—but instead, he comes back holding a pair of cuffs.

Not the kind you buy in a novelty shop. Not soft, not playful. These are real—cold, heavy, the kind he uses for work. Their whole design is meant to restrain, not entice. The kind that doesn't give you a chance to change your mind once they're on.

The sight of them steals the air from my lungs.

"You have a choice baby. I can gag you, so the world doesn't hear you shatter, but then, I won't stop until I'm satisfied. Or you can scream for me and have a safeword," He thrums, brushing the cuffs against my cheek.

A rush of heat surges through me, fast and dizzying. For a moment I can't tell where fear ends and want begins; all I know is that my pulse isn't panicked anymore—it's hungry.

Still, beneath the pulse of adrenaline, a thread of reason holds tight. I need something that's mine, a boundary in the middle of the chaos. A way to stop this if the pain goes too far.

"I want a safeword," I half groan, half whisper.

He cocks a brow, happy with my choice, probably because he wants to hear every scream I have to give him.

"Your safeword is sheriff. Say stop and I won't. Say no and I won't stop. But say sheriff and it ends immediately," He rasps, seriousness starting to take form on his expression. "Tell me you understand."

"I do," I whisper.

"Say it again," he hums, a smile forming on his lips.

"I do," I say louder.

"Mmm, one day you'll say that at the end of an aisle, promising your life, your very fucking soul to me. But for now—" He spanks my ass, "get on the bed, climb up to the headboard."

I do as I'm told and get into position. He comes next to me, threading the cuffs through the back of the bed, he puts the left one on first, the one that's below the steel bar, and then the right that hangs over it. He checks the cuffs, making sure they're not digging into my skin. As though he isn't about to inflict pain—and pleasure—on my body.

"That's right," he groans. "Now bend over and let me see that pretty little ass."

I do as he asks without question. He threads his hands between my thighs and opens me wider. Then moves his hands up to open my cheeks. A sensation works up the back of my leg, toward my ass, and before I can question it, I realize it's his tongue.

He makes his way to my entrance, licking and spitting.

He uses his fingers to take some of my arousal and massages it into the tight ring. I clench on contact, and he tuts.

"I know this hasn't been claimed," he rasps, voice low and visceral. "And tonight—it's mine."

The words hit like a shockwave. I jolt beneath him, instinctively fighting what my body already knows is inevitable. This isn't something I've ever imagined—something even Constance, with all her whispered confessions, has never dared to mention.

"You're only going to make it hurt more baby. Relax. Give it to me," he rumbles.

I let out a moan as he scoops more of my arousal, using it to slide a single digit into me. The sensation feels odd. An invasion of a place that I never thought I'd allow. But somehow, it feels... good.

"Fuck Summer, you don't know how good you look like this."

I let out a moan as he uses his other hand to play with my clit. He circles faster, dragging pleasure to the center of me until my body starts to tremble. Then—he moves. I feel the shift, the air changing with him, the promise of what's coming tightening every muscle in my body, but he keeps his fingers on my clit. I feel the heat of his erection circling the entrance—part of me wants to scream sheriff, the other half wants to experience this with him and only him.

"What's your safeword?" he whispers, voice still edged with command.

"Sheriff," I choke out, the word trembling past my lips.

I open my legs wider, an invitation for him to enter—and he does.

He starts slow, pushing just the tip into me, the stretch burning and feeling uncomfortable. I let out a hiss.

"Shh baby, this is the worst part."

And he moves deeper, working in and out as he goes, inch by inch. The further he gets, the more my body adjusts to him. The pain is overwhelming, but the pleasure is building up inside of me. I push back slightly, as though I'm trying to take more of him and he hums in approval.

"Fuck," he moans as he goes deeper and deeper.

"Oh, fuck Jacob," I moan, "fuck it hurts. I'm too full. It's too much."

But that sends him into a frenzy, in one swift motion he pushes himself the rest of the way. A scream erupts from me, so loud it hurts the back of my throat.

"Jacob—" My eyes roll to the back of my head. The sensation heightening me to a level I never thought I'd know. The pain is devastating, but the pleasure is so intense that I don't want it to stop.

He pulls almost all the way out and pounds back into me, the feeling sending my eyes rolling to the back of my head—pain, burning, pleasure. All mingling into one huge form of pressure that builds inside of me.

I scream, deeper and louder than ever before.

He continues his assault on my clit, although his strides alter—he's feral with pleasure.

"Mine," he moans. "Fucking mine." He parts my cheeks wider and pushes in so hard and so deep that I feel the smack of his balls on my front entrance. The sensation feels incredible.

"Yes. Just like that," I moan "Fuck... Fuck... Fuck!" I scream.

He moves fast, pumping in and out of me quickly, his balls slapping onto me every time he pumps into me. The pain subsides and I'm overcome with pleasure. I scream into the pillow, trying not to wake the whole damn town with the sound of my own destruction. But he yanks it away, leaving me exposed—nothing but the mattress beneath me, too low to muffle the noise.

He wants to hear it. Every gasp. Every broken sound. He wants to hear me unravel while he destroys me.

I'm so full, my pussy so wet. Tears trickle down my face—my throat feels like the screams are razorblades.

He adjusts behind me; I think he gets to one knee and continues at a new angle.

"Fuuuuu—" I start to roar, before the orgasm hits and hot fluid comes rushing from me. It sprays on the bed, coating the mattress beneath us. Everything is drenched, slick heat spreading beneath us, and when he drives harder, more spills out—like my body's surrender made visible.

My legs are gone, I'm unable to hold my weight up after my ruin, so he holds my hips up and continues to pound into me.

"Fuck Summer…. My dirty little slut. Look at you fucking pouring for me."

A tiny, pathetic yelp comes out, for a second, I think I'm going to pass out. Then he roars.

"FUCK!" he screams, louder than any bellow I've heard come from him, as he explodes, pulsing inside of me, filling me with his hot seed.

He stays there for a moment, chest rising against my back, catching his breath. Then he pulls out slowly and presses a towel between my cheeks. He tucks it beneath me with quiet care before moving to undo the cuffs.

Through the haze, I still notice the shift in his expression—the flicker of concern when he sees the raw marks circling my wrists where the metal bit into my skin.

"I'm sorry," he says, over and over, as he raises them to his mouth, kissing the red areas over and over.

I roll onto my back—unable to speak a word—and pass out into a long, and restless sleep.

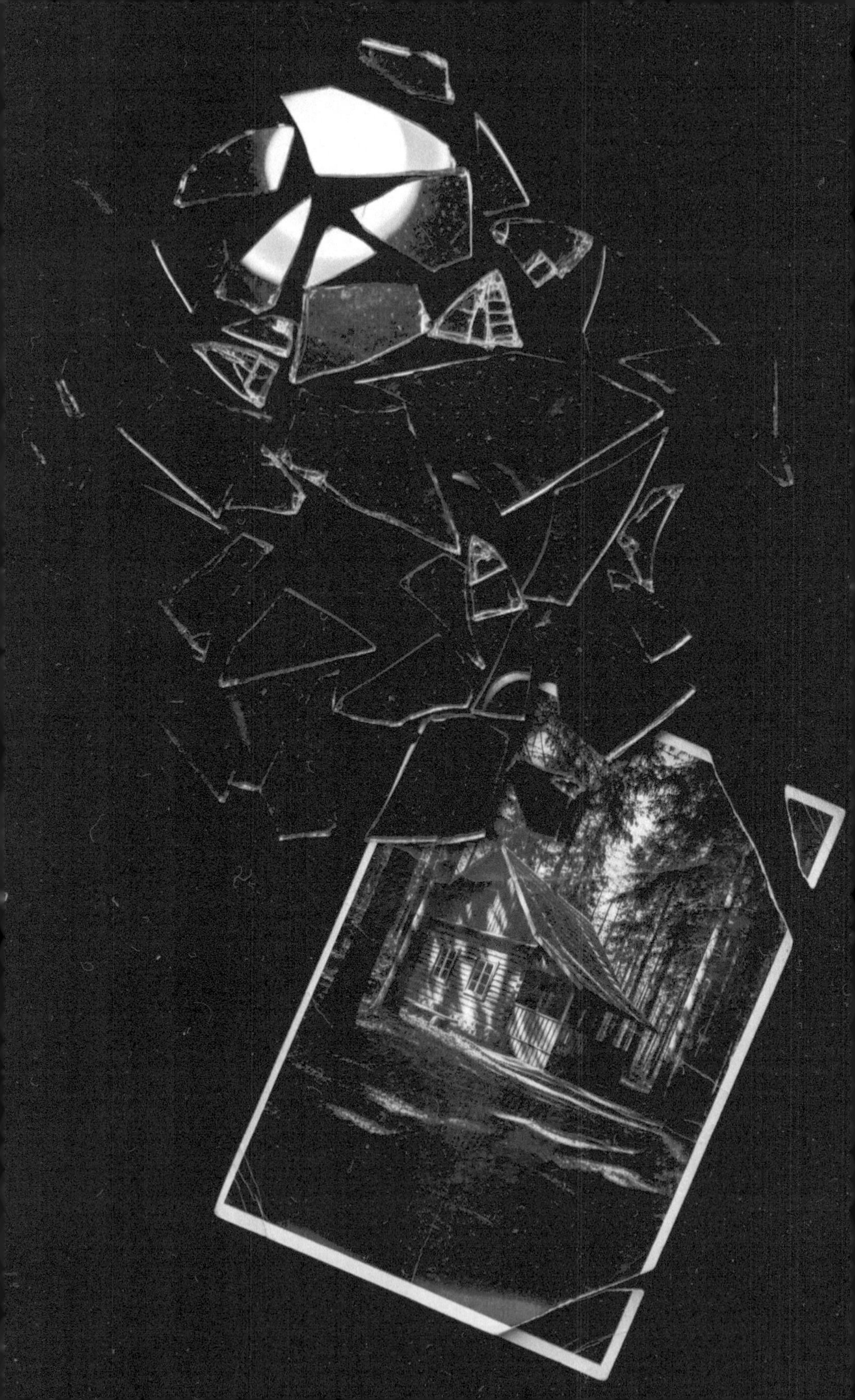

Chapter 18
Ashes At The Door
Summer

The phone rips through the silence like a knife. Shrill. Violent. Too loud for the hour, too piercing for the fragile threads holding the night together. I freeze under the covers, heart jerking hard enough to ache.

I reach over to put my arm over Jacob, but he already sits on the edge of the bed, boots propped, like he's been waiting for this exact sound.

He answers on the second ring.

His voice drops, a graveled growl meant only for whoever's on the other end. Too low for me to catch words, but the silence between them tells me more than words could.

His shoulders tighten. His jaw works once, twice, hard enough I hear the faint grind of teeth.

"No, I'll handle it," he says, and hangs up.

When he turns, his eyes skim the bed, locking on me even in the dark. That stare—it stills the blood in my veins. For a heartbeat, I think he'll speak. That he'll explain where he's going. But he doesn't.

"I love you," he whispers, before he stands, fluid, efficient, no wasted motion. He shrugs into his coat, holsters his gun with the ease of muscle memory, and stalks toward the door.

The slam echoes through the walls, rattling them like a warning.

I sit up, breath caught tight in my throat. The silence he leaves behind feels louder than the call that pulled him away. I'm still aching—muscles sore, wrists throbbing where the metal bit into my skin. The marks sting now, and I know by morning they'll bloom into bruises.

He said sorry. For the first time, he actually apologized for hurting me. For marking me. The sound of that word still echoes, like he wasn't sure how it was supposed to feel on his tongue.

Maybe it's just kids causing trouble somewhere in town, I tell myself. Maybe that's all it is. But he's the sheriff—he has deputies for that. If he left without a word, it means something bigger. Something bad.

I wish I'd stopped him. Asked him where he was going, when he'd be back. Instead, I just watched him go, too stunned, too raw to speak.

I could call him. I could. But if it's serious—if it's something that needs the sheriff himself—he won't want me to disturb him. So, I stay where I am— staring at ceiling—the quiet pressing down on me. My body aches, my mind won't stop replaying the way he looked at me before he left, and I know I won't drift back to sleep.

I climb out of bed, the cool air biting against my skin as I move toward the en-suite. The light flickers once before steadying, and I stand there for a moment, staring at my reflection—hair tangled, eyes hollow. I reach for a towel, for something to do with my hands, anything to make the silence less suffocating.

When I clean myself up, the sting coupled with the sight of red on the tissue twists something in my stomach. I turn on the shower and step under the water, letting it run until the warmth blurs the edges of everything. I stay there longer than I should, until the steam fogs the mirror and my skin starts to prickle.

When I finally walk back into the bedroom, the space still feels empty without him, but heavier than before, like his presence still clings to the air. There's a weight in my chest I can't name, a cold certainty pressing at the edge of thought. Something's wrong. Whether it's already happened or still waiting to, I can feel it moving closer.

I whisper into the empty room: He'll be back in an hour. It's nothing. It has nothing to do with me.

I pace. Five steps across the room, turn, five steps back. My skin feels too tight, nerves twitching under it like live wires. The boards creak beneath my feet, loud in the silence.

The clock ticks louder. My ears strain for the sound of boots on the porch, the slam of the door, his voice cutting through the dark. Anything is better than this silence, but no sound comes.

Then, as though my prayers are answered, I hear an engine roaring up the road—by the time headlights sweep across the glass, I'm already at the door. Relief slams into me, fierce and overwhelming. Jacob is back.

I reach for the handle, desperate for his voice, his presence. Anything to break this unbearable emptiness. But something stops me in my tracks. Something feels—odd.

I hear the breaks of the truck, then the driver door opens and slams shut. Boots sound on the porch, then the knock comes once. But Jacob doesn't knock. It's a single rap, almost hesitant.

"Summer!" I hear, a crackled deep male voice, calling my name.

A familiar voice.

Benny.

I open the door and there he stands.

His skin is chalk-white in the porch light, his hair damp with sweat. His chest rises and falls like he's run a marathon. His eyes— wide, shining, almost breaking—fix on me with pity so striking it feels like cruelty.

"Summer," he whispers, like my name itself is a wound. "I came as soon as I could."

Confusion washes over me. "What's going on?"

He looks past me, into the house, into the hollowness Jacob left behind. His jaw hardens. When his gaze returns, it slices straight through me.

"You don't know, do you?" he asks, half concerned, half angry.

The words land like ice water down my spine. My heart jerks.

"For Christ's sake Benny, what?"

His face twists, disbelief cutting through his features. He drags a hand over his mouth, like he can't quite believe the words coming out of it.

"Fuck." A sudden shake of his head follows. "He hasn't told you?" The laugh that slips out isn't really a laugh at all—just a jagged sound, bitter and hollow.

His shoulders sag, his whole frame seeming to fold under the weight of it. He exhales through clenched teeth, then steps closer.

"I shouldn't be the one saying this." His voice breaks on the words. "But someone has to." His eyes hold mine. "It's your parents," he whispers, voice cracking. "Their house... there were perimeters everywhere. Cop cars, the fire department were there. There was still smoke coming from the building when I saw."

I pause, waiting for him to say my worst nightmare.

"They didn't make it out, Summer. I waited. Wanted to help, but Jacob sent me away." His voice dips even lower, gentle, coaxing. "They're gone."

The air leaves my lungs in a single violent rush. My stomach knots, twisting so hard I double over. The floor tilts, and tilts, until I'm sure I'll collapse straight through it.

"No." My head shakes, frantic, wild. "No, you're wrong."

"I wish I was." He steps closer, his voice low and thick, dripping with sorrow. "God, I wish I was."

And then the images hit.

Flames swallowing the old wooden beams, orange and alive, roaring as they climb. The wallpaper blistering, curling black. My mother's voice shrieking my name from behind walls that crack and groan as they collapse. My father pounding fists against a window that won't shatter, the glass glowing hot before it explodes inward. The smoke choking them. The heat eating their skin. Their hands reaching for a door that won't open, until the fire swallows them whole.

The scream that tears from me doesn't sound human.

Benny catches me before I hit the ground. His arms wrap around me, strong, unshakable, pulling me into the solid press of his chest. I claw at him, fists tight in his shirt, trying to find something alive when the only images in my head are of my parents burning.

"It's okay," he murmurs, rocking me, voice breaking into something soft, something warm. "You're safe. I've got you. You're not alone in this."

I sob against him until my body convulses, until bile burns the back of my throat. The smell of smoke clings to my imagination so thick I swear I can taste it, bitter and acrid on my tongue. And then he leans down, his breath brushing my ear, low enough to feel like a secret.

"That son of a bitch didn't tell you," he whispers, "he left you here alone."

The words slide into me like poison. I push myself away from him, backing off like a child who's just find out the lap they're sitting on isn't the real Santa.

"Jacob loves me. Don't you dare—" I sob, uncontrollable anger pouring from every word.

"Then where is he, Summer?" he shrugs, frustration radiating from him as he pulls me back into his arms.

And he's right. Where is he? He's gone. Leaving me to shatter in Benny's arms. He holds tighter, sealing the crack he's pried open with his hands.

But it isn't enough. No arms can hold the weight of this.

"I need to see them." The words crackle out between sobs, half-choked, half-mad. I wrench at his grip, shoving hard against his chest until I'm on my feet. My body sways, knees trembling, vision blurring with tears. "I need to go. Now. I need to see them—"

"Summer—"

"I have to!" My voice splinters, piercing, shrill. My hand slams against the doorknob, slippery with sweat, rattling hard enough the metal clinks. "They can't just—I can't just—I have to see them!"

Benny's hand snaps over mine. Holding me in place and forcing me to look to him.

"No."

The word detonates in me, I yank my hands free of his grasp.

"Don't you tell me no!" I whirl on him, wild, unsteady, chest heaving.

My hands slam against his chest, fists beating uselessly against muscle that won't give.

"They're my parents. My parents! You can't stop me—"

"Listen to me." His voice cracks through mine, low but harsh enough to slice. He grabs my wrists mid-swing, holding them firm, holding me still. His face is close, too close, eyes searing into mine. "If you run out there right now, you'll see nothing but ashes. Do you understand? Ashes." He runs a hand through his hair. "Your parents were taken away by the coroner. They won't let you see them, not until after the cops carry out their investigation."

Benny lowers me carefully, like he's guiding me down rather than letting me fall. I'm shaking so hard my teeth clatter. My stomach knots and twists, and then bile surges up my throat. I lurch sideways, heaving, retching onto the floor until acid burns my tongue.

Benny is there, pulling my hair back, murmuring, "It's okay, I've got you, just breathe, darlin', just breathe." His voice is low, steady, coaxing me through the violence of my own body.

"You'll see them," Benny whispers, rocking me against him once more. "But not like this. Not tonight." His hand cups my jaw, thumb stroking away tears and sweat. His voice softens until it's almost tender. "He should have told you. God, I wouldn't have left you alone to find out like this. I wouldn't have run off and abandoned you. But he did. I'm here. I'll be the one to take you when the time's right."

The words sink deep, cutting through the haze of grief, leaving raw edges behind.

He did.

The truth of it is undeniable. I watched Jacob walk out that door, watched his back vanish into the night without a word, without a glance. He didn't tell me. He didn't stay. He left, even after everything he said. After everything we shared. After telling me he loved me before he turned and walked out of that door.

My voice cracks when it comes out. "You—you don't know my parents. You don't know where they live, or anything about them?"

Benny's hand stills. His body stiffens for a fraction of a second before he exhales slow, like the question itself wounds him. He leans back enough to meet my eyes, thumb brushing my cheek as though to soften the blow.

"Deputy Thompson called me," he says quietly. "My cousin."

I blink at him, stunned.

"He was one of the first on scene," Benny continues, voice low, careful. "I told him about you. About the dance." His gaze holds mine, unflinching, burning with sincerity. "And he knew Jacob was on his way. I… I told him… about us… about how I care—" He shakes his head. Halting before stepping too far.

"You deserve more than silence," Benny murmurs, softer now, coaxing, almost tender. "You deserve someone who won't disappear when everything falls apart. Someone who will stay. Someone who'll hold you when you're like this." His voice dips, earnest, trembling. "That's me. Not him."

It fits. Too neatly. Too easily.

I try to step back from him, but he cups my face, lowering his forehead to mine. "You don't have to question this. You don't have to think right now. Just let me take care of you until you're strong enough. That's what you need. Me."

His words pour over me, like honey laced with razor blades. Sweet. Soothing. Cutting me as it seeps in.

"Summer," he murmurs, his voice a low, steady rumble—too calm, too sure. His thumb catches another tear as it slips down my cheek. "You don't have to do this here. Not alone. Not in his house."

My breath snags, chest tightening.

"Jacob doesn't love you," Benny says, quieter now, the edges of his voice smoothing into something dangerous and kind. "If he did, he wouldn't have walked out. He wouldn't have left you here to fall apart. He'd have told you. He'd have stayed."

His thumb traces the wet path down my face, pausing at the corner of my mouth. His breath mingles with mine, warm and close enough to steal. "You deserve more than that, Summer."

I want to fight him—to tell him he's wrong, that Jacob's silence is its own kind of love, brutal and confusing but real. But the words catch somewhere between my ribs. Because Benny's voice is soft enough to sound like comfort, and his lies come sweet enough to swallow.

"Come with me."

The words are whispered, but they slice through me. I blink up at him, dazed.

"What?"

"Come back to my trailer." His hand strokes down my arm, gentle, steady. "You shouldn't be here when you're like this. You'll fall apart in these walls, Summer. Let me take you somewhere safe. Let me take care of you. Somewhere away from this."

My stomach clenches. The thought of leaving this house—Jacob's house, our house—feels like the ultimate betrayal—a step that would ruin everything, a step that would put Benny in a body bag.

"I can't."

"Yes, you can." Benny's tone is soft, but steel runs beneath it. "You think he'll come back and hold you? No. He's drowning you in darkness Summer, fucking with your mind." His hand cups my face again, tilting me to look at him. "But I won't. I'll give you light, Summer. I'll give you somewhere you can breathe. Time to process this, to grieve properly."

The tears spill over again. My chest caves around a sob, but it isn't grief this time. It's confusion. A crushing, suffocating confusion that makes me want to run in every direction at once.

He presses a kiss to my hairline, featherlight. "Please. Come with me tonight. Don't deal with this alone. We can collect your friends on the way if you'd like that."

I close my eyes, trembling in his arms. My parents are gone. Jacob left me alone. And I need comfort. I need Constance and Adelaide.

My lips part, a whisper breaking free. "Okay."

Benny exhales like he's been holding his breath for hours. Relief softens his whole frame, but his grip tightens like victory.

He kisses my hair again, lingering this time. "That's it. I've got you. You'll be safe with me."

His hand finds mine, fingers interlacing, tugging me gently but insistently toward the door. My chest is hollow, my mind numb. I move because I can't think of another option.

The air outside bites cold against my wet skin. Gravel crunches under our steps. Benny's grip is steady, pulling me toward his truck. I glance back at the house, looming dark and silent behind us. The walls feel like they're watching me walk away. Those walls hold memories. The fights, the violence, but also the place I learned that I could love a monster. The place he stroked my hair and kissed my neck. The place we made love for the first time.

Benny squeezes my hand. "Don't look back," he murmurs.

The words cut, but I let him keep pulling me forward. One step. Then another. My chest aches, but I push it down.

I'm about to turn back to the house. To tell Benny no—to tell him I want to wait for Jacob—when headlights flare at the end of the drive.

I freeze. My heart lurches, wild, desperate. The familiar growl of an engine follows, low and rumbling, pulling closer. Dust kicks up behind the beam of light, sweeping across the yard until it lands square on us.

Jacob's truck.

I want to run to him. I want to slap him. I want to claw his fucking throat out and tell him I hate him. But I also want to feel his arms around me. To hear him tell Benny he's wrong.

The tires crunch against gravel as it rolls to a stop. The driver's door jolts open and Jacob steps out, the porch light catching on the hard set of his jaw, the dark fire burning in his eyes as they lock onto me. Then down—to Benny's hand gripping mine.

My stomach plummets.

Benny's fingers tighten around me, possessive, defiant, but I struggle and pull my hand free.

The silence between the three of us is a live wire, humming and sparking, ready to set everything alight.

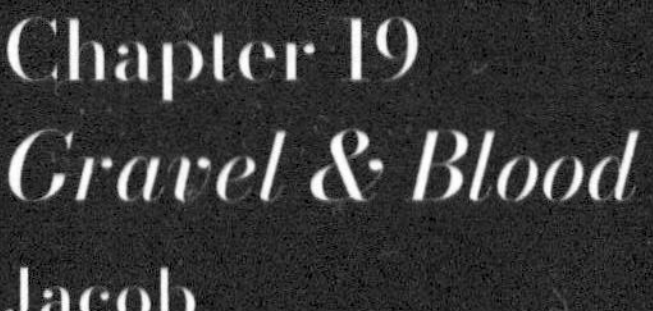

Chapter 19
Gravel & Blood
Jacob

I check the CCTV the second I get to her parents' place, but the feed's dead. Must've busted it when I threw the chair—sent the whole setup crashing down.

When I realize the feed's gone—when I know there's no way to keep eyes on her—dread crawls up my spine. I finish up as fast as I can and head home.

I don't want to see her face when I tell her that her parents were murdered. But she needs to know. And she needs to hear it from me.

I slam the accelerator—tires screaming against asphalt—all the way home to her.

As the house comes into view, a truck sits in the drive. Anger tightens in my chest, burning and heavy. My hands grip the wheel so hard I'm surprised it doesn't snap beneath them.

The second I see his hand on her, I stop being human.

Benny fucking Harrow. Standing on my drive with his fingers locked around Summer's, like he's got some claim, like he's earned the right to put his dirty hands on her skin.

I don't hear the engine cut. Don't feel the door slam. Just heat—black, blistering rage that climbs my throat until there's nothing left to do but break him. Summer pulls away from him and steps back. She knows what's coming and she doesn't want to taste the dirt.

Smart girl.

Three strides and I've got him.

His back hits gravel, skull cracking against stone. My fist follows. Cartilage gives under my knuckles with a wet pop, blood spraying across my hand. He jerks, wheezes, but I ride him down, knees pinning his hips, another punch collapsing his nose sideways.

He coughs blood in my face. I slam his jaw. Bone shifts and a gurgling noise rattles out of him, and it makes me smile, because that's the sound of him breaking where he thought he was solid.

"You think you can slither in while I'm gone?" My knuckles split on his cheekbone, skin tearing. "Crawl into her grief like a parasite?" Another blow. "I'll fucking kill you."

His lip bursts. Teeth loosen under the next strike. I hear one crack and roll across his tongue. He chokes on it, eyes wide, blood bubbling from his nose and mouth. Good. Let him taste himself.

Summer screams my name, but she's a ghost at the edge of this fire. All I see is him. All I hear is the crunch of his body folding under mine. All I feel is the life leaving him blow by blow.

He groans, some pathetic wheeze, and it stirs something savage in me. I hammer his ribs until one gives, deep as a gunshot. His body bows, desperate for air. I press my forearm to his throat, lean down until he can't miss the promise in my eyes.

Summer's hands are on me now, clawing, pulling, her voice shredded from screaming. "Stop! You're killing him!"

"That's the point," I spit, and smash his brow open. Blood runs into his eyes, blinding him. He tries to lift his arm—pathetic, slow— and I break the attempt with another hit. My knuckles are raw meat, slick with him, but I don't stop.

Her fists slam my shoulders, my back. "My parents are dead, and you weren't there! He came to check on me, he came to do the right thing!"

The words hit harder than Benny ever could. For a breath, my fist freezes above his face. The night presses in, hot and suffocating. Weren't there.

He sees it—the hitch in me. He tries a laugh, wet, broken. "Sum—"

His mouth caves under the heel of my palm, jaw sliding wrong. He gags, choking blood, eyes rolling. I lean close, so he hears it through the ringing in his skull.

"You don't get to say her name. You don't get to fucking breathe it."

Summer hits me—open palm, wild, cracking against my back. My head whips sideways. Her voice cuts me deeper than her hand ever could.

"You left me, Jacob! You left me when they died! You didn't even fucking tell me! You…." She steps back. "I hate you. And I promise… I swear… I am leaving."

The rage flares, colliding with the guilt already gutting me. My hands go to her wrists before I know it, I pull her down onto the ground, pinning her small body against mine so she can't swing again. Her chest heaves against me, hot, frantic. Her eyes—red, wet, furious—make me want to break and bleed at the same time.

"Summer." My voice is a rasp, fraying. "Stop."

"No!" She thrashes, hair wild, tears streaking her face. "Not after this. Not after them. You can hunt me, you can chase me, but I will never ever forgive you for this."

She thrashes under me, wrists twisting, body bucking, but my grip doesn't slip. My hands are iron around her. She wriggles, claws, kicks—small, frantic bursts of fight that can't touch the strength pinning her down. Then her head snaps forward. Teeth sink into my shoulder.

White-hot pain explodes, intense enough to drag a grunt from my chest. My hold tightens instinctively, muscle clamping down, but she only grows wilder—nails raking fire down my arms, her sobs jagged, feral, tearing at the air between us.

And through it—through the chaos, through the burn of her teeth—I see them.

Her parents.

Slumped in their living room chairs, heads dropped heavy, eyes gone glassy. One neat hole in each skull, the carpet dark beneath them. The flames I told myself were real—just theater. A curtain of smoke to hide the truth.

Execution.

My stomach lurches, vision splitting. For the first time tonight, guilt claws louder than rage. My grip falters.

My breath hitches hard enough to shake me. She feels it. Rips free. Shoves me with every ounce of her fury, and I roll back, shoulder screaming, blood slick on my arms.

Then she's gone.

Bolting across the yard, into the trees. Her sobs carry after her, shredded echoes in the black. I manage to get to my knees in the dirt, the taste of iron in my mouth, the stink of blood clinging to my hands —Benny's blood. My shoulder burns where her teeth branded me, my chest caves around the single truth.

I left her.

My chest feels carved open. Summer's voice is in my ears—her scream, her sobs, her fists against my skin. "My parents are dead, and you weren't there."

The words hit harder than any punch ever has or ever could.

And they don't let go.

I pull myself to my feet and chase after her. I push into the woods. Branches whip my arms, thorns bite my forearm, but I don't stop. The dark swallows me whole, but I don't need light. I know these trees. I've hunted through them, bled in them, buried men in them. They bend to me.

"Summer!" My voice cracks the night. I hear nothing back—just her breathing, faint, frantic, like a deer cornered.

I stop. Listen. Silence isn't empty. It has weight. It has shape. And in that shape, I find her. A sudden snap of a twig, too quick, too clumsy. She's running blind. Barefoot. I picture the ground splitting her soles open, rocks and glass biting at her skin. I picture her blood painting a trail for anyone who wants her.

It makes me fucking insane.

I follow the sound, my breath hot, my shoulder throbbing. Pain is good. Pain reminds me she fought me. Pain reminds me she's not weak. But her words live rent free in my mind.

I'll never forgive you.

The truth is, I'll never forgive myself.

But God help the man who took her parent's lives, because I'll find him. I'll peel him, piece by piece, until every nerve in his body learns what it means to beg. When he's ash, when even the earth doesn't want his bones, maybe then I'll breathe again.

"Summer," I call, softer now. Not sheriff. Not monster. Just man. Just me. "Stop running baby."

A shape flares in the corner of my vision—her calf, catching the moonlight, pale as glass. She's crouched behind a fallen trunk, trying to vanish. My chest cracks. She's so close, and she's so fucking far.

I take a step toward her, the forest closing in around us, thick with memories I can't shake. The last time we were here flashes behind my eyes—the way she looked up at me, trembling, when I held her down; the way her voice cracked when she told me she was falling for me.

The lump in my throat swells until it's hard to breathe. A bitter sting bites the back of my nose, and before I can stop it, my vision blurs with unshed tears.

I'm not just sad. I'm furious. I'm wrecked. Every emotion bleeds into the next until I can't tell where rage ends and heartbreak begins.

All I want—all I fucking want—is to go back. To crawl into that bed with her, feel her warmth against me, and live the night over again like it never ended. Like I never walked out that door without waking her and telling her that I was headed to her parents' home.

"Don't you dare fucking touch me," she sobs. Folding in on herself, she catches her breath.

I move closer, slow enough that she can see every step I take, and stop at the tree between us. My palm finds the rough bark, fingers spread wide, showing her my empty hand.

"I'm not touching you," I rasp, voice raw from everything I'm holding back. "Not unless you let me."

The silence that follows is thick, alive with the sound of her breath—fast, shallow, uneven. It breaks something in me just hearing it.

"You weren't there," she says at last, her voice splintering in the dark.

"I know," I whisper, the admission tearing through me. "I know."

"Did they—" Her voice cracks. "Was it the fire that killed my parents? Was it an accident?"

"No." The word rips out of me, raw and unwilling.

She makes a sound that isn't human—half sob, half animal—and the trees seem to lean in with it.

"Moore's men?" she asks, brittle now, testing the edges of what she already fears.

"I don't know," I answer honestly. The truth is all she gets from me, even if it paints me black. "But I'll find out."

A beat, then the knife slides in deeper—quieter, thinner: "Benny."

My jaw locks. His name in her mouth is a blade. It burns.

"He's alive," I say. "For now. But he won't be when I'm finished."

"No." Her voice breaks, but there's iron beneath the crack. "Don't kill him."

The fact that she still cares about him—despite everything—twists something inside me until my teeth grind. I want to tear his insides out and make him eat them.

"I'll deal with him," I snap, every syllable brittle with promise. "But he won't touch you again."

She stares at me, a flicker of something like relief and terror fighting in her eyes. I press my palm flat to the tree, feel the rough grain under my skin, and for a second I let the calm pretend to sit on top of the hunger. Then I meet her gaze and mean it: I will find out who did this. I will burn whatever needs burning to keep her safe.

Her weight shifts, subtle but there—she's closer, the night air pulling tight between us.

"I was going to go with him," she whispers. No guilt. No softness. Just the raw edge of truth. "He knew about my parents. He was taking me to Constance and Adelaide. I still want to—"

The words land like a bullet. I don't dodge.

"I didn't know," I rasp, cutting her off. "I swear to Christ, Summer, I didn't want to believe that they were dead. The call said a house fire, two casualties. I left you here because I thought I had time. I thought I could stand in both places. Protect you and save them. I was wrong."

My hand slams into the tree beside me, splinters driving into my palm, but I don't care. Pain's the only thing that makes sense.

"And I came straight back once it was confirmed, to hold you, to tell you myself. Instead, I came back to find him holding you like you belonged to him."

Her breath trembles, uneven, misting in the moonlight.

"You don't understand," she says, voice shaking. "I needed someone. And he—he told me they were gone. I crumbled, Jacob. He held me because I could hardly stand. Because my whole world fell apart back there and he was there for me."

She's right—I know she is. My fingers skimming the top of her shoulder.

Her face twists, salt tracks streaking pale cheeks.

"I need space," she says, the words breaking on a sob. "I need… time."

Her voice trembles, thin and frayed, and I can see how much effort it takes just to keep breathing.

"Too much has happened this week. Me and you… and now my parents." She wipes at her face, but the tears just keep coming. "I know we didn't have the best relationship—I swore I'd never forgive them for handing me over to you." Her voice catches, softening to something fragile. "But they're still—" She presses her fist against her mouth, choking back the rest. "Mama and Papa," she whispers, the words shattering as another sob tears through her.

Every part of me wants to close the distance—wrench her into my arms and smother the world with her until the tears stop. I want to cradle her, warm her, never let anything touch her. Instead, I watch the line in her eyes, the hard steel threaded through the grief, and for the first time I see how shattered she really is. The woman who is my whole goddamn world is cracking at the seams, and every inch of me wants to fix her.

My breath comes ragged; my fists hover useless at my sides, trembling like something animal and young.

"Not touching you," I rasp, each word scraping out of me, "when all I want is to hold you—it's torture." The admission is a confession *and* a threat. It tastes like rust.

But then I make myself do the only thing that still means something in this mess. I lower my hands to my sides, feel the roughness of dried blood my skin like a promise I can't afford to break. I force my voice down until it is nothing but stone. "Just… come back to the house, Summer, I'll keep my word. You have it. We can fix this. We can work it out. I'll tell you everything," I promise, the words spilling out fast, unfiltered. "Everything you need to know about your parents—no more half-truths, no more secrets. You deserve that much."

I take another step, careful, slow. "Just come back with me. Please. Let me make this right."

She hesitates—just long enough for me to think she'll turn away again—then gives a small, broken nod. No words. Just surrender.

We move through the trees, not together, not apart, but somewhere inbetween. The forest groans beneath us, branches snapping underfoot, leaves whispering secrets we can't bear to hear. The night seems to close in, heavy and suffocating, swallowing every sound except our uneven steps.

Our shadows stretch ahead of us, long and crooked, staggering like the ghosts we've become—always near, never touching.

When the house finally rises through the darkness, the porch light flickers an ugly, sickly yellow, casting the yard in shades of orange and gold. The gravel drive lies open before us, a gaping mouth waiting to devour whatever's left of us.

And then I see what remains of him.

Benny.

Sprawled. Broken. A heap of ruin under the porch light, blood dark against the stones. Summer stops dead beside me, a gasp cutting through the stillness. Steam curls from his skin in the cold, blood dark and sticky beneath him. He's nothing but noise dying out.

Her chin lifts, defiant, even with her face streaked in dirt and salt.

"Can we get him some help?" she asks, voice trembling but hard beneath it. "An ambulance. Something. Just some help."

For a long beat, I don't move. The world tilts, the sound of the wind and the hum of insects fading until it's just her and me and the body on the ground between us. Her eyes find mine—wild, pleading, burning with the kind of fear that still trusts me to fix this.

I give one harsh nod. It's all she needs.

"Go inside, Summer," I say quietly, steady enough to hide the storm breaking behind it. "Stay there. Do whatever you need to do to get through the next half hour. I'll be as quick as I can." I hold her gaze a second longer, making sure she hears the weight behind it. "Do not open the door to anyone."

She hesitates, trembling, then backs away toward the house.

The moment she's gone, the world exhales again. I cross the gravel, the stones crunching beneath my boots, a grim rhythm counting down what's left of the man lying there.

Benny's chest lifts in shallow, ragged breaths. His eyes flutter, glazed and unfocused, the whites—now red—catching what little light spills from the porch. His lips crack open, dry and trembling, trying to form a single sound—her name.

Summer.

It comes out as a rasp, and I can feel the fury in me ignite all over again.

Pathetic.

I fist his ankle and drag. His body scrapes hard across the stones, a smear of red marking his path. He groans—weak, broken—the sound thin and animal.

I haul him up into the bed of the truck like garbage, his arm flopping useless over the side.

I climb in, the engine growling to life under my hands. As the gravel crunches beneath the tires, I make myself one promise— louder than the guilt, stronger than the rage:

I will find the man who put those bullets in her parents. I'll take his life in pieces so small the devil won't know what to do with them.

Chapter 20
Ghost With a Badge

Jacob

The road is quiet when I dump Benny's carcass on the shoulder. The headlights bleach him pale, every bruise a dark brand across his face.

"Crawl if you want to live," I mutter. Then I spit on the gravel, slide back behind the wheel, and dial.

It takes two rings before I hear the voice I want. "Sheriff."

"Carter." My tone is iron. He's the only one I call when I need things handled. My right hand. My clean-up man. He's been with me long enough to know what I need.

"Where are you?" he asks, low, cautious.

"I've got a problem." My knuckles ache on the wheel. I flex them, feel the split skin stretch, the sting of exposed flesh. A reminder of how close I came to killing Harrow right there in the dirt. "I had to make an example tonight. Kid won't be walking straight for months. You understand me?"

A beat of silence, then a sigh. "Yeah…. You want me to make it disappear."

"I want it buried," I correct him. "I want it stitched so tight no one ever finds the thread. You're going to say you saw him drunk, got into a bar fight, wandered into the wrong end of town. I don't care. Just make it stick."

"I can do that Sheriff, where do I need to be?" Carter asks. His tone is steady, the way it always is when he's locking away his conscience.

That's why I trust him. He doesn't waste time on right and wrong. He knows the only laws that matters are mine.

"Good," I rasp. "I'm on Herringhorn Highway, about... 3 miles past the trailer park. Now tell me something. Other than me, you, and the two boys who stood in that living room, who else knows Elaine and Michael Miller are dead?"

"Got it boss," Carter answers instantly. "Not a chance anyone knows jack shit. We locked it down. No reports filed yet, no chatter on the wire. Just us."

"Then explain to me," I bite out, leaning into the wheel, "how dipshit Benny Harrow showed up at my fucking house tonight with the news in his mouth."

Carter goes quiet. I hear him breathing, slow and measured, like he's running every possibility through his head. Finally: "I don't know, Sheriff. If he knows, it didn't come from us. I'd bet my badge on it."

My jaw locks. That's not good enough.

"You'd better be right," I growl. "Because if there's a leak in my department, I'll find it. And when I do, there won't be enough left of them to require a coffin."

"Understood," Carter says, clipped. He's not stupid—he knows a promise when he hears it.

I hang up, slam the phone down, and sit there for a moment, fists tightening around the wheel until the leather groans. Fury claws up my throat, mixes with confusion until it's poison. I could wait for Carter, but Summer is alone, and with everything that's happened, I need to be home with her.

Fuck Benny. He can rot out here waiting for Carter. Maybe he'll crawl into the road and get taken out by one of the HGV's that frequent this road.

Hell, I would pay a year's salary to watch this son of a bitch be mowed down by one of Mr. McGallie's wagons.

I start my engine, pressing the pedal to speed back onto the dirt road. The shoulder swallows my headlights as I pull away, leaving Harrow to bleed into the ditch and bargain with whatever God has planned for him. The road opens like a vein. I ride it hard.

No one should've known. No one. And yet Benny did. Which means either Carter's wrong—or there's something far worse in play.

Carter's last words grind in my skull: Not a chance anyone knows jack shit.

Then how the hell did Benny?

The wheel creaks under my grip. My knuckles complain—split skin stretching, heat flaring. I flex, slow, until the sting spikes and settles, a clean pain I can stack others on. The truck smells like gun oil and iron and her—shampoo and salt and that small, wild thing she turned into when she bit me.

At the next turn, I catch myself in the rearview. The bite is already blooming—violet bruising under crescent teeth marks, a map of her fury pressed into me. I roll my shoulder, and it answers with a pulse that says remember what you did to make her do this. Good. I deserve the reminder. I deserve every brand she gives me.

The rearview throws another gift: my face. Blood dried along my jaw like I shaved with a knife. Eyes gone dark enough to be animals. I look like what I am. A man who put his hands where the law won't. A man who came home to find his girl held by another and decided to make an example.

If no one else could have known about Elaine and Michael, then that leaves two options: a leak I'll cut out of my department with pliers, or Benny knew it was going to happen.

I don't like either.

Gravel pops when I rip into the drive. The porch light stares. The house feels like it's bracing. I kill the engine and sit one breath longer. Then I climb out of my truck and go straight in.

The air inside is warm, steam heavy—as if the walls have lungs. Water runs somewhere deeper in the house. I follow the sound. The bathroom door is closed. The handle is warm under my palm. It's locked.

I shoulder the door, busting the lock on my way through.

Steam punches out into the hall, thick with the smell of soap and heat. The mirror is a smeared moon, the old tile slick with condensation. Summer is a pale shape in the claw-foot tub, knees up, arms wrapped tight over them, hair sticking to the sides of her face.

She jerks when the door bangs, green eyes flashing like a trap's teeth.

"Get out—"

"No." The word is a flat blade. "We're not doing locked doors."

Her chin snaps up. "Then get out and learn how to knock and I'll let you in when I'm ready"

"I need you to answer a question."

"I don't care what you need." Her voice goes brittle. She reaches for the towel on the rim of the tub, drags it against her chest like armor. "Get. Out."

"One question, Summer. And so help me God, you will answer me," I say, and the mirror clears enough to give me my eyes again— black, unblinking. "How did he know?"

Her lashes flickers. Confusion, then wariness, then anger bathing up through both. "Jacob—"

"Tell me… Benny." I take another step, and the tile whispers under my boot. The heat in here makes the bruised bite throb. "How did he know about your parents before anyone else? Who told him?"

She sucks in a breath that's more a gasp than air. Tears jump back into eyes that were dry for half a minute, and I hate that I put them there.

"His cousin," she says, quick, as if speed makes it truer. "Deputy Thompson. He called Benny. He came straight here."

I stare at her, and for a beat, I don't hear the water at all. Only my pulse.

"There is no Deputy Thompson," I say.

Her face cracks, not with grief—something uglier. Disbelief, offended. "Don't—don't do that. Don't pretend you don't know your own damn department just because you can't stand the idea of someone else being decent."

"I know every badge in this county." My voice is quiet now, deeper, more dangerous. "I know the shape of their signatures and the weight of their mistakes. There is no Thompson wearing a star under me."

She shakes her head, fast, water darkening the towel. "But—he said—"

"He lied."

"No," she says it like a curse. "why would he—"

I move, and the steam parts in my approach. I stop an arm's reach from the tub. I can see the tremor in her fingers where they clutch the towel hanging off the side of the tub. I can see the ring of pink where hot water has kissed her skin. I can see the place on her shin where the woods put a new cut in her. Every detail is a violence I can't unsee.

"I got the call from Carter," I cut her off. "Two men went to meet him at the scene. Me and Wyatt. No reports were made up to me leaving. No calls. No chatter." I let the absence hang. "No Thompson."

"Look at me." It comes out rougher than I intend. I tame it with effort. "Summer. Look at me."

She says nothing. The drip of condensation ticks on porcelain. The hot tap hisses a little, empty threat.

"I will find out," I tell her. "I'll put my ear to every door he's opened in his life until one of them gives. And when I find the mouth that fed him, I'm taking the teeth too."

Her throat moves. The first tear falls again, not a sob—just surrender. "He said… he said he got the call. He said Thompson was family. He said he thought—" She swallows. The next words scrape. "He said he thought you would have already told me. He said… he couldn't believe you left me."

"Did he name where Thompson works?" I ask.

"No." She drags another breath. "He said deputy. He said cousin. He said you left. I promise you Jacob. I—I'm not keeping anything from you. This is the truth. Yes, I was upset… yes, I was angry… but I heard what I heard. And after he said you'd left me—"

I do the worst thing I can do when she's shaking in hot water and tears. I laugh. It's short and humorless, and I hate that it comes out sounding like relief because it's not. It's clarity.

"He wanted that part to land," I say. "And it did. He made sure of it."

Her head jerks, eyes flaring. "Because it's true."

"I know." The words grate. "I know it's true."

"Then don't act like I'm stupid for believing the rest."

I step back because the temptation to touch her forearms—to slide my hands over the points of her elbows and hold her until she stops shaking—is a danger to both of us. I put my shoulder to the door instead, the bite mark erupts pain, a brand mark still hot from the fire.

"You're not stupid," I say. "You're grieving, you're in shock. And he knows how to dress a lie in a grief coat."

Her chin lifts in a defiant angle I recognize from the day she first walked into my station and spit in my coffee.

"You almost killed him, Jacob. Hell, you might have succeeded… and all out of jealousy."

I shake my head, a slow smile tugging at my lips. I won't even give her the satisfaction of an answer.

This isn't jealousy—it's possession.

She watches me, unblinking, steam curling around her face like smoke rising from a fire I lit.

"I'm going to ask Carter to pull tower pings," I say, already building it in my head, the tree of time and signal. "Harrow's phone. The men who were on scene. Every badge on duty within two towns. I'm going to rip the timestamps off the calls and I'm going to lay them on the table in a line that makes sense. If a deputy I don't own touched a phone to tell him about your parents, I'll know what tower carried it." I bring my eyes back to hers, and my voice drops to a growl. "When I find the son of a bitch who told him—" I stop myself. She doesn't need to hear any more.

I lean in until my breath grazes her temple. "You don't have to see what's coming next, Summer. You just need to understand that there's no safe place left but me. I will burn every bridge, salt every field, erase every name until you're the last thing standing next to me. And when I'm finished…." My eyes drag across her face, that mix of terror and disbelief that only makes me want her more. "…

You'll never have to be afraid again. Because there won't be anything left to be afraid of."

She closes her eyes. The water breaks against her knees in small, uneven sounds. Silence crawls up the tiled walls with the steam and hangs beneath the ceiling, listening.

"Please," she whispers. "Just— give me some space."

I hold her gaze one beat too long, feeling her imploding against it, then nod and step back through the steam. The ruined door groans as I pull it almost shut—but not all the way. Not tonight. Not while a man with a steady hand and a love of fire is still breathing my air.

I leave her wrapped in steam and grief and lies that don't belong to her. I don't trust myself to sit in that room any longer, not when I'm this close to tearing the walls down just to prove there are no shadows hiding a man named Thompson.

The hallway feels colder. My shirt clings to me with damp, her bite a steady throb under the fabric. I head down the hall, the clock in the kitchen ticks too loud, each second a hammer striking steel. I don't go to the sink, don't wash the blood off my knuckles. I want it there. I want the reminder that I caved his fucking face in.

But I need to find out about this Thompson fella. I'm certain I'm right, that this guy is a fabrication in a story Benny fed her. I need to know how he knew. How he got here so fast.

My gut tells me that he was the one to start the fire. But that seems too... drastic. But it's too coincidental that the son of a bitch would know and get here so fast.

I pull out my phone and hit speed dial.

"Sheriff." Carter sounds alert now, more honed than before. Probably still out in his truck, circling the crime scene, waiting for me to tell him where to bury the rest.

"You pick him up?" I don't waste time.

There's a pause, a careful exhale. "Yeah. Found him about two miles up, crawling like a dog. Left eye's ballooned shut, ribs cracked, couple teeth gone. I took him to St. Luke's. They're patching him. Said something about pneumo-something. He won't be dancing any time soon."

"Pneumothorax." I let out a low laugh. "Means I smashed his ribs into his lung."

"Jeez, boss."

My teeth grind. I picture Benny on a hospital bed, nurses clucking over him, hands touching what I broke. A part of me wants to storm the ER and finish the job. Another part knows it's better this way. He'll linger, stew in pain, have time to think about the moment he lied to her and made her believe it.

"Did he talk?" I ask.

"Not much. They dosed him pretty quick. Kept mumbling about Summer, though." Carter hesitates. "Sheriff… you want me to keep him quiet? There are ways."

"No," I say instantly, then slow it down. "Not yet. Let him breathe. Let him think he's safe. I want his tongue working when I'm ready to cut the truth out of him."

Silence stretches on the line. Carter doesn't push. He never does. He knows when I say not yet, it doesn't mean mercy. It means I'm building something worse.

"Now listen close," I continue, lowering my voice though the house is empty except for the sound of her in the bath upstairs. "You ever heard of a Deputy Thompson?"

There's a beat, then Carter barks a laugh that dies fast. "No way. I'd know. Hell, you'd know. We're not exactly a big outfit."

Thought so.

"She says Harrow claimed a cousin in the department called him. Gave him the news," I say. "But there's no Thompson. Not on my payroll, not in this county."

"That's calculated," he says finally. "Not… sloppy. He wanted her to think it came from inside. That's—"

War.

"Yeah," I bite out. "And he picked the right wound to dig in."

"Want me to pull phone records anyway? Make sure none of my men slipped up?"

"Do it," I snap. "Tower pings, call logs, everything. I don't care if it takes you all night. If someone so much as sneezed in Harrow's direction with a badge on, I want to know which nostril it came out of."

"You'll have it by morning," he promises.

"Good." I exhale through my teeth, the fury simmering instead of boiling now. "And Carter—"

"Yeah?"

"If it turns out there is no leak… if it's exactly what it looks like—if he took out her parents or knows who did—you let me handle him. Personally."

I don't wait for his agreement. I hang up.

The silence afterward is heavier than the conversation. The house groans under it, every floorboard a witness. I set the phone down, flex my fingers, watch fresh blood bead across split skin.

No Deputy Thompson. Never was. Which means Benny Harrow thought he could create a man out of smoke, drape him in a badge, and make her doubt me.

It almost worked.

I shove off the counter and make my way down the hall. The hallway is thick with steam spilling from the bathroom, but the water's off now. I push the door open again without knocking.

She's there. Standing by the basin, dripping, wrapped in the towel she's holding too tight across her chest. Wet hair hangs down her shoulders, sticking to the pale line of her throat. Her skin glows pink from the heat, damp, fragile, like she's been scalded into porcelain.

She jumps when she sees me, then hardens instantly. Chin up, lips pressed flat.

"You can't just keep barging in—"

"There is no Thompson," I snarl, cutting her off. "Carter confirmed what I already knew. There's no deputy by that name anywhere near my department. Harrow fed you a ghost."

She tightens the towel, her knuckles white where they grip it. "He said—"

"He said what he needed to say." My voice lowers, darker. "He wanted you to doubt me, and he knew exactly where to cut. He knew I wasn't here when you needed me, so he invented a man in uniform to make me the villain."

"Well either way, he knew. He was trying to help me, he came so I wasn't alone," she spits, voice trembling around the edges.

"And he filled the space." The words rip out of me, rough, jagged. "That's his game. Sliding in where I'm not. Dressing himself in family ties and badges he doesn't own, making himself look like the savior you think you need. But tell me this, Summer—" I lean in, forcing her to meet my eyes. "If Thompson doesn't exist, what does that make Benny?"

No sound comes from her parted lips.

"Exactly what he is," I answer for her, my voice dropping to a growl. "A liar with a pretty face and just enough charm to make you forget you're standing over a pit of snakes."

Her chest rises and falls too fast beneath the towel, her fingers clawing into the fabric like it's the only thing tethering her. She shakes her head again, but slower now, like she's not sure she believes herself anymore.

"You want to hate me because I wasn't there?" I say, softer, deadlier. "Fine. Hate me. Bite me. Bleed me dry. But don't you dare hand him the power to write our story with a name that doesn't exist."

The bathroom is silent except for the drip of water from her hair hitting tile.

Her lips tremble. For the first time since I came in, her eyes look less like knives and more like something breaking.

I take one step back, enough to let her breathe, enough to keep myself from touching her when she's still wrapped in lies and wet terrycloth.

She shakes her head as I step back. As though she doesn't want me to walk away from her. But doesn't want me close either.

The towel slips enough when she shakes her head that I lose the last of my restraint. In two strides I've got her against the wall, plaster cool at her back, my hand crushing the edge of the towel into her chest.

Her gasp breaks in my mouth when I kiss her. Hard. Messy. All teeth and fury, salt from her tears mixing with the copper still on my lips. She shoves at me with one hand, fists the towel with the other, but when I force her mouth open, she breaks into me like she's been starving too.

I taste the anger first. Then the grief. The part she won't admit—that she wants me to steal the ground out from under her, so she doesn't have to stand in it alone.

When I pull back, we're both breathing like we just fought our way out of fire. Her cheeks are wet, tears cutting clean tracks through the steam. I press my forehead to hers, close enough to feel her shaking.

My voice comes out rough, every word scraped raw. "He knew before I did, it's the only explanation," I breathe, the confession more like a curse. "Either he did this himself, or he's tied to the men who did. Because tell me, Summer—" My voice cracks, rising, desperate, "how the hell else would he know before me?"

She jerks her head, eyes wide, tears spilling in fast. "No... no, he wouldn't—"

"He would," I cut in, my grip closing around her wrist before I realize it, before I can stop it. "He's in their pockets or standing right beside them. Maybe he didn't strike the match, but he knew it was coming. And then he ran here—straight into our house—with a story meant to turn you against me."

Her lips part like she wants to argue, but nothing comes out. The truth—or the shape of it—hangs between us, heavy enough to crush the air.

"I'm not asking you to believe me because you want to. I'm telling you the truth because I need you to. Harrow is not the man you think he is. He's a vindictive, lying cunt who played a part."

"Why does it feel like I'm losing everything?" she whispers, broken.

"You're not." I shove the words between us, hard, brutal, because I need her to believe them as much as I need them to be true. "You still have me. You have our home. Our life together."

Her breathing slows enough that I feel the question before she whispers it.

"So... what next?" Her voice is sandpaper, scraped raw. Her

eyes, rimmed red, look up at me with something that isn't trust but isn't doubt either. It's a bleeding thing caught in the middle.

I don't hesitate. "I'm going to the hospital." The words land like a hammer. "I'm going to walk into his room, and I'm going to make Harrow tell me exactly how the fuck he knew before I did."

Her whole body stiffens under my hand. "No."

It's a small word, but it hits harder than a gunshot.

My jaw locks. "No?"

She shakes her head, towel slipping at her collarbone. "Not you… me… I should go."

The laugh that rips out of me is jagged, dangerous. "You think I'm letting you walk into a room with the man who might have killed your parents?"

"I think he'll talk to me," she shoots back, voice cracking but fierce. "He'll tell me what he won't tell you. And you—" She presses a trembling hand to my chest, holding me back like I'm the fire she's trying not to burn in, "—you can wait right outside. Close enough to hear every word."

I stare at her, fury and disbelief colliding in my veins. "You're asking me to stand on the other side of a wall while you sit with him? After tonight?"

Her eyes glisten, stubborn as hell through the tears. "I'm not asking. I'm telling you this is the only way we'll know. The only way he'll talk. The only way I'll get any sense of closure from this. I need to see my parents. I need to grieve them. But… I need to do this first."

I slam my palm against the wall beside her head, close enough that the towel trembles against her chest. "You're fucking playing with fire, Summer."

"I know," she whispers. "But you'll be there. Won't you?"

The answer is already carved into me. Of course I will. I'll be outside that door, close enough to count every lie in Harrow's throat, close enough to break his jaw the second he tries to twist her again.

Chapter 21
Make Him Talk
Summer

My clothes are still damp from the towel I peeled off too soon, hair dripping down my neck, soaking patches into the fabric. The cold crawls over me as we step outside, but I barely feel it—my body's too heavy, too numb.

Jacob stalks ahead, shoulders rigid, fists flexing like he's still tasting Benny's blood in his knuckles. He doesn't look back at me once.

I'm halfway across the driveway when headlights flare down the drive.

My chest seizes.

The car jerks to a stop, gravel spitting beneath its tires, and then both doors fly open.

Constance is out first, Adelaide right behind her, and they're both crying.

"Summer!"

Constance's arms wrap around me so tight I nearly lose my footing. She smells like lavender and coffee, warm and safe, and it cracks something open in me I thought was already gone. Adelaide presses in from the side, clinging like she can anchor me by sheer force of touch.

Tears spill hot down my cheeks. My throat burns as I choke on them, my sobs heaving into their sweaters until I can't tell whose arms are whose.

Constance rocks me gently, whispering broken apologies. "I'm so sorry, sweetheart. I'm so, so sorry. I can't believe—oh God, Summer…." Her voice fractures around my name.

Adelaide's smaller hands squeeze mine, her own shoulders shaking. Her eyes are swollen, her face blotched red.

"We came as soon as we heard. We didn't even think—we just had to get to you."

I can't answer. My voice is gone. All I can do is clutch at them, fists tight in Constance's sleeves, body collapsing against theirs like they're the only thing keeping me standing.

For one fractured second, it almost feels like I can sink into them. Like maybe I'm still a woman who can be held by friends and soothed back into herself.

Constance lifts her head and notices Jacob. She stiffens, though she doesn't let go of me. Adelaide glances too, her expression faltering, but neither of them says his name. They don't have to. The weight of him is already heavy enough in the air.

Constance cups my face in her hands, forcing me to look at her. Her own cheeks are streaked with tears.

"We're here now, Summer. You don't have to go through this alone."

I nod weakly, even as my gaze slides past her, back to him. And he sees it. Of course he does.

My sobs slow, thinning into tremors that wrack through me. Constance squeezes me tighter, Adelaide kissing my damp hair like she can will me back into safety, but my feet shift without meaning to. One step. Just one step out of their arms and closer to him.

Constance's breath catches, jagged enough to pierce. Adelaide's lip trembles, eyes filling again.

I can't meet their gazes. I can't bear the disappointment there. So, I keep my eyes on him. Always him. And when I move fully out of their embrace and toward the truck, I hear Constance let out a sob that feels like betrayal made flesh. But I don't stop. I can't.

Constance wipes her face with her sleeve, still clutching at my hand like she doesn't want to let me go.

"Summer, wait. Where are you going? You can't just—"

I stop when my hand touches the handle of the truck. Flashbacks come over me, buzzing through my mind like electricity. Me, Constance, Adelaide, running through the yard, Papa spraying us with the water hose. Mama baking us cookies, still warm and gooey and bringing them out and placing them on our picnic blanket.

My parents weren't just special to me. They played a huge part in Adelaide and Constance's lives, too. I owe it to them. For the memories. For the love they felt for my parents.

I shake my head and release the handle. I turn to face them both, the tears still flowing down my cheeks, crisping in the cold air. My voice rasps out broken.

"Okay," I almost say to myself. "Let's just... go inside."

They glance at each other, uncertain, but when Jacob stalks around the truck and wraps an arm around my shoulder, they follow us back toward the house.

The silence in the kitchen is too loud. Every surface gleams, too clean, too still, like it doesn't belong to me at all. I need something to fill the air. Something to stop the echo of Adelaide's sob.

I go to the counter and fill the water container for coffee. The familiar click, the rising hum—it should be nothing. Just an ordinary sound. But then my vision blurs. The kitchen fades. I'm there—in my parents' burning house. The smoke rolls thick, choking me, burning my throat. The walls groan like they're about to collapse, flames licking higher. I curl in on myself, heaping on the floor, hands over my ears, sobbing so violently I can't breathe. My chest convulses, every breath a war.

Footsteps thunder. And then he's there. Jacob. Dropping to the ground, wrapping his arms around me before I even know it.

"Summer. Christ—Summer." His voice is rough, desperate, cutting through the smoke in my head.

I sob harder, burying my face against his chest, clawing at his shirt like I'll drown if I don't hold on. He doesn't hesitate. He scoops me up, lifting me as if I weigh nothing, carrying me into the sitting room with a fury that makes my head spin.

The sofa catches us as he sinks down, but he doesn't let me go. He cradles me against him, strong arms wrapping tight around my shaking body. His lips press to my temple, then my hair, then my damp cheeks, over and over like he can kiss away the fire.

"I've got you," he murmurs, fierce and low, like a promise. "You're safe. I've got you, baby."

My sobs tear out of me, unstoppable. Every kiss he lays on me is a brand, searing, grounding me back into this body, this moment.

I feel other hands then—softer, tentative. Constance crouches beside us, brushing her fingers over my arm, whispering my name through her own tears.

Adelaide hovers close, her palm on my knee, her voice trembling as she says, "We're here too. We're here, Summer."

Jacob rocks me against his chest, kissing the top of my head, again and again, his breath ragged. His heartbeat thunders under my ear, fierce and unyielding, the only sound loud enough to drown out the echo of my mother's screams. It's his arms that stop the fire.

And I can't let go.

The storm inside me begins to ebb. The sobs taper into broken breaths, then shallow hiccups. My chest still aches, my throat raw, but the fire recedes under Jacob's heartbeat. His warmth wraps around me, steady and solid, and for the first time since the phone call I feel something that almost resembles safety.

Adelaide has slid close on the sofa, her hand moving gently through my damp hair, smoothing it back from my face. Her touch is feather-light, the opposite of Jacob's iron hold, but together they cocoon me, pinning me in two different worlds.

From the kitchen, I hear Constance moving—mugs clinking, the coffee machine hissing, this time muffled by distance. The sound doesn't choke me now. The smoke has gone.

Jacob shifts slightly, his chin brushing the top of my head. His arms loosen just enough to let me breathe without shuddering.

By the time Constance returns, the tray rattling in her hands, my body feels heavier than stone. She sets it carefully on the coffee table, the scent of tea rising in a cloud that makes my stomach twist with grief but not panic this time.

"Here, just how you like it." She sets a mug down within reach, then straightens, her eyes flicking warily to Jacob before softening again on me.

Slowly, I shift. Jacob's hand tenses as I move, but I don't leave him completely. I slide off his lap, settling beside him instead, my hip brushing his thigh, his arm draping possessively along the back of the sofa as if to remind everyone I'm still his.

I wrap my hands around the mug, letting the heat seep into my fingers. For a moment I just stare into the swirling surface, gathering the courage to break the silence.

Then I speak. My voice trembles, but the words come anyway.

"Benny came. Just after Jacob left."

Constance frowns. "Benny did?"

Adelaide blinks, confusion rippling across her tear-streaked face. "I—I don't understand. Why would he—?"

I swallow hard, my throat burning again. "He said he knew. About my parents. He told me... that they'd died." My grip tightens on the mug, heat biting into my palms. "He said... his cousin... Deputy Thompson told him."

Constance's mouth opens, then shuts again, as if she doesn't know where to begin. Adelaide looks from me to Jacob, wide-eyed, searching for someone to explain.

Jacob leans forward, his voice cutting through the stillness like a blade. "There is no Deputy Thompson."

Both girls whip their heads toward him, stunned.

Adelaide shakes her head slowly. "But—he must've meant—"

"He didn't mean anything," Jacob snaps, his eyes burning into me, not them. "He lied. Or he slipped. Either way, Harrow knew before I did, and I was second on scene. No one, other than fire fighters entered that building before me."

Constance stiffens, her hand pressed against her chest. "That doesn't make sense. How could he—"

Jacob doesn't look at her. He doesn't look at either of them. Only me.

His voice drops lower, almost a growl. "He did it… or he knows who did. That's the only explanation."

"That's where we were headed. To ask him… to get answers" I say.

Jacob shifts closer, his arm tightening along the back of the sofa, his presence overwhelming, dark and immovable. "We will find out what's going on, Summer, I promise."

"I need to look him in the eye and find out the truth," I say, my voice stripped down to something cold and steady.

Constance clears her throat, her hand still pressed against her chest. Her voice is soft at first but steadying with each word. "You shouldn't go alone. You know the sorts of men who hang around the Dogwood. And even though you—"

My head jerks up. "He's not in Dogwood, or his trailer."

Constance arches a brow, her voice cutting through the thick quiet. "Then… where is he?"

Adelaide glances between us, her confusion plain, eyes darting from my face to Summer's like she's trying to piece together a puzzle she doesn't want to finish.

I feel the question land, heavy and pointed. The kind that doesn't need to be shouted to draw blood.

"Where is he, Jacob?" Constance repeats, slower this time, suspicion curling around every syllable.

"He's in St. Luke's Hospital," Jacob responds, each word flat, measured, the calm that comes after the storm. I meet their eyes one by one. "You think I was going to let that piece of shit come to my home, put his hands on my girl, make me out to be the devil and walk away?"

The room goes still. Even the clock seems to stop ticking. Constance's lips part like she's about to speak but nothing comes out. Adelaide just stares, the color draining from her face.

"We're going there," he says, voice low but unwavering. "And I'll wait outside the room while Summer talks to him." His jaw tightens, the muscle ticking as he forces the next words out. "I'm not happy about it—but it's the right choice."

"No," Constance interrupts, steel threaded through her tears.

"Benny would know something was wrong if she went in by herself. He's not stupid. He'd smell it on her." She swallows, eyes flicking to me, full of stubborn love. "But if Adelaide and I go with her… he'll believe it. We'll make him think we're just there to comfort her. That we brought her to see him and are waiting outside to give her space. He… he knows how close we are. We saw him in The Dogwood, we—" Adelaide nudges her, as if telling her not to speak about my confession of the dance to them, only a few nights ago.

"This isn't the time, Connie!" Adelaide interrupts. "But yes. It'll look natural. Like we just came with her because she needed friends around her… which isn't a lie." She shoots Jacob a look. "Because we didn't want her alone right now."

Jacob grinds his teeth. His hand tightens on the back of the sofa until the leather creaks.

Constance see's Jacob's reaction—the space between them sparks, so hot I can barely breathe. Jacob's look of disgust lashes out like a whip, but Constance doesn't back down. Not this time.

I stare into my mug, the liquid trembling with the shaking of my hands. I don't want to go. God, I don't want to. The thought of looking into Benny's eyes again makes bile climb my throat.

But then Mama's screams echo in my head, dragging me back into the smoke. Papa's silence follows, heavy as stone.

I force myself to lift my head. My voice comes out hoarse, but it cuts through the room. "I'll do it. But Jacob comes and waits outside too."

"Summer, you don't have to—" Adelaide starts.

"I do." I shake my head, clutching the mug tighter, as if the heat will anchor me. "I don't want to. I don't want any of this. But if there's even a chance it helps us find out who did this to Mama and Papa—" My voice fractures, shattering on their names. I swallow hard and push the words out anyway. "Then I'll do it."

Constance's hand finds mine, gripping tight. "We'll be with you. Every second. He'll believe it."

Adelaide nods, her lip trembling, but she doesn't let go of me either.

The night feels heavier when we finally move toward the door.

Every step aches, like grief has seeped into my bones, slowing me down, weighing me down. Constance wraps her arm around me as we leave the warmth of the house. Adelaide hovers at my other side, clutching her sweater tight, her wide eyes darting between me and the darkness beyond the porch. And Jacob— he doesn't touch me this time. He just walks ahead, his shoulders broad, his presence filling the space like a warning carved into the night itself.

My chest tightens as I glance back at the house—at the soft glow of the kitchen light spilling through the window. The last place Mama and I shared a hot drink. The last place Papa told me he loved me. Now they're gone. Gone in blood, smoke and silence.

I bite the inside of my cheek until I taste metal. My throat burns, but I keep moving.

Because I'm not alone.

They're here—these three. The only three who matter now.

Constance, solid and stubborn, holding me up when I want to collapse. Adelaide, soft and shaking but still with me, still refusing to let me face this without her. And Jacob. Dark. Relentless. Dangerous. But mine.

They're all I've got left. The only reason I can force air into my lungs. The only reason I can keep walking toward the truck instead of crawling into bed and letting the world continue to turn without me.

I cared for Benny. God, I cared. Enough to dream about escape. Enough to believe in softness. But Jacob's words keep echoing in my head, gnawing at me like teeth.

He knew before I did. How?

The question digs deeper with every step. I try to shake it, to shove Benny back into the box of things I can't bear to think about. But the doubt won't stay quiet. Jacob is right.

How could Benny have known?

Constance steadies me, her arm tightening around my waist. She holds me closer, whispering softly, "Almost there, sweetheart. Just a few more steps."

The truck looms ahead, dark metal glinting under the porch light. Jacob moves toward it without a word, yanking the door open with a fast motion, like even the hinges should fear him. For a heartbeat, I want to turn back. To run upstairs, bury myself under the covers. But I don't.

Because Mama and Papa deserve more than silence.

Because Constance and Adelaide deserve the truth.

Because Jacob—God, help me—deserves to be right.

Chapter 22
The Stranger in His Bed
Summer

The glass doors slide shut behind us. The light inside is too bright, the hospital scent fills my nostrils, smelling of bleach and something metallic that makes my stomach churn. Constance and Adelaide flank me like guards, but it doesn't help. My skin prickles with unease as we approach the reception desk. The woman behind the counter smiles automatically, then blinks at me—my red-rimmed eyes, damp hair sticking to my cheeks—and her smile falters.

"I'm looking for Benedict Harrow," I manage, voice raw. "He was brought in tonight."

Her fingers hesitate over the keyboard. She types, pauses, her expression pinching like she's holding something back. She forces a tight smile. "One moment, please."

Constance shrugs and Adelaide makes a confused face.

She disappears through the door behind her desk. The seconds stretch, too long. My stomach knots tighter.

The door opens again—but it isn't the receptionist.

It's a man in uniform. Boots striking tile. A badge glinting under fluorescent light. His eyes sweep the room, then lock on me.

"You," he says, pointing, already closing the distance. "Come with me."

Before I can even breathe, his hand clamps around my arm. Firm. Unyielding.

Shock tears through me.

"What—wait—"

"Get the fuck off her...." Constance shouts, pulling on his hand. Adelaide stands in shock, not saying a word.

The receptionist looks over, phone in hand, likely ready to call for security.

The deputy pushes Constance's hand away and tugs me forward, hard enough to jerk me off balance. Panic flares, my heart lurching—

And then a snarl cuts the air.

"Get your fucking hands off her."

I whip my head around. Jacob.

He's come from the vending machine at the corner, a can slipping from his hand, fizz hissing across the floor. His eyes are locked where the deputy's hand bruises my arm. Then he's moving. Constance releases her hand and immediately retreats, making sure she's not caught in the middle of a storm.

The crash echoes through the reception as Jacob slams into the deputy, ripping his hand off me. Papers scatter, the receptionist shrieks. Every head in the waiting room snaps toward us.

Jacob pins him against the counter with his forearm, his voice a low, venomous growl. "You got a death wish, touching my woman like that?"

The deputy gasps, caught between shock and panic. "Sheriff—I didn't—I didn't know—"

"Didn't know what?" Jacob snarls, pressing harder. "Didn't know you were one grab away from leaving here in a body bag?"

"Jacob, don't make this any worse than it already is," Adelaide says, resting a hand on his shoulder.

He shrugs her hand off. "It's Sheriff Darnell to you," he says, slow, menacing. "Especially in front of my men."

"Please—" the deputy stammers, hands raised, eyes darting to the frozen staff around us. "Sir, I just need to speak with her. Privately."

"Fine, but you don't take her anywhere without me." Jacob's lip curls, eyes black with rage. "Ladies, wait here."

Constance nods. Adelaide still unable to make eye contact.

"Sheriff," the deputy pleads, sweat beading his forehead. "Just give me five minutes. Not here. A quiet room. It's not—" he swallows, voice cracking. "It's not about her. It's about him."

The word hangs heavy.

Jacob studies him, like he's deciding whether to break his jaw anyway. Then, finally, with a growl deep in his throat, he shoves the deputy off.

"Five minutes," Jacob says, voice like steel. "And if you so much as glance at her wrong again...."

The deputy nods frantically, rubbing at his throat. "It won't happen, Sheriff. Please... this way."

The deputy stands stiff-backed as he holds open the door to the corridor, like a man who's wandered into a lion's den and knows it. His eyes avoid Jacob, avoid me, as though the truth he's about to spill is too heavy to look anyone in the face.

"This way, sheriff." He gestures, and I notice the red blemish of embarrassment and fear crawling up his cheeks.

He shows us into a room that's just at the back of the reception area. It's small, with only room for a hospital examination bed, a computer that sits on a desk and two chairs. Jacob leans against the hospital bed, but I remain standing next to him.

The deputy clears his throat. "The man in ICU... he... he isn't Benedict Harrow."

The words seem to suck all the air out of the room.

My pulse slams in my ears.

"That's... no." I laugh, "That's not possible."

The deputy drags a hand across the back of his neck, eyes flicking to Jacob before landing uneasily on me.

"The John Doe came in rough, sir. Real rough. Carter's the one who brought him—said he found him collapsed near a bar on Main." He pauses, glancing down at the clipboard in his hands, as though the paper might soften the blow. "Doctors said his injuries were bad enough they had to put him into an induced coma. Safer that way."

Jacob's jaw tightens, the muscle twitching. "Go on."

The deputy nods quickly. "The hospital contacted Benedict Harrow's next of kin. He's been listed missing for months, so they came in hoping…." He swallows. "But after seeing him, both of them said the same thing."

His voice drops."That man in the bed isn't their Benny."

My stomach twists. "But… I saw him. I know him. I—"

The deputy cuts in. "The real Benedict Harrow vanished six months ago. No leads, no sightings. Whoever this guy is… he walked into town wearing Benny's identity like a second skin. On paper it's airtight—ID, payroll, everything."

Jacob's hands ball into fists. "So someone used a dead man's name and slid right under my nose?"

I press my palms against my knees, trying to hold myself still, but my whole-body trembles. Every time I thought Benny was saving me, listening to me, caring for me—he wasn't Benny at all.

Who was he?

"I trusted him," I whisper, bile burning my throat. "God, I trusted him."

Jacob doesn't take his eyes off the deputy. His voice drops lower, darker, like it's being dragged from somewhere dangerous. "And your first move was to drag her in here? To put hands on her like she's your suspect?"

The deputy swallows hard, his Adam's apple bobbing. "Ma'am, I apologize for the way I approached you. It wasn't right—"

"Enough," Jacob snaps, stepping closer until the man's back hits the wall. His size, his fury, swallows the room whole. "Not one word in her direction. Not one fucking breath."

The deputy's gaze flickers, caught between fear and pleading. "Sheriff—"

Jacob leans in, his words a hiss, vicious and final. "Just remember, she's my woman. And I own your fucking badge. You want to keep it, then every question you have for her, you ask through me."

"Yes, Sheriff." He nods, stumbling for the door. His boots squeak on the tile as he vanishes. The door shuts.

And suddenly it's just me and Jacob, the fluorescent light buzzing, my chest heaving like I've been drowning.

I whisper, barely audible, "If he's not Benny…." My throat tightens, tears threatening. "Then who is he? There must be a mistake."

Finally, Jacob stands and turns to look at me. His eyes are dark enough to burn. He leans, bracing his hands on the wall either side of me.

"I don't know." His voice is steady, lethal. "But I'll find out. And when I do…." His jaw flexes, every word bitten off with promise.

We make our way back toward the reception, the sterile hum of the hospital lights filling the corridor. Constance and Adelaide are exactly where I knew they'd be—slouched in the plastic chairs by the vending machine, arms folded, legs crossed, expressions thunderous.

A laugh almost escapes me. The sight drags me straight back to high school, to the times they sat outside the principal's office after being caught sneaking out or mouthing off. Same postures, same defiance—just older now, sharper around the edges.

Constance was always the worst of the two, never able to stomach authority or take no for an answer. Adelaide followed her lead more often than she'd admit. So, the image of Jacob storming through earlier—taking me and a deputy with him while leaving them behind—must've burned.

The moment they see us, the storm clouds break. Both women shoot to their feet in perfect sync, anger and relief warring across their faces.

"Hey, what was that about?" Constance asks, concern radiating from her expression.

"It was nothing, just a formality," Jacob answers for me. "It's all under control. But now, we're heading up to Harrow. He's in a coma, so no need for you two to stick around."

I look to Jacob, confusion pulsing through me, but then remember who he is. The Sheriff of Rosefield. He's used to keeping things under wraps until he has the whole story and every ounce of information. Plus, he's trying to protect me. He wants me to head into Benny's room with a clear head. He wants to avoid any more mental conflict and what ifs.

"No, we'll wait." Adelaide says softly, forcing a small smile. "We'll be right here for you Summer."

I nod my head, and lean forward, putting my head between my two best friends and wrapping an arm around each of their shoulders. They both hug me back, Adelaide plants a kiss on my ear and whispers "We've got you."

When I pull away and turn back to Jacob, he's stood, arms folded, looking bored. I pull a *what the fuck is your problem* face and move to him. He immediately unfolds his arms and holds one out to me. Embracing me when I get to him.

"ICU is on the second floor. We can wait for the elevator, but it's a shit show here, always one out. Stairs might be best?"

"How do you—"

"Most crimes end in injury Summer. I spend more time here than you'd like to think."

Obviously, I hadn't considered that his role involves regular hospital questioning. Nevertheless, he guides me with his arm.

"This way, baby."

I turn to my girls and give them both a thank you smile. They both throw one back at me.

The door creaks open, the smell of antiseptic rushing out like a wave. Machines beep in slow rhythm, too steady for how violently my heart is pounding.

I step in first. And stop. The sight of him knocks the breath from my lungs.

Benny—no, *not* Benny—lies there like something already half gone. His face is covered with swollen bruises, purple and black blooming across the bones I used to know. His lip is split, his cheek stitched. A rigid white band circles his mouth, holding a plastic tube in place that hisses with each breath the machine forces into him.

His chest rises shallowly. Drops.

A nurse at his bedside checks the monitor with brisk efficiency.

"He came in with a punctured lung," she says matter of fact, like she's reporting the weather. "Multiple rib fractures. Trauma to the head. Whoever did this…." She frowns, noting something down on her clipboard. "Well, it looks like he was attacked by a gang, at least three of them, I'd guess."

Her words rattle around in my skull. Three of them. But I know the truth. There was only one.

I glance sideways. Jacob stands just inside the door, broad shoulders filling the frame, his expression smoothed into professional neutrality. But his eyes betray him. A flicker of pride. Satisfaction. The tiniest curl at the corner of his mouth.

The nurse doesn't see it. But I do and my stomach twists violently.

She finishes her notes, adjusts the line running into his arm, and finally slips out with a soft, "I'll give you some time."

The door clicks shut and silence presses down.

I stare at the man in the bed. The stranger I thought I knew. Jacob's hand covers mine, warm, firm. He leans close enough that his breath brushes my ear.

"It'll be okay," he murmurs, low enough only I can hear. His thumb strokes slow circles into my skin, the softness at war with the steel in his voice. "I'll find out what's going on. I promise."

I swallow hard, my throat raw. My eyes flick back to the battered body on the bed.

And for the first time, I don't know if I want him to wake up at all.

The hallway feels longer on the way out. My legs drag, every step weighted with what I've just seen. The smell of antiseptic clings to my skin, and in my head, I still hear the hiss of that machine pushing breath into him.

Jacob's hand is a steady weight against my back as we push through the double doors into the waiting area.

Constance and Adelaide are already on their feet, faces pale, eyes wide. They rush toward us the second they see us, questions spilling out before we even reach them.

"What happened? How is he?" Constance's eyes dart between us.

I stand there, frozen. My mouth opens, but nothing comes out.

Adelaide grips my hands, her touch warm but shaking. "Summer… please. Talk to us."

Jacob steps forward, cutting through the panic. His voice is blunt. "He's not Benny."

Constance blinks at him, confusion hollowing her eyes. "What? What do you mean?"

Adelaide looks between us, swallowing hard. "Summer?…"

I force the words out, my voice barely my own.

"The hospital called Benny's brother. He came in tonight." A breath shudders through me. "He said the man in that bed isn't him."

Adelaide's grip on me falters, her hand slipping from mine like she's lost her anchor. Constance sits back into her chair, eyes hollow, mouth parted. Confusion adorning her face.

Jacob doesn't give them time to argue. He strides to the front desk, each step heavy, controlled, a predator moving through prey. The receptionist straightens, nervous under his shadow.

"The second that man opens his eyes," Jacob says, his voice low and lethal, "I want a call. Direct to me. No one else."

The woman swallows, nodding quickly. "Yes, Sheriff."

He leans in just a fraction, his stare pinning her in place. "If someone else hears about it before I do, I'll know."

She scribbles his number down, cheeks flushed, and nods again. Satisfied, Jacob turns back, his gaze sweeping over me, Constance, Adelaide.

I wrap my arms around myself—all I can see is the battered stranger lying in that bed, breathing through a machine, carrying Benny's name like a stolen coat.

And I wonder if I ever knew him at all.

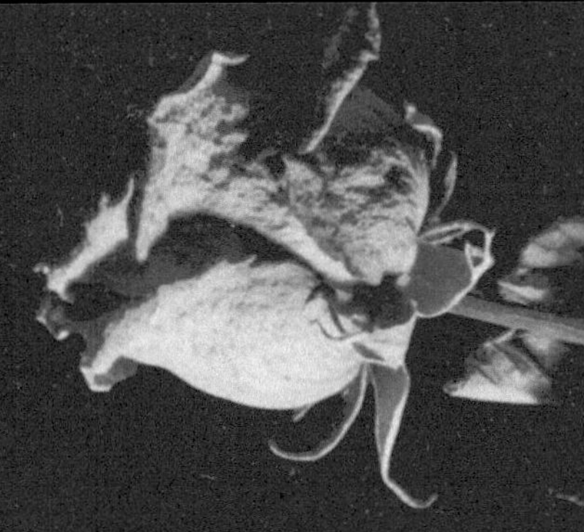

Chapter 23
Jackson Moore
Summer

The coffee machine hisses like it's mocking me, the burnt scent clawing at the back of my throat. I watch the plastic cup fill halfway before the liquid sputters, brown foam sloshing against flimsy edges. My hand shakes when I reach for it. I'm not sure if it's grief, or adrenaline, or both.

Headlights slash across the polished floor-to-ceiling windows. A black SUV pulls into the space closest to the entrance. The engine cuts. Two doors open. Two people step out.

Not in uniforms. Not nurses. Not hurried visitors clutching flowers or takeout bags. No, these two are different. They move the way hunters do when the chase is over—steady, unhurried, certain the prey is theirs.

The first is tall, broad through the shoulders, his stubble catching the glow from the overhead lamps. His eyes cut like flint when they lift toward the building, cold and assessing. Even from here, even through the glass, I can feel the weight of them.

The second is a woman, smaller, her movements quieter but no less certain. Her hair is pulled tight at the nape of her neck, her coat fitted and neat. She glances at the man beside her once, the briefest flicker of communication, before they cross the lot in step.

My stomach knots. Something in me whispers: not right.

The automatic doors slide open as they get close to the entrance, the rush of night air pushing against my face.

They don't hesitate when they enter, they don't scan the signs for direction. The man walks ahead—he reaches the receptionist and flashes his badge, just long enough to confirm what I already suspect. Detectives.

My skin prickles. Detectives. Here. For him. For the man in ICU who isn't Benny Harrow.

I force a sip of coffee, nearly gagging at the taste. My pulse won't calm, won't slow. I glance down the hall, searching for Jacob. He disappeared ten minutes ago to corner his deputy, his boots echoing into the distance. He should be here. He has to be here. Because suddenly, I feel exposed.

The detectives split the room with their presence. The man plants himself near the desk, leaning an elbow like he has every right to bend the space around him. The woman stays standing, scanning. Eyes solid, watchful. They're not looking for trouble. They're expecting it.

"Sheriff Darnell," the male says, his voice gravel and smoke.

And my blood chills—because Jacob headed to make a phone call five minutes ago and hasn't returned.

The receptionist stutters, eyes wide. "He's… I can call him—"

"No need." The reply doesn't come from her. It comes from behind me.

Jacob.

His hand flexes once, twice, before his gaze locks on the detectives. His entire body is tension coiled tight, his jaw rigid enough to crack.

He plants himself next to the male detective without speaking another word.

The detective smirks faintly. "Convenient as ever, sir."

The female detective steps forward, her voice calmer, precise. "We need to speak with you, Sheriff. In private."

"Down the hall." Jacob's voice is the low thunder of a storm. "Second door on the left."

They both nod and head toward the room.

Jacob comes to me. He holds out his hand. I take it immediately.

"What you hear in this room might not be pleasant, baby. You don't have to come," he says.

Constance and Adelaide both look in our direction, confused. They've been sat reading magazines and drinking soda. I thought they would have gone home by now, but then, I know they'd never leave me when my world is crumbling. I also know part of them wants the truth about Benny. As much as it hurts me that he's lied about his identity, he's lied to them too. They were trying to help me. Trying to be there for me. And in doing so, they'd crossed paths with… Benny.

They met him. They talked about my life with him. Part of me knows they feel just as blindsided as I do.

"No, I'm coming," I say, cutting off whatever protest Jacob was about to make. I fall into step beside him as we head toward room, trailing after the detectives.

The woman's gaze flicks to me first—not pitying, not cruel, just sudden and appraising, like she's weighing exactly how much truth I already hold. I clutch the cup of coffee tighter, the heat biting into my palms, grounding me in the only way I can manage.

The male detective sighs, dragging a hand over the stubble on his jaw before extending it toward Jacob. "Sheriff."

Jacob hesitates, then takes it, the handshake brief, strained.

"Maddox, Navarro," Jacob says flatly, his tone clipped and cold. "What brings you here?"

Maddox's eyes narrow slightly. "Sir, the girl. Is she—"

"She's my fiancée. She stays," Jacob cuts in, tone harsh and final.

For a second, I think I've misheard him. Fiancée?

The word slams into me, heavy and disorienting. My breath catches somewhere between my chest and throat. He says it like it's fact, like it's something that's always been true.

I stare at him, but he doesn't look my way. Doesn't offer so much as a flicker of explanation. Just stands there—calm, commanding, completely unbothered—while I'm left reeling, trying to figure out when exactly I agreed to belong to him like that.

I'm snapped back to reality when Maddox clears his throat and continues.

"The patient upstairs, Sheriff—" he stops mid-sentence. His attention flicks to me. But Jacob doesn't move. Doesn't even blink. He just stands there—still as stone—like he's been expecting this all along.

Navarro tilts her head, assessing. "Sheriff, we need to be clear about the importance of identifying the man upstairs." Her gaze locks on me.

My knees weaken. The mug trembles in my hands, coffee spilling over the rim and scalding my skin, but I barely feel it. Jacob shifts just enough for his arm to brush mine—a silent anchor, a warning, maybe both. He doesn't look at me. Doesn't need to. His stare stays fixed on Maddox, jaw tight, unreadable.

And yet, both of them—Maddox and the Navarro—keep watching me like I'm something fragile and dangerous all at once. Like they know they're about to startle me and can't anticipate how I'll react.

"Get to the point," Jacob says, low. Dangerous.

Maddox doesn't blink. "Sheriff, there's been an incident handed over from Broadachre County." His voice dips, grave. "Jackson Moore."

My heart stops.

Navarro takes over, her tone softer, though the words hit like bullets. "Moore was transferred for an appeal hearing yesterday. On the return trip, the transport bus was ambushed. Officers killed. Prisoners injured. Moore was taken."

No.

No.

My chest hollows, empties. I hear the words, but they don't fit inside my head. Jackson Moore. Gone.

Navarro's mouth presses tight. "We believe the man upstairs may be connected. Whether as an accomplice… or a witness. Which means we need to speak to him the moment he regains consciousness. All of the paperwork is on your desk, sir."

I can't breathe.

Moore, the man, the men. My parents' deaths. It's all too coincidental. The cup slips from my hand, coffee splattering across the tile.

Jacob's arm snaps around my waist before I fall, his grip iron. His voice, when it comes, is low, lethal, vibrating against my spine.

"Why the fuck wasn't I made aware of this yesterday?" Jacob snarls. His hands remain around me, I hear his heartbeat quicken in his chest, his breathing rate increasing.

"It was handed over to the department an hour ago. You weren't in the office — "

"If Moore's out," Jacob interrupts, "He's coming for her."

And the way he says it — the way his voice coils around me like chains — makes me know he believes it. Every word.

The world tilts from the truth hanging in the air like smoke. Jackson Moore — escaped. He's out there somewhere. Breathing the same night air as me.

"I want every man, woman and dog hunting that fucker down. I don't give a fuck about budgets. Pull in every resource we have to get that son of a bitch."

Maddox doesn't blink. His presence is a slab of concrete, heavy and immovable. "Sheriff, we have a dead driver, two dead prison guards. Broadachre County want in, too... Moore was in their jail, their jurisdiction, we're involved because of his motives. Because they think he'll come back here... And Sheriff, we need to consider that Moore was involved with the murders that occurred last night."

"They were my fucking parents," I snap.

Maddox and Navarro both look to each other immediately.

"My apologies, Miss Miller." Maddox says, sympathy radiating from his expression.

I nod my head, accepting his apology and wipe my nose on my sleeve. The tears have been flowing without me even realizing. I seem to have become accustomed to the sensation.

Navarro steps closer. Her voice is silk, meant to calm, but it cuts all the same. "We need your cooperation. The patient upstairs — " she glances at me before finishing, " — he might be the only thread we have to getting Moore."

I swallow hard. My throat burns. "But he's unconscious. He... he might not even survive." My voice cracks at the memory of that machine forcing breath into his lungs. "How can he help? And what makes you think he's linked to Jackson?" I ask

Navarro folds her arms, her expression a shade softer, though her words aren't any easier. "Men tied to Moore have a history of running under stolen names. It's a pattern. Fraudulent IDs, ghost addresses, burner phones. He fits that pattern. And when Moore's convoy got hit, every alias even remotely associated with that circle lit up on our radar."

Maddox's mouth tightens into a grim line. "Doesn't mean he was at the ambush. Doesn't mean he pulled the trigger. But if he's not who he says he is, and he's moving in the same shadows as Moore, then yeah—there's reason to believe there's a connection."

Jacob steps forward. Maddox's jaw works.

"We're doing everything we can to contain this, Sheriff." His voice is flat, precise—police-speak meant to steady things.

Jacob closes the distance until there's only centimetres between them. The smile that touches his mouth isn't a smile. "No, Detective. That isn't good enough."

Navarro steps in, palms up like she's holding the temperature down. Her eyes flick between Jacob and Maddox, even-toned.

"We're on the same side, Sheriff. We're doing our jobs. You know you can trust us— When have we ever let you down?" The words are professional, but there's a softness there for him that I imagine she doesn't use for anyone else.

The promise lands hollow. It's the way they move around him— deferential, familiar—that makes my skin go cold. They'll follow any order he gives them and never even stop to question it.

I can't move. My pulse bangs behind my eyes and the name keeps coming—Jackson Moore—over and over, a drumbeat that won't stop. He's not supposed to be out. He's supposed to be in a cell rotting.

"We can make arrangements for a safe house for you, Summer," Navarro says, voice smooth as silk. "Somewhere out of sight. We'll keep you safe."

Jacob's glare drops on them like a hammer—an animal warning.

He's not amused; he's offended. "You think anyone can keep her safer than me, Navarro?"

Her eyes flick everywhere, searching for an exit. She swallows, the small human sound of someone who knows she's poked a sleeping thing. "No, Sheriff. I just— I thought—"

"Listen to me," Jacob says, each word a tightened wire against my ribs. "And listen very fucking carefully—Summer does not leave my side until that son of a bitch is in cuffs, or under the ground. Got it?" His hand presses against my hip, a possession and a promise in the same motion. "But mark my words: if I find him first...." He lets the sentence hang, slow and black.

Navarro goes still. Maddox's jaw works but he doesn't say a word.

The hospital lights buzz above us and for a second everything feels thin—like paper stretched over a bone. My breath comes shallow and fast. I don't know whether to be comforted or terrified that the man who says he loves me is also the one threatening to burn a county to save me.

The silence presses in, deep enough that my breath comes shallow, like my lungs are refusing to expand. My throat burns. My full body shaking— a tremor I can't stop.

"Jacob...." My voice is a whisper, barely there. "Jacob... I'm scared."

His head snaps toward me like he'd forgotten I was standing here. His eyes burn into mine, dark and fierce. And for the first time, I see something behind the fury.

Fear.

Real, bone-deep fear.

Chapter 24
Eternity, if I Have To
Jacob

She doesn't see it, but my whole fucking body fractures when she says my name like that. Weak. Shaking. Terrified.

I want to tear their throats out just for putting that look in her eyes. But it's not their fault. They're two of my best detectives and—if anything—I'm grateful it's them managing the case.

Summer is trembling with fear. I want to crush my mouth against hers just to stop the sound of it. To give her an escape, to give her some of my strength.

Navarro clears her throat, glancing at me. "Sheriff, do you want us to move forward with the hospital interview once the patient's stable?"

"No. Hold off until I say otherwise. Priority is getting Benny to talk and that will only happen if Summer goes in." I turn my face away from her, hiding the inner turmoil it causes me when I think of her and him in the same room, especially now I know he could be linked to Moore. "I want eyes on him every hour of the day. Anyone comes to visit; I want their plates logged."

"Yes, Sheriff," Navarro says, already thumbing notes into her phone.

Maddox nods. "We'll rotate shifts with Harper and Rio. We'll make sure he's never out of sight."

My hand twitches toward them. "Good. And if he so much as blinks, I want to know about it. Understood?"

"Understood," Maddox answers without a hint of a smile this time.

Summer grips my arm, nails biting through fabric. She doesn't realize she's doing it.

I tilt my head down, catch her wide, wet eyes. She's breaking. Just the name Jackson Moore has her in a frenzy.

I swear to God, if Benny… if whoever-the-fuck-he-is… had anything to do with this—if he knew Moore's escape was coming— then I'll finish what I started in my driveway. ICU bed or not.

The detectives finally peel off, their polished shoes clicking across linoleum until the doors swallow them whole.

The silence left behind is suffocating. Summer's nails are still hooked in my arm, pointed little crescents through the fabric. I catch her wrist before she can speak, my fingers closing around it— not harsh, just enough to steer her.

A doctor knocks on the door, needing to use the room for his clinic.

I don't want her back in the waiting room. I don't want the world to see her like this.

"This way," I mutter, pulling her down a narrow side corridor away from the hospital room and the eyes waiting there.

She stumbles once, catching herself, her bare shoulders grazing the sterile walls as we move. Her hair comes loose from her ponytail —dry now, curling in loose, untamed waves. The scent of her shampoo clings faintly to the air, something soft and familiar in a place that smells like bleach and steel.

She stops so suddenly that I almost collide with her. Her back hits the wall, and before I can think, my hands plant themselves flat beside her head, caging her in. She looks up at me—eyes swollen, cheeks flushed. And even broken like this, she's achingly beautiful— raw, unguarded, real.

"I need to know everything about my parents' deaths," she says, voice shredded to ribbons. "I need to hear it from you. Tell me every- thing. I don't want to hear it from the cops."

I drag in a breath, press my forehead to hers, trying to hold her still, to stop the tremor running through both of us. "Summer, not here. Not like this —"

"No." Her tone cuts, the crack of authority in it cutting through the air. "You will tell me. And you'll tell me now."

I exhale hard, running a hand through my hair, searching for words that won't destroy her more than she already is. But the memory rises up anyway — vivid, merciless.

Smoke curling off blackened beams. The hiss of heat eating glass.

"Whoever did it got in through a back dining room window," I start, my voice rough. "Your parents were in the sitting area. The fire started in the kitchen — it was deliberate." My throat tightens, bile clawing up as I force the words out. "They both had a single shot to the head. Clean. Quick. They wouldn't have felt a thing."

Her breath shudders, tears streaming freely now, but I keep going, steady, the words scraping like gravel from my mouth. "The fire department got there before it spread that far. It wasn't meant to destroy anything. It was meant to be seen. A beacon to draw in the authorities." I pull in another ragged breath. "They wanted us to see it, Summer. They wanted us to know it wasn't an accident."

She lets out a quiet sob, her head collapsing against my chest. For a moment, neither of us speaks — the room holding its breath around us. When she finally looks up, her eyes are wet, rimmed with fear.

"Is that how you think they'll come for me too?" she whispers.

The thought of losing her breaks something in my soul, and before I think any better, I crush my mouth against hers. I swallow her sobs, taste her tears, pin her so tight to the wall she can barely breathe.

She fights me, fists caught in my grip. Her body shakes against mine, grief and rage spilling out into my kiss.

I pull away from her, my lips remaining close to hers. "I love you," I hum, "and no one, not even God himself, will take you from me. Because even in the next lifetime, I will hunt you. I'll find you. And I will spend eternity protecting you."

Chapter 25
Only Ever Yours
Summer

The car ride home is silent except for the low hum of the engine and the occasional hiss of the tires slicing through wet asphalt. My teeth chattering. I've been trembling since the hospital, since the detectives looked at me with those eyes that already decided Benny was tied to the kind of monsters who murdered my parents.

Constance and Adelaide had waited for us in the reception area. Their faces had broken into dismay when Jacob told them that Moore was out.

Now, they sit pressed close to each other in the back seat, their heads bent together, whispering things I can't make out. Maybe comfort. Maybe fear. Maybe both. When we turn down their street, Constance squeezes my shoulder.

"You should stay with us tonight," I whisper, like an offering I know she won't accept.

"No, Summer. We all need to process this. We all need our own beds for the night." She shakes her head. "And as much as it pains me to say—you're in good hands."

I nod my head, acknowledging that she's right. With Jacob is the safest I will ever be—I realize that now. When we pull up outside Constance's house, Adelaide opens the door, but before she steps out, she turns to me.

"We love you and we're always here… no matter what." Adelaide croaks, glancing back at me, eyes red, before she hooks her arm through Constance's.

I watch them walk to the porch, their shadows stretched long and thin under the yellow streetlamp. I don't breathe until they're both inside, the door shutting quietly behind them.

When we pull into the drive, the house—our house—looms ahead. Silent, familiar, yet somehow foreign now. Jacob cuts the engine, the sudden quiet ringing in my ears. He turns to me, his expression unreadable.

"Stay here," he says.

I part my lips to argue, to tell him I don't care if the house is safe or not, that I can't sit here doing nothing—but the look in his eyes stops me cold. It's harsh, commanding, edged with something close to fear. I just nod, wrapping my arms around myself as he opens the door and steps out.

The car locks with a double click—then another, his thumb pressing the fob again and again, as if repetition could make it safer.

Through the windshield, I watch him cross the yard, a dark silhouette against the weak glow of the porch light. His shadow stretches long across the gravel before he disappears inside, leaving me alone with the steady thud of my heart and the whisper of wind against the glass.

Time blurs. Seconds, minutes—I can't tell which. Then the door creaks open again.

He emerges from the house, striding across the yard with purpose. The porch light catches his face for a split second—hard, set, unreadable—before he reaches the car.

"Come here," he mutters, and before I can even move, he's lifting me into his arms.

The world tilts around me. My cheek presses to his chest, where his heart beats steady, brutal, certain. The tears return, hot against my skin.

He carries me inside like I'm weightless. Like the weight of grief and rage and ruin I feel is easy for him to carry.

He places me gently on the sofa, then moves away. I hear the shuffle of a blanket being pulled from the back of a chair. A moment later, it's wrapped around me, his hands tucking it in with a care that makes my chest ache harder.

"Stay put," he orders softly. Then his footsteps retreat upstairs.

I curl into the blanket, my knees to my chest, the scent of him clinging to the fabric. Cedarwood and smoke.

When he returns, he's carrying a folded set of pajamas. He kneels in front of me, places them in my lap.

"Change," he says. Not harsh, not demanding—like he can't stand the sight of me sitting here in uncomfortable clothes.

My fingers tremble as I reach for them, they're so numb I can barely work the buttons on the pajama top. Jacob watches, crouched low, his arms resting on his knees, but he doesn't move to help. He's giving me space. He's letting me ask for help before he intervenes.

When I finally fumble the last button, he stands and leaves the room. It's the kind of courtesy I wouldn't expect from him, the kind that makes my throat close. I slip out of my old clothes, the fabric heavy with the smell of hospital antiseptic, and slide into the soft cotton of the pajamas. They're much too big for me, hanging loose at the wrists and ankles, and that's how I know they're his.

When I whisper, "I'm done," he re-enters the room.

Without a word, he gathers the discarded clothes into his fist and sets them aside, like he can erase the night with the sweep of his hand.

"Relax," he murmurs.

I want to laugh at the word. Relax. When my parents are dead. When the boy I thought might save me turned out to be nothing but another lie. When Jacob himself—this towering, merciless man that I spent years running from— is my safety, and the man I'm falling so hopelessly and desperately in love with after all.

But I don't laugh—I just let out a shaking breath as stands.

He heads toward the door and disappears into the kitchen. I hear him rummaging through drawers, opening and closing one at a time.

"Where the fuck is it?" he mutters under his breath, voice low but edged with frustration.

Despite everything—despite the tension coiling through my chest

—I almost laugh. For all his control, all his darkness, he's still a man. A stubborn, impossible man who can stare down killers without flinching but can't find whatever it is he's looking for without tearing the house apart.

He returns with my pink hairbrush clutched in his hand. It looks absurd in his scarred grip. He climbs over me and sits behind me on the sofa, shifting me between his knees.

"Head forward," he orders.

My muscles resist, but I obey, letting my head bow. The first drag of bristles through my hair makes me gasp. It hurts. He's not careful enough, not practiced. But every time the brush catches a knot, he slows. He tries.

It's a strange kind of tenderness—this brutal man, this sheriff who bleeds violence, sitting here with a hairbrush and untangling me piece by piece.

I close my eyes. The brush pulls, then eases, then pulls again. The rhythm is hypnotic. And slowly, the trembling in my hands begins to fade. When he's finished, he sets the brush down, his fingers brushing the back of my neck. My skin erupts in goosebumps.

I lean my head back without thinking, resting it against his chest. He exhales, rough, like the air is burning on its way out. His lips press to the crown of my head—just a graze—and then lower to my temple, then my cheek.

I turn my body to face him and climb to straddle him on the sofa. I press my lips to his and kiss him. I expect his return to be fierce and claiming, but he's softer than I expect. Like he's fighting his own nature to give me something he doesn't even know he has inside him.

When he pulls back, his forehead rests against mine. "I know you hate me," he whispers. "Because I left you. Because I wasn't here when—"

"Stop." My voice is ragged. I bury my face against his neck, inhaling smoke and pine and him. "I don't hate you," I whisper into his skin. "I just never understood why you left without telling me."

His arms tighten around me, crushing, like he's trying to fuse me into him.

"But I know now, you didn't know they were gone. You rushed

off to save them. Because that's who you are. You're the savior, the protector. You look after this town and care for everyone—well, most—people in it," I say, tears soaking into his shirt. "And you've always been my safety. I just didn't see it before."

He doesn't speak, but the tremor in his chest tells me he heard.

I press my lips against his throat, a desperate kiss, a vow. "And you never gave up on me. Not for a single second." I swallow hard. "Jacob—I love you."

His lack of response is deafening. But I can feel it in the way his grip tightens around me, in the way his chest rises rough and heavy beneath my cheek. He heard me. He just doesn't know what to do with it.

I lift my head, force him to look at me. His eyes are fire and ruin, storms bottled in ice. He looks like a man about to come apart at the seams.

"I mean it," I whisper. "I'm so deeply in love with you it burns my fucking soul."

The muscles in his jaw flex. His lips part, close, part again. His hand slides up my spine, slow and possessive, curling around the back of my neck. He pulls me forward, crashing his mouth to mine. It's not gentle this time. It's punishing. Consuming. Like he's trying to drown himself in me before the world takes me away.

I gasp against him, my nails digging into his shoulders, but he doesn't stop. His tongue claims, his teeth graze, his growl vibrates through my chest. I feel myself unravelling, piece by piece, giving myself to him, wholly, completely. Mind, body and fucking soul.

When he finally breaks, his forehead presses to mine, breath ragged.

"Don't you ever say that to me unless you're ready to live with it," he snarls, voice raw. "Because I'll never let you take it back."

I choke out a sob, half fear, half relief. "I don't want to take it back."

His eyes close, like the words are too much, too dangerous. When they open again, they're darker. Hungrier.

"Christ, Summer...." His voice cracks around my name. "You have no fucking idea what you've just done."

He doesn't give me a chance to answer. His hands seize my hips, dragging me tighter against him. Heat floods through me at the hard press of him beneath the thin cotton barrier.

My breath stutters, body arching instinctively.

"Jacob—"

He cuts me off with another kiss, this one deeper, slower, but no less brutal. His hands roam, sliding under the hem of the pajama top, palms rough against my skin. Every touch is a contradiction—too harsh, too desperate, yet trembling with restraint, like he's terrified he'll break me if he doesn't hold back.

I clutch his face, forcing his gaze to stay on mine. "You're not going to break me," I whisper against his lips. "You'll never break me."

Tears stream down my face, but I don't care. I drag his mouth back to mine, kissing him deeper through the sobs, desperate and messy. He groans into me, the sound torn from somewhere deep and dangerous. When he finally pulls back, his breath scorches my lips. His eyes burn into mine—furious, starving, shattered.

"I need you," I whisper, trembling. "And if you meant what you said earlier—if you want me to be your fiancée, then my answer is yes."

His hand fists in my hair, dragging my head back so I have no choice but to meet his gaze. His mouth hovers over mine, dangerous and reverent all at once.

"You have no idea how many times I've dreamed you'd say those words."

"I'm yours," I breathe. "Only ever yours."

His earlier restraint disappears, and he kisses like a man who refuses to let me piece myself back together without him. He releases me and drags his teeth over my throat like he's branding me.

I moan, my body arching helplessly against his. My fingers clutch at his shoulders needing him closer even as he tears me apart.

"You own me, Jacob."

His growl is from the depths of hell, like my confession is gasoline thrown on open flame. He shoves me deeper into the cushions, his weight crushing, his heat surrounding me until there's nothing left but him.

"Say it again," his words are guttural, straight from his heart.

"I'm yours," I choke out, tears burning hot down my face. "I've always been yours. Deep down. I've denied it. I've hated you. But… I'm yours, Jacob. And I love you."

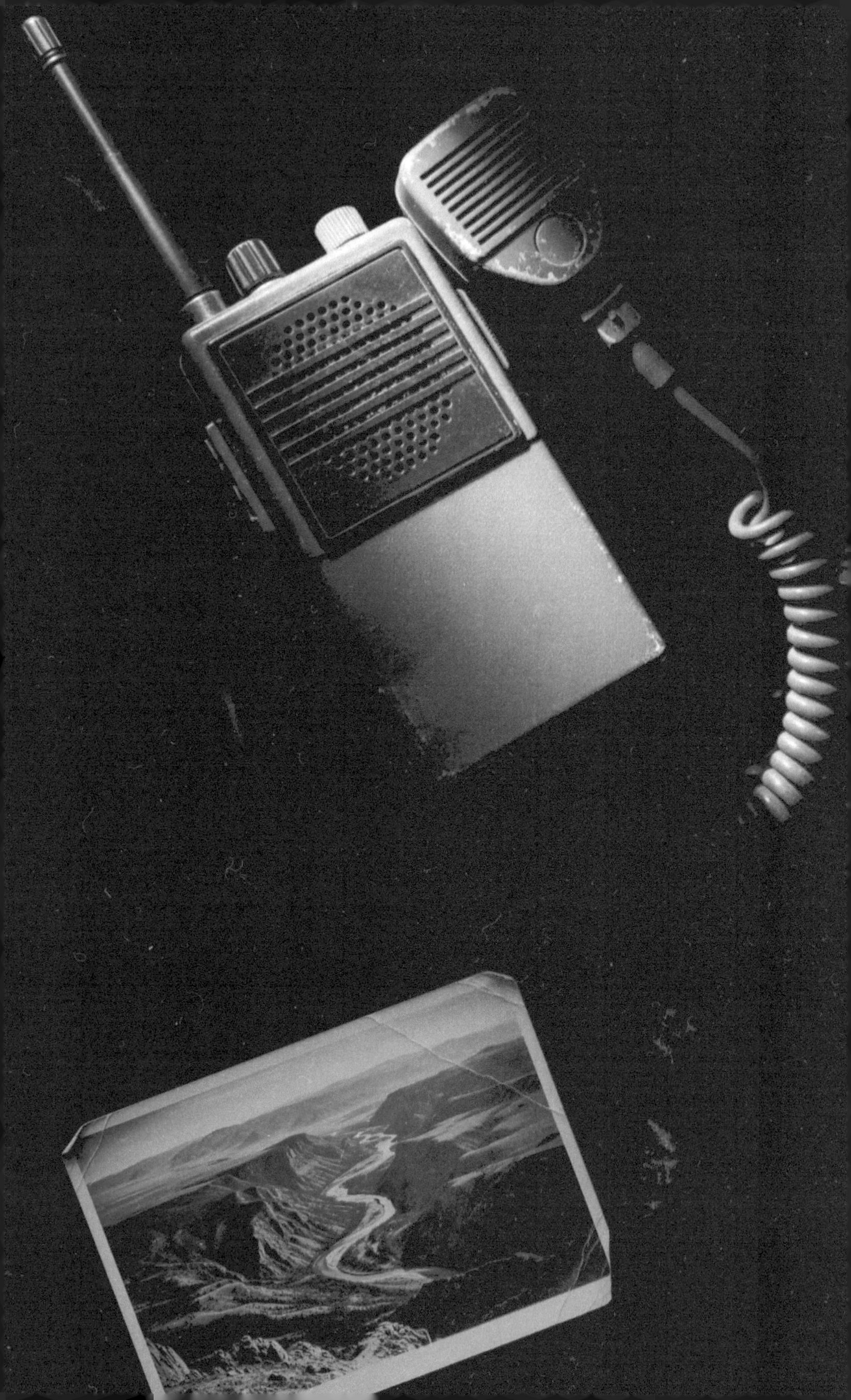

Chapter 26
The Knife and The Noose
Jacob

She said it. She fucking *said* it.

"I love you."

Those three words out of her mouth… they could drop me to my knees faster than any blade shoved into my ribs. Hell, she even said she'd marry me.

It keeps replaying in my skull, a broken record that doesn't grate—it brands. Her voice, wrecked and trembling. That little quiver in her throat like she was scared of saying it. Because she knows my feelings for her go beyond obsession. Fuck, I told her I loved her. She knows how I feel. But she held back. She's tried to fight it. The same way she tried to fight how badly her body craved me.

I've got her. All of her. Body and fucking soul.

Summer Miller told me she loves me, and I believe her. No lies in her eyes. No manipulation. No strings attached. Just the girl I tore out of her own life, who somehow still found a way to look at me like I was the one thing keeping her from drowning.

Christ, if anyone else had told me this morning that this day would end with her lips saying those words to me, I'd have laughed in their face and broken their jaw for mocking me. Men like me don't get love. We get violence. We get fear. We get power and blood and the silence of graves. But never love. But now it's mine. Her love. Her body. Her soul. I've been claiming all of it piece by piece, and tonight, she handed me the last fragment willingly.

My chest feels like it's going to split wide open. I can't breathe. For the first time in my entire life, I feel like I could break down and cry. Not shed a fragment of a tear, but really, completely break down and sob.

But I don't. I won't. Because she doesn't need a man who weeps. She needs a monster who will stand, teeth bared, between her and the fire.

So, I make the promise. Quietly. Brutally. The kind of vow that isn't spoken but etched into the marrow of my bones. Every single day from this one until the day I'm put in the ground—she's it. The axis I spin on. The reason I wake, the reason I fight, the reason I keep breathing.

I won't turn soft. She doesn't want that. My girl loves pain, loves my roughness, my obsession. She drinks down every jagged edge I give her. But I'll still change. Not in who I am—I'll never stop being the sheriff, the monster, the man who puts bodies in the dirt when they get too close. No, I'll change in 'why'.

Every bullet I fire will be for her.

Every son of a bitch I take down will be for her.

Every decision I make, every law I bend, every life I end—all of it, hers.

She's curled against me, her body slack with exhaustion. I can feel the faint tremor of her breaths against my chest, the warmth of her cheek pressed to the hollow of my collarbone. Every once in a while, her lips twitch, like she's about to speak, but sleep drags her under before the words can escape.

I should close my eyes. I should let my body rest—God knows I need it. My knuckles are torn open, my muscles ache, and my head's a warzone of voices. But I don't. Instead, I study her like a starving man memorizing the shape of bread.

I rise from the seat, careful not to wake her, and lift her in one motion. She grunts but doesn't fully wake. I carry her to my bed. No

—our bed. The bed where we will make our babies. Where we will sleep, fuck, and sleep again.

Me and my *wife*.

Her hair spreads over the pillow, strands curling from where I brushed it out earlier. I smile at the memory. The noise she made as it combed through her softness and released some of the tension she had built up from the worst day of her life.

Part of me feels jealous. I should have just pulled my fingers through her hair, to feel every single molecule of her being and not let anything else ever touch her. I almost laugh at the thought. Jealous of a goddamn hairbrush. What the fuck is wrong with me?

But then she shifts, sighs in her sleep, and the sound strips me raw. I reach out, careful, dragging the back of my knuckles along her jaw. Light enough not to wake her. Gentle—a word I don't know how to wear, but I force it on anyway.

Her skin is warm, soft, a balm I don't deserve. My chest tightens so hard I think my ribs might crack.

"Summer," I murmur, my voice a rasp, just for her ears even if she's too deep under to hear me. "You have no fucking idea what you've done to me." I shake my head and laugh, but without a trace of humor. "I've broken men without blinking. Put bullets between eyes without a flicker of regret. But three words from you—three— I'm on my knees. You think you love me now? You wait and see what I do with it."

I brush her hair back from her face, fingers sinking into the strands like roots. If another man ever hears her say "I love you," it'll be the last sound they ever hear. That, or the gunshot firing through their skull. But then I think, maybe she should say it to another boy, maybe she should say it to our son.

The image of a miniature version of me flashes through my mind, wearing the Sheriffs hat I refuse to don— riding a pretend horse through the yard. I'd give my son the life I should have had, the life I deserved. Not a life of fearing his father—of wondering whether he'd get the belt for not cleaning the porch just right. No—he would be loved, cherished and would grow to be a better man than me.

"One day," I whisper.

She exhales, soft and shuddering, like her body knows the future I've planned for us, even if her mind's too far gone to process it. I tuck the blanket tighter around her, press my mouth to the top of her head, and let the vow settle deep in my bones.

The vibration rattles against the nightstand, loud enough to slice through the silence. My heart doesn't just skip—it fucking stops.

I rip the phone up before it can wake her. Carter's name flashes across the screen, and every instinct in me turns to stone.

"Sheriff," his voice crackles, too rushed, too clipped. "We've had a call from a neighbour. Black SUV parked outside Constance Bishop's place. Reports of shouting, glass breaking. Possible domestic disturbance."

My blood goes cold. Not a chill. A freeze that locks every muscle tight.

Constance. Adelaide.

I glance down at Summer—at the woman curled into me, finally breathing easy, finally letting herself rest. My woman, who I swore I'd never fail again.

And yet here I am, staring at the knife-edge of failure.

If I wake her, I rip her peace away. I throw her headfirst back into panic, back into the kind of nightmares I've been fighting to burn out of her.

But if I don't….

My hand shakes against the phone, but my voice doesn't. "How long ago?"

"It was called in four minutes ago," Carter answers. "Units enroute, but…." He hesitates, and that hesitation is a death sentence. "Sheriff, neighbour said the SUV was tinted. They didn't see anyone leave. No plates, either. It's likely it could be—"

"Moore," I snarl. The name tears out of me before I can stop it.

Summer shifts against my chest, murmuring something in her sleep. I freeze. Hold her tighter. Pray she doesn't wake.

I'm split in half. One side of me is the man she just confessed to loving, the man who swore his world would spin around her. The other is the sheriff, the predator, the monster who knows the hunt has already come knocking at our door.

And I don't know how the fuck to tell her.

What do I do? Wake her? Lie to her? Leave her behind and deal with it myself like I did last time?

Every option tastes like blood. But I do the only thing I can think of doing.

Carter's still in my ear, waiting for orders, but my brain's already running ten steps ahead. I know these roads like the veins in my hands. If I push my truck, I can get to Constance's place in under six minutes. Maybe less if I don't give a shit about the lights.

"Carter," I bark on a whisper when he answers. "Get Haywood to my house. Now."

There's a pause, hesitation on the line. "Sheriff—"

"Don't fucking argue. Summer knows him. He's one of the only men I trust. Tell him I'll be back in half an hour," I whisper, making sure she doesn't hear.

"Sir—"

"Half an hour." My voice is quiet but steel, final, the kind that doesn't leave room for anything but obedience.

He swallows whatever argument he has and hangs up.

I turn my gaze back to Summer. She hasn't stirred. Her face is soft, lips parted, a little crease in her brow like she's fighting shadows even in sleep. Christ, she's been through hell. And I'm about to drag her deeper into it if I tell her now.

It's **2:30 a.m.** The world outside is dead quiet. The chances of her waking in the next thirty minutes are slim.

I'll lock every door. Leave the hall light on so it looks like I'm still home. Haywood will park out front in his truck, the sight of it enough to make anyone think twice.

She'll be safe. She'll sleep. And I'll sort this before she even knows there's a threat.

Because if Moore is at Constance's house—if he's waiting there with his hands around the throats of the only two people Summer still has left—then I know exactly how this will play out.

He'll threaten to kill them. He'll dangle their lives in front of me like bait, make me hand Summer over in exchange. And here's the truth I can't even say out loud. The thought that would scorch me if she ever knew. I'd kill the girls myself before I let Moore touch Summer. I'd snap their necks, bleed them out on the floor, if it meant keeping her safe. Because Summer isn't just mine. She is me. My axis. My obsession. My only reason for breathing.

~

The night air cuts against my skin as I step onto the porch. It smells like damp earth and woodsmoke, but underneath it all I swear I can taste blood, like my body already knows what's waiting. I pace once, twice, my boots grinding against the boards, then stop when headlights swing around the corner.

Haywood's cruiser.

I glance at my watch. **2:34 a.m.** Four minutes. That's all it took him to haul his ass out here. I'll remember that. Loyalty like that means something in a world where I can't trust a goddamn soul.

His cruiser crunches up the drive and idles in front of the house. Haywood steps out, uniform still crisp despite the hour, hand hovering near his belt like he's already anticipating a fight. Good. I need that kind of edge right now.

"Sheriff," he says, nodding once.

I step down off the porch, closing the distance until I'm right in front of him. My voice is low, jagged enough to cut. "She's inside. Asleep."

His gaze flicks to the windows, back to me. "You want me inside or posted out front?"

"Inside." I don't hesitate. "Lock the doors behind me. She knows you, trusts you. But listen to me, Haywood—" I lean in, my stare pinning him harder than any hand could. "No matter what happens, you keep her safe. That's all that matters. You hear me?"

"Yes, sir."

I grab his shoulder, fingers digging hard enough to leave marks. "No matter what. Do not wake her up. If she wakes on her own, you tell her I'll be back soon. But you do not mention Constance's home. Not under any circumstances."

His brows twitch, just slightly, but he doesn't question me. Smart man.

"I don't give a fuck if the world's burning down," I growl. "You don't let her walk out that door."

"Yes, Sheriff."

I hold him there a moment longer, making damn sure he understands the weight of what I'm putting on him. Because this isn't just a job. It's a death sentence if he screws it up.

Finally, I let go, exhale deeply through my nose. "Thank you," I mutter, the words foreign in my mouth, but true. "For coming."

Haywood nods again, more firmly this time. "You can count on me, boss."

I step back, scanning the house one last time. The hall light glows warm through the curtains, casting the illusion of home, of safety. She'll think I'm still here if she stirs. She'll roll over, see the glow, and believe. That'll have to be enough.

Because I'm the sheriff, and I'm going hunting.

I head for my truck, keys already biting into my palm, my heart beating in time with the ticking of my watch.

2:36 a.m.

Every second from here could mean the difference between life and death. And if Moore's touched her friends… if he's waiting for me inside that house…. He's already a dead man.

I drive like a fucking man possessed. Speedometer needle pinned, tires eating asphalt, siren lighting up the night. The truck bucks under me, engine growling like it knows the rage burning through my blood. By the time I barrel onto Constance's street, my watch reads **2:41 a.m.**

Two patrol cars already sit crooked at the curb, lights spinning red and blue across the clapboard houses. I kill my siren and leap out before the cruiser's fully stopped, boots hitting gravel hard enough to shake my teeth.

The officers straighten when they see me, but I don't waste breath on pleasantries. "Debrief."

One clears his throat. "Nothing to report, Sheriff. House is dark. Silent."

Silent. The word slithers down my spine, wrong. Too neat. Too clean.

"Put the door in," I order. My voice is a growl, final.

We move fast. Guns drawn. One officer rams the door with his shoulder until the frame splinters, and then we're inside, shouting commands into shadows.

"Sheriff's department! Hands where I can see 'em!"

Nothing.

I stalk down the hall, past the sagging wallpaper and overturned shoe rack, every sense on edge. When I hit the kitchen, the world stills.

On the counter, beneath the dim light of a single bulb, lies a knife. Clean. Laid out deliberate. Waiting.

And beside it—three Polaroids.

My stomach drops into ice as I step closer.

Elaine. Dead.

Michael. Dead.

And then—fuck.

Summer.

Her picture isn't new; I recognize the background. The diner. But it isn't just the photo. Someone's taken a marker to it. Drawn a thick black noose around her neck, the rope trailing off the edge of the paper. My hand shakes. My vision tunnels.

"Sheriff!" an officer calls from deeper in the house. "Empty! No one's here."

Empty.

No. This isn't nothing. This isn't silence. This is a message. A warning.

A trap.

I step back, chest heaving, sweat prickling across my shoulders even as the air feels like ice.

2:49 a.m.

I glance at my watch again. Time slipping away too fast.

I tear my phone from my pocket, thumb hitting Haywood's number before the thought fully forms.

It rings. And rings. And rings.

Panic claws at me, something I've spent my whole life keeping buried, but it's here now, bleeding into every crack.

Then—finally—an answer.

But it's not Haywood's voice.

Chapter 27
Ten Seconds
Summer

The shout wakes me first—a deep, guttural sound that splits the silence clean in two.

Then comes the bang. Loud. Violent. It rips through the dark.

The walls shake with it. My body jerks upright, heart clawing its way into my throat. For a second, I can't breathe, can't even process what's happening—until the next sound comes.

A gunshot. Loud and close.

"Jacob?" The whisper rips out of me before I can stop it, raw and useless in the empty room.

No answer.

My chest tightens until it feels like my ribs are caving in. I stumble out of bed, feet tangling in the sheets, nearly crashing to the floor as the realization hits me like a knife to the gut.

What if it's him? What if Jacob's been shot?

He's always promised me the house was safe, untouchable, like no one could ever break through these walls. But he never told me what to do if someone did. He never gave me a plan. Because he never expected to leave me alone to deal with it.

And now—God—maybe he's not just gone. Maybe he's dead.

I stagger into the en-suite, slam the door shut, and lock it with trembling hands. My back presses against the wood, my breath a

1

stuttered gasp. Silence stretches thin, brittle. My pulse is too loud, crashing in my ears.

Then—screams.

Not Jacob.

Other voices. High. Terrified.

Female.

Constance? Adelaide?

No. No, they're safe at home.

My legs shake, and I slide down the door, palms pressed over my mouth to smother the sobs. The screams keep coming, clawing at the walls, closer, closer—until the sound turns jagged and raw and the house doesn't feel like a house anymore.

It feels like a slaughterhouse, and I'm the next animal in line.

I press my ear to the door, straining so hard the wood digs into my skin.

Nothing.

The screams have stopped. The silence is worse—thick, suffocating. Like someone waiting. I force myself to my feet, legs trembling, and creep toward the window. Every board of the floor groans like it's betraying me. My hands shake as I peel back the curtain just enough to peek outside.

A cop car. But it's not Jacobs.

I scan the road again, breath fogging the glass. That's when I see it.

A black SUV. Its windows are tinted, the kind of dark that swallows light. My heart lurches. Detectives. Maybe it's them. Maybe Maddox or Navarro came back to check on me. Maybe Jacob sent them. The hope is weak, but it's enough to keep me standing.

Then a phone rings. It shrieks through the house, loud and violent, so out of place it makes me jump. The sound drills into my skull, bouncing off the walls, echoing in every corner.

Ring. Ring. Ring.

I freeze, staring at the shadow of the handset in the hall below, just visible through the crack in the bedroom door. Should I make a run and grab the device and beg whoever's on the other end for help?

The ringing claws through me, dragging me toward it, but my feet won't move.

And then—silence.

A breathless second of relief.

Until a new sound slips through the line, low and jagged, amplified by the stillness of the house.

A voice.

"Hello, Sheriff."

Deep. Male. Drawn-out like he knows exactly how those two words will land.

The air leaves my lungs all at once. A warmth spreads down my thighs before I even realize what's happened. My body's given up on me, humiliating me as if to remind me I'm prey. Just prey.

The sound of a cell being tossed to the floor rattles through my bones, but the voice doesn't vanish. I hear it again.

Low. Groaning. Coming from the hall.

I stumble backward, shaking so hard I slam into the vanity. My breath tears ragged through my throat as the truth detonates in my chest.

Jacob isn't here.

My fingers scrabble for the lock, twisting it hard enough to bite into my skin. The bolt slides home with a loud click.

I sink down against door, pulse thrashing. My body curls in on itself, rocking, rocking, as I press my hand over my mouth to keep from screaming.

Because now I know. This house isn't impenetrable. Not without him.

The first slam rattles the frame. The second makes the mirror over the sink jump against the wall. By the third, my heart is beating so hard I'm convinced it'll burst through my ribs.

The window. It's small, too small, but it's the only chance I have. I grab the chrome counter mirror, hands slick with sweat, and hurl it against the glass. The mirror explodes in my grip, shards biting into my palms, skin splitting. Blood slicks my fingers instantly, dripping down onto the tiles. I don't feel it. Don't care. I snatch what's left and smash again, and again, desperation pounding through me harder than the fists at the door.

Another slam. Another crack of wood splintering.

I scream as the bolt tears free, the door flying open with a violence that shakes the walls.

"No, no, no—" The words tumble out broken, useless, as I turn toward them.

And then I see them. Three men.

Two of them with their fists wrapped tight in hair, yanking heads back. Knives pressed to pale throats.

Constance. Adelaide.

The world tilts. My stomach twists so violently I choke.

Constance's face is a mess, smeared red across her cheek, her lip split and swelling.

Adelaide's hair is wild and tangled, strands wrapped through the fingers of the beast who holds her there. Their eyes are wide, wild, locked on me—they make my soul splinter.

They fought. God, they fought. And now they're here. Held like offerings.

The third man steps forward.

Long, dark curls hang damp around his face, shadowing eyes that gleam with something colder than death. His lips twist, slow, deliberate, into a smile that doesn't reach his eyes.

He doesn't need to speak. His presence alone fills the room, crawling over my skin like oil. Every instinct in me screams to back away, but there's nowhere to go. The broken window behind me is jagged teeth, the air reeking of blood and fear, and the only thing standing between me and them is distance—and distance means nothing.

I press my bleeding hands to the counter, shaking so violently the shards grind deeper into my skin. My pulse hammers in my ears, drowning out everything but the sound of Constance's choked whimper, Adelaide's gut-wrenching gasp as the knives press harder. And still—he walks closer.

The man with the long dark curls and a devastating jawline. But it's his eyes that finish me.

Blue. Not just blue—scorching, searing, the hot side of a flame. Eyes I've seen before. Eyes that danced when they looked at me, that pretended to care. Eyes I trusted.

Benny's eyes.

My breath tears out of me like I've been punched.

"Summer," he says, and the name sounds wrong in his mouth, twisted, cruel. He spreads his arms, as if this is some long-awaited reunion. "We finally get to meet in person." His grin widens, merciless. "I'm Jackson. These delightful gentlemen are Donnie and Vince." He jerks his head at the men restraining Constance and Adelaide. Their knives glint under the bathroom light, pressed tighter to the girls' pale throats.

My heart detonates in my chest.

Jackson.

It's him.

Alive. Here. In my house.

His gaze never leaves mine as he continues, calm, almost casual. "Now, we've got about four minutes before your boyfriend stomps back through that door, so I won't waste time. Come with us. No fight, no screaming." He flicks his fingers toward Constance and Adelaide. "Or their throats are cut and we take you anyway. Simple as that."

My knees buckle, my body shaking so hard I have to grip the counter to stay upright. Blood drips from my torn hands onto the tiles, each drop loud in the silence.

He lifts his wrist, admiring the sleek black watch glinting against his skin. "You've got ten seconds." He snarls, as he starts to count down.

"Ten."

Constance thrashes, shaking her head violently, eyes wide, begging me not to move.

"Nine."

Adelaide tries to scream, but it's muffled by the rough hand clamped over her mouth. Her eyes glisten, terror spilling out in fat tears.

"Eight."

The sound tears out of me, raw and broken. "Stop."

"Seven."

Donnie—the fatter one, with a scruffy beard and eyes that shine with sick delight—drags the blade from Adelaide's throat and licks it, slow, obscene, before pressing it back against her skin.

"Six."

Adelaide convulses, a muffled cry spilling into the hand crushing her face.

"Five."

I can't breathe. The room is spinning, my chest caving in.

"Four."

Constance whimpers, shaking so hard the knife nicks her skin. A drop of blood slides down her neck.

"Three."

The knife presses deeper against Adelaide's fragile throat, blood starting to seep around the knife.

"Two."

My whole world cracks.

"Okay!" I scream, the sound ripping out of me so loud it scrapes my throat raw.

"Okay—I'll come!"

The word hangs in the air, broken and desperate, sealing my fate.

Chapter 28
Where is She?

Jacob

My foot is welded to the gas pedal, the engine howling so loud it drowns the pounding in my skull. The night is a blur—trees, streetlights, shadows streaking past like ghosts I can't outrun.

My chest is heaving, every breath a jagged knife carving me open from the inside. Tears prick my eyes before I can stop them, and then they're burning hot trails down my face. I can't wipe them. Can't see straight. Can't think of anything but her.

Summer.

Her laugh—soft, disbelieving the first time it ever slipped past her lips when I teased her.

Her hair—the way the light caught it that afternoon in her daddy's garden, when I knew, knew, she was mine whether she wanted to be or not.

Her mouth—the way it shaped my name last night when she told me she loved me.

The memory guts me, rips me raw. Because that might've been the first and last time I'll hear it.

My grip tightens on the wheel until my knuckles scream, but it doesn't matter. Nothing matters except the sound of that voice on the phone.

That voice.

Jackson.

I know it like I know the sound of my own gun loading. Rough. Mocking. That bastard's laugh still rattles in my bones from all those years ago when I first heard it echo through the courthouse.

He was in my house.

With her.

My stomach heaves. Rage and terror choke me so hard my vision goes white. I swerve, nearly clipping a tree, the branches scraping across the roof with a metallic shriek. I slam the wheel back straight, the tires screaming across gravel, only to fishtail near a dustbin and clip it hard. It skids, toppling behind me, scattering trash across the street.

I don't slow down.

I can't.

I can't get the picture out of my head—Summer, barefoot, bleeding, with that fucker's knife at her throat. Her wide eyes locked on me in terror I swore she'd never wear again.

My chest collapses, sobs tearing loose from somewhere deep and savage. I'm fucking crying—me. I never cry. But now? I can't stop. My vision blurs with salt, hands slippery on the wheel, my body shaking apart.

Because the man who's got her—the man who's touching her—is the one ghost I never thought I'd face again.

Jackson fucking Moore.

I've burned the radio lines raw, my voice still rattling inside my head as I gun it down the last stretch of road. Carter. Haywood. Every goddamn deputy I can reach.

Get there. Don't let anything happen to her.

If they've done their job, she'll be safe. She'll be on the sofa when I walk in—hair tangled from sleep, eyes wet with fear and anger, ready to scream at me for not telling her the truth about Constance and Adelaide. I'll take it. I'll take every ounce of her fury if it means she's still breathing.

We can get through anything. We have to.

I want to tell her that we'll move away. We'll start a new life. I'll give up my badge and we can stop running. Let's do it all properly. Let's do it her way. But I need to get back to her first.

I tear down the bend, back tires spitting gravel like shrapnel, and skid into the driveway. Headlights flash against steel.

I kill the engine and fling myself out of the truck, barely aware of the slam of the door behind me. My boots hit gravel, crunching hard, lungs burning as I sprint toward the porch. Relief flickers for half a second. They're here. She's safe.

Then my stomach drops. The front door yawns open. Not kicked. Not forced. Just open. Waiting.

"Fuck," I breathe, already moving faster, already knowing.

The first thing that hits me when I cross the threshold isn't sight —it's smell.

Thick. Metallic. The putrid stench of iron that no amount of bleach can hide. Blood.

The world narrows. My vision tunnels.

Haywood is slumped against the wall a few feet away, mouth open, a string of blood still trailing from the corner down his chin. There's a black hole in his chest the size of my fist. His gun's still in his hand, but cold.

For a second—one terrible, suspended second—I can't move. My deputy. My friend. Cut down in my house like he was nothing.

And then I hear it.

A muffled sound, wet with panic. A strangled cry that slices right through the haze.

Female.

Summer.

"SUMMER!" My throat rips as I scream her name, raw, primal. The walls shake with it. I'm already moving, boots pounding against the hardwood, my breath tearing out of me like gunfire.

I take the stairs three at a time, my body running on nothing but terror. My chest is a furnace, every inhale thick and choking. Her name leaves me again, louder, broken: "SUMMER!"

The door to my bedroom is shut. I slam through it so hard the hinges shriek. And what I see….

Constance and Adelaide.

They're on the floor, bound with rope that's dug into their wrists until they're bleeding. Gags stuffed into their mouths; their faces streaked with tears. Constance's nose is bloodied, her left eye swollen shut. Adelaide's hair is a tangled mess, chunks missing like someone's ripped it out by the fistful. Their eyes dart up to me the second I burst in, wide with desperation, screaming silently behind the cloth.

The air is thick with the smell of sweat and rope and fear.

But she isn't there. Summer isn't there.

My heart stops.

The world tilts sideways, the sound sucked right out of it.

My chest caves, but the next breath explodes out of me as a roar so violent it feels like it cracks my ribs. "WHERE IS SHE?!"

I tear across the room, my boots kicking the floor, the blood in my ears so loud it drowns out their muffled sobs.

I drop to my knees beside Constance, rip the gag out of her mouth so hard she cries out, spittle and blood streaking her chin. She gasps, choking, eyes wild.

But I don't hear her words. I only hear silence.

Because Summer's gone.

I pull out my pocketknife and slice through the rope that has her bound, and then she does the same for Adelaide.

Constance rips the gag out of Adelaide's mouth and pulls her close, trying to calm her, but the second her eyes lock on me she snaps. She's up in my face, shoving at my chest with all the strength she's got left. Adelaide staggers forward too, both of them pushing me, their voices like knives.

Constance screams. Her voice cracks. "You weren't here!"

Adelaide's hands are bloody, trembling as she shoves at me, shrieking.

But their words don't land.

Nothing lands.

There's only this high-pitched shriek drilling through my skull—like tinnitus cranked up until it feels like my brain's splitting. I press my palms to my ears, but it doesn't stop. The whole world is nothing but static.

My body moves on autopilot, staggering past them. I hit the en-suite doorway.

And freeze.

Blood.

It's everywhere. Smeared across the tile. Spattered up the wall. A mirror lies shattered across the floor, glittering with red where it caught her skin.

And the window—Christ. The tiny bathroom window is cracked, glass fractured like she tried to fight her way out. Even her small frame would never have fit. She must've known that. Must've been desperate enough to try anyway. She knew they were here. She fought to get away.

My knees give out.

I collapse onto the cold tile, my hands shaking as I reach out. My fingers land in the still-wet smear of her blood. It coats me instantly —tacky, warm. Proof.

Proof that I wasn't here. Proof that they touched her. Proof that I fucking failed.

My chest convulses and I fold in on myself, dragging my bloody hand over my face. The sob rips out of me before I can stop it, raw and animal, tearing my throat apart.

I don't care that Adelaide is screaming. I don't care that Constance is pounding her fists against my back. I don't care that Haywood is lying dead downstairs.

All I see is red.

All I hear is her voice, her laugh, her whispers tangled in my sheets, her saying she loved me.

And now silence.

Silence and blood.

I curl into the mess of it, my hand still buried in the stain she left behind, and I fucking sob. Not just in sadness. No. With the fury of a thousand wars carried in one body.

Carter bursts in, three more of my men on his heels. His face is pale, eyes blown wide when he takes in the blood, the smashed mirror, the wreckage of me curled on the tile like a fucking child.

He mutters something inaudible —then he's on me. A jug from

the sink slams against my skin, icy water spilling down my head and soaking through my shirt. The shock rips the static out of me in one savage tear, dragging the world back into focus.

"Snap the fuck out of it!" Carter roars, grabbing my collar, shaking me hard enough to rattle my teeth. "This isn't going to help her!"

And he's right. God help me, he's right.

My lungs claw for air, rage scorching through the grief. My body jerks upright before I even know I'm moving. My bloodied hand shoots out, finds Constance. I fist her collar, slam her back against the wall so hard the plaster cracks.

Her scream pierces the room, high and desperate.

"What the fuck happened?!" I bellow, the sound tearing out of my chest like it might rip me open. My grip on her tightens, too tight, and her small frame buckles under my hold. "TELL ME!"

Adelaide tries to drag me off, slapping at my arm, sobbing, "You're hurting her! Stop—please!"

But I can't stop. The need to know, to see, to understand what they did to Summer shreds through me. Constance's voice breaks as the words spill out in a torrent, every syllable a knife.

"They came—" She's choking, gasping around my grip. "They came to our house. Forced their way in—three of them—"

"Who?" My spit sprays her face, the snarl unrecognizable even to me.

"One was lanky—strong—he said his name was Vince. One was fat—rugged—Donnie. And then…." She whimpers. "Then there was Jackson."

The name is gasoline on open flame. My knuckles dig into her shoulder blades as I shove her harder against the wall, fury pounding through me.

Her head jerks in a desperate nod. "He was… big—dark curly hair—"

Images of him slam into me. His efforts to fight me off when I put him in cuffs. His smug face at the courthouse. Then I stop for a moment, and it hits me— his eyes. His features. He looked a lot like — Benny in a peculiar sort of way.

No. Surely not.

Adelaide's voice cuts in, frantic, breaking. "Donnie and Vince — th-they came for us. We — we tried, Jacob. We tried. But they were stronger."

Constance's body shakes in my grip as she blurts the rest, words tumbling over one another, a confession, an execution.

"They brought us here. We sat in the dark — watched you drive away. The second you were gone, they pulled in. We screamed — we fought — God, we fought. But Jackson...." Her voice cracks, dissolves into sobs — "He gave her a choice."

My blood freezes.

"What. Choice."

Constance sobs so hard she can barely breathe. "He said — he said if she didn't go with them — he'd cut our throats and take her anyway."

Her knees buckle under my grip. Adelaide sobs harder, covering her mouth.

"She handed herself over, Jacob," Constance cries, words tearing out of her like flesh from bone. "We tried — we tried — we begged her not to — but she handed herself over."

Silence drops like a guillotine. Her words cut deep. I feel it split me down the middle, leaving nothing but blood and hate in the hollowed-out cage of my chest.

Summer. My Summer. Choosing chains over their death. Offering herself up like a lamb to the slaughter.

And I wasn't here. I wasn't fucking here.

My grip slackens. Constance collapses against the wall, clutching her throat, sobbing. Adelaide hauls her into her arms, their bodies folding together on the bloody tile.

I stagger back. The room tilts. I press my palm to the wall, my breath tearing, and I swear I can still hear Summer's voice — her soft, trembling "I love you" — before she was dragged into the dark.

The sound nearly buckles me. But then the rage fills the cracks. Jackson Moore has her.

And I will tear this earth apart until I get her back.

Chapter 29
Hell Has a Door
Summer

Hands tear at me before the word is even out of my mouth.

"Okay."

That's all it takes.

My scalp screams as fingers twist into my hair, yanking me down the stairs so hard my knees buckle. My bare feet skid across tile, then scrape raw against gravel. I can't see Constance or Adelaide anymore—I hear them though, muffled shouts cracking through gags.

Their voices stab into me deeper than any knife. They drag me through the hall, and I see Officer Haywood, slumped against the wall, a gun in his hand and a hole in his chest. Smoke still rises from the open cavity, and the smell— blood, burnt hair, rotting meat all combined into one sour scent.

The night is black and wide and cruel. Waiting at the edge of the driveway is the SUV. Black paint, black windows, a beast crouched in the dark with its mouth open.

I'm shoved inside. My shoulder slams against metal, pain biting up my arm. The stench hits instantly—cigarettes, stale sweat, leather that's soaked up too much history.

The locks drop down. That sound is louder than the slam of the door. Louder than my heartbeat that booms in my chest.

I'm pinned between bodies, knees jammed into my thighs, a gun resting casual against my side as if it belongs there. The weight of it is worse than the cold. Worse than the stink.

I can't breathe. My chest tries, ribs wrenching apart, but the air tastes poisoned.

The SUV hums to life. Gravel crunches. My stomach tips as the house slides away behind us, shrinking, shrinking—until it's gone.

And that's when the real pain starts.

It isn't knives or fists. It's in my head. The moment Jacob pulls into the drive, he's going to know something's wrong. He's going to see Constance and Adelaide bound and gagged. He's going to see blood smeared on the en-suite tile. He's going to realize I'm not there.

I see it in my mind—his face shattering.

My throat closes around a sob. I bite down hard, clench my jaw until my teeth ache. I can't cry. If I cry, they win.

"Sensitive," one of them mutters.

The other drags on his cigarette, exhales into the stale air. Smoke curls and twists, stinging my eyes until they water. No one says Jacob's name. No one needs to. He's the ghost in the backseat with me, the one thing tethering me to the world.

And then— "Good girl. You came without so much as a scream."

His words are low, deadly. And that voice. Jackson's voice sends a shiver crawling through my core.

The car bumps over a pothole, jolting me forward. My knees scrape against vinyl. The gun digs harder into my ribs, and I hold my breath, waiting for the bang that doesn't come.

The SUV settles back into a steady growl, chewing up the miles, carrying me further from Jacob with every heartbeat.

And still—no one talks.

Not like men. Not like humans. Just fragments. Laughter. Snorts. The kind of sounds wolves make before they eat.

My body feels wrong, too big and too small at once. My skin doesn't fit anymore. I keep thinking if I just move, if I just shift an inch, I might slip out of myself altogether and leave this shell behind.

I press my forehead against the glass. Cold seeps into my skull, numbing. Outside there's nothing—fields, trees, shadows layered over shadows. The world looks empty, like it's already written me off.

But Jacob will come.

I whisper it in my head, over and over, timing the words with my breaths.

Jacob will come. Jacob will come. Jacob will come.

But the SUV doesn't slow.

And Jackson doesn't speak again.

The SUV rocks around a bend. My shoulder scrapes the door. My palms itch for Jacob's grip, Jacob's steadiness, Jacob's voice telling me what to do.

Another drag of smoke. Another laugh. Then—Jackson finally speaks again.

"Funny thing," he murmurs, almost to himself. "I thought you'd put up a fight."

Heat floods my face. My nails dig into the vinyl seat.

"But you just walked out," he laughs, a deep, guttural sound.

The others snicker, low and evil.

"Don't mistake her, boss" he says. "I bet she's got claws."

"I know," Jackson replies, smooth as honey laced with glass. "But claws are nothing if they don't draw blood."

I squeeze my eyes shut. His words crawl over me, hot and cruel, seeping under my skin like poison.

"The sheriff's not coming."

I snap my head around before I can stop myself. His eyes catch mine—blue, bright, merciless. And he smiles.

"He's already lost." A pause. "You know what fascinates me, Summer?" he asks. "Choice. People always think they have one. Like you, back in that bathroom. Thought you were saving those girls." He flicks the bud of his cigarette out of the window then turns back to look at me.

My chest locks tight. My pulse slams so hard it aches in my teeth.

He leans into me, taking up too much space. I don't have to look to know his face is close. His breath touches the side of my neck, hot and sour with smoke.

"But you didn't save them. Did you?" His tone curls, almost gentle. "You just postponed it. The same way daddy's death was postponed. It's a shame your mother was there. I didn't want her—not really. Too old to sell. Too ugly to fuck."

I bite my lip until the skin splits. He wants me to answer. He wants me to break my vow of silence.

Jackson doesn't let up.

"And those two girls… they'll still die—they know too much. You just won't be there to see it. And you'll never know when. That's the worst part, isn't it? You'll picture it every night. Them screaming. Them dying. And you'll wonder if it happened already. Or if it's happening right then. While you're locked in a room, praying your sheriff still cares."

I squeeze my hands into fists in my lap, nails carving crescents into my palms. I don't want to imagine it, but I do. Constance's big eyes, wide with terror. Adelaide's hair yanked, her throat cut open while I sit here useless. My stomach twists so hard I gag.

The man beside me laughs under his breath.

Jackson keeps going, unhurried.

"Thing is, you think you made a sacrifice," he hums, his tone soft as he reaches to stroke a hand over my shoulder. "That's sweet. That's noble. But you don't get to make noble choices in my world. Every choice is a trap. A leash. And you just put the collar on yourself."

I don't answer, don't shrug him away, I just stare at my reflection in the window — pale skin, hair falling in my face, eyes hollow. A woman I almost don't recognize. A woman Jacob promised he'd protect.

Jacob.

He'll come. He'll come. He'll come.

The mantra stutters now, tripping over itself. Jackson's voice gnaws at the edges.

"You think Jacob's strong?" he asks suddenly, like he's plucked the thought right out of me. "That uniform makes him something more than a man? It doesn't. He's just meat with a badge. And meat rots."

"Shut up."

The words rip out before I can stop them. Small. Shaky. But they're there.

Jackson laughs softly, the sound like broken glass underfoot.

"There she is," he murmurs. "I was waiting for her."

His hand moves fast. Fingers tighten on my shoulder as he pulls me, forcing me to face him. His eyes burn blue in the dim light, bright as the flame he wants me to walk into.

"Don't tell me to shut up," he says, low and rough. "Not unless you want to lose your tongue."

My lungs claw for air. My jaw aches under his grip. But I don't look away. If I look away, I lose.

He shoves me back against the seat. My skull cracks against the window, stars bursting in my vision. The others laugh. My throat burns. My eyes sting. I force the tears back.

And Jackson leans away, satisfied. He lights a cigarette like he didn't just crush me in his hand. Smoke swirls, thick and choking, filling the SUV until every breath tastes like ash.

"Jacob will find me." My voice is raw, hoarse. But steady.

Jackson exhales smoke toward the roof, lazy and amused.

"Jacob will die trying." He laughs. "You know what the best part is?" His voice is a snake winding closer. "You'll hate me. You'll fight me. And then, piece by piece, you'll need me. You'll beg for my attention. My approval. My touch. That's how this works. That's how Jacob did it, right?"

My mouth floods with bile. I swallow it back, choking on it.

"Once I've broken you," Jackson breathes, "you won't remember he ever existed."

Headlights sweep across corrugated steel. Not a home. Not even a ruin. A warehouse. A place built to store cargo, not people. And yet it's waiting for me like a coffin with its lid already half-open.

The engine dies. And the driver steps out. He slams his door and comes to open ours. Child-locked I presume, designed to stop me from trying to escape. But I wasn't stupid enough to even try. The cold night air pours in before I can brace for it. A hand fists around my bicep and yanks me out into the gravel. My knees hit jagged stone, skin tearing through thin fabric. I don't make a sound. Not because it doesn't hurt, but because I won't give them my pain.

The warehouse looms closer with every drag of their hands on my arms. Its steel siding is new—too new. I catch it in the light, panels without rust, bolts that still gleam. Fresh padlocks on the side doors.

The main entrance yawns open with a groan, metal on metal. A stench rushes out—bleach and sweat and something underneath both, sour and alive. My stomach rolls, bile working its way up my throat, leaving me no choice but to throw up into the gravel. Donnie and Vince laugh at me, but Jackson hands me a handkerchief. I wipe my mouth with it, then throw it back at him, hitting his chest before he catches it— stopping it from landing in the dirt.

He shakes his head, then clicks his fingers and gestures toward the entrance. A hand finds my arm again and pulls me toward the open doors.

Inside, it doesn't look like a warehouse. The floor has been scrubbed to concrete shine. Fluorescents burn down in strips, bright enough to erase shadow but not enough to feel like daylight. The air is wrong—dead air, recirculated through fans too small for the space. And everywhere I look, pieces of someone else's nightmare.

A row of mattresses on the floor, lined up military neat. Stained, sagging, each with a blanket folded at the end like a joke. Folding chairs stacked in one corner. A long table covered in bottles of water, makeup palettes, scissors. A mirror propped against the wall, streaked with powder and fingerprints.

And the women. At least a dozen. Huddled together on one side like cattle corralled against the railings. Thin. Silent. Their eyes flicker up, then down again, as if looking too long might earn punishment. Some wear dresses that aren't theirs, fabric too tight across their shoulders. One of them clutches another's hand so hard their knuckles are white.

My knees lock. My lungs hitch. This isn't a holding cell. It's a showroom.

Vince whistles low. "Look at 'em, Summer. Your new sorority."

Donnie snorts, dragging a cigarette out of his pocket. "Sororities for college girls. These are just playthings."

Their laughter ricochets off the walls, too loud, too casual. Like this is normal. Like this is what every Tuesday looks like to them.

Jackson doesn't laugh. He watches me take it all in; head tilted like he's studying, waiting for the precise second I'll crack.

"You see it now," he says softly. "You thought Jacob's world was the worst it could get. But Jacob kept you in a dollhouse. This—" He gestures to the warehouse, to the rows, to the eyes that don't dare rise. "—this is what happens when the door to Hell opens."

His voice isn't raised—it doesn't need to be. It lands in me, hitting me straight in the empty shell of my chest, the cavity where my heart once lived. But now, my heart belongs to Jacob, he holds it in his hands, and until he finds me—until I'm back in his arms—the space will remain empty.

They pull me forward, past the girls, toward a staircase that doesn't belong in this place. Steel, bolted to the wall, leading up to a second-floor platform with glass-walled rooms overlooking the floor like observation decks. Offices, probably, before. Now—control towers.

Every step echoes. My bare feet hurt on the grated steel, but the hand pushing me forward keeps me moving. I catch glimpses as we climb—another door, barred from the outside; cameras mounted high on every corner; a red light blinking like a pulse.

Jackson walks behind me, close enough that I feel his presence like static, close enough that if I stumble, he'll be the one to catch me just so he can drop me harder.

At the top, a glass-fronted room. It's empty except for a chair, a table, and a rack of clothing draped in silk and lace. Dresses hung by color, lingerie folded in neat piles. Like a boutique carved into the bones of a slaughterhouse.

Waiting for me.

A woman appears. Too much makeup plastered over a face carved by decades. Hair fried into tight curls, skin leathered and orange. She chews her gum slow, eyes flat, like she's clocked out of her own body years ago.

"Got another one for you, Brenda" Vince says, shoving me toward her.

"This is the girl I was telling you about…. The one for me," Jackson announces with his chin tipped too high, like he's just accomplished the ultimate mission.

Brenda doesn't blink, looking me up and down like I'm a mannequin she's already bored of. "Needs paint," she mutters. "And red."

She plucks a dress from the rack; Silk, crimson, slit up the thigh and tosses it on the chair. Then sets down a tray—powder, brushes, tubes of lipstick like scalpels.

Jackson leans on the glass, arms folded, watching everything. He doesn't interfere. He doesn't need to. His presence alone pins me in place.

Brenda jerks her chin at me. "Clothes off."

The words land like a whip crack. I don't move. I swallow hard as my throat tightens.

Donnie laughs. "She's shy."

"Leave," Jackson snaps, his eyes never leaving me. "All of you, out."

Donnie and Brenda look at each other, and then back at Jackson. He raises his brows at them, frustration building from impatience. Eventually, they do as he asks and leave the room.

As soon as the door clicks, he speaks, "From this moment on, the only person to see you bare will be me. Your skin is mine. For my eyes only." His eyes trail the shape of my body, the pajamas Jacob gave me still hang loose on me. "Now… change," he orders.

I look for the door, for the idea of finding any way out, but there's nowhere. Even if I got out of this room, they'd chase me, catch me, and maybe the dark web booking system would re-open. From what he's saying, he wants me to himself, and that gives me more opportunity to eventually escape. If he wants me, and only me, he won't leave me here, maybe he'll take me somewhere else, somewhere I can run from. Somewhere I stand a chance of escape.

He pulls his pistol from his back and places it on his lap. A warning without words.

So, my hands shake as I reach for the hem of Jacob's nightshirt. I tell myself its survival. Just survival. Not submission. My skin crawls under his stare as each layer peels away.

Jackson's never looks away for a second. He doesn't smirk. He doesn't leer. He studies. Like he's mapping out where to cut first. And when the last piece of fabric hits the floor, he speaks.

"Perfect," he says softly. "Just the way I pictured."

SHERIFF
ROSEFIELD

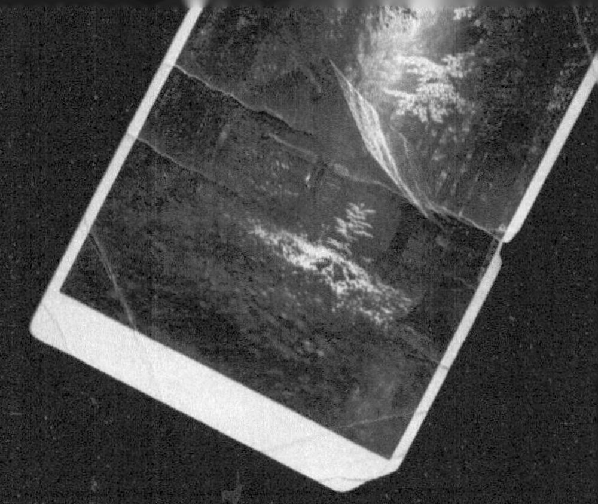

Chapter 30
Find Me Anywhere
Jacob

The station reeks of burnt coffee and sweat. Too bright. Too loud. Phones ringing, printers stuttering, radios spitting static. Every sound chews through my skull.

Constance and Adelaide are at the hospital. Navarro and Maddox, along with some Broadachre badges, have gone to see them. To see if they can dig out any information I might have missed.

I've been staring at the same bank of CCTV monitors for an hour, and I still can't see her. Nothing but headlights and shadows. SUVs. Pickups. Same body shapes, same goddamn plates that come up clean. Too clean. Stolen. Swapped. Scrubbed.

Jackson Moore didn't claw his way out of a maximum-security cell just to leave me breadcrumbs.

"Roll back camera six," I bark, throat raw.

Carter's at the keyboard. His hands don't shake, but his jaw does. He hasn't looked me in the eye once since we walked in here. He pulls the footage back, frame by frame. Grainy, washed-out, some gas station outside town. An SUV pulling through. License plate crystal clear. Useless. It belongs to a grandma three counties over who hasn't left her damn driveway in a year.

I slam my fist into the table. The monitor's flicker. My knuckles split open again, blood slick against the steel edge.

"Fuck!"

"Sheriff—" Carter starts, but I turn so fast he shuts up.

There are three others in the room. Young deputies. Fresh. Faces pale like they've seen ghosts just being in here with me. Maybe they have.

"Run the plate against out-of-state databases," I snarl.

"We already did," one of them says quietly. "Nothing. It's clean."

Of course it is. Of course it fucking is.

I throw my chair back, rise to my feet and pace back and forth. The walls are closing in, suffocating me with the hum of machines and the stench of failure. Every second she's out there with him— every second—it's a knife turning deeper. I see her face, her hair, the first time I saw her in her parents' garden. That smile that ruined me before I even knew her name. And now she's with him. With Jackson. My tears sting but they don't fall. Not here. Not in front of them.

I spin and sweep the desk clear with both arms. Paper, coffee cups, radios, files—everything crashes to the floor. The monitors rattle, one topples, screen splintering into spiderweb glass.

"Sheriff!" Carter barks.

I grab the edge of the next desk and flip it, wood splintering, metal legs screeching against tile. One of the young ones jolts back so fast he trips over his own chair.

"WHERE THE FUCK IS HE?" I roar, voice tearing out of me. "WHERE THE FUCK DID HE TAKE HER?"

Nobody answers.

Because they don't know.

Because Jackson will always be five steps ahead.

Because I should've seen this coming.

I drive my fist into the drywall. It caves, dust spilling down, blood smearing into white. I don't stop. I punch again, again, until my knuckles are pulp and the hole's wide enough to shove my whole arm through.

"Sheriff—stop," Carter snaps, grabbing at my shoulder. I whirl, grab his shirtfront, slam him into the wall so hard his head bounces off the plaster. His eyes widen but he doesn't raise a hand. Doesn't fight me.

"She handed herself over," I snarl, the words ripping out of me before I can stop them. My breath comes out ragged, splintering on the edges. "She walked out that door willingly. To save her friends."

The fury builds, choking me. "She sacrificed herself," I hiss, stepping closer. "Handed the damn axe to the executioner and bowed her head to the block."

The room goes still, the echo of my voice hanging between us like smoke.

Carter swallows. His throat bobs against my grip. His voice stays steady. "Then you'd better keep your head if you want to get her back."

I shove him away like he burned me. My chest heaves. My hands shake with blood and plaster dust. The room's silent now, except for the buzz of the monitors that survived my tantrum.

I drag both hands down my face, smearing red across my skin. The taste of iron lingers on my lips where it seeped into the cracks of my knuckles.

Carter straightens his shirt. He doesn't look at me with fear, not like the others. Just exhaustion. The same exhaustion I feel grinding me down to the bone.

"They moved everything," I mutter. "The warehouse, the women —wherever they were keeping them before, it's gone. They wouldn't risk it while Jackson was inside. But now—"

"Now he's out," Carter finishes for me.

I nod once. Slow. Final.

"He'll want somewhere temporary. Somewhere no one's watching. Close enough to move fast. Far enough nobody stumbles on it by accident."

The others exchange glances. One pipes up, voice uncertain. "It's going to take time to find it, boss. Finding where he's at isn't going to be easy. He could be anywhere."

I turn on him, slow. His face drains of colour.

"Then find me anywhere," I growl.

Nobody moves. Nobody breathes.

I know the truth. Jackson's not going to slip up. He's not going to leave a trail. And every wasted minute brings me closer to the one image I can't erase—the look in her eyes when she realizes I didn't come in time.

I grip the back of a chair and squeeze until the metal groans.

Carter clears his throat, rubbing the back of his neck. His voice cuts through the static in my skull.

"There are more men here tonight," he says, quieter now. "Not all of them active. Not all of them… official."

I lift my head. My vision blurs with fury and plaster dust, but I focus on him. "What the fuck does that mean?"

He doesn't flinch. He just jerks his chin toward the far end of the hall. Through the glass, I see two figures sitting in the dark—shadows hunched over paper cups, cigarette smoke curling like ghosts above their heads.

Carter steps closer, lowering his voice like he's letting me in on something no one else is meant to hear.

"Mason's here. You remember him."

Of course, I remember Mason. Thickset, always chewing toothpicks, retired five years back. He looks older now, shoulders bent under grief he never put down. His hand trembles when he lifts the cup. Not with age. With rage.

"His girl," Carter reminds me, eyes heavy, "was nine years old when a stray bullet from one of Jackson's men tore through their house. Playing with dolls on the goddamn floor. Mason's never let it go."

My chest tightens. I remember the call. The body bag so small it barely filled the stretcher. Mason's wife screaming until her voice broke.

"And Grove," Carter adds.

Grove was tall, wiry, the kind of man who carries his grief like a noose around his neck.

"His daughter dated Jackson," Carter says flatly. "For a few months. Thought he was some charming bastard. Then one day—she was gone. No sign of her. No evidence. Just… gone. Grove's been chasing whispers ever since."

Mason and Grove aren't lawmen tonight. They're executioners waiting for the rope.

I drag my hand over my mouth, smearing blood and sweat. My heartbeat's a hammer, pounding harder with every breath.

"They want in," Carter says. "They've been waiting for the opportunity to get their hands on him. For years."

I study them through the glass. The way Mason leans forward, elbows on his knees, eyes burning through the smoke. The way Grove's still as a predator, coiled tight, waiting for the signal.

They don't want justice. They want vengeance. And for the first time tonight, I don't feel so goddamn alone in mine.

I push off the wall, my boots crunching over broken glass from the monitor I smashed. My voice is a rasp, torn raw.

"Then brief them."

Carter hesitates. "Sheriff, we need to—"

"I. Want. Them. In."

He jerks his chin to one of the younger deputies, who bolts out the door to fetch them.

When Mason steps in, the room shifts. His presence is heavy, a storm carried on thick shoulders. He spits his toothpick into the trash and plants himself at the table, eyes never leaving mine. Grove follows, quieter, like glass hidden in sand. His face is gaunt, his hands white-knuckled around his cup. He doesn't blink. Just stares through the smoke like he's already seeing Jackson's corpse.

Both men carry grief like it's fused to their bones. Both men would burn this town to ash for one clean shot at Jackson Moore.

And right now, they're mine.

The office door slams open so hard the glass rattles in its frame.

Haywood's wife storms in, hair tangled, eyes swollen red like she's been drowning in her own tears. She doesn't even hesitate—she makes straight for me, her hand already arcing up.

I catch her wrist mid-swing. My grip is iron, my pulse a war drum in my ears.

"You son of a bitch!" she screams, voice cracked and raw. She thrashes against me, nails clawing at air, trying to land another hit.

Her grief is a wild animal. A mother bear with her cub ripped from her.

Carter's moving instantly, but I don't let go.

Her heel slams into my shin, hard enough to make bone vibrate. She doesn't want words—she wants blood. My blood.

Her breath is ragged, soaked in whiskey and salt. "You killed him! You fucking killed him!"

I grit my teeth so hard I feel enamel grind. "He was guarding Summer," I snap back. "He died doing his job."

"Job?" Her laugh is broken glass. Her eyes lock on mine—full of hate, full of agony. "You call it a job? He died because of her."

The room goes quiet. Mason shifts in his chair. Grove's jaw ticks. Even Carter stiffens.

Her finger jabs the air, trembling, like she can stab me from across the room. "All this death. All this blood. For what? For a bit of young, pretty pussy you couldn't resist? For some girl half your age instead of a decent woman who could've given you a real life?"

Her words detonate in me. Every syllable is napalm.

Summer's face flashes in my head—terrified, brave, stubborn, hers—and then it's drowned by the image of her in Jackson's hands.

I see red.

My voice rips out of me, low, guttural, a threat cut straight from hell.

"You ever speak about her like that again," I snarl, yanking her closer, "and I will remove your fucking voice box with my bare hands."

Her mouth falls open, a ragged inhale like she's choking on air. The whole room freezes. Even Carter looks at me like I've just drawn a line we can't ever walk back from.

"Sheriff," Carter snaps, stepping in between us, his hand on my chest, pushing me back. His tone isn't a plea. It's a warning. "Enough."

I let go of her wrist. She stumbles back, clutching it to her chest like I've broken her bones. Tears streak down her cheeks, streaks of mascara bleeding into skin.

"You're a monster," she whispers. Her voice is thin, brittle, but it cuts. "You brought him to his grave."

She turns on her heel and bolts, the echo of her sobs tearing down the hallway like sirens, then silence drops heavy.

My hands shake. Not from regret. Not from shame. From the fact that she's half-right. Haywood is dead. And Summer —

I shove a chair so hard it splinters against the wall. The sound makes everyone flinch, but I don't care.

Carter exhales through his nose, deep, steadying. He nods to Mason and Grove, like telling them silently: this is what we're working with.

And Mason, the old bastard, just leans forward, his voice gravel and hate.

"Good," he mutters. "Because if she thinks this is about pussy, she doesn't know what kind of hell Jackson Moore's about to bring down. You don't stop him now, Sheriff—every man in this room is gonna be worrying about more than pussy."

The words settle like stone, and I know he's right.

Chapter 31
A Life in Velvet & Chains
Summer

They drag me out of the office like I'm nothing but luggage. My heels skid across the floor, wrists bruised from where they've been gripping me. The black SUV waits by the door like a hearse.

"Get in," Donnie barks, shoving me forward.

I stumble, slam into the metal, the chill biting straight through my skin. The door yanks open and I'm shoved inside. Donnie slides into the driver's seat, keys already in his hand, humming like this is just another job.

Jackson climbs in beside me. Too close. His dark curls fall across his face, eyes catching mine like hooks. He doesn't look tired. He doesn't look scared. He looks thrilled.

He's seen me bare, and since that very moment his pupils have exploded—his eyes not leaving my body for more than a second.

Vince leans against the front passenger door. He's grinning, already lighting another cigarette. "I'll catch up later," he drawls. His gaze slides past me to the cluster of women still huddled on the sofa inside. His tongue wets his bottom lip. "That brunette's still got a little fire in her. I'll put it out."

My stomach lurches. Acid burns my throat. I want to scream, to claw his eyes out, to drag her out of this hellhole myself—but the door slams and he's gone. And I'm trapped.

The SUV rumbles to life, gravel spitting under the tyres as Donnie pulls us away. My pulse hammers so hard I feel it in my teeth.

Then Jackson leans back, stretching out like he owns the world. His arm rests against the tinted window. The other hand drops low —landing heavy on my thigh.

I freeze. Every nerve in my body screams at once.

His thumb strokes once, slow, a mockery of tenderness. "You're prettier up close," he murmurs, voice dripping heat and rot. "Thought maybe he exaggerated."

I snap before I can stop myself. I spit—hot, fast—right into his smug, flame-blue eyes.

For a heartbeat, silence.

Then his palm cracks across my face so hard the world tilts sideways. My cheek burns. The sting echoes through my skull.

But he's smiling. Wide. Wicked. "Mmm," he hums, leaning closer, breath hot against my ear. "I love a woman with fight."

I press back against the door, ribs aching, the taste of iron on my tongue. My voice shakes, but I force it out anyway. "Don't touch me."

He laughs. It's soft, almost sweet—and that makes it worse. "Touching you is just the start, sweetheart." His hand snakes higher, gripping, squeezing. "Where we're going? No one will hear your screams. Not the cops. Not your sheriff. Not a single soul. There won't be an inch of your body that I haven't had in my hands."

Donnie chuckles up front, tapping the steering wheel in rhythm with my heart. "She'll learn," he mutters.

And I know he's right. Out here, no one can hear me.

No one but them.

Jackson's hand presses back on my thigh like he's staking his claim. The leather of the seat squeaks with each bump of the road, the SUV growling low as Donnie takes us further from anything familiar. My cheek burns where he hit me, the heat crawling into my jaw.

My voice comes out raw. "Why?" I manage. My throat tightens, but I force it out again, louder. "Why take me there? Why dress me up like some —" I choke on the word. "—like some whore?"

Jackson turns his head slow, like a cat who's already decided the mouse has nowhere left to run. His grin doesn't falter. If anything, it culminates.

"Because, sweetheart," he drawls, his voice sliding under my skin like oil, "you needed to look the part when you arrive. First impressions matter. When you meet the staff, they'll expect you polished. Perfect. Not rocking up wearing another man's pajamas."

My blood goes cold. "Staff?" The word scrapes like glass up my throat.

He leans closer, his curls brushing my shoulder, breath hot against my ear. "Oh yes. Staff. Who'll take care of your daily needs in your new home. The kind of place where ladies like you stay nice and safe… as long as they behave."

His fingers tap-tap-tap against my thigh, a rhythm as steady as a metronome, each beat a threat.

"And if I don't?" My voice is too quick, too sudden, but I can't swallow the question back.

His eyes spark like blue flame. He tilts his head, amused, almost gentle—like he's explaining bedtime rules to a child. "That little warehouse you just saw? With the lingerie racks, the bruised-up pets, the ones too broken to lift their heads?" His smile widens, but there's nothing human in it. "That's where you'll end up. Passed around until there's nothing left worth selling."

The air punches out of me. My stomach twists so hard I think I'll vomit right there in his lap.

He notices. Of course he does. He drags his hand higher up my leg, squeezing until I can't tell if I'm shaking from rage or terror. "I wanted you to see it," he says softly. "I wanted you to know what happens when a woman thinks she's braver than she really is."

My nails dig into the cracked leather of the seat until I feel them bend. My chest heaves, but I keep my chin up, keep my eyes locked on the blur of road outside the window. If I look at him again, I'll break.

Jackson doesn't need me to answer. He leans back, satisfied, his hand finally retreating. But his words cling to me like smoke.

A home.

Staff.

Behave, or rot with the others.

Others who shouldn't be there.

~

It feels like we've been driving forever. Roads blur into each other, long ribbons of black hemmed in by trees that look the same no matter how far we go. Time doesn't move normally anymore. It stretches, warps, coils around my ribs like barbed wire.

When the SUV finally slows, my heart stutters. Gravel crunches under the tires, louder than gunfire. I lift my head, eyes straining past the smear of my own reflection in the window.

A country house. Not a house—a mansion. Pale stone, sprawling wings, windows that gleam like eyes. At the gates, tall and electric, a buzzing sound splits the silence before we even stop. They swing open like jaws, welcoming us inside.

The driveway is long enough to feel like another trap. Lined trees bow inward, their branches clasped like skeletal fingers. A fountain rises in the center—three tiers of carved marble, water spilling endlessly into a pool wide enough to drown a dozen bodies in. The SUV circles it, gliding to a stop.

"Welcome home, Summer," Jackson murmurs.

I shudder before I can stop myself, and his grin widens, like he's felt the tremor run through me.

The engine dies, and I can't tell if it's better or worse that I'm not trapped in that warehouse with the broken girls. I know I should feel relief—lucky, even—that I'm not already bleeding out on a stained mattress or crumpled in some basement corner. But the thought curdles in me.

Because if Jacob hadn't hidden me, if he hadn't locked me away in his twisted idea of safety, then maybe the other women wouldn't be there. Maybe if he'd kept investigating instead of protecting me, fewer of them would be whispering prayers into their own wrists tonight.

The guilt crushes me, bitter and black, still, I choke it back before it can show on my face.

My voice cracks when I speak. "Why now? Why come for me now? My parents. You killed them. Isn't that enough?"

For a moment, silence stretches. Donnie twists the key out of the ignition. The ticking of the engine cooling fills the space, like a clock running out.

Then Jackson leans forward. His arm drapes along the back of the seat, casual, like we're just on a late-night drive. His eyes gleam in the dashboard light, too blue, too bright.

"You want to know why?" His voice drops low, soft, almost tender. "Because, sweetheart, I've been counting the days."

He taps a slow rhythm on the seat, each knock deliberate, like the tick of a metronome.

"Months in a cell. Every second of every fucking day, I swore two things. First, that I'd kill Michael Miller for putting me there. Second…." His lips curl, wolfish. "That I'd get you."

My throat dries, tongue heavy. "Why?"

He laughs softly, shaking his head. "Don't play dumb, Summer, you know why. Your fucking father is the reason I went to that hell hole, Jacob was the one who put me in cuffs. Originally, my men were going to take you, sell you. Make a bit of money. But after my time inside, and with him protecting you… well… I've had time to plan this out."

His hand lifts, hovers, then brushes against my cheek — the same side he slapped earlier. My stomach lurches, but I don't pull away. He leans closer, his breath tinged with smoke and something metallic, like the tang of blood.

"Here," he says, gesturing toward the house, his voice smooth as silk, "is a life where you won't have to want for anything again — as long as you follow my orders." He leans closer. "This place dresses itself in velvet and chandeliers, but don't be fooled. Every gilded room has its predator. And darling… you're looking at him."

Donnie snorts as he steps out of the truck, but Jackson doesn't glance at him. His eyes stay pinned to me, burning.

"I told myself every night, when the lights went out in that cell, that I'd find you. That when I did, I'd make sure you'd be mine. They thought the bars kept me in. No. They just gave me time to plan."

The SUV door clicks as Donnie pushes his door open. Icy air spills in, cold enough to sting my lungs.

Jackson leans back finally, giving me space. "Now," he says, gesturing toward the door with a flick of his hand. "Time to meet your new home."

The words hang in the air like smoke, impossible to breathe, impossible to escape.

And I know that this is only the beginning.

Chapter 32
This Little Piggy

Jacob

The office door slams open so hard the glass rattles.

"Sheriff—I came as soon as I knew."

It's Deputy Calder Briggs, sweat streaking down his face, breath stuttering like he's run from the lot. He's clutching a folder so tight the edges are bent, and his eyes are lit with something close to desperation.

"What?" I bark.

"George Johnson," he blurts. "One of Jackson's men. I pulled him a couple days ago on a traffic stop. Brought him in, ran his prints. Got his last known address. He won't have had time to move."

The room stills. The men inside—Carter, Mason, Grove, and the others—turn toward him, like bloodhounds catching a scent.

"Show me," I say.

Calder's already moving, snapping the file open across the desk, shoving papers toward me. Mugshot. Print card. The name scrawled across the top in heavy black ink.

George Johnson.

"This guy might not know shit," Calder admits, voice low. "But he might. And right now, he's the only thread we've got."

I don't waste time. I glance around at the men—my men. Some

retired, some barely hanging on to their oaths, all of them united by one thing: hatred for Jackson Moore.

Mason's jaw ticks, that familiar haunted look tightening his face. His daughter's blood has never left his hands. Grove leans against the wall, arms crossed, his stare as dead as the memory of the daughter he never got back. Carter's already strapping on his vest.

I slam the folder shut. "Gear up. Now."

The room explodes into motion. Drawers fly open. Weapons checked, magazines slammed home, radios clipped. Not one of them hesitates.

By the time we roll into the lot, the air's thick with the weight of it, like the ground itself knows we're heading into a fight. Two trucks idle, exhaust curling into the night. Carter and Calder lean against the hood, rifles slung, boots restless. Mason checks and re-checks the chamber of his sidearm while Grove keeps his jaw locked, staring straight ahead.

Hayes stands off to the side, calm as stone, his shotgun balanced easy in hands that have gutted more deer than most of us have seen. Beside him, Vance paces tight circles, shoulders twitching, a kid itching for his first real scar. Reyes lingers in the shadows, silent, scar tissue twisting up his cheek. Nobody mentions it. Nobody ever does.

Before anyone climbs in, I stop them.

"Listen," I say, my voice carrying over the rumble. They freeze, eyes locked on me. "I won't beat around the bush. What I'm planning—it isn't lawful."

No one blinks.

I let it hang for a moment, let them understand. "This isn't about due process. This isn't about the system. This is about Jackson Moore. About ending him. About bringing Summer back alive. That's it."

My throat tightens, rage pressing hot against my ribs. "If any of you can't stomach that, say it now. Because once we get in those trucks, there's no going back. We find him. We tear his world apart. And we put him in the fucking ground."

Silence. Heavy. Unflinching.

Then Mason steps forward. His voice is gravel. "That bastard's been in my nightmares for years. My little girl was nine, Sheriff. Nine. Bullet in her chest because of his men. You think I give a fuck about lawful?"

Grove spits into the dirt, eyes burning. "I'll watch that fucker burn. For justice. For my daughter."

Carter nods once, clipped. "Whatever it takes."

Reyes cracks his knuckles. "I'm in. For your girls." He gestures to Mason and Hayes. "And for Summer."

One by one, heads bow in agreement. No hesitation. No dissent.

I feel something pointy twist inside me. Not relief. Not hope. Something darker.

"All right then," I say. "Let's hunt."

We split, boots pounding the asphalt, loading into the trucks like wolves scenting blood. The lot fills with the growl of engines, and for the first time tonight, I feel alive.

Because this — this right here — isn't law. It's vengeance.

And vengeance is all I have left.

The drive out is long enough for the air in the cab to sour. No one speaks. Not Carter riding shotgun, not Mason, Hayes and Reyes who ride in the back. Every man grips steel like it's the only thing tethering them to sanity. My own knuckles are white on the wheel. The glow of the dash paints us in sickly green, like ghosts on their way to haunt.

Calder rides tail in the second truck, headlights bobbing in my mirror. Vance rides shotgun with him and Grove rides in the back.

By the time we crawl off the highway and down into the backroads, I can smell the rot of poverty through the vents. This is the kind of place George Johnson would call home. Forgotten. Left to fester.

The house is squatting at the end of a dirt drive. Paint peeling, porch light swinging in the night wind, yard littered with old cans and tyres. A graveyard for lives long since abandoned.

I kill the engine. One by one, doors open.

Carter at my side. Mason hefting the battering ram. Grove spitting into the dirt. Reyes silent as a shadow. Calder and the others fan out from the second truck.

"Two round the back," I order, voice low but firm. "Reyes. Hayes. Don't let him rabbit."

They nod, disappearing into the dark like they were born for it.

The rest of us stalk toward the porch. Masons got the ram slung like a weapon, but my blood's running too hot for protocol. The second my boot hits that step, I don't wait. I plant myself square at the door and drive my heel into the frame.

It explodes inward with a crack that echoes like a gunshot. The men glance at each other—one heartbeat of shock—before storming in.

The house smells like mold and piss. Hallway lined with broken picture frames. A TV still humming static in the corner. Movement at the far end. The scuffle of feet.

"Back!" Grove growls, charging down the hall. Carter follows, gun raised.

There's a crash. A shout. Then Reyes drags him out—George Johnson, wiry and greasy, his shirt half off like he'd been caught mid-flight. His face slams against the doorframe once, hard enough to leave a smear of blood, before Reyes yanks him upright again.

But it's not just him.

There's a girl.

Christ—she can't be older than eighteen. Thin as bones under skin, pupils blown wide, sweat slicking her face. She's screaming, slurring, clawing at the air.

"You need a fuckin' warrant!" she shrieks, voice cracking like glass. "You—You can't just—"

Before she can finish, Mason snaps. He grips her by the waist like she weighs nothing and hurls her against the wall. Her body hits plaster with a thud.

She crumples, gasping, wide-eyed, every ounce of fight knocked clean out of her.

"I'll be quiet," she babbles, shaking. "I'll be quiet, I swear—*please* don't—"

I don't look in that direction again.

George spits onto the floor, snarling like a cornered rat. "You got no right—"

My fist connects with his jaw before he can finish. The crack rings through the house, and his knees buckle.

"Rights?" I growl, hauling him upright by his collar. "You think you've got rights, you piece of shit? You run with Jackson Moore. That strips you of every fucking one."

He knows fighting is useless — he's outnumbered eight to one. In truth, he knows even one to one he wouldn't stand a fucking chance against me, or any of my men for that matter.

The others are on him in seconds. Carter shackles his wrists behind his back. Grove digs the muzzle of his pistol into George's spine like a cattle prod.

We drag him through the front door, his heels scraping over the porch steps, and hurl him into the back of the truck like garbage.

The sounds of the woman still whimpering inside, curled against the wall like she's trying to disappear into the plaster. She won't. She'll remember this. She'll remember us.

But tonight, I don't care.

George Johnson is ours.

And he's going to fucking talk.

Mason's workshop sits half a mile out of town, tucked into the woods where no headlights wander by accident. From the outside it looks harmless — sloped roof, stacks of firewood piled neatly along the wall, a porch light flickering yellow. But inside? Inside, it smells like sawdust and oil. Old blood and new purpose.

We drag George across the dirt floor. His boots scuff, voice hoarse from yelling the whole drive. Carter and Grove shove him down into the heavy chair Mason uses for sanding. Thick, sturdy, made to take pressure. Rope bites into his wrists as they tie him down tight.

He thrashes once, twice. Then glares at me. "You ain't gettin' shit from me."

Carter shoots me a warning look. "Boss, remember the plan. Don't kill him. Not yet."

I nod once.

I crouch in front of George. He stinks — sweat and fear and blood drying at the corner of his mouth. "You'll talk," I say quietly. Calm. Like I'm promising the weather.

He laughs. It's ugly, broken. He spits, the glob landing just shy of my boot. "You might scare other folk in this town but you sure as hell don't scare me."

Wrong thing to say.

My eyes wander the workbench. Chisels. Mallets. Planers. And there — set gleaming under the overhead light — a pair of bolt cutters, heavy and razored at the jaws. I pick them up, test the weight in my hand. Perfect.

I step toward George and pin his left hand flat against the chair arm. The ropes strain as he jerks, muscles twitching uselessly. His pinky trembles under the steel, a pathetic little spasm that only makes me press harder.

"You'll talk." My voice is flat. "Or this little piggy goes to market."

The cutters bite down, inflicting pain but not cutting through bone. Yet.

"Where the fuck is Moore?" I bellow

His laugh is half pain, half humor, "I aint telling you shit, sheriff." He spits.

The snap is brutal, brittle — bone breaking like a dry twig. He doesn't even process it until the blood sprays warm across the wood. Then it hits him. His scream rips through the rafters, high and raw, a sound that doesn't sound human anymore.

I let the ruined finger drop, flesh and nail skittering across the floorboards.

"This little piggy went to market."

His chest convulses, air wheezing through his teeth. His eyes bulge, veins crawling red across the whites. Spit strings from his mouth as he shakes his head, babbling, "Fuck you, I don't know —"

I don't wait.

The cutters shift, jaws opening around the next finger. My hand is steady, my grip unyielding.

"This little piggy stayed home."

The crack this time is wetter. Louder. Blood sheets down from his hand, soaking the rope until it runs black. His scream curdles, breaking into jagged gasps that scrape his throat raw.

Behind me, I hear someone gag, retching into the dirt. Boots scrape as Carter shifts, like he might step forward, but he doesn't. Mason doesn't blink.

George thrashes, the chair legs rattling against the floor. His head whips, spit flying, eyes rolling wide. "Stop! Stop! I'll tell you — I'll tell you everything — "

I lean in until my mouth brushes his ear, my words a blade sliding under skin.

"Then talk."

He sobs, voice tumbling over itself. "The warehouse — the new one — they moved everything — off the interstate, by the old mill road. That's all I know, I swear — "

I stare him down. His lips quiver, spit glistening at the corners. His chest heaves shallow, rank breath puffing lies into the air between us.

"He isn't going to stay in the warehouse... he has somewhere else... Where?" I snarl through gritted teeth.

He shakes his head, tears streaming down his cheeks and snot flooding from his nose. He tries to let out a silent scream, a saliva bubble popping when he opens his mouth.

The cutters bite down on the next finger, jaws grinding against bone, slick with blood. Red drips thick onto the sawdust, soaking it in clumps.

"This little piggy had roast beef — "

"Wait! Wait!" George howls, jerking so hard the ropes burn his skin raw. "He's at Sebastian Vale's! Jackson — he's hiding at Vale's place, I swear it — I swear it on my fuckin' life!"

The men still. Carter's gaze snaps to me, unreadable. Mason's jaw knots hard, a vein ticking. The name cuts through the air like a blade. Vale. Connected. Dangerous.

I don't stop.

The cutters snap shut. His middle finger tears loose, drops to the floor with a slap that splatters the boards. George's scream breaks, high and cracked, curdling into something animal.

"I told you man…. I fucking told you."

Behind me, Grove stumbles out the door, boots scraping, gagging until his stomach empties into the dirt. Hayes follows, muttering a prayer between heaves. Rayes and Vance are already out there—they left the second I put the cutters to his pinkie.

Inside, George's sobbing drowns the silence, thick, choking, begging in words that collapse over themselves. Noise. Nothing but noise.

"Enough," Mason cuts in, stepping forward. His voice is iron, cold. "We've got what we need."

I rise. My hand drips red, sticky to the knuckles. My chest heaves once. Twice. Then still.

The gun clears leather.

George's eyes bulge, wild and wet. "No—wait—"

One shot. Clean. The crack shakes the rafters, echoes tearing into the walls. His head snaps back, then drops, chin sagging to his chest. Blood sprays across the sawdust, steam curling off it in the cold air. The stink of piss hits a beat later, bitter and acrid, cutting through copper.

The chair creaks under his dead weight, groaning like it's tired of holding him up.

I wipe my hands down my jeans. The blood clings, tacky and stubborn.

"We've got a name," I rasp, voice rough, ground to rust. "Sebastian Vale."

The men shift like the name itself unsettles them. Even Carter steady, unflinching Carter—looks at me like I've just spoken the devil's name out loud.

"Vale," Mason mutters, jaw tightening until it pops. "Of course it's him."

I turn on him. "The name's familiar, but I can't place him."

"You know him, boss.," Mason snaps. "Defense lawyer. Big-shot bastard who moved from out of state last year. He represented Moore against the state. He's kept half these animals out of prison since. Always two steps ahead. Always clean. You think Jackson's smart? Vale's smarter. He doesn't just cover tracks—" Mason spits into the sawdust, eyes burning. "—he buys the whole fucking road."

A bitter laugh scrapes out of Grove. "And he's untouchable. Money, politics, judges in his pocket. You can't put a man like that in cuffs."

I slam the side of my fist into the workbench. Tools rattle. Wood splinters. "I'm not putting him in cuffs."

Silence settles, heavy as lead.

Carter clears his throat, steps closer. "So, Vale's the one harbouring Jackson? That's where Summer is?"

I meet his eyes. "That's what George said. And if he's lying, he's dead anyway."

The words taste like iron.

The men exchange glances. None of them argue. They don't want justice anymore. They want retribution.

Something in me splits wide open—an animal tearing free of its cage. The thought of her in their hands, their mouths on her skin, those bastards touching her. I see them passing her between them, using her, breaking her, and it burns through me until all that's left is violence.

I holster my gun, my voice flat.

"Then let's go find the son of a bitch."

Chapter 33
Pieces He Gave You
Summer

The front doors swing wide. They're carved wood, taller than any I've ever seen, etched with vines and roses. A man in a perfectly pressed black suit stands waiting. White gloves. His face is weathered, sagging like melted wax, but his eyes are blue glass under pressure—cold, brittle, ready to break.

"We've been expecting you, Miss Miller," he says, his voice crisp, rehearsed.

My stomach folds in on itself. Expecting me. Like this is an appointment. Like I'm a delivery scheduled for a Tuesday afternoon.

"Thank you, Harris," Jackson says smoothly, the name rolling from his tongue like he's rehearsed it too. He even dips his head, all courtly and charming.

But Harris—he doesn't smile. He only bows, stiff, mechanical. I catch the flicker in his eyes when they slide to me. Pity. It's gone in an instant, smoothed over with professionalism, but I saw it.

Behind him, a woman emerges. She's tall, thin, her black hair scraped into a bun so tight it drags her brows up into arches. Her apron is spotless. Her hands folded.

"This is Mrs. Dorsey," Jackson says. "She'll make sure you're comfortable."

Comfortable. The word sticks like glass in my throat.

And then another appears—a man this time, shorter, wide through the middle, with dark skin and gentle eyes that don't belong in this place. He wipes his hands on a flour-dusted towel knotted at his waist.

"Mr. Lyle," Jackson says warmly. "The heart of this home."

Lyle dips his head in acknowledgement. He doesn't meet my eyes long. But in the second he does, I feel it. The pity again. The 'I'm sorry' he can't say out loud.

Jackson releases me, his palm sliding down my arm, like it's a caress instead of a command. "Mrs. Dorsey, if you'd be so kind, give our guest a tour. Donnie will accompany you."

I almost laugh. A tour. Like I'm a bride seeing my new house. Not a prisoner being marched deeper into her cage.

"Yes, sir," Mrs. Dorsey replies. Her voice is flat. Dutiful. But her gaze cuts past Jackson to me. Her lips press tight, and I know she wants to say more. She doesn't.

We move.

The marble floors stretch beneath feet, veined with silver that catches the light from chandeliers. The ceilings soar high enough to echo. The walls are pale, broken by oil paintings—men with stern faces, women draped in pearls, none of them smiling. Their eyes follow. Judge. Condemn.

Donnie lumbers behind us, hands shoved in his pockets, whistling off-key. A watchdog with too many teeth.

Mrs. Dorsey walks briskly, pointing out rooms like this is all perfectly normal. The library, lined with shelves and leather armchairs. The dining hall—a table long enough to seat thirty. A ballroom with polished floors that gleam like ice.

My pulse drums hard in my ears.

"This wing is private," Mrs. Dorsey says quickly, regaining her composure. She doesn't look at me. She doesn't have to. The tension in her jaw says enough. Don't ask. Don't look. Don't push.

We keep walking.

Every step makes me smaller, even though the house is too big, too open. There's nowhere to hide. Nowhere to breathe.

Mrs. Dorsey's heels click on the marble as she leads me deeper into the house. I'm barely listening to her soft, practised words anymore— something about the East Wing being quieter, more private. My stomach is a knot, twisted so tight it might snap. Every hallway looks the same—long stretches of pale walls, thick rugs muffling steps, chandeliers dripping with crystals that sparkle like they're laughing at me.

Finally, she stops in front of a door. It's white, carved with delicate flowers and painted gold at the edges. Too soft. Too pretty. Like it's waiting for a little girl to skip through it, not a prisoner being shoved inside.

Mrs. Dorsey opens it. "This will be your room," she says, voice clipped.

The space is enormous. My breath stutters when I step inside. A four-poster bed dominates the center, its frame carved from dark mahogany with a canopy draped in sheer white curtains. At the foot sits a velvet chaise in blood-red. The wallpaper is pale cream, patterned with gold vines that twist like chains. A chandelier dangles low, scattering light across polished floorboards and a massive armoire with brass handles.

It's beautiful. Too beautiful. Which makes it worse.

Because I can already see myself locked in here, the walls closing in. The pretty details morphing into prison bars. The curtains like gauze thrown over a body.

Mrs. Dorsey hesitates. Her mouth parts like she wants to say something, but Donnie shifts behind us, clearing his throat. She stiffens and smooths her apron instead. "If you need anything, ring the bell beside the bed."

I nod, my throat raw.

And then she leaves. Donnie leaves too. The heavy click of the lock echoes through the silence, and my chest constricts.

I'm alone at least for a moment.

But I know—I know—he's coming.

I pace the room, my hands shaking. My eyes catch on the objects around me, desperate for a weapon. The only thing that looks remotely useful is the silver candelabra sitting on the dresser. Heavy, ornate, its arms curling into jagged points.

I grip it with both hands, hiding in the middle of the room, staring at the door.

It doesn't take long.

The handle turns. Slowly. Then the door opens and Jackson steps in.

He fills the doorway like a shadow dragged into flesh. His frame is tall, broad, but it's his face that makes my blood curdle. His hair is thick, dark, and curls messily around his temples. There's a heaviness to his jaw, covered with a day's stubble. His lips are cut into a mocking smile, but it's his eyes—the same blue flames I saw before—that strip the breath from my lungs. They're too bright, too alive, too cruel.

"Planning to set the mood, Summer?" His gaze drops to the candelabra trembling in my grip. He laughs. Not loud. Just low and amused, like I'm a child waving a stick at a wolf.

"Stay back," I whisper. My voice cracks.

In one stride, he's on me. His hand shoots out, snatching the candelabra from mine in a single motion. Metal scrapes as he tosses it across the room—it clatters against the floorboards, useless.

Then he turns me around so fast my breath bursts. His chest presses into my back, hot, suffocating. His mouth is at my ear. His breath fans against my skin, slow, deliberate.

"I don't plan to rush this," he murmurs, voice low enough to slide down my spine. "Do you know how many men would kill to have you? How much they'd pay just to touch you?"

He sniffs the side of my hair, taking his time to work his way around to my ear.

"Your father…. He crossed too many people. I could get millions for you… in less than five minutes. But no one will so much as get a whiff of you. You belong to me… and so help me God, I will enjoy every second of your company."

My stomach heaves. My knees threaten to buckle. But something snaps inside me—I twist my heel down hard, stomping onto his foot.

He grunts, a deep sound that rumbles in my bones. In an instant, his hand shoves me forward. I stumble onto the bed, the mattress dipping beneath me.

Looming above me. Shoulders squared, head tilted slightly, lips curved in a cruel half-thought. His eyes—glacial blue—scorch into me, narrowing, dissecting. The muscle in his jaw ticks, the cords in his arms drawn tight as though one wrong breath from me will snap the restraint holding him back.

I go still. My pulse slams against my ribs, so loud I swear the room can hear it.

His stare lingers. Unblinking. Weighing. Measuring. For a heartbeat too long, I'm certain he's deciding whether to break me here and now, to scatter me across the floorboards just to prove he can.

"So fucking beautiful," he murmurs, his voice a low growl as he brushes a strand of hair away from my eyes.

Then, slowly, he eases upright. Shoulders roll back. His hands smooth the front of his shirt in deliberate, precise movements, as though I'm nothing but grit he brushed from his skin.

At the doorway he halts, one hand curling around the frame. His gaze slices back over me—brutal, knowing, a warning wrapped in silence.

"Dinner will be ready in thirty minutes."

The slam of the door rattles the walls. The lock turns with a final, metallic click that echoes in my chest.

And then—nothing.

Just me. The four walls. The throb of my pulse filling the space where he'd been.

Alone.

I don't want to eat. I can't think of anything worse right now. My stomach twists with every heartbeat, nausea rising like bile. The thought of sitting at a table across from him—pretending this is some sort of dinner party instead of a nightmare—makes me want to claw my own skin off.

I search the room instead, bare feet whispering across the polished floorboards. My eyes scan everything, desperate, frantic. I pull open the closet. Dresses, blouses, skirts—rows of them, all my size. Neatly folded underwear in the drawers, some modest cotton, others lacey and obscene, meant for display, not comfort. My chest tightens.

The bathroom is the same—stocked like it's been prepared for me. A toothbrush already unwrapped, moisturisers and expensive creams lined up like an offering. Even tampons, tucked neatly in a basket. The realization slams into me harder than any slap—this wasn't improvised. This wasn't chance. They've been waiting for me.

I drop to my knees, searching under the bed, running my hands over the floorboards, tugging at the edges of the rug. I fling open cupboards, rattle drawers, tap the walls—looking for hidden cameras, for wires, for something. But the room just stares back, pristine and suffocating.

Then—A knock at the door.

I freeze, breath lodged in my throat. My heart slams so hard against my ribs it hurts.

I don't move.

The knock comes again, harder.

I still don't answer.

The door bursts open.

Donnie storms inside, his bulk filling the doorway like a wall. His scruffy beard glistens with sweat, his shirt stretched across his gut. He doesn't speak—he just grabs a fistful of my hair and yanks. Pain tears across my scalp and I stumble forward, screaming.

"Dinner's ready," he grunts, dragging me like a ragdoll.

"I don't want to go!" My voice cracks, useless against his strength. I claw at his wrist, try to pry his fingers from my hair, but he just pulls harder, my neck snapping back.

The hallway blurs as he hauls me through it. By the time he shoves me into the dining room, my scalp is on fire and my knees ache from stumbling against the floor. He forces me down into a chair, hard enough that I bite my tongue.

I blink through the sting of tears.

Jackson sits at the head of the table, waiting. The table is set like something out of a catalogue. Crystal glasses, polished silverware lined up in neat rows—more forks and knives than I even know what to do with. Plates gleam beneath the light of the chandelier overhead.

Jackson's smile spikes when he sees me.

"Donnie," he says lightly, swirling the stem of his glass, "not like that. Not unless I tell you."

The words slither across my skin. Donnie snorts, releasing me and dropping into his own chair further down the table. My hair falls limp across my face, and I fight to steady my breathing.

Jackson lifts his glass, holding it toward me. A mockery of a toast. "To us."

"Fuck you," I snarl.

He pulls his gun from his side and places it on the table in front of him. A threat. But I don't care. He could shoot me. He could end it all right now. Truth is, I couldn't care less if my life is stripped from me right now.

But then I remember. Jacob will be on his way. And I will get out of here. Jacob will kill Jackson, and all of this will be a bad memory. I just need to survive this first.

Harris enters, carrying a tray. Mrs Dorsey follows with plates. The cook, a plump, soft-eyed woman with hands that look like they've kneaded bread their whole lives, sets the first dish down in front of me. She gives me a look—quick, pitying—and for a second, the scent of roasted meat and herbs fills my lungs, warm and comforting.

The thought of eating makes me want to gag. But I know I have to. I'll need strength if I'm ever going to get out of here. My hands tremble as I pick up the fork, my lips dry as I force a bite into my mouth.

Jackson watches. Smiling. Always smiling.

His jaw is defined, like Benny's. The way his hair curls at the edges, unruly but deliberate. The flame-blue of his eyes, too bright, too alive. It's wrong. It's horrifying. But it's there.

He looks so similar to Benny. Just with a slightly different nose and more stubble. The thought hits me like a blow to the chest.

I drop my fork. "You... you look like him," I whisper. My voice barely carries. "Like... Benny."

For the first time, Jackson's smile softens—though it doesn't reach his eyes. He leans back in his chair, swirling his drink. "That's because he's my brother."

My stomach flips. "What?"

"You obviously know by now that his real name isn't Benny." He tilts his head, almost amused. "His name is Kurt. Kurt Moore."

The air leaves my lungs in a rush.

"He was part of the plan," Jackson goes on, calm, wiping the remnants of food from his mouth with a napkin. "You really think he just stumbled into your life? You think he was your hero?" His laugh cuts. "Every week, Summer. Every damn week he came to see me. We spoke in riddles, so the guards didn't ask questions, kept it quiet. And do you know what we spoke about most?"

His gaze pins me in place. My fork trembles in my hand.

"You."

I feel stupid. Violated. Like my entire world has been peeled back to reveal nothing but decay underneath.

All those conversations. All those smiles. All those promises.

Lies. Because Benny was never real. The freedom he made me crave would have led me straight to Jackson. To this prison I've found myself trapped in.

My chest aches so badly it feels like I'm splintering from the inside.

"He told me everything," Jackson goes on, smooth as silk, cruel as a blade. "The way you laughed. The way you cried. The way you sat on his lap and Jacob saw you. Now that—that was funny.... He gave me pieces of you long before I could ever touch you." He leans forward now, elbows on the table, eyes burning into mine. "By the time I got out, Summer, I already knew you."

My chest caves in. Every memory of Benny—no, Kurt—twists into poison. Every smile, every soft word, every promise he made me, it all unravels into lies.

"Good actor, isn't he?" His smile sharpens again. "Tell me, when he held you, didn't it feel like something was missing? When he came for you in the bar, didn't it feel... rehearsed?" He tilts his head, mocking. "That's because it was. He was a messenger. Nothing more."

I can't breathe.

The walls press in, marble floors gleaming too bright, chandelier lights blinding. My fork clatters from my hand and I grip the edge of the table to steady myself.

He leans closer, voice dropping, venom disguised as velvet. "And here's the best part, Summer. He loved you, in his way. He thought he could have you for himself. Poor, stupid Kurt. He even asked me if I'd let him have you. I said no, obviously—he thought he could outsmart me. But you?" His gaze pins me in place, freezing me to my seat. "You were never gonna belong to that dumb fuck… or the sheriff, for that matter."

The cook clears her throat in the kitchen, a nervous sound, but Jackson doesn't look away from me.

"I don't belong to anyone, I'm not a fucking possession. What is it with you… fucking… men," I manage, my voice hoarse. "You all think you have some say over my life. Well, let me tell you something. Jacob is coming. He will kill you. And then he'll take me home."

Jackson smiles, wide and slow, like a predator baring its teeth. "You really are something."

And I flash back to the night outside the bar. When Benny—no, Kurt—said exactly the same thing to me, the first night I met him.

Chapter 34
Tear Down The Gates.

Jacob

The engines roar as both trucks tear down the road, headlights slicing through the dark. Mason's behind the wheel of mine, his jaw set, eyes locked forward. The men in the back are quiet, the kind of silence that feels heavy, like it's bracing for impact.

My fists clench so hard I don't feel the split until I smell it—copper in the confined cab. Blood pools in my palm, runs sticky between my fingers, drips onto the floor mat. I don't wipe it. I don't fucking care.

"We'll get her back," one of the men in the back mutters. It's Carter. His voice is low but certain, like he believes saying it enough will make it true.

I don't turn around. My voice cuts flat, hollow. "You can't promise me that." A beat of silence.

Then Carter again, quieter. "But we'll do everything we can. They won't know we know where they are. Killing George… was a smart move."

Mason snorts, almost bitter, breaking the tension. "Yeah, smart move. Except now I gotta clean out my fucking woodwork shed." His knuckles tighten around the steering wheel, but there's no heat behind the words. Just exhaustion.

"Send me the bill," I mutter.

Mason's hand leaves the wheel for a second, clamping my shoulder. "I was joking, Sheriff. I don't give a shit about the blood. But if someone else could maybe pick up the fingers for me...." He grimaces, his face twitching like he's actually picturing it.

A laugh bursts out of me. Short. Wrong. For a half-second, it almost feels good to let it out.

Then guilt floods in like poison.

What the fuck am I laughing for when Summer's in Jackson's hands, probably crying, probably screaming, probably already broken? I bite down hard, swallowing it, the taste of iron and ash thick in my mouth.

I press my forehead to the window, watching the blur of trees rush by. The vibration rattles my skull. All I can see is her face when she told me she loved me. That small, fragile moment when I thought maybe I could actually be worth something to someone.

The other truck trails in the dark behind us, headlights bouncing on the bends, never too close, never too far. A convoy without fanfare, the way it has to be. Jackson's men could be anywhere—posted on a ridge, hiding in the trees, watching for patterns. And if they see us all together, it's over before it starts.

Mason drives like the devil's on his bumper, fists locked tight around the wheel, the veins in his forearms standing out in the glow of the dash. The road coils and jerks, blacktop snaking through the hills, each bend more angled than the last. The truck throws us side to side, but none of the men complain. The silence is suffocating, heavy with the weight of what we're heading toward.

I keep my fists tight in my lap. The cuts send pulses of pain up to my wrists, but I need it. Pain keeps me steady. Pain reminds me of her.

Summer.

Christ. Her name alone feels like someone splitting me down the middle.

But Jackson doesn't deserve my grief.

I've spent years cleaning up his messes. The trafficking, the prostitution, the drugs, the murders. The women who went missing. The women who came back broken shells. The bodies dumped in rivers and fields. Everyone in this truck knows what he's capable of. Some of them have bled because of him. Some have lost family.

And if Jackson lays one fucking hand on her, I'll—

"Boss. What you said earlier. No, I can't promise we will get her back." He swallows, keeps his eyes forward, the dash light painting his jaw in honed angles. "But I can promise we'll die trying."

I nod my head, accepting his words—knowing he means every one of them.

The rest of the drive is a coffin of silence. Tires hum over twisting roads, engines growl under the weight of every mile, but no one speaks. Words feel pointless when all I can hear is Summer's scream echoing in my skull.

When the convoy finally slows, it's like the world holds its breath. The house rises out of the dark, tall and looming, a shadow fortress behind wrought-iron gates. Spotlights sweep lazy arcs over the front lot, and for a heartbeat, it feels like we've rolled straight into Hell's courtyard.

"Big place," Mason mutters, his voice sandpaper as he edges the wheel, steering us to a hidden spot behind the line of trees.

"Too big," Carter answers, his hand already brushing the grip of his sidearm.

We pull up just out of sight, engines killed, trucks cooling to silence. My fists ache from clenching the wheel. Knuckles split open again, blood sticky against the leather.

Mason exhales loudly, the sound heavy with anticipation, before unclipping his belt and pushing open the door. "Ready, Sheriff?" he asks.

I nod once.

Carter, Hayes, and Grove move with me, our doors opening in near-perfect unison. Behind us, the rumble of the second truck fades as Calder, Vance, and Reyes climb out, boots hitting the dirt almost in rhythm with ours.

We huddle around the hood, breath ghosting in the night. The air smells like pine, damp earth, and gun oil. I sketch the layout quick and hard—main gates locked, front exposure heavy. If we go loud, we need to go fast. If we try quiet, we're fucked the second someone slips.

"We've got two options," I say. "Cut through the woods and breach the back—or…." My gaze slides to Grove. "We take out the front guards and blow it wide open. Once the men hit the ground, we drive the truck through and wrench the gates open."

Grove grins, but it never reaches his eyes. He'd served his country long before finishing his term and joining my department, a man known for his precision and calm under fire.

The trunk pops open, and he lifts out the case, snapping the latches with practiced ease. In seconds, he's assembling the sniper rifle—each motion fluid, mechanical, familiar. The scope catches the faint wash of moonlight, a brief flash before the darkness swallows it again.

"We'll need cover fire the second those bodies hit the dirt," Mason says.

I nod. "Then we storm it. No hesitation. Summer's in there. We don't give them a chance to move her."

Everyone murmurs agreement, low and final. The sound of safeties clicking off is louder than gunfire in the quiet.

We edge forward, trucks rolling slow until the iron gates loom just ahead. Two guards stand flanking the entrance, rifles slung casual.

"Grove," I whisper. "Whenever you're ready."

The sniper barrel rests across the bonnet, his body stretched behind it, every muscle steady. He exhales once, long and slow. The shot cracks, piercing as bone breaking. First guard drops like a puppet cut from strings. The second barely has time to look surprised before Grove's finger squeezes again.

Both men crumple into the gravel.

Alarms scream to life, shrill and furious, flooding the night with chaos. Red strobes blink along the roofline. Dogs bark inside. Shouts rise from within.

No more time for planning.

"Now!" I bellow.

Metal screams as the truck tears the gate down, the whole frame shuddering under the strain. The gate buckles, hinges shrieking, chains snapping like gunfire. Steel folds in on itself until we're able to climb through.

The air fills with sparks and dust. The gate lies mangled in the dirt, a carcass of bent metal and the road ahead yawns open.

We surge forward, guns raised, adrenaline flooding like fire through veins. The night explodes with noise—alarms, boots pounding earth, my pulse roaring in my ears.

We tear through the open yard, boots hammering the gravel, breath coming in short savage bursts. The alarms wail louder, lights flooding the grounds like daylight. From the shadows, more of Moore's men surge forward. Gunfire cracks through the night, hot metal whistling past.

Reyes drops with a scream, clutching his side. Mason grabs his collar, drags him behind a stone planter, returning fire with a roar. My vision tunnels red. Every second wasted is a second Summer is in there, with them.

We push harder, bullets shredding air. Bodies hit the dirt. Moore's guards fall one by one, their rifles clattering against marble steps. The rest scatter inside like cockroaches.

"Door!" I shout.

Mason, Carter, and Grove converge, shouldering the thick mahogany double doors. They don't budge. I slam my boot into it— wood splinters, but the frame holds. Again. Again. Nothing. It's reinforced, iron hidden beneath the finish. The fuckers have thought of everything. This is a fortress.

"Windows!" Carter yells, already pivoting toward the tall panes lining the front.

We unleash hell. Gunfire hits the glass—but when the smoke clears, it's still intact.

The bullets sink but don't break through. My chest heaves with rage. Bulletproof. Every inch of this fucking place is indestructible.

"Vale had too many enemies to play stupid," Mason snarls, spitting into the dirt. "This house is a goddamn bunker."

We spread, circling fast. The perimeter is sprawling, but we don't have time to slow down.

"Eyes up!" someone shouts.

I jerk my head back just in time to see the muzzle flash. A sniper on the roof. The shot tears through the night—and through Calder's chest. He goes down without a sound, blood soaking the gravel.

"Fuck!" Carter fires upward, Grove already dropping to a knee, sighting in. One pull of the trigger, and the sniper folds, tumbling off the roof like dead weight.

But my heart isn't slowing. If Moore had one on the roof, there'll be more. This isn't a skirmish—it's a goddamn gauntlet.

We push around the rear of the mansion, shadows flickering against brick and hedges. My boots hit mud, my breath tearing out of me, lungs burning. And then I hear it.

A sound that doesn't belong.

A mechanical hum, low at first. Growing. A whirr.

My blood turns to ice.

"No," I breathe, my legs moving before my mind can catch up. "No, no, no—"

I run. Faster than I ever have. My chest feels like it's splitting open, heart clawing at my ribs, but I don't stop. Because I know that sound.

SHERIFF
ROSEFIELD

Chapter 35
The Distance Between Us
Summer

The fork slips from my hand when the alarm splits through the house. A shrill, mechanical wail that rattles the crystal glasses on the table. My chest jerks tight—I don't even know what it means—but Jackson does. His chair scrapes back violently, and before I can blink, his hand fists my arm, yanking me to my feet.

"Move," he growls, dragging me so hard my shoulder burns.

I stumble, try to twist free, nails clawing against his grip, but he's too strong. His body is a wall, his hands like iron. When I dig my heels into the polished marble floor, desperate to slow him, he doesn't falter—he just bends, hooks an arm around my waist, and hauls me up onto his shoulder like a ragdoll.

The world flips upside down. My hair whips into my face, the blood rushing to my head as he carries me, his stride unshaken by my thrashing. I pound my fists against his back, claw at his shirt until threads come loose. I kick, I scream, but it only earns me a slap across the back of my thigh that stings so much I cry out.

"If you don't cut it out," he warns, his voice low and thick with menace, "I'll give you to Donnie for the night. You think I'm scary, Princess? He'll split you in half and leave you begging for death."

I freeze, nausea flooding me. The words hit harder than the sting of his hand. He knows exactly how to shut me up.

He chuckles darkly, patting the back of my leg like I'm a child throwing a tantrum. "That's better."

The house is chaos around us. Staff scatter through the halls, their polished composure fractured into panic. Harris—so stiff and proper at dinner—nearly collides with us, his silver hair dishevelled, eyes darting like a trapped animal. The cook grips the edge of the counter for support, his lips pressed together in terror. Mrs Dorsey clutches her apron, frozen, trembling.

I lift my head enough to look at them. Please. My lips move soundlessly, my wide, wet eyes begging them to do something, anything. To stop him.

But none of them move.

Harris bows his head as if ashamed, the cook turns away, and Mrs Dorsey wrings her hands until her knuckles are white. They can't look at me for more than a second. And in that one second, I see it clearly—pity. Pity and fear.

They won't help me. They can't. Jackson owns them. I don't know if it's money, threats, or blood on their hands, but whatever it is, it's enough to keep them silent.

The hopelessness burns through me hotter than the slap on my skin.

And all I can do is hang over his shoulder, helpless, as he carries me deeper into whatever nightmare he's planned.

The sound cuts through me before I even know what it is— gunfire. Short, brutal cracks that rattle the air, followed by men's screams. My blood freezes, then surges, and I know. I know.

Jacob is here.

A scream tears out of my throat, louder than I've ever screamed in my life. My lungs burn with it, my chest shakes with it. "Jacob!" I don't even know if his name makes it past my lips or if it's just sound, but I scream again, thrashing, fighting with everything I have left.

Jackson's entire body jolts, a guttural snarl ripping from him. He jerks me higher on his shoulder, his arm tightening around my waist until it feels like my ribs will splinter. The pressure makes me gasp, spots pricking my vision. He squeezes harder, bruising me, as if he could strangle the fight out of me with just his grip.

But I keep screaming. Kicking. Clawing. Jacob is here.

For a second, the chaos in the house fades—the alarm, the pounding of boots, the echo of gunshots—and all I hear is the drum of my own heartbeat hammering in time with his. He's close. He's so close.

And then I hear it.

A sound I can't place at first—low, mechanical, growing louder, stronger. Then the whirring whips into a frenzy, blades cutting through the night air. My stomach plunges. A helicopter.

"No—" The word scrapes out of me, but Jackson doesn't let me finish. He swings me off his shoulder and hurls me into the passenger seat of the machine with such force my body smacks against the cold plexiglass window. Pain explodes through my shoulder. I gasp, choking on it, tears flooding my vision.

I lift my head just in time to see him—Jacob.

He's a blur of fury and desperation, running toward me like the earth itself might swallow him if he slows down. His eyes lock on mine even through the chaos, even through the night, and my soul claws to get to him.

My hands slam against the glass.

"Jacob!"

Jackson yanks me back hard, strapping me in with the belt so tight I can't breathe. My arms thrash, nails tearing at his hands, but he shoves the heavy headset over my ears, clamping it down.

I rip it straight back off.

His hand clamps around my throat in a lightning-fast grip, his eyes searing into mine, cold and blazing all at once. His lips form the words slowly, deliberately, so there's no mistaking them.

Put. It. On.

My lungs convulse under his grip. My fingers tremble. I do as he says, sliding the headset back on, hating myself for obeying, but terrified of what will happen if I don't.

"Do you want to be deaf?" his voice snarls into my ears, like he thinks he's doing me a favor. His hand releases my throat, leaving phantom bruises already pulsing beneath my skin.

The floor drops away as the helicopter lifts. The noise is deafening, even with the headset, the vibration shaking every bone in my body. The world tilts, and the house shrinks beneath me.

And Jacob — Jacob is still running.

He doesn't stop, doesn't slow. He sprints across the gravel like a man possessed, screaming my name, his hands reaching for me even though I'm already too high, already slipping away.

Then, mid-stride, his body buckles. He falls to his knees, his fists slamming into the earth, his face lifting to the sky with a roar that cracks something inside me.

I slam my palms against the window, claw at it, sobbing so violently my chest feels like it's tearing in two.

"Jacob!" My voice is swallowed by the propellers, but I keep screaming anyway, because I have nothing else.

The helicopter banks, turning, pulling me away from him. My body lurches with the motion, but my eyes stay fixed on him until he's nothing but a shrinking shadow on the ground.

Jackson's laugh lands in my ear — wet, delighted — and for a split second, Jacob's broken shape flares behind my eyelids: the way he threw himself to the ground, the way he tried to reach for me even when he knew I was too far away. It stacks on top of everything else until something inside me fractures.

"Well, well, well… looks like the Sheriff can sniff you out, Princess."

Red crawls along the edges of my vision and my body moves on its own. My fist lashes out, swinging from my seat I can't fully turn in; knuckles smash into Jackson's jaw with a dull, sick crunch. My free hand claws at his face, nails ripping skin, and a hot ribbon of blood streaks from his cheek to his mouth. His laugh dies into a raw, animal noise.

One of his hands clamps my wrist with the force of a vice; he jerks and bends my fingers back so quickly that a white, clean snap lights up my skull.

Two fingers go wrong under the pressure, pins and pain flaring bright and immediate. He shoves me until the harness grinds into my collarbone and my cheek slams into the cold composite wall. The impact knocks the air from me; warm liquid beads at my lip and I taste iron. He pins me with an elbow across my chest, breath hot and ragged at my neck, and the straps bite deeper as he leans in—close enough that I can feel the rasp of his words against my skin. My hands tremble, useless inside his hold, and every beat of the rotor seems to match the jagged pace of my heartbeat.

The helicopter tilts; the world outside tilts with it, men shrinking in the wind, but inside that small, thudding cage there's only sound and the geometry of damage: the sting of bitten knuckles, the electric flare of broken bone.

And all I can do is sob.

A hand slides up my dress, finding my entrance.

I flinch violently, trying to twist away from his touch, but Jackson doesn't move his hand away. His elbow presses deeper into my spine, rough and unrelenting, as I fight against it. Blood drips from my nose, warm and metallic, sliding over my lips before I can breathe it away. The taste fills my mouth, whetted and bitter, mixing with the panic clawing at my throat.

"Do you always get this wet when you're angry," he says through the headset, his voice dripping with a mockery of calm. He pushes a finger inside of me, my body trying to reject him.

Jackson squeezes my thigh, hard enough that I wince. "Don't go quiet on me, Princess. Don't stop fighting me now."

He releases his elbow enough to allow me to whip my head back toward him, but my chest still pressed hard against the cold surface, tears still dripping down my cheeks. "Stop." My voice is hoarse, raw.

His mouth curls into a smile, slow and serpentine. His teeth catch the faint cabin light, pointed, white. His eyes—those searing blue flames—study me like I'm prey he's been stalking for years. The blood on his cheek is smeared, though drying into his skin.

"No," he says, leaning closer, his breath hot against my ear even through the headset, "You're a fucking goddess. And this," he curls his finger upward "is mine now." His tongue darts across his lips, a quick flicker that makes my skin crawl.

"Please," I whisper, though my voice quivers.

His laugh is low, rich, cruel. He pushes off me and leans back in his seat, removing his finger from me and spreading his legs wide like he owns the entire helicopter. I push myself away from the wall, but gather myself against it, crossing my legs and backing up as far away from him as I can. Tears fill my eyes as I cradle my broken fingers and wipe the blood from my nose.

"Princess," he says, almost tender, almost mocking, "The sooner you realize there's no escape the better." Then he raises his fingers to his mouth and sucks my taste from them.

I look away, jaw tight, refusing to meet his gaze as he makes a low, satisfied sound that curdles my stomach.

I shut my eyes and whisper Jacob's name, barely a breath, like saying it might anchor me to something real.

When I open them again, Jackson is still smiling—patient, cruel, and certain he's already won.

Acknowledgments

To Dahlia of Spite and Spine Ink — my PA, proofreader, chaos-manager, and unofficial emotional support human. Thank you for keeping me grounded when my brain was sprinting in twelve directions at once. You're the quiet backbone behind this book.

To Ellie of Refine and Format, my editor, for reading the absolute disaster of a first draft and somehow seeing gold in the rubble. You believed in this story before it even knew what it wanted to be. You are worth your weight in gold!

To Tocororo, my artist — you have gone so far above and beyond that "thank you" doesn't feel big enough. Your talent built a world around my words, and you are genuinely one of the best artists walking this earth. No arguments. No exaggeration.

To the Indie Author Revolution, thank you for opening your arms, your DMs, and your chaotic group chats to me. I've never felt more at home.

To my husband, for not being too jealous of the unhinged, morally grey men who live rent-free in my imagination. Thank you for cheering me on, even when I'm writing scenes you definitely shouldn't analyze too deeply.

To my parents for being the total legends they are. For not judging, for backing me, and telling everyone how proud of me they are. Love you beyond words!

To my friends and family, thank you for every "keep going," every "you've got this," and for never letting me doubt myself — not even for a second.

To my Kickstarter backers — thank you for taking a chance on me before this book even existed in the world. Your faith, your excitement, and your support made this possible. You were the spark behind this entire journey.

And finally, to my readers — the ones who laughed, cried, screamed, and let this dark little story crawl under their skin…

You're the reason any of this exists.

You're the reason Summer has a voice.

You're the reason Jacob is allowed to be… *well*, Jacob.

Thank you for every page you turned and every moment you gave this book.

See you in Book Two — Rosefield isn't finished with you yet.

About the Author

Rebecca Dale writes dark, emotional romance rooted in tension, obsession, and characters who blur every line they touch. A Yorkshire girl through and through, she brings grit, warmth, and a stubborn heartbeat to the stories she creates.

When she's not buried in fictional chaos, Rebecca is juggling real life — kids, dogs, caffeine, and the beautiful disaster of being a writer who can't switch her brain off. She has a deep love for small towns, morally grey men, complicated heroines, and love stories that aren't afraid to get a little messy.

Her debut novel, The Fall of Summer, launches The Reckoning Duet — a world where loyalty is dangerous, desire is unpredictable, and nothing is ever as safe as it looks.

Rebecca shares behind-the-scenes updates, teasers, and far too much unhinged book energy on social media.

Follow her on TikTok and Instagram @rebeccadale_author for exclusive content, upcoming releases, and a front-row seat to the madness.

Scan to continue the journey with early access to Book Two of the duet.